What people are saying about

TO SKIN A CAT

If you've never treated yourself to a Joe Box mystery before, then it's high time—and *To Skin a Cat* is a great place to start. John Robinson's hero is a GI Joe turned PI Joe—a Vietnam vet with a tough hide and a soft center. The dialogue crackles with attitude and energy, the plot is hard edged and fast paced, and the suspense is excruciating. Read it now and thank me later.

—JIM DENNEY
AUTHOR OF THE TIMEBENDERS SERIES

Move over! There's a new detective in town and his name is Joe Box. Rough, hard-nosed, and utterly engaging, Joe is on the case in a story crackling with action and razor-sharp prose. In this, the third novel in the series, John Robinson establishes the indelible Joe Box as one of the most engaging characters in the genre while masterfully balancing the story with just the right amount of faith. Whether your hero is Monk, Miss Marple, or Magnum PI, you will love private investigator Joe Box.

—WANDA DYSON
AUTHOR OF *INTIMIDATION*

Enter the world of PI Joe Box and prepare to stay through the last page. *To Skin a Cat* is author John Robinson at his finest. A genuine, nonstop page-turner.

—DOUGLAS HIRT
AUTHOR OF THE CRADLELAND CHRONICLES SERIES

A JOE BOX MYSTERY

TO SKIN A CAT

JOHN ROBINSON

RiverOak®

Good News in Fiction

COOK COMMUNICATIONS MINISTRIES
Colorado Springs, Colorado • Paris, Ontario
KINGSWAY COMMUNICATIONS LTD
Eastbourne, England

RiverOak® is an imprint of
Cook Communications Ministries, Colorado Springs, CO 80918
Cook Communications, Paris, Ontario
Kingsway Communications, Eastbourne, England

TO SKIN A CAT

Published in association with the literary agency of Hartline Literary Agency,
123 Queenston Dr., Pittsburgh, PA 15235.

This story is a work of fiction. All characters and events are the product of the
author's imagination. Any resemblance to any person, living or dead, is coincidental.

Cover Design: BMB Design

First Printing, 2006
Printed in the United States of America

1 2 3 4 5 6 7 8 9 10 Printing/Year 10 09 08 07 06

Scripture quotations are from the King James Version of the Bible. (Public Domain.)

"Karn Evil 9 First Impression" © K. Emerson and G. Lake, Arrangers' Publishing Co.

"Wild Frontier" by Randy Stonehill, © 1986 Stonehilliam Music/Word Music
(a division of Word Inc.)

ISBN-13: 978-1-58919-076-4
ISBN-10: 1-58919-076-9

LCCN: 2006925229

Welcome back my friends, to the show that never ends.
We're so glad you could attend,
Come inside, come inside …

Pictures at an Exhibition
Emerson, Lake and Palmer

To embrace this grand illusion
Is to know the living death.

The Wild Frontier
Randy Stonehill

1

*T*he faces in the wall were back. Burning. Jeering. Taunting.

I jumped up, balling my fists as I stared around, wide-eyed.

They were everywhere, ominously floating. Shifting and silently moaning. That was always the worst part. Their mouths moved in the flames, but no sound could be heard. My hands were clenched so tight I felt my nails drawing blood. Some of the visages before me looked hauntingly familiar: guys I'd served with in the war, or as a cop on the force. Sometimes even my wife and son.

The problem was, they were all faces of the long-ago dead.

Through the ocher walls came their grasping hands, beckoning me to join them. Up through the floor came more gray, ethereal fingers, plucking at my clothes and grabbing at me. With every bit of self-will I possessed I stood stock-still.

"It's not real," I said out loud. "None of this is real. There aren't any faces. There aren't any hands. There aren't." But it didn't seem to be working. Still they called me, like the Sirens to Ulysses.

I felt my resolution crumbling, turning to powder like old plaster. That's when inexplicably the hands retreated, and the faces faded.

Once more I found myself alone in the dank room, drawing in gasping, shuddering breaths. Knees weak, I leaned against the wall, now bare of phantoms, willing my pounding heart to slow down before it tore itself apart.

I couldn't take much more of this. One of these times they weren't going to leave. Not until they took me with them.

Almost surrendering to despair, it was all I could do not to hang my head and weep. A part of me sneered in derision. Joe Box, tough guy. Vietnam vet. Former cop. Hard-nosed private eye. Look at him. About to cry like a little girl.

Yeah, what of it? I almost answered, checking my reply at the last second. I had to watch that. Talking to myself, especially here in this dark realm, could be habit-forming. It seemed to me that all I needed to make it through this was a friend. Just one tiny friend …

I got my wish.

Under the wooden door, slithering into the room, came a small green garter snake. His skin was cartoon-bright, and like a cartoon, his face carried a happy smile.

I returned it, grateful for the company. As a kid growing up in the hills of eastern Kentucky, I'd kept garter snakes as pets, lots of them. The last one I'd owned, right before my dad and Granny and me had moved up to Cincinnati, I'd named Lester. This little guy here looked just like Lester.

I bent low, offering him my hand. The snake ignored me, instead curling itself around my ankle. I smiled again. That was so much like Lester too.

"Hey, Lester," I said. "Want to take a walk around the room? Like we used to?"

Lester didn't answer. He never did. But this time there was a reason.

He was morphing.

The creature looped around my ankle wasn't a green garter snake anymore. It was a small black python. When it looked up, its eyes glowed with lovely cold fire.

Slowly, almost casually Lester began climbing. And as he climbed, he began growing and thickening. He was eight feet long now, and as thick as my arm as he coiled himself around my body.

Then in a slow, mesmerizing rhythm, Lester began pulsating with dark rich colors. Blood red. Jet black. A two-tone palette running from his head to his tail.

This wasn't so bad. Kind of pretty. His weight felt good too. Good old Lester … I started to stroke him.

And that's when things went south.

The snake's eyes locking hard onto mine, he started to squeeze. The breath exploded from my lungs as my eyes bulged. What the—? This wasn't even close to being right. Why was Lester trying to kill me?

I didn't know, and didn't have time to ponder it. Whipping my body from side to side, I struggled to free myself from his death grip. To no avail. I was running out of time. Fast. Sliding my hands down Lester's body, frantically I sought some kind of purchase on his smooth skin. Anything. A couple of feet from his neck, I found it. A soft, mealy spot. My thumbs sunk deep. Heartsick, and with everything I had, I ripped poor Lester open. His flesh parted beneath my hands like cold, wet newspaper, and the snake shuddered. That should have ended it. But it didn't.

Through the rents in Lester's sides erupted a horde of scorpions.

There were dozens of them, hundreds, each as big as my thumb and as black as sin. They kept coming, now crawling all over me with spiky feet. Everywhere they touched, their stingers felt like the blue-white tips of acetylene torches, searing and cooking my flesh.

Helpless, I screamed in fear, rage, and agony.

The scorpions screamed back, a piercing cacophony, joined by the Lester-thing. The faces in the wall had returned, and they'd found their voices, laughing maniacally.

In the midst of the madness, I fought to stay sane. "Come on, man, wake up," I said. "This isn't real." And it wasn't. I awoke with a start.

Jumping up off the couch and staggering to my feet, I found myself drenched in cold sweat, shaking like an aspen. The images of the nightmare still fresh in my mind, I ran my fingers through my hair. I couldn't take much more of this. Three nights in a row now. Three.

♦ ◊ ♦

October, to my thinking, is the best month of the year. By then the harsh heat and heavy humidity of the Cincinnati summer is gone, and winter's nasty grasp hasn't yet begun. Although from time to time you can hear it cracking its knuckles in anticipation.

Earlier that morning I'd spent some time downtown at the Cincinnati Police Department headquarters, giving a bored detective there the final particulars of how my last case had gone. The corpulent body of the villain who'd caused everyone involved such misery was still missing somewhere at the bottom of Lake Herrington, and likely would stay that way. I'm not sure what good the cop thought my testimony would be; possibly none, as sixty minutes later I was done and back outside, enjoying the weather.

On the other side of my office window, the sky above the neighborhood of Mount Healthy where I worked (strange name, I know; don't ask) had gradually eased from that white kilnlike color the summer heat paints it to the deep, azure blue it only gets in late fall. I had the window cracked just a bit to let in the cool gentle breeze as I went over some paperwork.

Another hour of this drudgery, then I'd pick up my fiancée Angela Swain for our date, which tonight would consist of a fine French meal at the Chez Maison, followed by what the critics were calling a pretty good comedy at the Playhouse in the Park. All that was needed to complete this tranquil scene was a little red-breasted robin trilling outside, a la Mary Poppins. I sighed in contentment.

The shrill, harsh ringing of my phone broke that serenity. Business always has an aggravating way of intruding. I picked up. "Box Investigations."

"Is this Mr. Joseph Box?" The voice was male, a bit older, breathy, pleasant.

"Yes. Who's this?"

"I'm in your lobby, sir. I was calling to see if you were in before I undertook the task of mounting your stairs. Good-bye."

"What?" But whoever it was had hung up. Oh well. If the guy really was in the lobby, the mystery would be solved soon enough.

A few moments later I heard the ponderous tread of someone starting to make his way up the stairwell. The man—if it was the same one who'd just called—was having a hard time of it. Thud, thud, and a pause. One riser conquered. Thud, thud, and another pause. I couldn't help humming "I've Been Working on the Railroad" in time to the sound.

This looked like it might take a while, so I folded my hands on the desk blotter in front of me, pasted on a bland expression, and waited.

The noises began growing louder, finally stopping outside my door. There was a pregnant pause, and then my doorknob turned. The door slowly opened, revealing a squat, heavyset man with a reddish face, whom I made for a little older than me. Midfifties maybe. He was pop-eyed and laboriously wheezing from the exertion of the climb.

"Excuse my unusual call from my cell phone," the man said. He was panting heavily. "But for obvious reasons I wanted to make sure you were in." He pointed to the chair in front of my desk. "Do you mind?"

"Sure thing," I nodded, wondering just who we had here.

My visitor plopped himself down with a grunt and a heavy sigh. I couldn't help but notice rivulets of silvery sweat-worms running down his florid face above his too-tight shirt collar. I hoped he wasn't about to have a thrombo. But if the expensive cut of the man's navy blue silk Saville Row suit over his black Bally shoes was any indication, I imagined that if he did keel over, the medical insurance he carried was first-rate.

I figured to let him speak first when he got his wind back. He didn't disappoint.

"A hard climb, Mr. Box." Sighing, the man pulled a fine white monogrammed handkerchief from his front pocket. He began wiping his face with it. "I'm not in the shape I was as a youth."

"Who is?" I concurred, figuring this fellow would get to it eventually. As I said, I needed to pick up Angela in an hour.

He folded the damp cloth back into a neat square before tucking it away. "I suppose introductions are in order. My name is Morris Lester Chalafant."

He proffered a hand, and I stretched across my desk and shook with him. Not surprisingly, his grip felt like warm, moist meat. I hate that. "Joe Box. But then you know that already."

"I do indeed, sir," he said, his breathing sounding better. "Even if your name wasn't posted on the sign downstairs, your fame, as they say, precedes you."

"'A good name is rather to be chosen than great riches,'" I said. "Proverbs 22:1, if I'm not mistaken."

The bulging effect in Chalafant's eyes was gone now, replaced by a merry gleam. "You're not mistaken. And you have both the name and the riches, if the stories are true."

"Stories?"

"You've heard them all, I'm sure, sir. Reporters being what they are, it was impossible to keep the tale under wraps for long. About how even before you became wealthy after your last case, you couldn't be bought."

I bristled at his gall, but kept quiet. My visitor continued, "And that brings up a rather odd counterpoint to my visit. With your new status, I would have thought you'd have foregone the hard daily grind of a private investigator's life."

I still didn't trust myself to answer. For being a complete stranger, this dude was treading perilously close to the edge.

"Perhaps now it's simply a lark for you. At any rate, I've heard that you're honest, tough, hardworking, and tenacious."

"Don't forget thrifty, brave, clean, and reverent," I said. "I haven't been a Boy Scout since I was twelve, Mr. Chalafant." Leaning toward him, my piercing gaze was steady. "And as far as my finances go, it's really none of your business."

He ignored that comment. "A Boy Scout isn't what's called for. But tenacity? Yes, tenacity is what is required." His cheery manner faded a bit. "That. And circumspection."

"A private investigator who can't keep his mouth shut doesn't last in this business. And I've been at it an awfully long time."

"Yes, going on fifteen years, isn't it? Before that you were a hopeless alcoholic."

That raised my eyebrows. Chalafant's exuberance returned. "Before that you were a Cincinnati street cop, and before that an infantry rifleman, a corporal serving in Vietnam. You're a widower of some twenty-five years, now engaged to a successful architect, whom you met at the church both of you attend." His good humor grew. "How am I doing so far?"

My manner chilled by half as I settled back in my creaky old desk chair. "Maybe we ought to switch seats, Mr. Chalafant. I'm thinking you should be the investigator."

"Now, Mr. Box, don't get upset with me, please. It's simply that my employer had you thoroughly vetted before he sent me here today. He's a very meticulous man."

"Your employer?"

"A singular individual. One whom I'll wager cash money you've heard of. And much like you, also a man whose fame precedes him." My visitor placidly folded his hands across his ample gut. "Cyrus Alan Tate."

"Cyrus Tate? The porno king? That guy they call Cat?" I almost laughed, only checking myself at the last second. Being found in the same category of human sludge as Cyrus Alan Tate would put a decided kink in my happy mood.

"Ah, I was right. You have heard of him." The other man chuckled, a wet rasping sound. "I know, it's silly the way the press, comprising his initials, quite a while ago hanged that nickname on him. But I've heard it bandied about that any publicity is good publicity, true?"

"I could make a fairly good case against that."

"Admittedly, at first it caused Mr. Tate no end of embarrassment. But after years of enduring that appellation, he seems to enjoy it now."

I'd progressed from chilly to downright cold. "Glad to hear it."

"Come, Mr. Box. Surely, you being an apparently healthy male, have from time to time in your more, shall we say"—Chalafant ran a glutinous tongue over his grayish, rubbery lips—"desperate moments, availed yourself of Mr. Tate's particular wares?"

My reply was terse. "No, can't say that I have. Call it a character flaw."

The other man laughed, slapping his hands down on his hamlike thighs in delight. "It would appear the stories I've heard about your new religious bent are also true."

This dude was getting on my last nerve. "What do you want, Mr. Chalafant?"

He settled his weight back into the chair, the wood creaking alarmingly. "You are aware of Mr. Tate's latest venture, are you not?"

"Let's say I'm not. Why don't you fill me in?"

"Very well." Tenting his fingers like an English professor, Chalafant said, "East of here, at the farthest edge of Claxton County, and practically on the Ohio River, my employer, Cyrus Alan Tate, has constructed what may well become the mecca of the sex industry as we know it."

"Son of a gun." Of course I'd heard all this on the news, but I wanted his take on it.

"Simply put," my visitor announced, "the project is a state-of-the-art building standing five stories high, and finishing out at nearly a quarter-mile in circumference. Inside it are seven large-screen high-definition movie complexes, various gift shops, and a walk-through exhibit, consisting of a combination theme park and animatronics tableau. This exhibit features famous sex workers through the ages, both male and female, some of them dating as far back as the Sumerian Empire."

"Yeah, I always heard the Sumerians were hot dates."

He ignored me. "In addition it houses fifty fully equipped, sound-deadened massage parlors, staffed by professionals. Also found there is the largest adult bookstore in the world, featuring books, special toys, interactive games, and DVDs. These have been gathered from the four corners of the earth. Most of them have never been seen by Western eyes."

"Let's hear it for smut," I quipped, but Chalafant heedlessly soldiered on.

"The building's crowning glory will be unveiled sometime soon. This experience will be something so wondrous, so marvelous, its very description beggars the imagination." He smiled thinly. "Unfortunately, I'm not yet at liberty to divulge exactly what it is."

I rested my chin on my fist. "Pity. I'm on tenterhooks too."

"All in good time, Mr. Box. If you choose to join us in our venture." The other man's look grew beatific. "The name of this structure is beauteous in its simplicity. Mr. Tate is calling his creation ..." he paused a pretentious beat, "PornUtopia."

Of course, I knew that, too, and I bit my tongue. The press had had a field day sniggering like schoolboys when they'd heard it. There really wasn't any reply, civil or otherwise, I could make to something so blatantly asinine, so I said nothing.

Chalafant took my silence as approval, and spread his plump, manicured, fish-belly white fingers. "Inside PornUtopia's walls will be found sensual delights of the flesh the likes of which can scarcely be dreamt of."

I picked up my black marble paperweight, enjoying its heft. Idly I wondered if I should try splitting this dude's skull with it. "Golly, sounds great. Can the missus and I bring the kids?"

That crack deflated the porcine jerk at last. He sighed like I was the class dullard. "I fear you're misunderstanding the scope of this project."

"Oh, I believe I understand it fine. What you're telling me is your boss has created a porn palace for fifteen-year-old boys in thirty-year-old bodies. If it wasn't so revolting it'd be pathetic."

"I'm afraid—" my visitor began, but I broke in on him.

"And that name." My look was disbelieving. "I mean, come on. PornUtopia? What IQ-challenged Madison Avenue whiz kid thought that up?"

Surprisingly, Chalafant appeared offended. For someone in the dirty book and movie business, I would have thought that was impossible. The expression on his face was like an undertaker who had just found he'd been stiffed on his bill. "Mr. Tate created that name himself."

"Oddly enough, I don't doubt it. Again, Chalafant, the question remains. What brings you into my establishment today?"

His answer was even. "Simple. A business offer. Mr. Tate wishes to hire you."

I laughed. "Good night, nurse. To do what, exactly?"

"You've conducted security work in the past, true?" I nodded, intrigued with where he could possibly be going with this, and Chalafant said, "That's what I'm here for."

"Kind of late in the game for that, isn't it? I would have thought Tate would hire a specialty firm for that. Any security work I've performed has been strictly small potatoes."

"Just so," the other man said, as if pleased I'd gotten it. But gotten what?

He went on, "The system installed in PornUtopia was contracted to a large company headquartered in Phoenix, Arizona. You may have heard of them. Apex Technologies."

"Yeah, I know them." I should. Apex was the most expensive private-security firm in the world. "They don't come much bigger. What could I possibly bring to the mix?"

"Mr. Tate is justly famous for considering every aspect of a problem, and building in redundant components to stave off future problems. Your task would simply be to verify the work done by the Apex workers. Another set of eyes, if you will."

I frowned. "I can't say I much like the idea of being a 'redundant component.'"

"Possibly a week would need to be allotted to complete your inspection." Chalafant was ignoring my comment, eyes dancing like a dashboard Chihuahua. "For that seven days' work, you would be paid the sum of ten thousand dollars."

Ten thousand bucks. *Wellsir.*

"Not to mention, of course, the expected on-site fringe benefits. Of the female persuasion." He paused once more. "Or male. Whichever mood suits."

I figured it was time to shut down this farce. "Not interested."

That seemed to shock him. "Sir—" he began, and again I broke in.

"Two things, Mr. Chalafant." I held up the correct amount of fingers on my left hand before ticking off the points with my right index. "One, I don't need, or want, your porn money. And two, as an opinion from a guy who's trying to be a fairly moral human being, what Tate's doing stinks." I shook my head. "Nope. Find yourself another boy."

"But—" the other man started one last time.

I slammed the paperweight down on my already scarred desktop. "We're done here." Chalafant still seemed utterly befuddled at my stupidity. I said to him pointedly, "Before you go though, answer this. Why me?"

He stayed mute. I went on, "I mean, if good old Cyrus had me checked out like you said, he must know I've changed my ways. And he must have known I'd say no." I narrowed my eyes as an evil thought wiggled in. "Or did he?"

"All men have their price, Mr. Box." My visitor was smiling again. "Even you."

The Tabasco sauce was coming up my legs. It was a moment before I trusted myself to speak. "Well, I'll be dogged. Forgive me for being slow. I get it now. Your boss is known for being high profile in his disdain for religion of any stripe. Am I right?"

The other man made no reply.

"Your visit here today was just a ploy to see if I'd rise to the bait," I continued. "If I took his job, Tate could crow that a Christian could be bought. If he made the bait sweet enough." In three strides I crossed the room, pulling open the door harder than I'd meant, rattling the smoked glass. "Good day, Mr. Chalafant."

"What?"

"Let me make it plainer. Beat feet."

"Oh, don't be ridiculous!" A vein was throbbing alarmingly on the side of the other man's head. It went like that a few seconds more before he seemed to calm himself. "All right. Let's say for argument's sake you're correct. That this offer was partly designed to show your faith in a bad light. If it was, so what?"

"Come again?" I wasn't sure I'd heard him right.

"I was told you're the best," Chalafant said. "And Mr. Tate always gets the best. Always."

As I glared ropes at him, my visitor's tone turned oily. "Please, sir, listen to reason. Forget your religious bigotry. Your so-called code of honor. Your outdated morals. Mr. Tate's cash will spend, Mr. Box, and spend well. Take the job." That smirk wasn't any nicer than it'd been earlier. "As long as you live, you'll never be part of anything bigger."

"That's wrong," I corrected. "I already am."

Chalafant stared, not understanding.

I used that lull to get in one final shot. "Something you said earlier has been bugging me. When I mentioned that proverb, you acted like you'd heard it before. You even went so far as to tell me I'd quoted it correctly. The thing is, you really don't strike me as the Bible-reading type, Chalafant. How did you know I got it right?"

"That's easy. In my youth, I was a student of Scripture." I frowned, and he went on, "I'm a Jew, Mr. Box. Or should I say, I was. Now I'm … something rather more."

I'll say. At long last, I'd had enough of this fool. I pulled the door open wider. "Like I said, time to get it in motion, jerk. Make sure this doesn't hit you on the way out."

Chalafant huffed out a breath. Minus his hollow smile, now he just looked slimy. "Very well. Obviously I'm wasting my time here. And Mr. Tate's."

That was the truest thing he'd said yet.

Struggling to his feet, he grunted, "Just one thing more. Since money isn't your hot button, is there anyone else you can recommend whose it is?"

I started to answer in the negative.

And then I remembered Billy Barnicke.

2

Angela Swain, my drop-dead gorgeous brunette fiancée (yes, I'm biased) leaned my way, a small piece of chateaubriand speared expertly on the tines of her fork. "Taste this. It's really very good."

I gave her a look. "I've got the same thing on my plate as you do. That's why they call it chateaubriand for two."

"Don't be a stick-in-the-mud. It's bad for your image. This is what lovers do, especially in five-star French restaurants like this. They offer each other bits of their foods to taste. It's sensual."

"Sensual?" To a hillbilly like me, sensual is when the country ham isn't too salty.

She bobbed her fork up and down. "Come on, Romeo. This is the first time either of us has eaten here. Let's get the full effect." She gave that look that makes me go weak in the knees. "Do it for me, big guy. Enjoy."

I paused another moment, then said, "Oh, why not?" Cranking my head over, I took the morsel of meat with my teeth. I started chewing it, wagging my eyebrows as I did. "Wow, you're right, Ange. This is a lot better than mine."

"Witty," she sighed, exasperated. "Very witty. No matter what, you'll always be a country boy, won't you? Even if your Kentucky accent is thirty years gone."

I grinned in reply, hoping there weren't steak fragments between my teeth. "It's part of my charm."

Angela shook her head, and I used that lull in the conversation to pick up the delicate white Limoges cup by its dinky little handle, taking another sip of Chez Maison's superb coffee. Setting it down, I said, "I had an interesting guest today."

"Interesting as in 'oh-brother-what-a-trip-he-was,' or really interesting?"

"The first. Guy had a weird name. Morris Chalafant."

"Chalafant … Why does that sound familiar?"

"What's weirder is who he works for." My fiancée looked puzzled, and I said, "Cyrus Alan Tate."

She set her fork down with a frown. "Cyrus Tate? The porno king?"

"The one and only."

"Good heavens. What did he want with you?" Her chuckle was less than heartfelt. "You're not thinking of changing careers on me, are you?"

"Not hardly," I laughed, trying—and failing—to paint a picture of that in my head. "His visit had to do with that smut sanctuary Tate's putting up out in Claxton County."

"I've heard of it." Angela shook her head again. "I can't believe the people there let it be built. Are they insane?"

"Times are hard all over," I shrugged. "In Claxton County as much as anywhere. The tax revenues from the thing alone will probably float half their economy."

My fiancée sniffed her disdain. "I can't imagine anyone wanting to work at a place like that. Not anyone self-respecting at any rate."

"Neither can I. But as the cowboys used to put it, sometimes a man's gotta do what a man's gotta do. Especially if he has a family to support."

Angela's violet eyes widened. "Don't tell me you condone that abomination."

"I didn't say that. All I'm saying is what some people might think."

"Well, I think it's sick."

"You won't get any argument from me. That's why I threw Chalafant out."

"Good." She nodded firmly, then said, "You never said what he wanted with you."

"It seems Tate's hired a pretty big out-of-town firm to do the security service there. Chalafant wanted to see if I'd be interested in vetting their work." My smile was sardonic. "Jerk had the nerve to call me a 'redundant component.'"

"Somebody needs to redundant *them*."

"That doesn't make any sense."

"You know what I mean." Angela tossed her napkin on the table. "Men like Tate steam me. He makes it all seem so perfectly harmless. But not just him. What about the men who'll go to his place? What about those who'll run it?"

I kept silent; when my sweetie goes on a tear, it's best just to let her run it out. "Worst of all," she said, "are the women who'll willingly let themselves be used like so many disposable paper cups."

Angela Swain is a justly famous architect. But before that, long before she had the encounter with God that would change her life so dramatically, she was something else. Something dark.

I knew I'd touched a sore spot with her, and regretted ever having mentioned Chalafant's visit in the first place. I figured anything I would say at this point would only make things worse, so we passed the next few moments in silence while we both sipped our coffee.

Angela broke the logjam, her grin tentative. "Threw him out, huh?"

"Well, not physically, of course. The shape Chalafant was in, that probably would have killed him. I just opened my door, and he got the idea." And then I said one of the stupider things I've ever uttered. "I referred him to Billy."

"You did *what?*" Angela's eyebrows headed north. *"Billy Barnicke?"*

Several disapproving stares from the diners around us were now directed our way. The maître d' materialized and scurried over, concern clouding his thin Gallic features. "Is there a problem, *Madame? Monsieur?"*

"No, we're fine," I lied. "The lady just got strangled on a green bean. She's OK now." I grinned, pointing at the meat with my fork. "Tell the cook this steak is *great.*"

He looked hard at me, then over at Angela, his Boston Blackie mustache quivering. "Very well. Please, enjoy your dinner. Call me if you need … anything more." With that he disappeared to wherever a maître d' in a fancy restaurant goes after he's finished dealing with the riffraff. What he'd left off saying was, *and for Pete's sake keep your voices down.*

Angela scowled, and not just because of my crack at her expense. "You're going to get us tossed out of here yet."

"Me? I wasn't the one raising my voice. Besides, it wouldn't be the first time I was ejected from an eatery. Story of my life." Figuring that was it, I began working on my steak once more. I was wrong.

"Don't act like this is over, hotshot," Angela fumed. "It isn't."

"It is as far as I'm concerned."

"It's not."

I shot her a look. "What the devil are you going on about?"

"I mean, how dare you sic that monster on Billy? I thought you liked him."

"I do like him. As much as I can like a competitor." I started cutting again.

"But he's your friend."

"Not really. Not anymore." I was still working away. "It's true that back in my drinking days we hoisted a few, but those times are long gone. Every now and then we'll refer clients to each other, but he probably ends up stealing as many from me as I give him."

She wasn't letting go of it. "I thought you PI types had a code."

"Code?"

"You know. Like how one private investigator always watches another one's back."

I stopped sawing and looked up, shaking my head, not getting it. "What the Sam Scratch does watching each other's backs have to do with anything?"

"For pity's sake! How plain do I need to make this, Joe?" Angela's voice dropped to a stage whisper. "You referred a porn trafficker to a friend!"

I'd begun transporting the bite of steak to my mouth, and stopped. "So?"

"Merciful Father! Don't you see the *wrongness* of that?"

I lowered the fork and leaned in. The rest of the diners didn't need to hear this.

"Ange, listen to me." I was speaking as quietly as I could. "Billy's a sometimes-friend, sometimes-competitor. Period. Nothing more. That's just the way this business is."

"Maybe your business isn't as clean as you'd like to believe."

I ignored that. "One day you're playing cards with a guy, the next you're trying to outbid him for a client. There's nothing nefarious about it." I could tell she wasn't buying this, and I figured to go for her heartstrings. "Besides, I know for a fact Billy's operation is struggling these days. He could really use the money. I just thought I'd cut the guy a break."

"Porn money," Angela said flatly. "And if you knew he was hurting financially, why didn't you just simply help him out yourself?"

"He's a grown man, and he has his pride," I shot back, growing defensive. And how stupid was that, me trying to defend Billy Barnicke? "Or rumor has it. He'll be fine."

Angela narrowed her beautiful eyes at me, as if taking my measure. And not overly impressed with what she saw. The problem is, I don't take that, not from anyone.

Mindful of the other diners, I quietly went on through gritted teeth. "Look, here's the deal. Billy'll walk around Tate's place for a week, pronounce Apex's work up to snuff, collect his ten grand, and everybody goes home happy. And that's all there is to it. Are we fairly clear on that?"

"No. You're spouting pure rationalization. Nothing more." Angela was speaking slowly, as if dealing with a dunce. Then she went for the throat. "If it's all so innocent, why is working for Tate fine for Billy, and bad for you?"

Well, nuts. No way around it, she had me on that point, but good.

My brain spun its wheels uselessly for a few seconds, seeking mental traction, while I tried to formulate an answer that would satisfy her. And truth be told, satisfy me as well. But none was forthcoming.

She nodded her head. "I thought so. Shot you down on that one, didn't I? But I'm not the one you have to make your case to. And God can be hard to convince."

I let that hang for a beat, before giving a noncommittal shrug. "Could be you're right. But in the end, that's really between me and him, isn't it?"

My fiancée paused as if I'd slapped her. Her reply was cool. "Why, yes it is. I apologize." Seething with anger she began aimlessly fooling with her water glass.

"Come on, let's both stop," I sighed after another moment. "It's too nice an evening to fight."

Still running her fingers around the rim of the glass, she cocked an eyebrow. "Is it?"

"Yeah, it is." I tried it again. "Look, all I'm trying to say is, I've got to make my own way in this. How am I ever going to learn for myself otherwise?"

There was another pause. I hoped I hadn't crossed the line.

Then with a slight shake of her head Angela took her hand off the glass and placed it over mine. The restaurant's soft lighting was doing extraordinary things to her brunette hair. "You're right, of course," she smiled. "Sometimes when I try to help, it just comes off as heavy-handed. As you're so fond of saying, son of a gun."

How about that? Amazing. It looked like our dinner was saved from disaster.

"Wait a minute," I laughed. "Not only are you trying to run my life, now you're stealing my lines. Have you no shame, woman?"

"*Mea culpa.*" Angela chuckled softly as she gently began stroking my hand. "And with the baggage from my past, I admit I really don't have much room to talk."

She was lightly running her fingertips back and forth across my scarred knuckles. "So as far as Billy's concerned, do whatever you feel is best, Joe. Whatever happens, I don't think there's any lasting harm done."

I met her eyes then, and my good mood faded. I could hardly get the next words past my teeth. "Yeah, well … there's where you're wrong."

Angela stopped the back-and-forth motion of her hand and didn't answer, waiting for the hit. She knows me too well.

"Right after Chalafant left, I called Billy to see if he might be interested." I leaned back and pinched the bridge of my nose. "The two of them talked, and he agreed to take the job."

3

*T*he rest of the evening progressed about like you'd imagine.

I don't think Angela was consciously trying to make me feel bad about me having involved Billy with Tate's operation—as a matter of fact, she didn't mention it again—but the undercurrent was there. Not even the decadent offerings from the Chez Maison's dessert tray could lighten things up; right then, decadence was the *last* thing I wanted to think about. And the play the two of us took in later, billed as a "rollicking comedy," for all I knew might have been a work pounded out by Ibsen in one of his darker moods.

After I dropped her back at her place, my sleep that night wasn't good.

I awoke foul-tempered and edgy. For yet another time this week, that same faces-in-the-walls nightmare had invaded my sleep. It was way past getting old.

Flipping the covers back, I crawled out of bed and raised the shade, peering out my window at the early dawn. The yellow sun was climbing, and high up in the red and gold trees the robins and finches were conducting their never-ending truce talks once again. At full volume. Sometimes, when I consider the propensity for violence the human race seems to possess in limitless measure, I remember the bird kingdom, and feel better about my kind.

A little more lighthearted now, I turned away and began moving down the hall. The first thing I needed to do after I'd fed my cat and had my morning caffeine jolt was to call Billy at his house and warn him off the job. If he'd listen to me. He didn't understand my new view of life. Worse, he didn't care. Like most of my friends, he considered it a useless aberration that would fade with time. But Billy, plainspoken as always, would have put his contempt in earthier terms.

Walking into the kitchen, I immediately knew something was wrong.

Normally when I come in, I have to shuffle my feet to avoid tripping over my cat. Although a runt, Noodles is still a chowhound of the first water, and being feline, he gets upset easily if his routine is disturbed. That's why every morning I fix his breakfast first, before getting my coffeepot going. Otherwise he'll howl and yowl and generally make such a racket that I'm forced to attend to him. And that's no way to start the day for either of us.

But this morning he wasn't there.

"Noodles? Where are you, boy?"

Reaching up into the cabinet above the stove, I pulled out the box of Kitten Kuddle cat food. It's the only brand he'll eat. The food truly is wretchedly off-brand, sold only at smaller stores, with its flavors limited to beef, chicken, or tuna. Where you or I would go off our nut eating the same dreary fare year after year, Noodles seems to thrive on the stuff. Which made his disappearance this morning all the more puzzling.

I shook the container, rattling the dry contents inside. Maybe he was using his litter box, which I keep next to the toilet. If so, he'd be out in a minute. I fluttered the box again. Nothing.

I called louder, shaking the box like a castanet player in a mariachi band. "Yo, Noodles. Breakfast is on." Still, silence. "What's gone with that cat, I wonder?"

Setting the box down on the counter, I walked down the hall toward the bathroom.

That's where I found him, slumped half in and half out of his litter box, his little body ominously still.

I dropped to my knees beside him. *What* the—? Was he—? I knew he was far from being a young cat, but— Dread gripped me. No, this couldn't be.

"Hey, Noodles? Buddy?" At the sound of my voice he managed to raise his head, giving out a shaky *mrowr-r-r.* Thank God, he was alive, but the poor little guy was trembling so hard it was like he was being zapped by a particularly ham-handed executioner.

With shaking hands I nervously wiped my mouth, taking in more details.

Dried saliva caked the left side of Noodle's face, and his eyes were milky and unfocused. Somewhere in this he'd also soiled himself. Valiantly he tried getting to his feet, but his rubbery legs failed him. He went limp and fell over, gazing up at me in abject misery.

Oh man. Tentatively I reached a hand toward him, before yanking it back. What the devil *was* this? Uncannily, it had all the earmarks of a human stroke. This wasn't good. This was as far from good as a thing could get. Years ago I'd rescued my cat from being tortured to death by a couple of drunks, and he was as close to family as I had left on this earth. Close, nuts. Noodles *was* family, and only twelve.

And I wasn't ready to let him go yet, not by a long shot. OK, no time to fool around here. I needed to call the vet.

◆ ◊ ◆

Dr. Tom Bagdasarian is normally a jovial sort, the kind of backslapping, twinkle-in-the-eye raconteur that kills them at cocktail parties, but he was all business as he heard me describe the condition of my cat.

"Is he still breathing?" he asked when I'd finished.

"I think so." I had the cordless phone with me in the bathroom, and I felt along Noodles' ribs. They were fluttering alarmingly, but thank heaven, moving just the same. "Yeah. He's breathing."

"Labored?"

"*I* don't know, Tom! What should I do?"

"First, calm yourself," he said evenly. "If you work yourself into a state, you'll do neither of you any good."

I drew a couple of deep breaths, as if I could save my cat through sheer osmosis. "OK."

"Here's what I want you to do. Open his mouth, and make sure there's no detritus blocking his airway."

"Detritus?"

"Vomit, food, whatever. It's vital to keep that passageway open. Especially if this is what I think it is."

"But what *is* it?"

"Do what I'm asking you to." Tom softened his tone. "Please, Joe."

I set the phone on the toilet and bent low, prying Noodles' mouth open. I peered inside. It looked clear.

I snatched the phone back up. "I think we're OK. Now what?"

"Wrap him in a soft towel. Gently. And get him here as fast as you possibly can."

I hung up without saying good-bye and pulled a large terry-cloth bath towel off the rack on the wall. I softly lifted Noodles from his litter box and began folding him in the towel. As I did he meowed pitifully, his shuddering rapidly growing worse.

From the depths of my gut I groaned a wordless prayer. I'm far from proud of it, but I'm pretty sure the gist was, *Don't do this to me. Not again.*

Hustling him out of my house, I ran down the front steps and to my car. As I laid Noodles on the seat, he howled again, but not as loudly as before. Was he growing weaker? Praying harder, I wrenched the ignition key.

Even now I can't recall the drive to Tom's office. I'm sure there were blaring horns, screeching brakes, and many an obscene gesture directed our way, but I honestly don't remember them. All I can say for sure is the twenty-minute trip from my Butler County home to Tom's practice next to Northgate Mall seemed to take all day.

My car laid a patch of rubber eight feet long behind it as I skidded to a stop in front of his door. Lifting Noodles from the Cougar's front seat, I ran with him into the waiting room like my hair was on fire.

At this point you may be judging my actions with pity or contempt. Maybe both. After all, he was just a stupid cat, right? Well, no, actually. He was my friend, and I nearly bowled over Tom's rail-thin nurse, Madge Adams, as I thundered down the hall.

But Madge must be a dab hand at dealing with frantic pet owners, because she didn't even blink. Adroitly recovering her equilibrium, she directed Noodles and me into the first examination room, where Tom was waiting, and then she followed us in.

"Let's see him," Tom said. Nervously I handed over the bundle containing my little buddy, trying not to think of how quiet he'd grown.

Tom put Noodles up on the table and unfolded the towel, bending close. He looked up at me. "You're in my light, Joe."

"Sorry." I moved back maybe an inch.

The vet's kind face creased in an understanding smile. "Sit down." He pointed to a chair beside a medicine cabinet on wheels. "Right there. OK?"

"OK." I did as he asked, lowering myself. "If you need me, I'll be right here."

He smiled again. "I know you will." Once more he bent over Noodles. "OK, let's see what we've got." Amazingly, as Tom prodded him, I heard my cat start to purr. I nearly lost it then. Tough little rascal. Tougher than his old man, that's for sure.

Another minute or two more of this, and Tom straightened his tall frame. "Well, it's what I thought, and I wish I was wrong. He's been poisoned."

That jerked me out of my chair like a water-skier on a rope. *"Poisoned?"*

"Sixth one I've heard about this week." His expression was grim. "All of them from your neighborhood."

"But ... what kind of person ..." I shook my head in disbelief. "Look at him, Tom. Hasn't he been through enough?"

Staring down at Noodles, all the vet could do was nod. I mentioned earlier that those drunks had tortured Noodles. I need to expand on that a bit. In truth, they'd tried to burn him to death. On his little body my cat bears the twisted skin and scars of their cruelty.

Leaning down, I scratched his ear stump. Noodles tried to purr louder, but he was suddenly racked by a wheezing cough that threatened to tear him apart. The paper on the examination table before him now bore flecks of pink, frothy blood.

"We're out of time," Tom muttered, scooping up Noodles and shoving me aside. "Madge!" he hollered as he ran down the hall, me right on his heels. "The chamber!"

Her reply was calm. "Already prepared, Doctor." Tom and I hustled into a smaller room at the end of the corridor.

The general impression I got was one of starkness. The walls were bare, and the only furniture in the room was a large table in the middle. On it squatted what looked like a smaller version of a 1950s-era iron lung. That was all the time I had to gawk as Tom hurriedly shoved Noodles inside, towel and all, slamming the door shut after him. Through a dinky glass window in the tank's side I could clearly see Noodles convulsing. Foamy blood now ran freely from between his clenched teeth.

"What's that thing you've got him in?" I yelled. "He's dying in there!"

Tom ignored me as he hit a switch on the tank's side. Somewhere below the floor I heard an air compressor kick in. While my frantic brain processed this, the vet bent down and began turning a black knob above the switch while he stared through the thick glass.

"What's—" I started again, but savagely he shushed me, all the time never taking his eyes off of Noodles.

A few painful, eternal seconds crawled by while I knotted my fists, knuckles white, praying silently in desperation. Some sage once said that God always hears the requests of children. I was hoping he'd add to the mix one coming in from a struggling private eye.

Time hung fire.

Then I leaned closer. Was that—? I felt a small flicker of hope forming.

A few more seconds passed, and now it was plain I hadn't been seeing things. Noodles had stopped his mindless thrashing. His body was quieting, and best of all the flow of blood was slowing down.

I released my breath. I hadn't realized I'd been holding it. I looked at Tom and blinked. Sweat beaded his forehead, his skin pale.

Straightening and turning to me, he met my eyes. "*That* was close."
Looking over at his nurse Madge, whom I hadn't known was still in the
room with us, he instructed her, "Keep an eye on him for the next
hour, and call the police. Joe and I will be in my office."

"Yes, Doctor."

A couple of minutes later we were in Tom's tasteful office, him
behind his desk, me in the visitor's chair in front. He ran a speckled
hand back through his thinning gray hair.

"That's about as near as I'd ever like to cut it," he said. "It's a
good thing I don't keep any liquor around here, because I could use
a drink."

"I would have told you to make it two, but I've sworn off the stuff."
I shifted my weight. "Tom, what the devil is going on here?"

"Something nasty. I'd mentioned it earlier." His voice went flat.
"Joe, your cat was poisoned."

I didn't answer, and he went on, "The story is making the rounds
of the vet circles, but unfortunately it hasn't hit the press yet. Bottom
line, it looks like some sick, sorry jerk up your way is having some fun
killing cats."

"I'd like five minutes alone with him." My racing heart had calmed
some, and I slumped back in my chair. "What would make someone
want to do that? And what's with him using poison? Is the guy some
kind of a crazy chemist with a death wish, or what?"

"I don't know." Wearily Tom pulled off his wire-frame glasses and
dry-washed his face. A couple of seconds passed, then he put his
cheaters back on and said, "It could be anybody. A mean kid, a little
old lady trying to protect the neighborhood birds, whatever. Maybe it's
just somebody with a cruel streak a mile wide and too much time on
their hands. The thing is, cats are usually the targets. Don't ask me why.
I can't answer."

"It could be it was an accident."

"No, it's deliberate. I'll bet you my fee it is."

"On the phone," I said, "when I called you. You knew."

"The symptoms were all there. The spasms, the voiding of the
bowels, the rapid breathing, the shuddering … it had all the markings

of metallic poisoning. The frothy blood erupting is what sealed it. That's why I had to put Noodles in the chamber as fast as I did."

"I was wondering about that."

"The hyperbaric chamber is patterned after the old iron lungs you and I remember as kids, when polio was running rampant and paralyzing people."

I knew it. "What does it do?"

"Metallic poisons drive themselves deep into the soft tissues, depriving them of oxygen. Left alone, they can kill pretty quickly. The chamber, with its higher pressure, forces the oxygenated blood in, and the poisons out. In theory."

I raised an eyebrow. "In theory?"

"As with any poison, it's a delicate dance between time and toxicity. I think we beat the reaper with Noodles. The next hour will tell. But even then, he's not out of the woods yet. It depends on how much poison he ingested."

"So what happens until I know for sure?"

"Stay in here. Relax, as much as you can. I understand you've found religion, so you might try praying for him."

"That's all I've been doing since I found him."

Tom's tired smile was kind as he stood. "Then I'd say your cat is in about as good a set of hands as I can imagine."

He came around to my side of the desk, patting me on the shoulder as he passed before pausing and flipping off the light. Then he softly shut the door behind himself, leaving me alone. Well, no, that's not true. I was far from alone, and I took up where I'd left off as I returned to praying for my little pal.

♦ ◊ ♦

An hour later, I heard the door open behind me, and I looked around.

Tom was walking in softly, carrying something quite small and very still, wrapped in the towel I'd brought. My heart thrust itself up into my throat. Was he—? I jumped to my feet.

"Shhh," the vet whispered. "He's sleeping. Pretty soundly too. He's been through quite a battle."

I gently lifted the bundle from Tom's hands and folded back a corner of the cotton towel. Noodles' eyes were shut, his breathing deep and regular, only every now and then interrupted by a shudder.

Reluctantly I met the other man's eyes. "What's the prognosis?"

"Better than I would have given you odds for when you first brought him in. After I removed him from the chamber, I gave him a broadband spectrum of antitoxin injections. Those should help counteract whatever it was he ate. The operative word being 'should.' This is one hard-nosed little fighter you've got here."

I put a forefinger against Noodles' cheek, ever so gently stroking it. As I did, he unconsciously moved his head a bit, rubbing me back. I smiled down at him.

"Don't get too comfortable with what you're seeing," the vet cautioned. "Like I said before, he's not out of the woods yet. Metallic poisons are awful. Think strychnine or arsenic, that'll give you an idea."

"Which one was given to him?"

"I don't know yet. I drew blood for a tox screen, but that takes time. I'll know something more concrete later today. I'm still trying to get a fix on how he ingested it. Do you let him out much?"

"Hardly ever. After what happened to him as a kitten, he prefers the indoors." I was still cradling Noodles. "But every now and then his feline nature steps up to the plate, and he acts like he wants to go out. If I'm not there to do it, my neighbor across the street has a key to my place. She said she's happy to let him run for an hour or so."

"And he was let out yesterday, right?"

"Last night, actually. I was working late at the office, and Beulah called me and said she saw him at my front window, howling to be let out. I told her to go ahead." I stared at the floor. "If I'd known what was going to happen—"

"Stop. There's no sense going there." Tom's look turned pensive. "This Beulah. How well do you know her?"

"Well enough to trust her with my cat's safety." The vet frowned, and I went on, "Tom, she's eighty-five years old. She's wrinkled. She makes Christmas cookies. She's your basic white-haired grandma straight out of central casting."

"And she may be a poisoner of small animals." I started to fire off an answer, and he held up a hand. "I'm just saying that appearances can be deceiving. In your line of work, you should know that better than anyone."

"Yeah," I sighed. "Yeah, maybe you're right." I looked down at my sleeping cat. "If he pulls through this, I'll never let anyone else have access to him again."

"I can't blame you there. Right now the immediate concern is getting him well. I'll keep him here for the next twenty-four hours for observation. That should tell the tale. When you do finally take him home, he's going to need rest, fluids, and plenty of TLC."

"I'm good for all three." Reaching around back for my wallet with my right hand I asked, "What's the damage today?"

Tom put a gentle restraining arm on my elbow. "Put it away. I'll send you a bill."

What he meant, without coming right out and saying it, was *Let's see if Noodles lives first.*

My thoughts against my cat's poisoner grew heavy. And very, very dark.

4

*H*ow you doing, buddy? Comfortable enough?"

In reply to my question, Noodles opened red-rimmed eyes, not even raising his head, regarding me silently from the makeshift bed where he reposed in the corner of my office. My stuffed sock monkey, Mister Monk Junior, stared down at him benignly from his home on top of my file cabinet. He's the last present my wife, Linda, had bought me, to replace the one I'd lost as a child. She and my unborn son had died in a Christmas Eve car crash nearly thirty years ago now, on her way back from buying it. A cheery sort, he helps me get past their loss. Sometimes.

The time was late morning of the following day, and earlier I'd picked up my cat from Tom's before bringing him here. As I watched, with a sigh he closed his eyes, pedaling his back legs a moment before growing still once more.

For seemingly the hundredth time since I'd put him there, I got up and went around the corner of my desk over to where he lay, bending low and stroking him. He sighed again. I hoped all this sighing was a good thing, that it meant he was getting plenty of oxygen. The last thing Tom had told me before I left his office was to keep Noodles closely monitored for the next twenty-four hours.

"No bright lights, no sudden noises," he warned. "Some of the effects of the poisons mimic epileptic seizures. They affect the flexor muscles."

"What are those?" I was getting an education in small animal husbandry. One I'd neither asked for nor wanted.

"Turn around." I did as Tom said, presenting him my back.

"They run here, and here," he said, lightly running his thumb down either side of my spine. "Any sudden change might trigger an episode."

I faced him again. "Episode? Like what? Growling, foaming at the mouth, what?"

"Probably not that. If it happens, there'll be no mistake. You'll know it. He'll arch his back like he's stretching, but it won't stop until he's completely rigid. I've heard stories of animals breaking their spines in such a fit."

I gave the vet a look. "Man, you're not sugarcoating it for me, are you? You're making it sound hopeless."

"I'm always straight with my patients. And their owners. In the end, it's kinder that way."

I hated to ask the next. "So what do I do if something triggers an ... what you said?"

Tom's weary eyes met mine. In them I saw candor. Too much of it. "Normally I'd have you bring him in, and I'd inject him with a muscle relaxant. Sometimes it works. If given in time."

"Then let me have some to take with me. In 'Nam, I saw our medic give guys plenty of injections. In the worst situations imaginable." Tom started to shake his head, and I broke in on him. "I know what you're going to say. How hard can it be to inject a cat?"

"It's not the difficulty, it's the futility." I obviously didn't get it, so he said, "Noodles suffered lung damage as a kitten in that fire those two drunks set. Surely you've heard him wheezing from time to time. Especially as he's gotten older."

"I've heard it. I was hoping it was my ears playing tricks on me."

"If something sets off an episode like I've described—and it's by no means certain he's been poisoned with what would cause one—an antispasm injection would be useless. His lungs couldn't take the strain. He'd be gone before it could take effect."

I must have looked really stricken by then, because Tom simply said in parting, "He's counting on you, Joe. Just love him."

Loving him wasn't even an issue. And praying I could do too. Not well, maybe, but what I lack in quality I make up for in determination.

I looked down where he lay as I continued to gently stoke his battered body. "You're not going to die, cat. Do you hear me? You are not ... going ... to die."

I stood up. OK, enough. I'd taken him to the vet, he'd been treated, and I would continue to pray for him. It was out of my hands now. I had a business to run. Again striding purposefully back around my desk, I tried not to let the phrase "whistling past the graveyard" take hold of my thinking.

I sat down and dialed Billy Barnicke's phone number. Two rings, three, and he picked up.

"National Investigations." Billy always did have grandiose visions for his practice.

"Billy? Joe."

"Hey, Jozefsky!" the other man boomed. I could picture him grinning and leaning back in the same style desk chair I have. I'd picked mine up at the Salvation Army store; I have no idea where Billy copped his. But it wouldn't surprise me to find a company called Sleazy Seats making them just for guys like us. "So to what do I owe the pleasure? Got another rich client you'd like to foist off?"

"No. But Tate's the reason I'm calling."

"Yeah?" I heard his lighter click as he lit a cigarette. "What about him?"

I paused. Now that I had Billy on the line, I was afraid the words weren't going to come out right.

So what if they don't? a part of me asked. *You knew you were going to feel like a fool when you picked up the phone. Just say it and be done.*

"Uh, it's ... uh ..." I was right. The vowels and consonants were sticking in my throat.

I could imagine a frown creasing Billy's desiccated German features as I heard him take in a drag, blow it out. "Tate's not thinking of backing out on the deal, is he?"

"No ..." Nuts. Why was I having such a hard time with this? "It's just that I don't think you should go ahead with it."

"What are you talking about?"

This was harder than I'd thought. "This thing that Tate's doing ... it's not right."

Billy chuckled. "Looks mighty right to me. I've been feeling lucky these past few days, but didn't have the scratch for the itch. Now I do. Riverboat, here I come."

"I think you should reconsider working with the guy, Billy. I really do."

His laugh was a study in smoker's rasp. "You always were a kidder, Joe."

My voice tightened. "Shut up and listen to me. I'm starting to get a bad feeling about this." And I was.

A word of explanation is called for. Ever since I was a kid, sometimes I've been able to tell beforehand whether or not a thing is about to go sour, for me or for someone else. More than once it saved my bacon in 'Nam. Afterward, too.

I'd thought my so-called gift would fade as I grew older. So far, it hasn't. The folks living in the hardscrabble coal-mining town where I grew up in eastern Kentucky have a name for it: *fey*. In my case the feeling manifests itself as an unpleasant ant-crawling sensation traversing up and down my spine. And right now, as I'd said those words to Billy, those ants were having themselves a time.

"Hold on." His tone had turned suspicious. "You're not trying to mess things up for your old pal Billy B. are you, Joe? Like maybe you've changed your mind about Tate's ten grand, and now you wanna snag it yourself? Tell me you're not trying to screw me over."

"You're talking crazy. It's just—"

"*I'm* taking crazy?" he broke in. "Seems to me I'm not the one trying to queer the deal."

"Queer the deal? I'm trying to save your life." And the weird thing was, somehow I knew I was right: if Billy took this job with Tate, his life really was over. How I knew, I can't exactly say, but I knew it just the same.

"Wait a minute, wait a minute, *now* I know what all this is." Billy's tone had turned sly. "Why, I do believe you're drinking again. I think old brother Holy Joe went and tied one on." His derisive laugh devolved into a cough. "My oh my, what *will* the church ladies say?"

I gripped the phone tighter. "Shut your trap and think a minute, Billy. Have I ever said anything like this to you?"

"No, can't say you have." His reply was flat, his fake good humor gone like ice in August. "But as the sixteen-year-old hooker said to the john, there's always the first time."

I almost tossed the receiver. He was refusing to get it. All Billy was seeing was dollar signs. I calmed myself and tried it again, this time from a different tack. "Listen, you were an altar boy, right?"

"This is stupid."

"Answer the question."

My friend blew out a breath. "Back in my misspent youth, yeah. Downtown. At Saint Peter in Chains. Three years." Billy's voice took on a different pitch, rougher. "It was kind of fun up until the day Father Kelsey tried to instruct me in something they don't teach at seminary. Why? What's that have to do with this?"

"I'm saying that as a Catholic in parochial school you were taught the difference between right and wrong."

"Tell that to Kelsey," Billy countered, but I ignored it.

"The word's called 'morality.'" Even as I said it I realized how pompous I sounded. And I knew I'd blown my only chance with him.

I was right. Billy jumped on it.

"Oh, man. I don't believe this. Joe, you got some major stones, lecturing *me* on morals. Tell me, is this the same Joe Box I used to pub-crawl with, the guy I had to take home so many times when he was blind drunk that I lost count?"

I didn't answer. Truth was truth, and Billy had skewered me with it like a piece of meat on a spit.

"I'm hanging up now," he said. "Nice try though."

The sound of his phone crashing down was so loud it was like I'd been hit in the head with it.

◆ ◊ ◆

The next few days passed uneventfully. And what do you know? Noodles didn't die.

To be sure, his recovery was a lot slower than suited me, but as Tom wisely counseled when I took my cat in for the follow-up exam, "Just be thankful he didn't end up like the others."

By "the others," Tom was referring to the three other cats the Butler County poisoner had nailed in the past seven days. It was in the news now. Out of a total of ten tries, he or she had been successful with nine. Noodles was the only one who'd made it. I don't know if that was due to Tom's skill as a vet, or divine intervention. Most likely both.

As far as the other thing, I'd pretty much resigned Billy to whatever fate awaited him. I'd tried to warn him, and he'd ignored me. Even though I still felt responsible, for good or ill, his bed was made; I hoped he'd find it comfortable.

Which made what happened next so strange.

It was Sunday morning, almost twelve noon straight up, and services at the church Angela and I attended had just let out. The temperature for mid-October was unexpectedly balmy, and the bright, Indian summer sunshine streaming down felt good on my face.

But I knew it was just illusion. Winter was patiently waiting for everyone's guard to drop. Then it would pounce.

As the two of us crossed the parking lot toward my car, my eye was drawn to an odd sight: a black stretch limo parked sideways across a couple of empty slots just down a ways from us. Behind the tinted glass I could make out the shadowy figure of the driver. He appeared enormous. Outside the car, a tall, elegantly dressed man in his late forties with razor-cut, jet-black hair leaned against the door. An insolent smile hung on his thin lips.

But what really drew my attention, along with the other folks walking along toward their own cars, were the companions flanking him.

Both were women, over six feet tall with wasp waists and swimmers' shoulders, the one on the man's left an icy Nordic blonde, the one on his right a rich ebony brunette. The females, put plainly, were insanely gorgeous, dressed in identical severely cut, dark-green business suits. Around me I could hear the church members chattering about this weird trio, and I knew without even having to be told that the dude in the middle was Cyrus Alan Tate.

As Angela and I approached my car, Tate pushed away from the limo and began strolling easily toward us, the two bookend women lagging a silent, respectful step behind.

Angela glanced at me as the three drew nearer. "Joe? Do you know these people?"

Keeping my eye on the trio, I simply nodded. "Yeah. I think I do. The guy anyway."

"But who—?" I ignored her as I stepped in front, trying to shield her.

The group reached us, and the man put out his hand in a smooth, practiced motion. "Joe Box?" His voice was low and well modulated.

"That's me," I answered, disregarding the proffered mitt. "And you must be Cyrus Tate."

Tate lowered his hand, but his evenly capped toothy smile stayed bright. "That's right. Obviously my aide, Morris Chalafant, described me when he visited you the other day. Or perhaps you've recently seen me in the news."

"No," I lied. I had, of course, but I kept my expression neutral. "Just a hunch."

"A man who pays attention to his hunches," he quipped. "I like that."

I said nothing, and Tate motioned to his compatriots. "But I'm being gauche. Allow me to introduce you to a couple of friends. Cindi and Candi, say hello to Mr. Box."

Cindi was the blonde, Candi the African American. Their nods at me were calculating, and neither cracked so much as the hint of a smile as they regarded Angela and me. And while Tate's lips were skinny, almost nonexistent, theirs were positively swollen. I reckoned between the two women there was enough injected collagen to decimate a third-world village.

I nodded at the blonde. "I'll bet you a manicure at your favorite salon your name ends in the letter *i.*" And to the other one: "So does yours."

The two Amazons didn't even lift an eyebrow, but Tate looked surprised, and he chuckled. "Not bad, Mr. Box. Not bad by half. How did you know?"

"Too many years of reading my cousin Ray's dirty magazines when I was a kid. I know a centerfold when I see one."

Angela turned toward me and gawped.

Tate tilted his head up to the sky and laughed, "ha-ha-ha," but the sound struck me as mechanical, like the windup box wedged in his throat had a crack in it. After the third "ha" he lowered his head and kept right on, as if he'd never laughed at all. "Since it's plain you're ahead of the curve, I'll bet you know why I'm here."

"Here, in this parking lot? Or here on this planet at all?" I didn't give him time to respond. "To number one, yeah, I think I know. Although why you felt you had to brace me in front of my church isn't clear. That is, unless you wanted to charm me personally, instead of taking a chance over the phone. To number two though, I don't have a clue."

My insult to their boss finally got a reaction from Cindi and Candi. They glanced at each other, and beneath their fine-cut clothes, I saw both of their bodies tense.

"It doesn't really matter," Tate said. "May I speak freely in front of your, ah—," he gave Angela a quick up and down, "—friend?"

"Best keep your eyes in your head, laddie," I smiled, "or you'll be wearing them as a bolo."

At that both of the women took a step toward me, but Tate, his gaze now locked on me, put his arms out to the side, laying the palms of his hands gently across their abdomens. The bodyguards—and that's what they had to be—halted instantly.

Still staring, he slowly lowered his hands and gave a tiny nod. "My apologies, Mr. Box. I should know better than anyone the folly of coming between a man and his ... desire."

"The word you're reaching for is 'love.'" I turned away from him, taking Angela's elbow. "And we're finished here."

"But—"

Forget this guy. We began heading toward my car, and were a few

43

steps away when Tate called out to our backs, "Please, Mr. Box? I've come quite a long way to see you."

"Joe, don't you dare," Angela whispered as we walked. "That man is poison."

"A moment more, that's all I ask," I heard him say. We kept moving.

"Something's gone wrong," he called again. "With your friend Mr. Barnicke."

That stopped me.

"Joe ..." Angela warned again, but too late. I was turning anyway. My sweetie did the same, but from the corner of my eye I could tell her look at me was replete with flared nostrils.

"What about Billy?" I asked. The other man and his two companions drew closer, near enough for me to touch—which wasn't something I was planning on doing. I'm not much into slime, or its carriers. "What's happened to him?"

Tate made a dismissive motion with his hand. "Not with him personally. I didn't mean to alarm you. I meant, something's wrong with the quality of his work." His chuckle was the essence of good-natured grace. "Sorry."

I felt my blood pressure climbing. "Just what kind of game are you playing?"

Tate's pale eyes were as wide and innocent as a newborn's. "Why, no game at all."

"Fine," I said, nodding curtly. "Then it's like I said earlier. We have nothing further to discuss."

"Please, Mr. Box." Tate made as if he were about to touch me on the arm, and then must have reconsidered. Good thing, too. The boy would have drawn back a bloody stump. "I need your help. Your friend's left us in quite a bind. I'm not sure where to go with this."

I blew out an exasperated breath. "With what, Tate?"

"It's ... well, it has to do with his drinking."

Billy and booze. I'd figured as much.

Tate went on, "Now, I'll be the last one to begrudge a man the freedom of doing whatever he wants to do in his off time. Why should

I? I've built my entire business around just that freedom. But when I hire someone to do a job, I expect them to do it sober."

My laugh was harsh. "I'm not his keeper. Why come to me about it?" Tate's expression turned shrewd. "I hired him on your recommendation, Mr. Box. Surely you feel some responsibility."

"No." My tone was cool. "Can't say that I do." Tate frowned, but I went on. "Let me tell you a story that relates. It's a corker too." I settled into it. "The first car I ever owned was a red '65 Mustang I bought from my cousin Ray when I got back from Vietnam in 1971. Man, that thing was one sweet ride." I grinned at the memory. "Holley carb *and* racing slicks. Anyway, one hot summer day the front end went out, and I took the car to a mechanic over in Goose Rock on the referral of a friend. What I didn't know was that same morning the mechanic's wife had left him for his best friend."

I caught Cindi and Candi exchanging glances, Cindi rolling her eyes, Candi shaking her head slightly. I smiled at them. "There's a point to this, girls. Trust me."

Turning my attention back to Tate I went on, "Bottom line, the guy worked on the 'Stang dead drunk. That night as I was coming home from work the steering linkage began rattling like crazy. Before I could even wonder what was happening, it broke completely free, leaving the wheel flopping around in my hands like the thing was coated in pig grease. A second later the car flipped end over end, and rolled down the Bitter Creek embankment. It was a miracle I didn't croak. So, was the mechanic at fault? Sure he was. But bad things happen, and later the guy made it right."

Tate's face clouded. "What in the world does that have to do with this?"

"Simple. Billy's a good investigator, but a weak man. Little things can send him into an alcoholic haze. Bad news can do it, or even good, like you paying him ten thousand bucks for a week's work." I shrugged. "But he's wired pretty plainly. It doesn't take much to keep him in line. What I'd do is warn him strongly, and then let him finish."

"It's a bit late for that. I've already fired him."

"Huh." I lightly rubbed the end of my nose. "Then if it's advice you're after, I'd say you'd better find yourself another PI."

"I was hoping I could get you." Tate's words were pointed. "After all, you're who I had in mind for the job in the first place. Morris must have told you that."

"Yeah. He also said it was mostly a stunt you'd cooked up to see if you could get a Christian on the payroll of Tate Enterprises. Kind of a feather in your cap." The other man started to reply, but I cut him off. "You know, Tate, Led Zepplin put it best, a long time ago: 'the song remains the same.' And so does my answer. Pal, I wouldn't work for you on a bet."

That shut the hambone up. Finally. As the three of them stood there, flatfooted at my brass, I turned to take Angela's arm.

"Let's go, babe," I told her. "Something around here stinks."

5

Later that evening, back at my house, Angela and I were playing a little Scrabble. I was already up by quite a bit, and really liking that a lot, when I laid down a z tile in triumph.

"Hah!" I exclaimed. "Zubex." I picked up the score pad and began writing. "Third game skunked, Ange. You ready to concede my incredible grasp of the English tongue?"

"I'm ready to grasp your English tongue and give it a good yank. What in the twelve moons of Saturn is a zubex?"

I raised my eyebrows. "Don't tell me you've never heard of a zubex. Lions eat them in Africa. They're kind of like a deer, only smaller."

"*Braaak!* Wrong answer." Her grin was savage. "I'm going to call you on this one, hotshot. You mean an ibex."

I squinted at her. "What the devil is an ibex? You're making that up."

"*I'm* making it up? You're the one who called an ibex a zubex."

"We'll let Mr. Webster settle this," I said stiffly, pulling the dictionary over to me.

"Look for ibex first," Angela coaxed as I riffled the pages. "Save yourself some time. Because I'll bet you a ham sandwich you won't find the word 'zubex' in there."

I went to the *i*'s and ran my finger down the page. A moment later I found it. I frowned. "Huh. Ibex. 'A small, deerlike animal whose main habitation is the African veldt ...'" I shook my head. "So OK, you were right." I flipped to the back of the book. "But now let's see what a zubex is. Because maybe I was wrong about it being an animal in Africa, but that doesn't mean a thing, as long as I spelled it right."

Angela was nonchalantly staring up at the ceiling. "You're not gonna *find* it ..." she sang as I came to the *z*'s.

Reaching the end of the listings I paused, and then stopped. "Well, lookee here, as I live and breathe. A zubex."

"What?"

She snatched for the dictionary, but I kept it close as I made like I was still reading. "The entry goes on, and I quote, 'The zubex is a small, warm-blooded animal mainly found along the Pacific Rim, and most closely related to the platypus.'"

"You're crazy. Let me see that."

Lunging, she tried to seize the book, but I lifted it higher, plowing on. "The zubex is best known for allowing Joseph Jebstuart Box the ability to retain his title of the world's number-one Scrabble champ, and in the process ticking off Angela Swain to no end—stop it!"

We were both laughing now as she dove across the table, making a final futile grab. The game board and tiles went flying as we tumbled down together. A moment later we found ourselves side by side on the floor, the tiles around us littering the area like wooden confetti. In that light, Angela looked good enough to eat.

"As long as we're down here," I said, "how about a kiss?"

"I don't kiss cheaters," she answered primly, just an inch away. "Scrabble cheaters especially. They are the lowest of the low."

"Chalk it up to a weak moment."

She cocked an eyebrow at me. "You seem to have a lot of those."

I waggled my eyebrows right back, giving her Groucho. "Yeah, and I'm having one right now ..." That's as far as I got as suddenly the phone rang in the kitchen. I rolled over on my back, looking up at the ceiling. "Perfect. Who could that be?"

"What time is it?" Angela pulled up her sleeve, checking her wristwatch. "Good grief. A little after ten."

"On a Sunday night yet. I'll make short work of this." Climbing to my feet, I pointed down to where she was pushing herself to her feet. "Stay right there."

"Can I at least get up on the couch? Your floor isn't exactly soft."

"OK. But no farther." I padded into the kitchen, where the phone was on its fifth ring. Checking the caller ID, my spine started tingling to beat the band, and its director.

The number was Billy's.

I snatched up the receiver before the answering machine could come on.

"Billy? Is that you? What's the matter?" Instead of a reply, there was a wet, gasping sound, like someone breathing through damp cloth. I gripped the phone tighter. "Talk to me, man."

By that time Angela had come into the room and stood by me. Obviously she'd heard my end of the conversation from the living room. "What's going on?"

I held up a forefinger, quieting her. "Listen, are—"

"Joe," I heard him whisper at last, painfully drawing my name out.

"Are you hurt?" I asked, my voice taut.

His reply didn't even sound human. "They ... I ... I ..."

Angela was practically pulling my sleeve off in her agitation. "Will you *please* tell me what's happening?"

I covered the mouthpiece with my hand. "It's Billy. He sounds like he's been run over by a truck."

She reached down, unclipping the cell phone from her belt. "Keep him on the line, and talking. I'm calling 911."

I nodded and turned my attention back to Billy. "Stay with us, man. Angela's calling the cops. You'll be all right."

"No cops!" I heard him rasp, with more strength than he'd had just moments before, and my eyes opened wide. Then he groaned and said more softly, "No cops ..." He pulled in another agonized breath. "They'll ... I can't take ... another one ..."

Another what? I had no idea if that last was directed at me, or just

Billy moaning in delirium. But my reply was soothing. "OK, no cops. I'm on my way."

"What?" Angela said. I shushed her again.

"I'll tell you in a minute," I muttered. Then I said to Billy, "Hang tight, pal. I'll be there in twenty." I hung up to find Angela staring at me in disbelief.

"Why aren't you calling the police? Shouldn't they help?"

I'd already snatched my jacket from the back of the kitchen chair and was slipping it on.

"I know what this is," I said, zipping up. "Pretty sure, anyway."

"What, for heaven's sake?"

"Billy's 'no cops' comment is what gave it away. I think a loan shark he's blown off sent some thugs over to his house, maybe to try and get a little payback." She frowned, not understanding, so I said, "Besides drinking, Billy's other weakness is gambling."

"Gambling? What kind?"

"It doesn't matter. With him it's all the same, spinning a roulette wheel on one of the riverboats, or pitching pennies in a back alley. The game's the thing. The problem is, he's not very good at it. It sounds like he's run afoul of some guy he owes money to."

"But meeting him at his place … could it be dangerous?"

"I doubt it. I've been through this before. I'll go over, ice his bruises, sit with him awhile. But I need you to promise not to call the cops while I'm gone, Ange. Things could get really messy for him if you do."

"All right." She sounded less than enthusiastic.

I felt in my pocket for my keys and turned to her. "You going to hang here until I get back, or head on home?"

She still sounded dubious. "This may take some time, so I might as well leave." Angela's look at me as she picked up her purse was a curious mix of aggravation and love. Touching my face in parting, she smiled. "You and your friends."

We walked out my front door together, and then she got in her car while I climbed in mine. Angela pulled out of the drive first, pointing her Saab toward Hamilton. I went the other way, turning my newly purchased, vintage 1968 candy-apple red Mercury

Cougar toward Cincinnati and the working-class neighborhood of Norwood.

♦ ◊ ♦

Almost twenty minutes later I turned onto Williams Avenue. Billy's little beat-up clapboard house was down two blocks, where Floral crossed, and at this time of night I had no problem finding a parking spot on the street right in front. As I got out and pocketed the keys, I noted that his dwelling was ominously dark.

I mounted the three rickety steps up to his front door. Knowing his doorbell hadn't worked in years, I reached out and gave the frame two sharp knocks, at the same time calling out, "Yo, Billy. It's Joe. Open up." I listened for movement inside. Nothing. The foreboding deepened.

Trying to be respectful of Billy's neighbors who were either asleep or watching TV, I raised my voice just a tad. "Come on, man. It's chilly out here." And it was. By the time the third week of October arrives in Cincinnati, it's not unusual to see light frost, especially at night. Right then, my jacket was having to battle against the upper-thirties temperature.

"Ah, the heck with this noise," I muttered as I reached above the doorframe where I knew Billy kept his spare key. Yes, as a PI he should have known what an obvious place that was for a thief to look, but Billy was never one to listen to good advice. I should talk.

Slipping the key into the lock, I turned the knob, opening the door a foot. Stepping inside, I shut it behind me and sang out, louder than before, "Billy?"

A low moan came from the kitchen.

Hearing that, I cursed my stupidity for not having brought along my .38. Double-timing the five steps through Billy's living room, I stormed past the cluttered foyer and on into the kitchen. Once there, by habit my hand found the worn push-button light switch. Clicking it on, I stared around the room. The place had been trashed

The door to Billy's old refrigerator stood open, and on the floor in front of it lay smashed eggs, broken beer bottles, and melting butter. The cabinets were flung wide, destroyed dishes crunching underfoot. Scattered around were ripped open cereal boxes and dented cans. It was as if the old-time Goths and Vandals had thrown a bachelor party here.

I looked down then, and that's when I saw him. My jaw dropped.

"Oh no ..." I whispered as I fell to my knees beside him.

Billy hadn't been just pummeled; he'd been beaten within an inch of his life.

My friend's face, never movie star handsome to start with, was almost unrecognizable. His left eye was swollen closed, his right nearly so. His nose was mashed flat, and one ear dangled from his head by a small flap of skin. His left hand had been crushed, plainly by someone's boot heel; I could make out the pattern mashed into his skin.

The fingers on Billy's right hand, except for the pinky, were all either broken or dislocated. How he'd managed to hold his phone in that hand, or even punch out my number with his one undamaged digit, was beyond me; it must have taken incredible grit. The blood, cuts, bruises, and contusions I could see were bad enough. Who knew what deeper damage his body had suffered?

I was wrong. This wasn't a beating. This was one step up from murder.

I lifted him gently into a semi-sitting position, taking care to make sure that any broken ribs he'd suffered wouldn't puncture a lung. Pulling his lower jaw open, I found a mess. His mouth was jam-packed with clotted blood and broken teeth. Using my finger I cleared out the worst of it. Right away his breath sounded a little bit better.

Billy's one remaining good eye rolled about in its socket a moment before looking up and finding mine.

"Joe ..." he groaned. Immediately he went into a wracking coughing fit.

"Shh, partner, go easy now." I looked around the room for something soft to cushion him. "Listen, I'm going to lay you back down a second while I call for help."

"No ... time ..." When he gasped this time, he sounded like a bagful of broken glass.

A chill coursed through me. From my time in Vietnam, and then later on the streets as a Cincinnati cop, I know a death rattle when I hear one. And I'd just heard one. It was certain Billy had only minutes left. I pulled him up higher, trying to ease his passing. But there was something I had to know first.

"Who did this?" A name came to me. "Was it Sal Battaglia?"

Earlier this spring Billy had had a run-in with the loan shark Battaglia and his crew that had resulted in a similar beating. Not a tenth as bad as this one though. So help me, I'd have an accounting of this. I'd ask my half-brother Vincent to help. He'd do it, though grudgingly. More on that later.

Surprisingly, Billy jerked his head. "Not ... Sal ..." He drew another agonized breath, and what he said next didn't shock me as much as I would have thought. *"Tate ... "*

I had to be sure. "Cyrus Tate had this done to you?"

Billy nodded painfully once.

"Why?" I demanded.

Instead of an answer, a freshet of hot coppery blood exploded from Billy's mouth, spraying my shirt crimson. And when he spoke for the final time, his words made no sense.

"The first two," he strangled out, and then, more softly, "the ... first two ..."

Lightly, I shook him. "What do you mean? The first two *what?*"

But Billy was past answering. Any reply he gave couldn't have been heard with natural ears.

6

Within five minutes of my 911 call, a city of Norwood life-squad unit and a CPD patrol car with a couple of uniforms inside had screeched up on the street outside of Billy's, parking behind my Cougar. It wasn't until I'd let in the EMTs with their gurney that I saw I'd been wrong about the cop car's occupants. One was a Cincinnati patrolman, sure enough.

The other was Lieutenant Jack Mulrooney, lead detective of the CPD vice squad. Swell, I sighed to myself. Just freaking dandy. The poet said there's a match for everyone in this world, and Jack and I sure proved it. We were each other's nemesis.

The day I graduated from the academy as a rookie cop, I'd been assigned to an older patrolman for mentoring. It was my good fortune to be handed over to Sergeant Tim Mulrooney, Jack's dad, for my street training. "Sarge" was savvy and beef-jerky tough, but that rough exterior couldn't hide a huge giving heart.

Sarge's training didn't end when our shift was over either. He and his wife, Helen, took me and my late wife, Linda, under their wing, almost as their own surrogate children. That's probably where their son Jack got his disdain for me. It was the classic Cain and Abel story: try as he might, Jack's get-ahead-at-any-price methods didn't do much to endear him to his father. But rather than making him reassess his tactics, all Jack had done in response to his dad's chastising was to do more of whatever it took to climb the CPD ladder.

The net effect was, by the time Jack turned thirty-five, he'd won the honor of becoming the youngest vice squad chief of detectives in the history of the department. In spite of that, ten years later, he still resented the affection his dad had for me. The fact that I'd left the force in the middle of my second year, four days after my wife's death in a car crash, didn't help. In Jack's eyes I was a quitter, beneath his contempt, and would always remain so.

My nod at him was noncommittal. "Lieutenant. To what do I owe the pleasure?"

His expression was cold. "Luck of the draw. I was at an FOP gathering tonight over on Sherman, and Officer Downs here was giving me a lift back downtown."

Dutifully standing off to the side, Downs was a dewy-cheeked youngster of twenty-two or so, and had to have been less than overjoyed at the prospect of chauffeuring the brass around. But he was smart enough to keep his expression bland. And unless I missed my guess, the "gathering" Jack had mentioned was nothing more than his weekly poker game.

The older man went on, "The Norwood PD took the squeal, and we caught it on the squad radio." His eyes grew even icier. "When I heard your name, I couldn't believe it. I told the dispatcher Downs and I would take it."

Lucky me. Of all the nights for Billy to up and croak, it would have to be when my sworn enemy was only five blocks away. Dawn would be a long time coming.

"So tell me, Box ..." Jack started, but his questioning was cut short as the EMTs began wheeling Billy's body back out of the kitchen and through the living room, past where the two cops and I stood. My one-time friend was covered by a sheet, and by the casual way the paramedics were moving him, I knew I'd called it right. Once he arrived at the hospital, on the records Billy Barnicke would be listed as DOA.

"Where are you taking him?" I asked them, my voice rough. The older of the two, a big, shambling guy with a button nose and thinning black hair, paused and answered.

"General. He'll be autopsied there. It's routine with cases like this." The guy's tone softened. "You a relative?"

"No." My tongue felt unaccountably thick. "Just a friend." Reaching out, I touched the material covering the body. The white cotton felt cool on my fingertips. "So long, Billy."

Without further comment the hulking EMT and his partner wheeled the cart out the door, down to the waiting ambulance.

I watched them load Billy in for a moment before I heard a movement, and I turned. It was Jack, smoothing his hair. I looked at him. "You were saying, Lieutenant?"

"I was saying, maybe we should continue this downtown."

"I don't think so. I remember the last session I had with you in the Dungeon. The basement interrogation room is still called the Dungeon, isn't it?"

Jack nodded at the memory.

I continued, "It went all night long, you blowing bad breath and cigarette smoke in my face, while all the time my wrist stayed manacled to a D-bolt in the floor. But what made the whole thing really out of line that night is as a vice cop you didn't have any more jurisdiction in that arson case than you have in homicide. You just shoehorned your way into the thing for grins, to cause me grief." My sigh was companionable. "The way I figure it, Jacko my boy, I don't have to say spit to you. So why don't you peddle your act to somebody who'll buy it."

"But that's wrong, you do have to answer to me," Jack said. "See, a guy carrying a gold shield—a guy like me, for instance—can stick his nose in just about anywhere he pleases. It's called departmental cooperation. Ever hear of it?" He snapped his fingers, his voice taking on a mocking tone as his hazel eyes went unreadable. "Oh yeah, I keep forgetting. You're not a cop anymore."

I ignored that. "As I further recall, your skills weren't as slick as you'd like to think. At the end of that session you weren't any closer to finding the person who'd blown up my apartment house than when you started."

Jack lightly rubbed his chin. From where I stood I could hear the rasp of late-night whiskers.

"It doesn't matter. Because it seems I'm always finding you around violence, Box." He motioned with his hand. "Look at yourself. You have enough gore on your shirt to qualify as a Jackson Pollock painting. And that body they just took out of here? That one you were alone with here for who knows how long? Cripes, I've seen less blood at a sausage factory." His sigh was pleasant, the epitome of ersatz friendliness. "To me, you're looking pretty good for this."

I addressed young Officer Downs. "Kid, let this be a lesson in how not to pursue a crime lead." He frowned, clearly not getting it, and I explained, "It's tempting, but never go with the first suspect handy. Especially when motive is lacking." I turned my attention back to the other man. "Jack, there was no reason for me to kill Billy."

"There's always a reason. You PI types are all alike. You spend all day digging around in people's garbage. Do enough of that, and pretty soon you start to smell like garbage yourself." He shrugged. "I dunno, maybe you found something on him, you came over here to make the guy pay you to keep quiet about it, and he fought back."

"You're reaching, Jack."

"Maybe it's drugs," he went on. "Maybe it's something else. Who knows, it could even be you two had a lovers' spat. So far as a motive goes, give me time. I'll find one."

"Or invent one."

Jack's face grew hard, and he turned to the younger cop. "Downs, frisk this idiot."

Not wanting to cause the kid grief, I played along and raised my hands to the side. Downs did the task quickly and thoroughly, a very professional job, then turned to his boss. "Nothing. This dude's as clean as my Aunt Minnie's thoughts, Lieutenant."

I grinned at the patrolman. "Say, that's pretty good. I'll need to remember that." Downs couldn't have known that in fact I had an

57

Aunt Minnie at one time, and usually her thoughts—and language—were anything but pure.

The kid grinned back in return, and Jack scowled. "Like I said, it doesn't matter. This is just the start of the fun for you, Box. And I would have bet a month's pay you were packing that old .38 of yours. How come you aren't? Barrel finally drop off?"

"I didn't figure I'd need it tonight."

"No, not with you as strong as you are physically, that's for sure. Beating a man to death, a gun would have been redundant." He motioned at my side. "Let's see 'em."

That threw me. "See what?"

"Your hands, dummy."

Sighing, I held them out.

Jack leaned close. Then shaking his head, he straightened. "OK, no marks. So you didn't use your hands. Still doesn't matter. I'm sure a cursory search around here will turn up a pipe, an ax handle, something."

"Maybe, but they won't have my prints on them."

"Not a problem. We'll find the rubber gloves you wore, and forensics can lift the prints from inside." The other man's chuckle was gravelly. "You've really hung yourself this time, my friend." Then he shrugged, "I suppose I can't fault you too much though. For being a transplanted hillbilly, you're just not that smart."

In light of that, my patience finally ran out with this goober.

"Great, Jack, then look for them," I shot back. "Find them. I hope you do. And that'll be a first, seeing as how it's known far and wide you couldn't locate your own fanny with a search warrant and a pack of dogs."

He opened his mouth, and I charged on, heedless. "Whatever you do, though, do it fast. You'll need every piece of evidence you can get to put Billy's killer away. Just make sure it's enough so that his door is permanently welded shut."

Again the other man started to speak, but I savagely cut him off. "I'm done screwing around with you. Charge me or spring me. Either way, I need to change my shirt."

The big blue vein pulsing in Jack's neck let me know I'd finally gotten to him. But he was a cool enough customer to take a patronizing tone.

"All right," he said. "We'll let it go. For now. But I need your word on something. Can I trust you to come downtown first thing in the morning to make a formal statement?"

My grin was more teeth than tact. "Sure, Jack. For you, anything."

The way he also pulled his lips away from his gums only qualified it as a smile in purely the physical sense. I was perversely pleased to see his neck vein still pumping merrily away, now enhanced by the large twin muscles on his jaw hinges standing out like Brazil nuts. Two more minutes of having to deal with me and Jack's head would fly off like a champagne bottle cork. Which is something I'd pay cash money to see.

He cocked a thumb toward the door. "Beat it, scumbag."

"I love it when you sweet-talk me," I said as I left.

7

I kept my word to the detective, showing up at District One headquarters on Ezzard Charles Drive the next morning at nine o'clock sharp. The fat old desk sergeant looked bored as he watched me sign my handgun over to him. He was as ancient as the building, and about as talkative, only grunting when I thanked him for the visitor's pass he gave me in return.

Clipping it to my shirt, I asked him, "Is Lieutenant Mulrooney's office still on the third floor?" Not that I was here to see him, Lord knows; I was just curious.

The sergeant had already lowered his head back down to his paperwork. "Yeah, yeah, same floor, same spot," he muttered.

"I'd heard some remodeling had been done since the last time I was down here, and I was just wondering—"

"The Loot's office wasn't one of the ones that got redone," the guard answered, still scribbling away at who knows what. So Jack's office got left out, huh? I nearly laughed out loud. I bet that pleased an ego-hound like him to no end. Not.

"Thanks, Sergeant," I said, turning away from him toward the elevator bank.

Reaching it, I gave the address board the once-over. It showed homicide had been moved from the second floor to the fourth and was now on the opposite end of the building from where it had been the last time I'd had to make use of it.

Was that three years ago already? That had been a real goat-grab of a case, way back before I'd met Angela. One day I might tell the thing, now that the last of the principals had died. Yes, I was talking about Billy.

Speaking of which, it was time to do what I'd come here for.

After getting in and riding the elevator up to the fourth floor, I exited and looked around. Across the hall I saw another information desk, smaller than the one at the front entrance. Walking up, I nodded at the older civilian woman seated behind the counter.

Her return look was cool and professional. "May I help you?"

"Yes, I was instructed to come down here this morning to make a statement on an open case. The Billy—I guess it's William—Barnicke investigation."

She turned to her computer terminal. "Your name, please?"

"Joe Box."

She typed for a moment, concentrating. "Oh yes, the homicide last night over on Williams Avenue." Pursing her lips, she stared at the screen. "Now how in the world did that one end up here? That's under the Norwood PD jurisdiction."

"You'd have to ask Lieutenant Jack Mulrooney about that. I'm just the one who found the body."

"Jack," she scowled, still typing, packing more disdain into that one syllable than I would have thought possible. It appeared I wasn't the only one around here to have issues with our ill-tempered vice-squad detective.

"Oh good," the receptionist said to the screen then, her face clearing. "According to this, the case has been assigned to Detective Pilley." She smiled slightly, and it did wonders for her. "The Pill's all right. Him, you can get along with." Pointing to her left she said, "Third door down. Just knock."

"Thanks." I pivoted and walked the ten steps or so down to the door she'd indicated. In spite of the newer décor that District One had recently undergone, I was pleased to see they'd kept the pebbled glass office door motif I remembered from my time on the force. I gave the door a polite rap, noticing that on it Pilley's first name was noted as Max.

"Come," I heard a baritone voice say from inside.

I opened the door, entering a medium-size room that wouldn't have looked out of place at a podiatrist's office.

"Detective Pilley?" I asked, approaching a large, thirtiesh, bull-necked man seated behind a pressboard desk that fairly screamed "bought in a lot of a dozen just like this."

"That's right." The man rose to his feet, his right hand extended, brown eyes questioning. Right there that earned him five points for friendliness. "And you are—?"

"Joe Box," I said gripping his hand. "Lieutenant Mulrooney asked me—well, told me, really—to come down to make a statement on the Barnicke case."

After a quick shake, Pilley said, "Yeah, the beating death last night. That's a strange one." He pointed to a visitor's chair next to me. "Please, have a seat." Taking his own advice, he settled his bulk into the ancient-looking chair on his side. The thing shrieked like a stepped-on puma.

Pilley must have noticed the look on my face.

"Noisy, isn't it?" he said, rubbing the chair's arms affectionately. "The department may have taken my old desk to the scrap heap when they moved us all up here, but by God, this chair I paid for myself. They can have it when I'm retired. Or dead."

"I know what you mean. I believe I have your chair's twin back in my office." *And Billy's chair made the third.* "Yours sounds as well broken-in as mine."

Pilley tented his fingers. "Office? What kind of work do you do?"

I steeled myself. Some cops don't like dealing with folks the likes of me. At all. "I'm an investigator. Private."

But the response he gave surprised me. "Interesting. I've often thought about getting my ticket for that. If and when the CPD ever decides I've overstayed my welcome."

"That's a bit like what happened to me when I was on the force here, back in the early seventies. It took my wife's death to finally make me walk."

Pilley cocked his head. "A lost member of the tribe, huh? How long were you in?"

"Not long. A little over two years. Like I said, that was nearly three decades ago. I was a rookie. Jack's dad was my partner."

Pilley's chuckled in disbelief. "Sergeant Tim Mulrooney was your partner?" I nodded, and he said, "Man, he's pretty much of a legend around these parts."

"I'll be sure to tell him that the next time I see him."

"He's still alive?" Pilley laughed. "What am I saying? Of course he's still alive. Guy like that's too tough to die."

Now I chuckled. "I'll tell him that, too."

Pilley's smile faded as he placed his hands flat on his desk. "So you're the one that got on Jack's bad side last night. Probably not the brightest move you ever made, Mr. Box."

"It's not the first time the two of us have crossed swords. I doubt it'll be the last."

"Lucky you. Are you always this careless in choosing your enemies?"

"He kind of chose me." I shook my head. "But that's beside the point. If you don't mind, I'd like to go ahead and make my statement. I have a fairly full day lined up." Which was an exaggeration, but he didn't need to know it.

"Not a problem." Reaching over, Pilley depressed the switch on the intercom sitting near the desk's corner. "Doris, could you come in here, please?"

"On my way," the machine's speaker crackled a moment later.

Pilley released the switch. "My secretary'll be here in a minute."

My look was one of fake disbelief. "The department doesn't make you take down your own witness statements? You must rate."

He shrugged. "My penmanship is lousy, while Doris's handwriting ought to go on baby announcement cards. A man should play to his strengths."

I was about to reply when Pilley's door opened, admitting a tall redheaded woman in her fifties, carrying a clipboard. The lady was as thin as a Chinese noodle, afflicted with a pinched face, and seemed harried. Nevertheless she flashed me a tired smile as she took the seat next to mine.

Pilley must have noticed her appearance. He glanced at me and then back at her. His words were tinged with compassion. "Man, Doris. Rough night?"

The woman nodded wearily. "Brandy had a rough night, so we all did." As if she felt that response required an explanation, she turned and faced me. "Brandy's our daughter, our only child, and has Kaposi's sarcoma. AIDS. She's dying."

That sucked the air out of the room as neatly as a wind tunnel. Since there was no earthly reply I could make to such a remark, I said nothing.

As if unaware of the impact her words had on me, Doris simply clicked her ballpoint pen and put tip to paper. "I'm ready when you are."

Trying not to appear as nonplussed as I felt, I related the previous night's events in almost a news anchor's tone. As I spoke, Doris wrote, dutifully pacing my speech as she took down every word. And for some reason, I found myself leaving out the final detail, the one where Billy's dying words had indicted Cyrus Tate for his beating. Why, I had no idea, unless I was reluctant to accuse a man without cause, even a slime like Tate. I'd want more proof before I'd give him up to the cops. Even then, the telling of the passing of Billy Barnicke took less than five minutes. And that's a lousy epitaph for any man's death.

Finally I was done, and I shrugged, meeting Pilley's eyes. "I guess that's it."

"You're sure?"

"I suppose I could tell you how Jack and I spent the rest of the night drinking tequila shooters and playing canasta, but I'd be lying." Doris's matter-of-fact words about her dying daughter had hit me harder than I thought.

Pilley blinked. "No need to get testy, Mr. Box."

"Sorry."

The secretary held the clipboard out to me, but her words were directed toward her boss. "OK to have him sign it?"

The detective studied me. "You're sure there's nothing else to add?"

"Yes." *Not yet, anyway.* "That's all."

Pilley nodded at her. Doris handed me the clipboard and pointed at a blank area beneath her exceedingly neat handwriting, tapping the paper with a brightly painted nail. "Anywhere there is fine."

Taking the pen, I signed my name with less than a flourish, then handed back both the document and the pen.

Doris gave the detective an inquiring look. "You need me for anything else, Max?"

"That'll be all. Thanks."

We waited until she'd left the room, then Pilley leaned in a bit over his desk, folding his calloused hands on it. "After what you went through last night with your friend, I guess Doris's words about her daughter hit you like a ton of bricks. I'm really sorry about that. She has her good days and bad. Like all of us, I guess."

"She seems somewhat OK with it. Which is kind of weird, in my opinion."

"Don't let her fool you. Like most of us assigned to homicide, she's learned to develop a fairly tough front."

"Yeah, but about her own daughter?"

"It's even worse than that. Brandy was a pretty good kid until she got mixed up with that Tate guy."

Deep inside my gut, a thermite device detonated, sending white-hot flames up my esophagus. Him again. I struggled to keep my voice neutral and my expression bland. "Tate guy?"

Pilley made a dismissive motion. "Cyrus Alan Tate. Surely you've heard of him. That two-bit peep-show barker that calls himself Cat."

"Yeah. Him. What, uh ..." *Brother.* If Tate figured into this mess, I needed to know it all. Now. I cleared my throat and tried it again. "What did he do to the daughter?"

Pilley got a sour expression on his face, as if he'd just bitten into a particularly vile persimmon. "Plenty. Killed her is all, only her body doesn't know it yet."

"What do you mean?"

The detective stared. "I can't imagine why you'd want to hear any of this."

I kept my answer simple. "The night my wife died in a car wreck, so did my unborn son. I have an idea of what Doris is going through."

That warranted a grunt. "Well, this whole mess is pretty sad. For what it's worth, things started going bad for Brandy about two years ago. The day she decided to go to an open call Tate was holding here in town, auditioning new models for his magazine."

"I remember that. It was summer. August if memory serves. And what he staged was nothing more than some bikini show-off extravaganza on Fountain Square. The press was all over it."

"Like dogs on meat," Pilley agreed.

"It was a real media circus. Lots of church groups showed up to protest that day. Feminist groups, women with kids in strollers, other kids carrying signs, all kinds of stuff."

"That's right."

I leaned back in my seat. It wasn't any less comfortable than the visitor's chair I keep at my own office. Trying to keep my tone casual, I asked, "So it worked? Brandy was chosen to be a Tate model?"

Pilley's jaw flexed in agitation. "Yeah, she was one of a dozen local gals that got the royal nod that day. That same afternoon Tate flew the whole lot of them off to LA to start prepping them for the photo shoot for that magazine of his. *The Cat's Meow.*"

"I've seen that rag on the newsstands. Stupid name."

"I tried telling Doris that it was a mistake. But she insisted the money Brandy was going to bring in would come in handy. Maybe help pay for college. Besides, she said, it was just a few skin shots. What was the big deal?"

I picked up the thread. "I'll bet I can guess the rest. Brandy goes to LA. She does the shoot, finds out she likes the attention. Not to mention the cash and goodies. Pretty soon she's in too deep to get out."

Pilley's gaze was straightforward. "That's exactly right. Not too long after that she becomes one of Tate's private harem he keeps at that estate of his out in Claxton County. She thinks she's died and gone to heaven; it turned out hell was closer to the truth of it. All the while Doris turns a blind eye to the whole thing, just pleased that her little girl seems so happy. Tate, of course, is pure charm, telling Brandy he's going to make her a movie star."

"And he does," I interjected, not missing a beat, "but the movies he puts her in aren't the kind you'll find at your local mom and pop video store."

The detective blew out a disgusted breath. "You should have stayed a cop, Mr. Box. Pretty soon Brandy's letters stop. Her phone calls stop. Doris's mail to her is returned unopened. Then, two months ago, one bright summer day Doris's little girl shows up on her mother's doorstep, skinny, strung out, and dying of AIDS."

I've heard so many despairing stories over the years, of just this type, I've lost count. In my book, Cyrus Alan Tate, and others of his ilk, were deserving of all the scorn society could dish out. "I suppose it's asking too much to try to find out who infected her."

Pilley barked a humorless laugh. "Why bother? She was a porn star. Do you have any idea how many partners she must have had, male and female, over the last two years?"

"I can imagine." I shook my head. "On second thought, I don't want to." I stood. "I guess things got pretty far afield from the reason I came down. Am I free to go?"

"Sure. Hey, listen, thanks for taking the time to stop by." Pilley said this without an ounce of disingenuousness, as if we'd just spent the last fifteen minutes jawing and pitching horseshoes. Either he really was a simple soul, or one of the coolest individuals ever to pin on a badge.

"I won't say it hasn't been fun," I said. "Because it hasn't. No offense."

"None taken."

I crossed the room. Reaching the door, I was pulling it open when something occurred to me. I turned back.

"A few minutes ago you said something that went right past me, Detective Pilley. You called Billy's death a 'strange one.'" I rubbed my chin. "Now this being an open investigation, you may not be able to answer what I'm about to ask. If so, I understand." My gaze at him was steady. "What makes Billy's death warrant the term 'strange'?"

Pilley didn't answer for a second. I waited. Then he looked past my shoulder, making a short spinning motion in midair with his index finger. "Shut the door."

I did as he asked and walked back over to his desk, standing next to the chair I'd been seated in. For a moment longer the detective shuffled some papers on his desk and said nothing. Maybe he'd changed his mind.

I nodded my encouragement. "Nobody here but us chickens. I'm all ears."

Pilley sighed. It seemed he'd reached his decision. When he leaned back in his chair, it screeched like a starling being killed. But instead of answering, he posed a question of his own. "How well did you know the deceased? I mean, *really* know him?"

That took me off guard. "Why?"

The detective shrugged his linebacker shoulders. "Call it Curious Cop Syndrome. Don't tell me you were never afflicted with it during your time on the job."

"Yeah. And it got me in plenty of trouble too. Still does. But your question is kind of along the same lines a conversation my fiancée and I had about Billy, just a few days ago. And I'll tell you what I told her. We weren't pals. We really never were."

Pilley crossed his legs, saying nothing.

"Billy and I were drinking and carousing buddies, nothing more," I went on. "What sent our relationship south was when I decided I'd drunk enough for this lifetime. Because of that, lately we were more like friendly competitors than anything else."

Pilley gave me cop eyes. "But that begs the question … why you?"

I frowned. "Pardon?"

His words were even. "What I mean is, why on earth would a dying man call up a guy that's barely more than an acquaintance, at the worst possible time in his life? Just because of a few laughs the two of them may have had together sometime in the past?"

Before I could reply, the other man said, "Surely you understand my dilemma. Of all the people William Barnicke could have tried to reach when his final hour arrived, he turns to a 'friendly competitor.' Now think about that. If the roles had been reversed, would *you* have made that call? See? It's hard to reconcile with natural human behavior."

"I can't answer that, Detective. And the problem is, the only one who can is cooling his heels on a slab down at the morgue. Is it really that important?"

"No, not right now." Pilley's look grew tight. "But later it just might be." Picking up his pen, he gave me a nod of dismissal, then looked down and started writing.

I stayed where I was. "I've answered your question. Please answer mine. Why did you term Billy's death 'strange'?"

A long moment passed, and then Pilley looked up and sighed. "All right. As one law enforcement professional to another, however far you've fallen, I owe you that much. Especially seeing how it's not all that germane to the case. Yet. But that's likely to change, the further we dig into the victim's past. So it goes without saying, this isn't for public dissemination."

"Agreed."

Once more he leaned forward. "This is only going to be said once in this room. So listen up. As much as those vultures in the press might love it to spike their ratings, whoever did this job on your guy didn't do it in a fit of rage."

That wasn't surprising. To me it seemed a pro hit, but I said, "What do you mean?"

When the cop replied this time, his tone was as dry as a sirocco wind.

"What I mean, Mr. Box, is that according to the coroner's report, William Barnicke was beaten clinically, repeatedly, and quite methodically, with what appears to be a heavy leather object, an object crowned with some kind of rounded tip. Some weird combination whip and ball-peen hammer is our best guess." Pilley's expression grew dark. "In the end, whatever this thing proves to be, it was used over the victim's entire body. Not an inch was missed. Not one square inch. Do you understand?"

"Yes," I said. "Somebody was sending a message. Using Billy."

Pilley plowed on. "William Barnicke's death wasn't meaningless. Far from it. It had a purpose. Quite a defined purpose. And sooner rather than later, we'll understand what it was." When the detective nodded at me in dismissal this time, I knew he meant it. "We'll speak of this again. Please stay available."

"Or ...?"

His expression wasn't nearly as pleasant as it had been when I first came in. "Do I need to spell it out?"

No, he really didn't. The situation was painfully obvious. Before this case got a whole lot older—and, once he got wind of it, much to Jack Mulrooney's glee—the prime suspect for Billy's death was going to turn out to be one Joseph Jebstuart Box.

If I didn't do something about it first.

8

*P*lanning was called for, and what better place to do it from than the comfort of my office?

I'd just flipped open my leather portfolio I keep on my desk when I heard a rustle from the far side of the room. From where I sat I looked over at the cardboard box Noodles had been using as his bed for the past week.

"So that was you, was it?" I asked. "How you doing? Feeling better?"

In response he gazed up at an invisible spider on the ceiling, utterly ignoring me.

My tone grew expansive. "Tell me, pal, how does it feel to have a cold-blooded murderer as your owner? Are you ill at ease with me now?" I harked back to an old piece of army doggerel I'd heard in Vietnam. "Does it make you nervous in the service? Does your liver quiver?"

He blinked over at me and meowed lustily. *"Naow?"*

"Yowza, that's the ticket. You're sounding like your old self."

Picking up a just-opened box of spicy Slim Jims where they reposed on my blotter, I pulled one out and peeled off the wrapper. Taking a bite, I called over to him, "By the way, sorry about the crack regarding your liver. For a cat on the mend, that was uncalled for."

Supremely bored with my conversation, Noodles yawned. Exiting his box, first he stretched his back, and then each of his legs luxuriously. With the threat of him going into a spasm while doing that now blessedly past, I could smile, instead of cringing in dread.

The brown and white Cap'n Crunch bowl I'd brought from home was empty of the few bits of food I'd placed there. Earlier that morning, before I'd left for police headquarters, I'd filled it. The Cap'n's face, now cat-food free at last, gazed blissfully up. The level of the water bowl beside it was down a tad as well.

"You ready for a little more Kitten Kuddle?" I opened the lower desk drawer where I'd been keeping the box of that dry food for the duration of my cat's recovery. "Or are you up for some of the Cap'n's finest instead?" Noodles is a nut for any sweet cereal, Cap'n Crunch in particular; hence the bowl.

Neither, I guess, as he jumped up on my lap and started kneading it with his paws. The past twenty-four hours or so my cat had grown unaccustomedly cuddly. I suppose that nearly dying will do that to a fellow, whether he's man or beast.

I leaned past him to start making some notes on my legal pad, when the phone rang. Even before I picked it up, I knew with a sinking feeling who it was.

"Hey, Ange," I said.

"Hey, yourself." Her tone carried more than a bit of an edge. "So why didn't you call me last night after you got back from Billy's? Is everything all right?"

Oh man. This wasn't going to be easy. On one level, Angela always pretty much just barely tolerated Billy. But on another, deeper one, she was savvy enough to recognize his self-destructive behavior for what it was. A cry for help.

I cleared my throat. "Well, uh … that is … What I mean is, he didn't make it."

She still sounded peeved. "Make it? Make what? A gambling bet?"

And then I heard her pull in a sharp breath as the penny dropped. "Oh no. Are you saying ...?"

"I'm saying he died, Ange. Last night. In my arms."

Immediately her words turned soft. "Oh mercy, Joe, I ..." Her voice caught, and I heard her swallow. "What can I ...? I am so, so sorry."

"It was in the *Enquirer* this morning. Second section, below the fold, down near the bottom. I picked up a copy from the news rack on the corner. I'm not sure if it made the TV reports yet. Put it this way, I didn't see it when I got up."

"So what are you going to do?"

"What do you mean, do? The man's dead. My part in it is over."

"Don't lie to me, Joe."

"Lie to you? What are you talking about?"

"Please don't act like you don't know what I mean. I deserve better. I know how you are."

"And I know how you are. Ain't that a beautiful thing?"

"No sarcasm. It isn't the time. You don't need that, and neither do I. Your friend is dead, and you're hurting. A smart mouth has always been your main line of defense when you're in pain."

Again I didn't reply. I've said it before, truth was truth.

She sounded resigned. "And I also know that it's not in your nature to just let any of this lie. As much as I might want it to be different, you're not going to walk away from this, are you? Not until you've dealt with Billy's death."

Although the subject matter was grim, I almost laughed. Dang, but the woman was good. She knew me better than I knew myself.

And she'd brought up a good point. Because here's the thing. Right up until that moment, I'd believed only my conscious, rational mind had been wrestling with the thorny problem of keeping myself as far as I could off the cops' radar screen.

But when Angela had just now pointed out my main character flaw, that of my always trying to right wrongs, something clicked inside. It was only then I realized what my subconscious, *irrational* mind had been trying to tell me all morning: the avenging of Billy's death, and the finding of his real killer, were two sides of the same dingy coin.

"Well? Are you going to answer me or not?" my fiancée pressed.

"Not," I replied truthfully. "Right at this second, babe, I'm not sure what I'm going to do. Whatever it is though, I'd better get moving on it quick. I've probably already made the CPD's short list of suspects."

"But I thought you said this attack on Billy was most likely the depredations of some lowlife moneylender he'd run afoul of."

I'd found out differently, of course. But I wasn't about to tell her that.

I could almost see her furrowing her pretty brow as she asked, "What's that term they say in those old gangster movies we like to watch? Getting vigorous?"

I did laugh then. "It's called 'taking vigorish.' And it's a real term."

"OK, taking vigorish, then."

"The phrase refers to the obscenely high interest rates a loan shark gets. When a shark gives a man a loan, the rates he quotes the victim are called 'vigorish.' Sometimes they can get as high as 20 percent." I paused. "A week."

"Twenty percent a week," Angela gasped. "That's terrible. Talk about usury."

She'd get no argument from me. I went on. "Remember in the Bible, when it talked about groups putting burdens on people they couldn't possibly bear? It mentioned the Israelites laboring under the pharaoh. Well, today we have loan sharks. Two crews, same effect."

"It's a miracle anybody could keep up with something like 20 percent a week," Angela allowed. "And not go crazy with worry. So what's it called when the victim can't make those payments?" Her voice once again had turned somber. "And he's beaten to death, like Billy was?"

"In the trade, they simply call it giving the guy a beating. But take it from me, Ange, a loan shark didn't do this."

"What do you mean? You sure were awfully confident of it last night."

"I mean, what happened to Billy doesn't fit their pattern."

"I don't understand."

"Breaking a vic's kneecaps. Or his thumbs. Or worse, burning down his house." I shrugged, although she couldn't see it. "That's just part of a loan shark's day-to-day. But killing his mark isn't. He does too much of that, and pretty soon the word gets out on the street. Before he knows it, there goes his customer base."

"Yes, but how do you *know* it wasn't a loan shark that killed Billy, in some fit of misplaced rage? Somebody whisper in your ear? Or what?"

She had me there. I wasn't about to relate to her Billy's dying words.

Back when Angela and I had first started getting serious, I'd made a vow that I'd do my best to keep her at arm's length—at all costs—from the seedier elements of my business. Now that we were engaged, that went double. Those blacker parts of my life and work, the down and dirty parts, were simply off-limits. I was used to dealing with the scum of the earth. She wasn't.

"That's not important," I evaded, my words unintentionally gruff. "Just accept the fact that I know what I'm talking about."

"All right, for heaven's sake. No need to tear my head off."

I sighed. "I'm sorry. It's just that you caught me at a really bad time here."

"Yes." Her one-word reply sounded ominously cool. "It seems I'm doing that more and more with you." She became brisk. "Well, no problem on my end, buddy-boy, none at all. Don't worry your grizzled head about it. I'm going now. I won't take up any more of your valuable time."

And before I could say another word, the line went dead.

Stupidly I looked at the now-silent instrument clutched in my hand, much like an Amazon headhunter might regard a first edition copy of *Moby Dick*. Both of us would have the same puzzled expressions on our mugs.

"Well, I'll be jigged," I said to no one in particular. "I did it again." Exasperated, I looked down at Noodles, who I swear was smiling at me. "You want to wipe that look off your face, smart guy?"

My cat began washing himself, supreme in his superiority over dull-witted men.

I hung up the phone, vowing to use it later for some much-needed fence mending. After Angela and I both had a chance to cool off.

Once more I pulled the legal pad over. Placing it in my left hand, I regarded it blankly.

Well? a part of me sneered. *You came here to plan. So plan.*

All right, let's just do that thing. Picking up my well-chewed yellow #2 Eberhard Faber pencil, I began to write.

But when I looked at what I'd written, somehow I found I'd only managed to put down two words. They were these: Vincent Scarpetti.

9

*L*ess than five minutes later, I'd cleaned Noodles' litter box, refilled his food and water bowls, and was back in my car. But I wasn't headed toward downtown and police HQ.

I was going the opposite way, both literally and figuratively. I was on my way over to Erie Avenue. Specifically to the Leaning Tower restaurant, home of overpriced ziti and piped-in opera. And to one Vincent Anthony Scarpetti, the next Mafia don of Cincinnati.

My half-brother.

Even now I still wrestle with that idea. I'd first met Vincent last spring, back while I was hip-deep in the Kitty Clark stalking case. I'd thought he looked pretty good for it, considering the relationship his father and Kitty had enjoyed. But what had started out as simply my less-than-enthusiastic efforts to discover who exactly was tormenting the famous, aging country music superstar quickly developed into something monstrously worse.

At its end, Kitty was dead, I was unexpectedly rich, and the mind-twisting discovery had hit that future organized crime chieftain Vincent Scarpetti and I shared something in common: our mother. Kitty Clark herself.

And don't think *that* didn't take some getting used to. For both of us.

Within twenty minutes I was there. Being a shade after ten in the morning, and thus still pre-lunch, parking in the Tower's too-small lot didn't prove to be an issue. I pulled the Cougar into the closest spot I could find, over by the door to the employees' entrance.

It was only after I was out and pocketing the keys that I noticed the space I'd used was Tony's ... Tony Scarpetti that is, Vincent's father. And, until his aging body finally succumbed to the raging syphilis that was mercilessly destroying it, still the titular head of the Cincinnati families.

I shrugged off my mistake as I began walking toward the sheltered overhang that shielded the back entrance. So I'd had the temerity to park in Tony's marked spot; so what? It was common knowledge that, due to diminished capacity, Tony hadn't driven himself anywhere in years. For that task, his soldiers—all large, tough, unsmiling men—were all too happy to help the *capo di tutti capo* (the "boss of bosses") whenever he snapped his fingers their way. On those odd days when his hands still worked.

I mounted the six concrete steps rising up off the apron, finding myself in front of a large, white painted metal door. On it the words "employees only" had been applied with military precision, using reflective stick-on letters.

This time I didn't even bother checking out the tiny security camera unobtrusively mounted high up, where the overhang joined the brick. That was the least of it, I knew. The last time I'd been here, over two months ago—on the day I revealed to the man our true relationship—Vincent had showed me all the top-of-the-line protection goodies he'd stashed in and around the place. He'd done that after first deciding that killing me would cause more problems than it would solve.

Although I knew I was on-screen somewhere, and so really didn't need to, I gave the door four sharp raps. Even before the sound of the last knock had faded, the thing opened silently on oiled hinges, revealing the unlikeliest greeter on planet Earth.

The man was called Carmine. If he had a last name, I'd never heard it; it could be that at birth his parents took one look and disavowed any further part in his upbringing. The guy was in the neighborhood of just under seven feet tall, about middling high for a current NBA forward. But the neighborhood that had watched him reach that height had never seen another like him.

Carmine was half as wide as he was tall, slow talking but quick moving despite his size, with thin black hair plastered above tiny, childlike ears. Dangling from the end of his shirtsleeves hung thick reddish hands the size of mid-city telephone directories. If that wasn't enough, his pebbled face could have been the pattern Karloff had used to fashion the Frankenstein monster. Just add in the requisite neck bolts, and there you'd have it.

In other words, he was Jack's giant, minus the beanstalk.

On our first meeting, back in the center of the Kitty Clark disaster, my visit had almost resulted in Carmine being instructed to take me down to a deserted area by the river wharves for a "session," as Tony Scarpetti had put it. I'd escaped that only when, right in the middle of our talk, Tony had suffered one of his disease-induced seizures, saving my bacon. If Carmine had been in the room with us while my fate was being discussed, he would have been highly disappointed to learn of my dodging that particular bullet.

But I also knew that however much Tony had spent on it, the security system here couldn't have been as good as he thought; I guess it's tough keeping secrets among thieves. Because shortly after I'd revealed to Vincent our blood relationship, I suddenly found myself on the receiving end of something both disturbing and hilarious.

It seemed that, with neither my knowledge nor approval, Vincent's troops had tacitly decided to treat me as an honorary *goombah*, a mafioso. And while I wasn't then, nor would I ever be, a true working member of the Scarpetti family, I also discovered something else.

I was Carmine's new "bestest pal."

His face lit up when he saw me, making his fissured, bony forehead crinkle in joy. Had there been someone suffering a chronic heart ailment standing close by, I would have advised him or her to turn away. Fast.

"Mr. Box!" the giant grinned, revealing a mouthful of large, over-lapping yellowish brown teeth. To him I was always "Mr. Box," never "Joe." Which was OK with me. I'd never really planned on being close friends with a Mafia hit man anyway.

"Good to see ya. Long time, huh?" Still grinning, he thrust his right hand out for a shake.

Forget that. All the guy would have to do with that mitt of his was to squeeze mine just a bit too tight, and from that day on you could call me Lefty.

In response, I patted his arm. Under the lush material of the man's ever-present white pinpoint Oxford shirt—no tie, at this hour—the limb felt as hard as baked asphalt.

"You're looking good, Carmine. New shirt?"

Shyly, he fingered it. "Yeah, the boss bought me a box of 'em for my birthday last month. Custom-made, like always. Said my old ones were shot."

By boss, Carmine meant Vincent. Until the old man finally died, to Carmine only Tony Senior would ever be worthy of the appellation "Mr. Scarpetti."

"Kinda nice, doncha think?" the hulk went on. Then he lifted his head, looking straight out, intoning the next words as if by rote. "The boss says every employee here needs to make a good first impression."

"The color looks good on you." Which was true. White couldn't have made him look any worse.

"Thanks," he said, and then he frowned. "Say, what're you doin' here, anyway? The boss send for ya? He didn't tell me you'd be comin'."

"It's kind of a surprise. Is he in?"

"For you? Sure."

Carmine always acted as if Vincent and I weren't only related, we were also friends. The truth of the matter was somewhat different. It was all we could do to barely stand being in the same room with one another.

"Thanks." I followed the thug through the door and on into the large, industrial kitchen on the other side.

Although lunchtime was still a couple of hours away, already the day crew was busily boiling pasta, making sauces, tearing lettuce, searing meat. As frantic as the scene was, I also knew it wasn't a patch on how it would look later in the afternoon, when the evening shift was in and zipping along like something out of a Mack Sennett movie.

We exited the kitchen and entered the restaurant proper. At this hour the piped-in opera was silent. The only sound was coming from the young busboys wiping stray spots off the water glasses at the tables, folding maroon-colored linen napkins, and giving each piece of shiny flatware a quick final polish before resting it in order at each place setting.

The only men in the room not moving were two larger, older, tough-looking guys, standing at either end with folded arms. I knew their names, which doubtless weren't the ones given to them at their christenings: Paulie and Skeet. They too—big surprise—were Scarpetti soldiers. They nodded at me in respect as I passed.

I glanced over at Carmine as we walked. "There's really no need to escort me. I know the way."

I should. And with my new "family" status, it probably wouldn't have been too much of a struggle to get Vincent to loan me a passkey that would allow me access to the private entrance to his office, and so avoid this roundabout route.

But I doubted I'd ever be interested enough in speaking to my half-brother, on any topic, to ask such a favor. No, continuing to cut through the kitchen and dining room the way we were doing would suit me right down to the ground.

"Hey, it's no problem escortin' you around, Mr. Box," Carmine said. "All part of the job."

I'd have bet that was true. As chief gatekeeper here, the idea of not accompanying visitors on their way to see "the boss" would most likely never have crossed what passed for the giant's mind. I just hoped Jack Mulrooney never found out about this.

A minute later we'd crossed the expanse of lush port-wine-colored carpet, arriving at an unmarked door, and Carmine twisted the knob. Standing aside, he pushed the portal open, his part done.

"Have a good visit," he said, with a total lack of guile.

What could I say, but "thanks," once again? I began strolling down the long hallway before me. Behind, I heard Carmine softly shut the door I'd just come through.

Here, in this space, the Mediterranean theme of the Leaning Tower simply ceased. Instead of muted carpeting, sobbing Italian sopranos, and Rococo artwork, what stretched away was a nondescript corridor done up with slate-blue painted Sheetrock walls, set off by darker blue carpeting. No paintings or statuary here, and the only sound to counterpoint my footfall was the soft electrical buzz coming from the fluorescent light fixtures overhead.

I only had to walk down maybe thirty feet, before coming to a final golden oak door. This one I rapped twice with my knuckles, even though I was sure the occupants on the other side were fully aware of who was there. What they couldn't have known was the why.

A second later the door swung wide, and I came face to face with the final soldier, and the one with the most important job. The man's name was Lou, and he was one of Vincent's personal bodyguards.

Why not use Carmine for that? you might ask. It's a fair question. After all, he was bigger by half than most men. True, but Carmine was also a force of nature: huge, sloppy, chaotic, like an earthquake. In other words, he was great to have around if a room needed clearing, or to give somebody a "session." Lou, on the other hand, was more my size, and moved with stealth, like a cheetah.

To say it another way: Carmine was the hand grenade. Lou was the stiletto.

The guard gave me a sullen stare. Of all of Vincent's boys, Lou was the only one to peg me right. We both knew I'd only be as civil to Vincent as I needed to be, and he with me, each to achieve our own ends.

"Mr. Box," he nodded. "You should have called before you came. Mr. Scarpetti has a full schedule today. He—"

"Oh, let him in, Lou," I heard a voice break in from farther back in the room.

As always, I marveled at its sound. I'm not sure if Vincent had taken vocal lessons to impart that tone, or if was God-given. Either way, the result was a smooth baritone, silky enough to rival any radio announcer from yesteryear. As nice as his voice was though, it couldn't disguise the man's aggravation with me.

Wordlessly Lou stepped aside, letting me pass.

The room I entered was dark and manly, full of mahogany paneling, rich-toned oil paintings of sailing ships, and expensive oxblood leather chairs studded with buffed brass buttons. At its far side, over a dozen feet away, sat an old teak desk the size of a piano crate.

Behind it, seated in a matching wingback, was a lean, polished, handsome man, his striking green eyes tucked far back beneath hoods of thin flesh.

Vincent Scarpetti, my brother.

10

*H*e sighed as I approached the desk. "What do you want, Joe?"

I'd noticed he hadn't risen to greet me. Psych games, establishing dominance. I grinned at him, shaking my head. "Man, you gotta love a guy that cuts right to it."

Vincent leaned back, folding his deceptively soft hands before him on the desk blotter. "Again. What do you want?"

I glanced back over my shoulder at the bodyguard, who was still standing by the door, his hand on the knob, and then back at my brother.

"Lou," Vincent called over to him. "We're fine here. Go grab a smoke."

The guard frowned. In response, my brother simply cleared his throat. That got him moving. "Right, Mr. Scarpetti. If you need me, just sing out." Giving me one more tough look, Lou pulled the door open and walked through it. A second later he tugged it closed. Hard.

I didn't even need to ask Vincent if Lou would obey and head outside as he was told, or if he'd remain on the other side of the door, listening. Strict obedience was a requirement of the Scarpetti troops. Anything less might result in a "session."

"All right, he's gone," Vincent stated, then added pensively, "You know, for the life of me, I don't know why I just don't have you clipped. I suppose you can thank our common blood for that. Yours more common than mine." He scowled. "Anyway, spell out what you came here for. Then leave. Like the man said, I have a lot to do today, and little time to do it."

"A miscreant's lot is not a happy one, huh?" I needled.

That got him. Although he tried to fight it, the ghost of a smile flickered around the corners of my brother's mouth. "Not bad, for a quip on the fly. Although if you're quoting the line from the *Pirates of Penzance*, the word is 'policeman.'"

"I didn't want to mention that term in this room. Didn't want you to croak."

Both of our smiles then faded as the gossamer-thin thread of fraternal bonds broke and slipped away. I got down to it. "How much do you know about the porn industry?"

If the question surprised Vincent, he didn't let on. "Simply that it's huge, and growing bigger by the day. Why?"

"Ever heard the name Cyrus Alan Tate?"

"Who hasn't? He's the biggest fish in the pond."

"More like a diseased channel cat in an industrial drainage pool. But I digress. Tate's the reason I'm here today, keeping you from making more ill-gotten gains."

Vincent's lips twisted up in a smirk. "I understand he gives good subscription deals on his magazine to morally superior PIs."

I let that slide. "Tell me about him."

"That may take some time, and time's one quantity I'm short of. Like you said, it's equated with money. Mine."

"Gosh, Vince, I didn't know you were strapped for cash. You should have said something." My voice was grave with fake concern as I made like I was reaching into my shirt pocket. "Look here, I'll write you a check. Ten bucks for ten minutes. That's sixty bucks an hour, psychiatrist's wages. How's that?" Lord knows a psychopathic bag of snakes like my brother could use all the head shrinking his cranium could take.

Vincent waved a dismissive hand, playing along. "You keep it. Regardless of your new financial status, I'm still richer than you are, or ever hope to be. Consider it a ... fraternal gesture." His look was wintry. "One brother to another."

That was pure Scarpetti bluff. Vincent had no idea how much I was worth. If he had, he would have pushed me in front of a bus.

"Fair enough." I settled into business mode. "Here's the deal. A week ago, Tate offered me a job."

That provoked a laugh. "Doing what? You don't strike me as the porn-actor type. Do you have a second career I should know about?"

"Golly, you're a stitch, Vince." He was still smirking as I went on, "No, the job had to do with vetting the security work on that new smut temple he's having built over in Claxton County. PornUtopia."

"Security work. Now that's more your speed. And PornUtopia I'm also familiar with. One of my local businesses, Tip-Top Concrete, received the contract for that job."

"Really. You underbid everybody, huh? That's a neat trick. What did you do? Make Tate an offer he couldn't refuse?"

"That wasn't funny back when Marlon Brando said it. It's grown less so over the years."

"Sorry." I wasn't sorry at all. "But I've heard Organization-owned front companies, especially construction firms, have been known to do less than sterling work. How did you manage to get past that? Give Tate a guarantee in writing?"

"At the price he got, a guarantee wasn't even an issue."

I didn't reply, and my brother went on, "Back to Tate's security position. What happened with it? Did he stiff you on the bill?"

"I never took the job. Not my cup of apple jack."

"Given your religious views, I'd imagine not."

"I referred the dude to a friend of mine in the business. A guy named Billy Barnicke."

"Barnicke ... Why does that name sound familiar?"

"Because he was in the news last night. He was beaten to death over in Norwood."

"Pity. So why are you linking his killing to a man like Tate?"

"Because Billy as much as told me Tate ordered the hit. He said it right before he died."

"Interesting." I must have finally gotten my brother's attention with that. "Go on."

"I'm trying to get a handle on the guy. What makes him tick. I already know about Tate's warped tastes concerning sex. What I need to know is more about the man himself."

"Why? Are you looking to 'make him pay' for icing your friend?" Vincent laughed in derision.

My answer was serene. "Don't worry about it, bro. It's not your concern."

The other man's humor vanished in a flash. "I've told you before. I'm not your 'bro.' Our common breeding from that manipulative country music hag notwithstanding."

"Gosh, don't hold back, Vince. Tell me how you really feel."

"Trust me, you wouldn't like that. At all." Again he folded his left hand in his right. "And just to make you aware, everything in this town concerns me."

I bared my teeth. "You sounded like your dad just then."

"I'll take your dig as a compliment. Because Pop taught me everything I know." Vincent lightly ran his fingertips over the desk's rich surface. "Or need to know."

"Including the porn business?"

"No." Vincent's fingers stopped moving as his face grew dark. "More's the pity."

"Now who's being cryptic?"

He leaned forward, his eyes as hard as steel shot. "Allow me to give you some free advice, Joe. Something to meditate on."

"Meditation is overrated."

"It's this. Don't ever feel you have the freedom to press your luck here. Because regardless of how you've managed to fool my men, you can't fool me."

"Fooling you was never my intention," I said truthfully.

"Any information I choose to give you is based strictly on how I might turn that to my advantage. Whatever I withhold is my affair."

"Fine," I shot back, my voice stony. "Now let me throw a few things right back at you. First off, I'm not afraid of you."

"You should be." Vincent's mercurial manner was suddenly casual again.

"I'll admit, the first time I was over here, and met you and your father, my knees were knocking like cowbells. And you played my fear for all you were worth, giving me that creepy Christopher Walken impersonation you're so good at."

Then I leaned in and placed my hands flat on his desk. "But here's the sad and simple fact of the matter before us, *bro*. I know, and more to the point, *you* know that I know, that you're just like me."

Vincent's reply was smooth. "You're insane."

"I'm not talking about our parents now, or how we both were raised. Disregarding the still-unbelievable fact that we had the same mother, we both had lousy fathers, and you know it. Mine was a raging hillbilly drunk. Yours was a coldhearted mob boss. I'd bet neither of us had sterling childhoods."

"You know nothing about me. Nothing. Presuming that you do will only lead you down a path you really don't want to tread. Believe me on this."

I pushed on. "The truth is, Vince, we're simply a couple of guys trying to go along and get along, against the day our final tally is drawn up. But on that day I'll have an Advocate. You'll have a Judge. Same guy, two different jobs."

My brother snorted. "It's worse than I thought. You're a fanatic."

"I've been called worse. And by better people. But I think that's enough screwing around, from the both of us. The question stands. Are you going to help me out here or not?"

Vincent cocked his head, turning sly. "What if I say no?"

I shrugged. "That's easy. I'll just let the word leak out that you turned down your own brother, when he came to you asking a favor." Gazing meaningfully at him, I went on. "Kind of a shabby way to treat a blood relative, isn't it?"

Vincent's voice turned frigid as his body tensed. "You wouldn't dare."

Raising almost-innocent hands, I said, "Hey, you're the one into this 'family ritual' razzamatazz, Vince, not me. How you choose to deal with the fallout is your business."

A long minute passed, while we stared at each other like gladiators squaring off in the sand. Maybe this Italian stuff was rubbing off on me after all.

Surprisingly, Vincent caved first. "All right. Fine. For my own reputation I'll tell you what I know about Tate. And then you're to leave. I mean it, Joe."

"All right."

My brother settled back in his chair, tenting his fingers, his voice still cold. "The information I have on him is fairly straightforward. I've had dossiers worked up on all my competitors, both present and future."

"That's interesting. Saves time on knowing who to hate, huh?"

He disregarded that. "And I have a photographic memory. Let me see ..."

Staring up at the ceiling, as if reading from a prompter, my brother began. "The only child of Henry and Eileen Tate, Cyrus Alan Tate was born on August 6, 1954, in Beckfield, Arkansas. His mother was a telephone operator, his father the pastor of the Beckfield Community Church."

"Wait a minute," I said. "Hold the phone. Did you say he was a *pastor*?"

Vincent bobbed his head, once again looking at me. "Not a very good one, if the stories are true. His church started small, and never got any bigger."

I grinned at the absurdity of it. "Son of a gun. Who'd a-thunk it. Cyrus Alan Tate's dad was a preacher."

"My sources tell me Tate's life permanently changed when he was twelve, the day he unexpectedly walked in on his father at the church office." Vincent's chuckle was nasty. "They say the boy caught him—" my brother put his first and second fingers up, making quote marks in the air—"'having relations with his secretary, right up on her desk.'"

I said nothing. Wellsir. That explained a *lot*.

Vincent continued. "Not surprisingly, the affair wrecked the Tate marriage. Henry resigned his position in shame, departing for parts unknown. He left behind a bewildered son, Cyrus, and a humiliated spouse, his wife Eileen. The woman suffered a complete nervous breakdown a few weeks later."

"Man, this just keeps getting worse."

"The wife, in one of her saner moments, realized she couldn't take care of the boy. So she sent him to live here, in Cincinnati, with her sister Peggy, and her husband, Elias. That couple's family name, interestingly, was Staub, not Tate. Cyrus only retook his original surname when his porn business began to flourish."

"To get back at his dad." It was starting to come together.

Now deep in his story, Vincent once more picked up the thread, the information accessed. "That move set the tone for the rest of Tate's life. Shortly after the boy's arrival, Uncle Eli introduced him to all the pleasures of the flesh. Drinking, drugs, rock music, sex. Especially sex." Vincent's shrug was almost Gallic. "Male, female, animal; it didn't matter. Whatever the diversion, Tate proved to be an apt pupil."

"It shows."

"After putting himself through Syracuse University, where he majored in abnormal psychology and minored in journalism, in 1975 Tate graduated at the top of his class, *summa cum laude.*"

"Who says pornographers are dumb?"

"That's when he created his first skin mag, *The Cat's Meow.* Tate was only twenty-one years old the year he launched it. He'd vowed to use the magazine to push the envelope of what the public would accept. And he did. It was like nothing ever seen before. The result of his daring surprised everyone but Tate himself. The journal was an instant media hit, and became the cornerstone for his later empire."

My brother stopped again. It appeared that was it.

"Well done," I said, my head spinning.

"But wait, there's just a little bit more." Vincent was obviously enjoying my discomfort. "There are some fairly strong indications that Tate is brewing up something brand-new out at his PornUtopia complex. My sources tell me it's something Tate believes will shake the world."

"New? I thought Tate had already exploited every perversion the human mind could come up with."

My brother's eye held an unhealthy twinkle. "Rumor has it this new development in sexual pleasure Tate is working on may not be entirely ..." He paused. "... human."

"Animals?" I said. "He's done it. Household items? Sick, but he's done that, too."

"Have you ever heard the term *artificial intelligence?*"

"I heard Spielberg did a film on it a while back. The thing tanked." Then I scowled. "Now wait just a minute, Vince. Are you trying to tell me Tate's creating *androids* out there? Sex robots? Love machines?" The idea was patently absurd.

"You have to admit, the idea's intriguing." Vincent's humor faded, leaving for better quarters. "No, I only know it has something to do with AI. Or a variant thereof."

I stared. "You're really serious." He nodded, and I went on. "It's not enough Tate's made it a point to torque off every family values group in the country. Now he's raising the stakes, trying to make himself out to be the Thomas Edison of porn."

"Cut it any way you wish, it's one way to be remembered."

"Yep. It is that. And speaking of which, what's your stake in this brave new world Tate's opening up?"

"Nothing at all." A beat passed. "For now."

I waited.

"Joe," Vincent said, "allow me to give you a true feel of what you're up against, both with me, and with Cyrus Tate."

"I'm listening."

"That's good. Because your health depends on it."

"Heavens."

"Beginning in the last century, the Scarpetti family has been a part of every illicit activity you can imagine. Gambling, drugs, extortion, whatever. Nothing, up to and including murder, has been beyond the pale for us."

"Listen, a small beginning is nothing to be ashamed of. As my Granny used to say, even roaches start out as eggs."

Vincent's aspect was as cold as ice. "Fortune and power are the foundations of the world, Joe. Something you'll never understand. And they always go together. Always."

I'd never heard it put quite that way, but I let it pass.

"The Scarpettis have a hand in things you can scarcely comprehend," Vincent said.

"Yeah? Like what?" But he paid me no heed. The Mafia chief was on a roll.

"When Pop finally passes, our power will only grow. Because, up until now, the only exception to our interests has been pornography. From Uncle Angelo, on down the line, and right up to my father, porn has always been the third rail. Untouchable."

I almost laughed. Had my brother, the mob boss, just said the word "untouchable"?

"In the old country, family was sacrosanct," he said. "Even when a man was out boffing some bim on the side, it was understood to all concerned that his faithful wife would simply turn a blind eye. Cheating was obvious. So obvious that no one noticed."

"Or chose not to."

"Exactly. Pornography was considered bad. Unmanly. A real man, when he felt the urge to get some strange, wouldn't turn to dirty books or adult movies. He'd get a real woman."

"And your father believed in this concept."

"He still does. And will. Until the day he dies."

"And that's when you start taking a long, hard look at Tate and his empire. Your Tip-Top Concrete thing was just a way to get your foot in the door, on your way to bigger things." I paused. "So tell me something else, Vince. Will you be going after it all, or just a part?"

His answer was oblique. "Let me tell you a story. An illustration of sorts." He settled back. "Once in the old country there was a young, smart farmer, a *paisan.*"

"Hey, a farm joke. I love a good farm joke."

My brother continued, unperturbed. "The young man wanted to grow his farm, but at the same time wished to give the appearance to his fellow villagers that he was humble. So one day he got an idea, and he prayed this prayer. 'Lord, I don't want all the land,' he said. 'I only want the piece of land that's next to mine.'" The Mafia chief waited for my reaction. I didn't disappoint.

"Seems I heard a version of that one before, as a country kid growing up on a hardscrabble plot of land myself."

The mafioso's eyes were as black and dead as a shark's. "Really."

"I think my Granny told it to me. The unsaid moral of the story was, as soon as the farmer got that piece of land, then the prayer he prayed would get him the piece next to that, and so on. Pretty soon, he'd own it all."

"That's exactly right." Vincent's smile was carnivorous. "You answered your own question."

"Yeah, I did. So what you're planning with Tate is a modern-day version of a Kentucky land grab."

"You may not be bright, Joe, but you do have a way with words."

"And as you said before, more's the pity. Because now knowing what you're up to, I simply can't let that happen." I sighed. "*Caramba*, bro. It looks like after I get done dealing with Tate and all of his perverted crap, then I have to come back and deal with you."

My brother grinned. "Joe, for you my door is always open, and you're certainly free to try." Then the grin faded. "Your odds of success though … that's not so certain."

Amazingly, I felt a twinge of pity, for both us. What a lousy hand we'd been dealt. "This warfare you're making us do. It's almost Shakespearean."

"True." Vincent's shrug was pure, fatalistic old country. "It was in the stars."

11

*T*he ride back to my office wasn't one of my better ones. It wasn't until I'd checked my watch that I found it was one o'clock, and that I'd missed lunch. For me, that's noteworthy.

Spying a fairly empty Skyline Chili coming up on the right, I pulled in next to the drive-up booth, ordering two cheese conies with extra mustard and onions and a large Coke from the vacant-eyed teen manning the till. When I paid him for my order, he was barely able to give me back the correct change. No thanks were given, of course. Not even a "have a reasonably good day."

Pulling back into midday traffic, I began scarfing the dogs, and idly wondered about that boy. Had porn, and Tate's products in particular, put that zoned stare into his eyes? Licking chili from my fingers, I scowled. No, that was patently silly on the face of it. Then I paused in my licking. Or was it?

The thought grew.

Could it be that porn was just a part of the general decay of society and traditional mores in this new millennium we'd all found ourselves in? Don't forget to add in disrespect for God and country, drugs, rebellion, and all the rest of the nasty package.

And if humanity really was being inundated by waves of filth and degradation, what by all that was holy were we regular folk going to do to stem the tide?

Right about then, another even worse notion occurred to me.

What if we were years too late in addressing the problems, and the words "we win—you lose" had already been scrawled over the lintel posts of our country, our world?

It was with that happy reflection dancing in my brain that I wheeled the Cougar into my office building's parking lot. Pulling into my slot, I got out and put the keys in my pocket.

Coming in the main door, I could hear the primary press of Pronto Printing, the neighboring business directly under my office, sounding rougher than usual. Pronto specializes in business cards, flyers, menus, what-have-you, and does a pretty fair trade. So the press, not surprisingly, is the business's backbone, and thus highly important.

A second later the thing hiccupped again, clanked hard, and then stalled altogether. Through the closed door of the shop I could hear its owner, a short, normally easygoing Chinese gentleman named Mr. Yee/Lee, begin heartily cussing it out in Mandarin.

At least I think it was Mandarin. Given the fact the owner has a severe speech impediment in the first place, he could have been speaking Farsi for all I knew. As I said, the man's name is either Mr. Yee or Mr. Lee, depending on his mood and the time of day (his first name I've never learned). As I also said, usually he's pretty even-tempered, except when his press goes on the fritz. Which it does, without fail, at least once a week. Then it's best to let him pull out his claw hammer and leave him to it.

I was doing just that, trying to ignore the loud banging and invectives coming from inside the shop. Sometimes I've known Mr. Yee/Lee to wail away on the thing for an hour or better, before he either gives it up as a lost cause for the day, or it starts running again.

As much as I like the old man, I wasn't in the mood now for that noisy nonsense. I needed to get my head into this case, so that hopefully I could keep it, and the rest of me, out of jail. But how? Maybe once I was behind my desk the answer would just appear, like a David Copperfield magic trick.

But oddly enough, the solution came to me quicker.

I had just begun mounting the staircase up to the second floor, where my office is, when I had a sudden flash of brilliance. These occur so infrequently I was nearly tempted to sit down on the steps and enjoy it. But this was too good to waste time on.

Turning to my left, I entered the office of the business right across from Pronto, Whizzer Jokes and Novelty. As the place is mainly a distribution house for magic and novelty shops, rather than a sure-enough store for the general public, there isn't a whole lot of merchandise out in the office proper. The good stuff, I knew, was in the back.

Coming in, I found it deserted. But that wasn't too big of a deal. I know the owner, like me, runs a one-person shop. I'd just started to call out when I spied a new item on the desk: an old-fashioned steel hotel bell, exactly like the ones the night clerk in classic movies uses when he wants to summon a young, sharply dressed bellboy wearing a pillbox hat.

Feeling jaunty, like William Powell in *The Thin Man*, I reached over and gave the metal button a firm smack. But instead of the normal ding I should have gotten, from a speaker hidden in the fake potted fern on the floor a loud, booming man's voice hollered out, "Somebody wants attention!"

It was a toss-up as to which would happen first, me keeling over in cardiac arrest, or messing my pants. Thankfully neither.

That's when I heard a woman behind me, laughing hard. "It works! It works!"

I turned and glared. "Toni, that one put blood in parts of my brain that's never been there before. You're gonna kill me with your pranks one of these days. One of these days you're gonna find me toes up on your floor, my heart stopped and a final look of terror plastered on my face. Just ship me to the boneyard then."

The woman's blue eyes twinkled in mirth. "Oh, I doubt it'll come to *that*," she said. "Now wetting yourself? Or filling your britches? That'd be good. Or how about both at once? A double-hitter. That'd be *great*."

I gave her the evil eye, which only caused her to laugh harder. "Now you quit with the dirty looks, Joe Box. Obviously, you don't get it. You've been awarded a great honor."

"Honor? What honor? Nearly making a fool of myself?"

"Ah, phooey." Toni waved her hand as if fanning off a stink. "My glowering friend, you've just been on the receiving end of one of my brand-new line of jokes."

"Lucky me."

"It was a good one, too, I have to say. I got the idea a week ago, and only this morning got it hooked up. You should have seen the look on your face. Priceless."

I glowered. "Yeah, priceless."

Her grin was purely sardonic. "Don't be that way. The word 'jokes' *is* part of the name of this joint. Right? And I have to try 'em out on somebody, don't I?" Toni's humorous smirk was more conspiratorial than anything else, as if the two of us had been in on the stupid prank together. "I love this job," she said.

In spite of myself, I found myself joining in her laughter. When something as idiotic as a glorified joy-buzzer works, you might as well be a man and admit it.

Toni Maroni—and that really is her name—is just that way. A happy-go-lucky, forty-year-old tomboy, who'd early on found out that her station in life consists simply of making people laugh. In her case, the more slapstick the gag, the better.

She's a tomboy, too, in her stature and appearance. Toni stands barely five feet tall, with red, frizzed, finger-in-the-light-socket hair topping a ruddy, gap-toothed face. But odd looks and offbeat humor aside, she really is a good-hearted soul, always ready to help out the needy or less fortunate.

When I was a kid down in Kentucky, my Granny used to call a person like Toni a "stray dog woman," for those very reasons. And maybe Toni's "stray dog" mentality is also the reason why she met, married, and then divorced three navy men before she was thirty.

Toni told me one time over a shared lunch that after the last sailor, she finally got the marrying itch out of her system. Maybe. Or maybe those swab boys just got tired of finding whoopee cushions on their kitchen chairs and preserved flies in their ice cubes.

Taking a seat in her own chair, she motioned me into her vinyl-clad visitor's seat next to her ancient rolltop desk. "You've got that look on your face again, Joe."

"What look?" I said as I sat.

"That I've-got-to-save-the-world-and-my-own-butt-at-the-same-time look."

"What, have you and Angela been comparing notes?"

"No. You're just easy to read. At least to me. Does it have to do with a case?"

"Kind of." I was as evasive with her as I usually am. "Listen, are you still involved in community theater?"

That seemed to surprise her. "Yeah, I am. We're doing *The Merchant of Venice* this Christmas. Why? Are you looking for a part? You'd make a killer Shylock."

"Perish the thought. But you still do the makeup work for them, right?"

"And the lighting. And the set design. We're not exactly overrun with staff."

"Well, makeup is what I'm needing," I said. "More to the point, a disguise."

"A disguise?" Toni sat up straighter, rubbing her hands together. "Hot buttered rum! You don't know how long I've waited for you to ask me that."

"Glad I could help. The thing is, I need something that'll really change my looks. And something simple that I'll be able to do by myself. Maybe repeatedly over a period of days."

Toni got up and came around to my side of the desk and circled me, stroking her chin like Sigmund Freud. "Stand up," she commanded.

I did, and she cocked her head from side to side like a bird.

"The height's going to be a major problem," she observed. "Short of cutting off your legs, there's no easy way of making you less than your normal six-foot-three stature."

"Cutting off my legs is out. I can pretty much assure you of that."

"Not a problem. If you're cool with it, I am. We'll let you hunch over as best as you can, and leave it at that." She regarded my face closely. "Anybody ever tell you that besides your killer green eyes, you have a strong jaw and cheekbones?"

"It's my hillbilly inbreeding. All of us Boxes are regular Dudley Do-Rights."

She wrinkled her brow. "Yeah, well, maybe, but those bones'll have to go."

"That sounds ominous."

"We'll use mouth appliances. Don't worry about it."

"Already I'm not liking this."

Toni directed her gaze to my scalp. "How would you like a haircut?"

"I just had one."

"No, I mean a short one. Really short. After that we'll do a dye job on it, take that salt and pepper stuff and darken it down good, make it as black as tar."

"You're really getting into this, aren't you?"

"After that, a fake mustache, a good one. I have the very thing in the back." I must have looked overwhelmed about then, because she said, "Don't worry, it goes on with spirit gum and comes off with acetone. Anybody can do it. Even you."

"*Acetone?*" I glanced at the door. "Maybe this wasn't as good an idea as I thought."

"Top that off by slapping a pair of black, plain-glass Buddy Holly horn-rims on your head, and from the neck up you've got it," she finished.

"You *have* done this before, right?"

Now she was staring at my midsection. "You work out, don't you?"

"An hour with the heavy bag at the Y every morning. Why?"

"Your gut. It's too flat."

"Angela doesn't think so."

"She's not the one you need to fool. Ever heard of a fat suit?"

"Not even in passing. But I'll bet you're about to enlighten me."

"They come in all sizes, from a simple prosthetic to full-body. Did you ever see *The Nutty Professor?*"

"What's Jerry Lewis got to do with it?"

"You really are out of the loop, aren't you? I meant the Eddie Murphy remake."

"Nope. Why?"

"They used one on him in the movie. You don't need one that elaborate, though, just a small one, for your belly. I think I have one around here somewhere from the last time we did *The Odd Couple*, for the Oscar Madison character. The actor we had was a beanpole, but that belly bag made him look like he drank a twelve pack of beer each day."

"Good grief. Anything else?"

"How do you feel about losing your left hand?"

"What?"

"I have a dandy Captain Hook prop left over from last year, when we did our children's theater production of *Peter Pan*. Only used once. We'll remove the frilly cuff."

"I'll pass. I'd like to keep both of my hands, thanks."

"Again, up to you. I just like to run a full-service shop."

"That's an understatement. Speaking of which, how much is all of this going to set me back?" Even as I said the words, I almost cringed at my penury. But given my poverty-stricken upbringing, I've found it's always a smart move to know how much something costs.

Toni seemed to have taken no notice. "Not a thin dime, Joe. Like I said, I've been dreaming of this since you first rented your office, twelve years ago. When I found out you were a PI, I almost had a fit." Amazingly, her tone turned almost shy. "Now, I know you keep to yourself regarding your cases. But I'd always hoped, just once, you'd come down here and ask me to help you out with a disguise. See, I'm really pretty good at it, y'know?"

I smiled. I guess that made me just another one of Toni's "stray dogs."

"So when do we kick off this *soirée*?" she asked.

"Tomorrow morning, I guess. I'll need to take Noodles home, arrange for Angela to watch him, and then pack. What time do you want to start?"

"We begin early and stay late in the theater biz. I'll need to show you how to put the stuff on by yourself so it'll look at least as good as the first time I do it. So, say, six a.m.?"

"Sounds good. Toni, this really means a lot to me."

She waved that off. "Forget it. 'Cause baby, this gig is like Christmas, the Fourth of July, and my birthday, all rolled into one." She paused. "There's just one thing."

Uh-oh. "What?"

"Just, ah ..."

Caramba. Was I wrong, or was Toni suddenly looking a mite teary-eyed?

She pulled herself up to her full height (what little there was of it), her eyes unnaturally shiny. "Whatever this is you're involved in, just come back to us. OK?"

12

*B*ack again in my office, I called Detective Pilley and told him I was going to be gone on a short trip. He didn't ask to where, and I didn't tell him. He did strongly encourage me to check in with him every couple of days. I agreed. I really didn't have much choice but to agree.

My next call was to my answering service, instructing them to take all incoming calls for the next few days. My orders were to tell whoever it was that I was unavailable, but would get back to them when I could.

That task done, I drew the shade, and then sat down at my heavy old desk. Flipping on the lamp and drawing the middle drawer out smoothly, from inside it I pulled out my .38 revolver and webbed shoulder holster.

Holding it down so the light hit it better, I opened the gun's cylinder and checked it. Good thing I'd refilled it with six of Mr. Remington's best cartridges. The last time I'd fired the pistol was a week ago, the day I was over at my friend Dave Harrow's gun shop. Below the shop Dave keeps a small shooting range available for his customers who want to either zero their weapons or just crank off a box of ammo. As always, the .38 had fired true.

I really, truly hoped I wouldn't find an occasion to use it on this trip.

About then Noodles looked up from where he lay in his box, giving me a sleepy, muzzy look. Then he saw what I was holding, and his eyes grew wide in puzzlement.

"Now don't be alarmed by the shootin' iron, son," I drawled, giving him my best Cowboy Bob voice. "I'm only a-goin' after varmints." I dropped the routine. "I hope."

Noodles still looked thrown for a loss, and no wonder. He'd never seen me holding a gun. And why would he? He's a cat, for Pete's sake. Still, he deserved an explanation.

"Here's my plan," I told him. "I couldn't tell our friend Toni, but I know I can trust you to keep your mouth shut. You're a cat of discretion. Right?"

In response he yawned so wide his head looked like a PEZ dispenser.

"Close enough for jazz," I nodded. Putting the gun down on the desk, I settled back in my chair. "Cyrus Alan Tate's name keeps popping up everywhere I look. It's like a ... well, like something that won't flush, no matter how hard I try."

Noodles began cleaning himself.

I went on, "It's well known that Tate's building a huge combination sex museum and brothel out in Claxton County. But I think something else is going on out there, something beyond a simple slap-and-tickle session for straying executives or over-the-road truckers. Something that got Billy killed when he discovered it."

Noodles was working on a knot in his back leg fur with his teeth. I trusted he was paying attention.

"Now the easy answer is for me to go out there and see for myself what's up." I leaned back, staring up at the ceiling. "But there's a problem with that. I'll be recognized as soon as Tate sees me. So it seems to me, the logical answer is for me to wear a disguise." I went back to looking at my cat. "How do you feel about disguises?"

Noodles had pulled the knot of hair free, but now couldn't get rid of it. It hung like a flag from the corner of his mouth.

"That's sick. Just spit the thing out, why don't you?"

Not him. He was trying to move it from one side of his mouth to the other with his tongue, each time shaking his head like the hair tasted bad.

"Oh, for crying in a bucket." I got up and walked over to where he lay, leaned down, and snatched the dripping mess off his chin with my fingers. He gave me a grateful look as I tossed the stuff into the wastebasket.

I was just walking back over to my desk when the cell phone on my belt went off. Only a handful of people know that number, and I had a feeling I knew who it was. Pulling the phone out of its clip, I checked the caller ID on the screen. Yep, it was Angela.

Wiping my hand on my pants first, I thumbed the button. "Hey, babe. I was just getting ready to call you."

"Was it about the story on the news?" She still sounded a bit cool for my taste.

"What story?"

"The Butler County cat poisoner. They caught him. That's why I called."

Grinning, I sat back down in my chair. "Son of a gun, that's all right. And about time too. It was some freak, I'll bet."

"Not even close. In the end it turned out to be kind of sad, actually."

"Sad? That an animal torturer was caught? What are you talking about?"

"The man's name is Spunkmeyer. He's a retired postman. And an amateur chemist."

"A chemist. Well, that fits in with my theory. So why the heck was the guy killing cats? Did he say?"

"That's just it. According to the report, the old man likes cats, but hates squirrels."

"Squirrels? What do squirrels have to do with it?"

"It seems Spunkmeyer has some kind of phobia about them. He got it when he was a boy. That part really wasn't clear."

"None of this is real clear yet," I said.

Angela went on. "What happened was, he made up some kind of metallic poison into pellets and planted the stuff near where squirrels would gather. Parks and the like."

"Metallic poison. It looks like Noodles' vet was right."

"Anyway, somehow Spunkmeyer fouled up the mixture. What the squirrels ate only made them a little sick. But when a cat would catch and eat one of those squirrels, the poison changed chemically and turned aggressive, attacking their nervous systems."

"Brother. Sounds like Noodles really dodged the bullet."

"They showed the poor man being arrested. He appeared to be in shock."

"Pity. Speaking of shock, I'm glad you called, because I need to ask you a favor."

"I already know what you're going to ask," Angela said. "You'd like me to watch Noodles while you're away. Because you're going to try to find Billy's killer."

For a moment I went as mute as a rock. My sweetie can do that so effortlessly. It was another second or two before I found my voice. "God tell you that, did he?"

"I didn't say that. It's just a feeling," Angela said.

Feelings. I knew all about those.

She went on. "But I have some peace about it, so I'll just have to go with that."

"Peace. Well, I'd say that's pretty good then. For once it looks like one of my cases will go easy."

Her tone turned dark. "I didn't say that."

A rapidly dropping elevator feeling suddenly assaulted my stomach. "Oh boy."

"There's a beautiful old hymn that's been around awhile," Angela said. "It's called 'Peace in the Midst of the Storm.' That's what I'm picking up here. That kind of peace."

"What are you talking about? Peace is peace, right?"

"Not in this instance." Her voice sounded strained. "There'll be peace at the end of this case, all right. But something is telling me you'll have to pass through hell to get it."

♦ ◊ ♦

We chatted a bit more about where I was going, how long I'd be staying, and so on. We even both had a strained laugh over the disguise

Toni was cooking up for me. But as we talked, Angela's "pass through hell" line was never far from my thoughts.

After hanging up, the thought hit me that there was one other person I needed to bring into this, somebody I really should have called at the beginning. My oldest friend, Sergeant Tim Mulrooney. As I'd told Detective Pilley, Sarge had been the partner I'd been assigned to the day I joined the Cincinnati police force. He and his wife, Helen, had been like my surrogate parents. And Sarge's street smarts, along with his seldom-miss insights into human behavior, were just what I needed before I headed out tomorrow.

Leaning back in my office chair, I punched out the Mulrooney's phone number and prepared to wait. They'd retired to Naples, Florida, years ago, and it might take him a while.

But it only rang twice before it was answered by a gravelly voice. "Hello?"

"Sarge?" I grinned. "Guess who this is."

"Ed McMahon, as I live and breathe. Listen, Ed, I bought all those stinking magazines you sent me. Now where's that million bucks you promised?"

"We're a bit short here today, Mr. Mulrooney. I'll have to write you an IOU."

"Nah, keep it, I'll just get it from Joe Box. He's good for it."

We both laughed, our skit done, and I said, "Man, it's good to hear your voice."

"Same here. We haven't talked since Helen and I were up your way last spring, the day you and Angela got engaged. How is she, anyway?"

"Pretty as ever, and raring to get hitched."

"The sooner the better. She needs to make an honest man of you, Joe. Besides which, Helen's laid up enough rice for the wedding to feed half of Hong Kong."

"Don't rush us. We'll get there."

"Spoken like a nervous man. So what's up?" Sarge always did cut right to it.

"It appears I've got myself into a little situation here."

"You never have 'little situations.' You have five-alarm catastrophes. What is it this time?"

Quickly I told him everything: Chalafant's visit and Tate's offer and Billy's death, and why it was I felt compelled to go beard the lion in his den. I even told him about my recurring nightmare.

"It could be the bad dream's a warning," Sarge said.

"A warning?"

"From your subconscious. Maybe even from God. To be on your guard. So as far as bearding lions goes, forget 'em. Lions don't even enter the equation."

"Angela's pretty exercised about all this. Why, I don't know. It's not like I haven't had rough cases before."

"You really don't know why she's upset?"

"Besides me facing a possible murder rap, not a clue. Sorry."

"I'd ask you to check your gender, but that'd be crass."

"Huh?"

Sarge's voice took a slow, patient quality. "You're a man, Joe. So am I. And you're getting ready to head full-force right into the most deadly ground a man can face."

"Deadly ground?" Don't think too badly of me that I still didn't get it. Remember, spiritually I'm still a work in progress.

"It's called lust," Sarge said bluntly.

"Lust?" I tried to keep a grin off my face. The word sounded out-of-date.

"You guessed 'er, Chester. And it's caused more heartache and pain both for the men it grabs and the women it uses, than you could ever imagine. Not to mention the kids caught in the middle."

"Lust-a-rama," I said again. "Well, sure. Tate's kind of famous for that."

"You're not understanding me."

Obviously not, because my old friend went on, "The air itself out there's gonna be saturated with it. Even when it's not right up in your face, you'll still sense it." I didn't say anything, and he continued, "It's kind of like … well, like plastic wrap."

"Plastic wrap?" I frowned. "Sorry. You lost me on that last turn."

"You know what I mean. The more you fool with the stuff, the more tangled and balled up it gets. You have to fight to keep it from sticking to you. And I kinda think that's what your nightmare is about. Something big is gaining on you, Joe, like Satchel Paige said. And if it gets you, you're a goner. The devil's gotten pretty good at that over the years."

"The *devil?*" I almost groaned. "Man alive. Isn't there *anything* that boy doesn't have a toehold in?"

"In this world, not much. Like I said, that's why you're gonna need to be on your guard out there. Because he's brought down bigger men than you."

That sounded a bit over the top. "You really think it's going to be that bad, huh?"

"I know it is. As one man to another, one brother to another, to make it through what you're about to start is gonna take a lot more than just happy thoughts."

While I chewed on that, Sarge went on, "Listen, is it OK with you if I pass this on to some other men I know? Don't worry, they're all good guys, and can keep their traps shut."

"Sure." My thoughts were flying eight different ways at once, but I tried to sound cheery. "The more the merrier, I guess."

"I'm not calling this little set-to merry," Sarge said. "But it's important."

That surprised me. That had been exactly my thought as well. Which is strange, as he's never said anything of the sort, about any of my cases. "What makes you say that?"

The older man turned pensive, his words slow. "I don't know. And I wish I did. Let's just say I got a bad feeling about it."

Feelings again. Him, too? What was next, sage advice from Noodles?

"Something dark is brewing up your way," Sarge said. "Something dark that's about to be exposed to the light." He paused, and then added, "And when it is, the cost to everyone concerned is gonna be awful."

13

An hour later Angela showed up. I helped pack Noodles off in her car, she carrying him out in his cardboard box bed, me bringing out his litter box and food and bowls.

After making sure he was comfortable on the passenger seat, I came around to her side. She was already behind the wheel, and I leaned in for a kiss.

"Thanks for taking care of him, babe. I appreciate it. You know he won't be any trouble. And I shouldn't be gone but a couple of days."

"Pack for longer," she said.

"Nah. I always go light on trips. Remember my Nashville jaunt last spring?"

Angela's fixed look was piercing. "I'm telling you, Joe. Pack for a longer trip. This isn't going to go as quickly, or as smoothly, as you think. As much as we'd both want it to."

I started to answer, but she interrupted me.

"Something else. There's going to come a time there when you're going to feel that you're all alone. You're not. Remember that." My mind was spinning as she went on. "And whatever you do, do this. Please." Her voice thickened. "Come back to me."

"Good grief, Ange." I was staring right back at her. "Why is everybody treating this thing like *Commandos Die at Dawn*? All I'm doing is going out to Tate's place incognito and see if there's enough I can dig up on the guy to get the cops looking at him for arranging Billy's death. That's all."

"You really believe that, don't you?" Before I could answer she reached up and pulled my face down to hers. "Give me a kiss. Right now. Before I beg you to stay."

My thoughts flying, I did as she said. As our lips pulled away from each other, on them I could taste Angela's salty tears.

"I love you, Joe," she said. "Be strong."

With that she put her car into gear and gave it the gas, pulling out of the driveway and wheeling into the street. A moment more and I'd lost her in the traffic. I stood there for a bit, watching the empty air, then turned away.

Trudging back into my office building, Angela's final words were rebounding in my mind. *Be strong?* What did she mean? Everyone seemed so concerned about the safety of my country hide. First her, and then Sarge, and then Toni Moroni, and then her again. The only one who hadn't thrown in his two cents yet was Noodles. And if I could have understood cat talk, I wouldn't have put it past him either.

Coming in my office door, I looked around. Noodles had only spent a week in here with me, but already the place felt vacant without him. And why did it seem so dark now?

A heaviness was settling in on me, like a wet blanket. No doubt about it, I could feel a case of the mulligrubs coming on, as Granny used to say. I needed to get out of this room. Because it also struck me that, after getting my gun and ammo off my desk and packed away, there wasn't a thing more I needed to do here.

Time to get after it, as my platoon leader, poor old dead Sergeant Nickerson, used to say to us every morning before we'd begin our daily patrol in Vietnam's lowlands.

So that's exactly what I did.

♦ ◊ ♦

My sleep that night was bad.

The faces-in-the-wall dream returned, now supplanted by something worse. In addition to the nightmare critters, the feeling was as if something dark and massive was behind me. All around me, and growing closer. Brother.

First light the next day, bright and early at six o'clock, I knocked on Toni's office door. She opened it with a grin. "Hey, Skeezix. I thought you might have chickened out."

"Chickened out? Why?"

"Have you ever put anything besides cheap aftershave on your face?"

"No."

Her Cheshire cat look expanded. "Well, big boy, you will today." Pulling her door wider, she motioned me in. "We're all set up. Have a seat over there under the light."

I did as she said, warily lowering myself into an uncomfortable-looking straight-back wooden chair with no arms, set out in the middle of the room. Beside it stood a powerful floor lamp. Next to that was a small table with various unknown items laid out in an orderly way. Some of them looked disturbingly like body parts. Hair and teeth and innards and such.

"Unbutton your collar and fold it in," Toni commanded.

"The last time I was this nervous was at the dentist's," I said, rolling my collar under. I was glad she'd pulled the shades closed.

"This won't hurt a bit," the woman said, bending close and intently gazing at my face. "Not to say it won't be uncomfortable to your manly presence."

"You know, that was absolutely the wrong thing to say," I said, beginning to rise.

She pushed me back down gently, tucking a paper towel securely under my chin. "Relax, galoot. You're in the hands of a professional here."

"I feel like the Dustin Hoffman character in *Marathon Man*."

"Nonsense," Toni said, picking up what appeared to be a big wad of Silly Putty off the table. "We'll start with this. Now open wide."

"Yep. That's what I'm feeling, all right. *Marathon Man* flashback here, big time. And you're the Laurence Olivier character, that crazy Nazi dentist." But I complied, cautiously ratcheting open my jaws.

Toni's voice was soothing. "That's good. Strict obedience to your makeup artist is the key." Then inserting the mass into my mouth, she took on an evil, Teutonic quality. *"So tell me. Iss it safe?"*

"Oh brother ..." I gurgled as she went to work.

♦ ◊ ♦

It wasn't as bad as I thought. Toni told me the Silly Putty stuff was really something else (I forget the name of it). The plasticlike goo was designed to change the shape of my face.

She'd placed larger wads of it in my lower jaws, between my cheeks and gums, and smaller wads topside. She said she did the goo first because it would firm up and custom mold itself to me while she did the rest. "The rest" consisted of more mundane things.

As promised, she gave me a short, almost military haircut, dying it a dark brown-black. After affixing an itchy matching mustache over my upper lip with spirit gum (she showed me it came off easily with what amounted to fingernail polish remover), Toni put a pair of black horn-rims on my face.

For the grand finale she placed a round makeup mirror in my hand. "Take a look."

I did. And almost dropped the thing. Gazing back out was a stranger.

The face before me was round and kind of puffy. With the black glasses and full mustache added in, it was somehow older-looking too, although the dark buzz cut would have made me figure it the other way around.

In short, Joe Box had ceased to exist. This guy had taken his place.

"Dang, gal, you're good," I said, almost reverently. Then I realized something else. "How come I sound so different?"

Toni smiled. "It's the mouth appliances. When the shape of your face changed, so did your voice. Not a lot, but enough. An ear, nose, and throat guy could explain it better."

Still staring into the mirror, I shook my head. "Unbelievable."

"OK, stand up and take off your shirt," she commanded.

Wondering what was next, I did as Toni said. A second later I found out.

From a box on the floor, she picked up a bladderlike thing festooned with straps.

"Know what this is?" she said.

"I wouldn't even hazard a guess."

"I told you yesterday. It's part of a fat suit. A fat belly, actually. It'll add twenty pounds, but it only weighs maybe two. Slip this baby on, and you'll look like a real couch potato."

"Let me see it." She handed the thing over, and I gave it a critical once-over. Its give as I pressed it under my thumbs felt realistic enough, but still I felt the need to crab. "I'll bet it's hot."

"Oh yeah, and sticky, too," Toni agreed, as she took it from me and deftly strapped it around my middle. "Didn't you ever hear of suffering for your art?"

Something else occurred to me. "What's inside it? Not liquid, I hope."

"No. Some space-age miracle sponge material. At least that's what the instruction manual claims. That's why it's so light." Her expression was puzzled. "Why?"

"Do you think I could cut a slit in it? From the back?"

"I don't see why not. Although it wouldn't make it any less hot to wear."

"I'm not looking to make it less hot. Though that's not to say after fifteen seconds of this I wouldn't like that a bunch. But that's not it. I may need to conceal something."

Toni's look was eager. "Yeah? Like what?"

"Like none of your beeswax, maybe."

"I'll bet it's a gun," she grinned.

She'd nailed it, but I wasn't about to let on. "Need to know, Toni. And you don't." Slipping my shirt back on (and with that sponge appliance there, it was very tight), I began buttoning it up. "OK, what's left?"

"Just this." She handed me a folded piece of paper and a small paper sack. "I've written the instructions down so you can do this yourself. The spirit gum and acetone are in the bag. There's enough for two weeks of application and removal of the mustache."

Two weeks. Surely that would be enough to get the goods on Billy's killer. Lord, let it be enough.

"The mouth appliances will fit easily into their places, so you'll know which goes where," Toni went on. "I've also tucked in a little bottle of hair dye, but watch it, it's messy. By then your hair will have started growing out, and your real color showing through."

"I hope I'm done way before that."

"Me too. But if you plan on staying at wherever it is you're going for any longer, and you run into a snag, you'd better find somebody there that can fix you up. Otherwise your cover is blown, bucko."

"My cover, huh?"

"Yep." Toni's gap-toothed grin was more insouciant than ever. "You don't know how long I've waited to do this, Joe. This is real James Bond stuff."

I took the sack and the paper from her. "You're sure I can't pay you for this, huh?"

She shook her head. "Nope. And what I said yesterday goes. Just come back home safe to your friends." She brightened. "Hey, maybe someday you'll put all this in a book."

14

After checking my car's odometer, I glanced at my watch.

I was forty-five minutes into the trip along US 52 east. Almost thirty miles gone. And, much as it hurts me to say so, I wasn't driving the Cougar, or my other car, a much-less-flashy-but-good-for-tailing-suspects 2003 Volkswagen Jetta.

No, for this trip I'd first stopped at a Rent-a-Heap Cheap place just across the river in Kentucky, because I needed the plates to match my ruse. After a bit of haggling, I got the pick of the litter. What I'd ended up with was a 1990 Buick Regal, and it's not too much of a stretch to say it was the sorriest vehicle I'd ever clapped eyes on. The car had once been silver, but except for the parts painted brown primer, it had faded to a dusty gray. The interior was just as bad. The seats were sprung and dirty, and the only good thing about the ragged header hanging down like a shroud on the passenger side was it almost obscured that part of the spider-cracked windshield.

In short, it was the perfect car for a down-on-his-luck hillbilly to be driving. Me.

The drive itself though was nice, the autumn air as crisp and clean as the Alps, the shimmering red and gold leaves on the trees making the world look like it was gloriously ablaze. The cloudless sky overhead was a deep cobalt blue, and with the warm temperature, the day was shaping up as a keeper. The newspaper ads for PornUtopia said it was less than an hour away from Cincinnati; I was about to see if that was so.

The disguise for the most part seemed to be not as big a deal as I'd thought it would be. The glass in the black horn-rims was nonprescription, and so posed no real hindrance to my looking through them. I'd passed on the idea of not wearing them, even when I was alone. To my thinking it seemed best to keep them on as if they were the real deal. Hopefully that would help to keep me in character.

The mouth appliances were a different matter. It wasn't that they hurt, exactly, but the hard rubber sensation was pretty uncomfortable all the same. I had to rely on Toni's expertise when she'd said they'd grow on me and fit better the longer I wore them. What hurt the worst was that she said I wouldn't be able to eat while wearing them, not a bite. I guess there's only so much you can ask of a disguise.

My fake mustache had grown less itchy during the drive. Thank the Lord. The only real pain of the whole getup, and that more in a mental sense than physical, was the foam "beer belly" I was wearing. The gadget itself was devilishly hard to get used to, with the straps holding it to my body chafing me like a bear. (I'd had to stop and buy a few extra baggy shirts before I left.) First chance I got, I'd put a T-shirt on under it.

When Toni had said the phrase "suffering for your art," she hadn't been kidding.

Risking another few seconds of taking my eyes off the curvy road, I checked the paper in my hand. Yesterday Mrs. Brake, my elderly friend at the Cincinnati public library, had gotten some info from the Internet about PornUtpoia, and then printed it off for me. (I still hadn't bought a computer for my own use. But I was weakening.) The paper showed Tate's complex was a mile this side of the next town coming up. A village called, in surely what had to be the macabre irony of the century, Sunnyvale.

I recalled the town's stats. Sunnyvale had originally begun in the early 1800s as a combination fort and trading post called Dutchman's

Landing, set hard along the Ohio River. In 1878 it took its present name, looking to attract settlers to its gently rolling valleys and ready water supply. Sunnyvale was the prototypical sleepy river town, growing slowly and steadily over the intervening century and a quarter into a friendly burg of approximately twenty-five hundred souls, give or take the odd dog or duck.

Then, eighteen months ago, Cyrus Tate arrived. And everything had changed.

Why did Tate pick Sunnyvale, of all places, to construct his sex temple? Did he own property in the area and figured he might as well put it to good use? Or was the reality simpler? That in his twisted way he just wanted to take good old Mayberry USA and turn it into Smut Central? That puzzle, among others, was what I was here to find the answers to. But then a second later everything fled as I rounded a curve and got my first look at PornUtopia.

Drawing near, mouth agape, unconsciously I slowed my car from the posted fifty-five to nearly forty. The news videos had hardly done it justice.

The building coming up was massive and circular, looking like nothing less than a small convention center. It was five stories tall, each story ringed by what appeared to be real stone columns, giving the thing a Roman arena feel. Big surprise. The news reports in the *Cincinnati Enquirer* had said that one of Tate's heroes was the sex-crazed emperor-fiend Caligula.

Across the top story, in ten-foot-high garish neon-blue letters, the name PornUtopia blazed out into the morning. Even though it wasn't yet ready for customers, and wouldn't be for at least a month or more, it was plain Tate was already conditioning the area populace for its twenty-four–seven operating status.

Besides the structure's size, two other things immediately jumped out. Flanking the long, gently curving driveway leading from the main road up to the huge parking area stood tall metal poles, crowned with flags from around the world. That was the first strange thing.

The second was that there wasn't one window in the building to be seen anywhere.

But the reason for the second thing, really, was self-evident. Question: Why aren't there ever any windows in a tavern? Answer: Because those inside don't want those outside to know what it is they're up to. The same thinking applied here, only on a scale I'd never seen before.

Slowing even more, I pulled into the drive, putting the car in park but leaving the engine running. Most of the heavy equipment was long gone, replaced by a landscaping crew putting in shrubs and saplings and rolls of zoysia sod. The groundskeeping, at least, appeared to be ahead of schedule.

Then I noticed something else, and wasn't too surprised. The "something else" was a beige golf cart hustling up the driveway toward me at a respectable speed. Behind the wheel I could make out a largish guy in a uniform, his partner beside him.

I knew what this was about. For a moment I was tempted to put the Regal back in gear and continue on my way to Sunnyvale. But I figured this meeting was inevitable, so I might as well get it over with. Let the games begin.

I calmly folded my hands in my lap as the cart pulled up to my driver's side door.

The wheelman exited the vehicle, leaving his partner where he was. Both appeared young, midthirties maybe, and fit. They wore mirrored state-trooper-style shades, and the one now rapping on my window was packing some heat on his hip, a nine-mil if I wasn't mistaken. I rolled down the glass and he leaned in, smiling.

"Good morning, sir. We're not open for business quite yet. I'm afraid I'm going to have to send you on your way." This guy's teeth were wonderful, a tribute to orthodontia, but his breath needed work. Beneath the off-brand cinnamon-mint mouthwash I could detect last night's supper—chili and onions if I knew my junk food. And I do.

I glanced at his shoulder patch. Apex Technologies, the ones Tate had wanted first me, and then Billy, to vet. So far, there was nothing out of the ordinary. The guard was polite and seemingly competent, if a bit bored. His partner back in the cart appeared to be staring straight at me, but behind his shades I couldn't tell if his eyes were open or closed.

The time had arrived for me to pull out my Rufus Corncob persona.

"Golly." I craned my neck past him. "I'd heard tell that thing was big, but I had no idea." My mouth appliances hadn't moved an inch as I spoke. It looked like my confidence in Toni's abilities was well placed.

The guard was still showing his teeth. "Yes sir, it's big all right. Now if I could just get you to—"

"Y'all got any girls in there yet?" I broke in, and gave him a lascivious grin. "My wife don't know I'm here."

The guard's demeanor slipped just a tad. "No sir, not yet. As I told you before—"

I whistled. "Dang, that place sure is somethin'. It surely is." I held out my right hand, which a second later the guard reluctantly shook. "My name's Sidney," I said. "Sidney Bean. Most folks just call me Sid."

The guard said nothing as we released hands, and past him I saw his partner stir. It was obviously taking longer to get rid of me than he thought.

"I really came here to find work," I prattled on. "I heard y'all might be hirin'. If so, that's when I figure on tellin' Edna. She's my wife, see. I been out of work durn near six months, and she's about frantic. I believe we'd both like it here fine." I grinned, giving him Gomer. "Yep, real fine."

"I'm with security, sir. I wouldn't know about any jobs."

"Hey, security, I've done that." I was making this up as I went. "Back home in Jackson I did six weeks of bank work at the Second National. Never had a sick day. Never had one robbery on my watch neither. Reckon I could wear me a gun like yours?"

"There aren't any openings in security." The man plainly was having his fill of me.

"Anything else then?" I chattered. "I'm a hard worker. Ask anybody in Jackson, and they'll say, yep, that Sid Bean, he's one hard worker." The chuckle I gave Mr. Nine Millimeter was salacious. "And I imagine the side benefits of slavin' away for good old Mr. Tate wouldn't be too hard to abide neither."

"The company personnel office is located in town. They might be able to help you out." He pointed. "That way. About a mile."

By now his partner was out of the cart and slowly coming over. And there was something else. I noticed he'd undone the flap on his holster. Interesting.

I pretended alarm.

"Hey now, boys, no need for that," I said, my eyes wide. "Good grief, I'm leavin', I'm leavin'. Just tryin' to be neighborly. Y'know?"

With that I put the Regal back in gear and did a hard three-point turn out onto the highway, goosing the throttle as if I was spooked. In my rearview mirror I could see the two guards talking to each other. The one I'd been speaking with pulled his shoulder mike close to his mouth and said something into it. As he did the other one laughed.

Another twenty seconds passed before I rounded the turn, and PornUtopia disappeared behind me. As it did I slowed to a more respectable speed. Something told me I'd stirred things up back there; I didn't really need a ticket now on top of it.

A minute later I came to the big Welcome to Sunnyvale sign. The thing was so doggone bright and cheery as I passed I half expected Robert Preston and Shirley Jones to step out from behind it and break into a rendition of "Seventy-six Trombones" from *The Music Man*.

I entered the village and began cruising slowly down Main Street, taking it all in. The town truly was a marvel, a hearty tribute to regional pride and spunk. The gas-lit avenue I was traversing was wide and smooth, with nary a crack, bump, or chuckhole to be felt.

The cheerful storefronts I passed were open and comely, each set off with blue awnings and painted window boxes festooned with a mixture of colorful mums and other fall foliage. Most of those windows held one of two signs, advertising either this year's United Way fund drive, or the big Halloween dance at the VFW coming up on Friday night.

The cross streets looked to be just as pretty and neat, as if the whole place had been laid out on a grid. Strolling along the tree-lined sidewalks I saw couples arm in arm, heads nuzzled close.

Laughing kids on bikes passed them, flanked by scruffy mutts cute enough to cause Benji to rethink his career. In fine and in sum, Sunnyvale was as good a piece of prime Americana as you'll see this side of Branson, Missouri.

So why was every internal alarm I possessed going off like the Russians had just launched a first strike?

It was time to find out. Seeing as how the guards had most likely already alerted their cohorts in town to be on the lookout for a nervous goober needing a job (me), I thought it best to park the car and see where the employment office was. They'd gone to the trouble of mentioning me; the least I could do was make my appearance.

I wheeled the car into an empty space on the street right behind an older but well-maintained Toyota Camry. Getting out, I walked around back and up onto the curb, the quarter for the meter already in my hand.

But there weren't any meters.

As I stood there puzzling that over, a man exited the place I'd just parked in front of. A glance up at the building's sign let me know that, whether by luck or design, I'd ended up in front of the town's hardware store. That was good. Through experience I've found that, in most small burgs at least, the twin hubs of information and idle gossip will always be located either at the hardware store or the barbershop.

Pulling the store's door securely closed behind him, the man smiled. "Whatcha looking for, mister?" The guy was gray-haired and blocky, heavyset like a butcher, but with merry blue eyes and an open, ruddy face.

I looked to my left and right up and down the street, returning the man's smile. "A parkin' meter. Don't you folks believe in 'em around here?"

He chuckled. "Nope. Not anymore. We found we don't need the aggravation. All the silly things do is either break or tick off the tourists."

"Huh." A town this size, voluntarily getting rid of their parking meters? That made no sense. Parking meters are mute, one-legged cash cows; every town father worth his salt knows that. Especially if out-of-state tourists are the ones feeding them. A hundred quarters in each one every day, multiplied by a couple hundred of the things, adds up to some serious jack. Why would they let that go?

Unless there'd soon be a bigger revenue stream coming in.

"Well, I'd say that's mighty friendly," I allowed.

"We aim to please." The man walked over to me. "My name's Evan Talbott. I own this establishment. Big, medium, or small, Talbott can do it all."

He cocked his thumb over his shoulder. Looking past him I found the store's sign did indeed read Talbott Hardware, with the homily he'd just quoted underneath.

Talbott shielded his eyes from the sunlight. "Haven't seen you around here before. You must be new to Sunnyvale."

"Yep, sure am." I found I was slipping effortlessly into my role. "My name's Sid Bean." We shook hands. "And you're right, first time here." I brightened up, still playing the fool. "Say, Mr. Talbott, since you're the owner of this store, maybe you can help me out. I'm fresh up from Kentucky just this mornin', and I need work. Bad."

The man was shaking his head even as I spoke. "That may be a problem. We're a pretty small town, and jobs around here just aren't that easy to come by. What we have usually goes to our own folks. I certainly don't have anything for you. Sorry."

"How about Tate Enterprises?" My expression and tone were as innocent as a Hallmark card. "They hirin'?"

I watched Talbott's face as I said that, alert for any eye shift. But his expression didn't change.

"Possibly," he shrugged. "But I heard they're close to the grand opening out there. I imagine they already have about all the help they're going to need. You're welcome to ask around, of course, but I'd doubt very much if they have anything for you either."

"Can't hurt to try, I reckon. You know where their office is?"

Talbott pointed to my left. "Half a block farther down, on this side. Their sign's pretty big. You can't miss it."

About then I heard steps approaching, and I turned my head.

An older gent was coming our way, wearing a gray herringbone suit thirty years out of date. An honest-to-Pete straw boater topped his head, and he smiled and nodded at Talbott as he sauntered between us. "Morning, Mr. Mayor. Glorious day we're having."

Talbott nodded back. "It is at that, Justin. It is at that."

The codger beamed as if he'd been blessed by the pope and kept moving down the sidewalk.

"Did I hear right?" I said. "Did that old feller just call you 'Mayor'?"

Talbott chucked lightly. "It's more an honorary title than anything else nowadays. Since Cyrus Tate came to our fair town, about all I do anymore is show up at church bazaars and bake sales." He laughed, patting his hard-looking belly. "As if I need more of that."

"Well, I'll be dogged." I shook my head in mock amazement. "Here I am, Sid Bean, talkin' to the sure-enough mayor of Sunnyvale."

Talbott looked past me, as if anxious to be on his way to wherever. "I must be off now, Mr. Bean, but best of luck to you. If you need me for anything else," he glanced back at his store, "well, you know where I'll be." With that he headed away from me down the sidewalk.

Belatedly I called out to his retreating back, "Thanks, Mr. Talbott!" He gave a cheery wave as he kept moving.

When I was sure the guy wasn't going to turn back around and catch me, I dropped my goofy grin. How about that? Talbott had practically told me that once Tate and his cash had come to Sunnyvale, his mayoral duties had dried up. For a hollow man, he sure hid his demotion well.

That had to have hurt. I've known a few small-town politicos in my time. Enough to know most of them don't relinquish their power without a fight. In my experience, the smaller the town, the bloodier the race. Usually nothing is off-limits, up to and including nasty slurs against an opponent's family, race, drinking habits, or sexual proclivity. But Talbott appeared as happy as a clam about his newly symbolic status, "appeared" being the operative term. Again, mighty odd.

Unless, that is, hard cash was the hook set tight in Talbott's jaw.

One of the Scriptures I'd run across just recently said—and I'm paraphrasing here—"money answers all things." It was a surprisingly cynical idea, especially coming from the Bible. But there it was in all its bald glory, and it was worth puzzling out. Maybe the answer to Evan Talbott really was as simple as that. Perhaps, like countless others before him, he'd laid his principles on the golden altar, and sold his soul for gelt.

If so, that made him a very dangerous man.

15

alking a half-block farther on, as promised I came to Tate Enterprises' employment office. The storefront was sandwiched between a dry cleaner's and a hat shop, and was as well kept as the others. In keeping with the small-town feel, I half expected to hear a bell dinging above the door when I went in. But there was nothing.

The place appeared deserted, and I decided to check it out before whoever worked here discovered me.

The office was fifteen by fifteen or so, with a half-dozen beige visitors' chairs lining the inside front wall, and a small dark-maple desk against the back one. At both ends of the row of chairs were matching end tables with a few magazines scattered on them.

I leaned over to the closest one and took a peek. Nope, none was a *Cat's Meow*, only a current *Time*, a week-old *People*, and last month's *Reader's Digest*.

The carpet was a short dark green, the walls off-white and hung with a few tasteful prints of riverboats and willow trees. The room was nice, but not overly so, and the fact that it was set up to recruit workers for a porn palace wasn't in evidence anywhere.

Surreptitiously I glanced up and around. Up near the far corner of the ceiling hung a miniature security camera, smaller than a pack of gum. I'd bet anything you'd care to name it belonged to Apex. Squinting, I could make out a tiny red light above it, and knew it was active. All I had to do now was wait.

It didn't take long. A moment later the door behind the receptionist's desk opened noiselessly, and through it came, of all people, Cindi, Tate's blonde bodyguard.

Assembling a bland smile, I tried to ignore the fact that my guts were rolling like potatoes in a barrel. Man, not her. I'd known the time was coming sooner or later when I'd have to see exactly how good Toni Maroni's makeup skills were, but I'd dreaded it all the same. And now I had to do it with Cindi-the-freaking-bodyguard.

Getting a better look at her than I did the first time we'd met, I still couldn't shake the feeling that something about this woman was *off*. It wasn't her severely cut business suit (cream colored this time) or spike heels. It also wasn't the fact that her jade-green Fu Manchu fingernails exactly matched her contact lenses.

What it was exactly, I wasn't sure, but it was there all the same. I'm sure the effect Cindi was going for was jaw-dropping devastation to any male who might clap eyes on her, but to me her clothes and manner made her appear predatory. In short, she creeped me out.

"Good afternoon." She pointed toward the visitor's chair. "Please, have a seat."

"Thanks." I hadn't heard her speak before. The timbre of her voice surprised me. It was a contralto, low and smoky and just a bit rough. But I did as she asked and lowered myself into the chair.

She folded her hands on the desk. "How may we at Tate Enterprises help you?"

I shrugged, giving her what I hoped was an open, boyish look. "Like the sign out front says, ma'am, I need a job."

"Hmm." She regarded me closely, but it was more as if she was taking my measure than as if she'd seen me somewhere before and was trying to place exactly where.

I rushed on. "My name's Sid Bean, and I'm a hard worker. It don't matter what it is, neither. Manual labor's my best suit. I may not be smart, but I can lift heavy things." I'd seen that on a T-shirt once, and its inherent silliness had cried out for its use. I could have picked a better time and place though.

"You know what PornUtopia is all about, correct?" she asked.

"Yes, ma'am."

"And you'd have no qualms about working there?"

I spread my hands. "Hey, it's only skin, right? And Lord knows, we all got skin."

That must have been the right answer, because Cindi smiled slightly even as her mood became brisk and businesslike. Picking up a clipboard with a piece of paper already fastened on it from the corner of her desk, she handed it to me.

"Unfortunately we have no openings at present. But please fill out this application as completely as you can. We'll hold it in our open files for six months. If something becomes available, you'll be contacted."

"Six months?" I tried to look crestfallen. "But I need work now."

"I'm sorry. It's the best we can do."

I brightened. "Hey, is Mr. Tate around? Maybe I can talk to the big boss himself. He might know of somethin'."

Cindi's smile turned into a smirk, though to her credit she tried to hide it. "I don't think so, Mr. Bean."

I handed the clipboard back. "I don't reckon this'll do me any good then."

She took it from me and stood. "Well, as you wish. Best of luck to you, at any rate."

I stayed where I was. It was plain she was anxious for me to leave. Perversely, I didn't want to. I gave it one more try. "You're sure I can't talk to him, huh?"

"I'm positive. Mr. Tate is a very busy man and spends most of his time these days readying PornUtopia for its grand opening. Have a good day."

"Thanks." Outwardly weary, I got to my feet. Inside, I was giving myself a high five. I'd gotten Cindi to reveal that Tate was in town. Later I'd figure out how and when to brace him. But for now, it was enough.

♦ ◊ ♦

Finding myself back out on the street, I checked my watch. Near on to lunchtime. I'd said earlier there are two places in any small town to get information, the hardware store and the barbershop. But I'd left out the third one: the town diner. Any burg the size of Sunnyvale had to have at least one place where the locals hung out to eat and chew the fat. Which, depending on the quality of chow served, sometimes is the same thing. And those diners are usually located one of two places. Either right in town or at the edge of it.

Since I was already near the center of Sunnyvale, and the day seemed right for it, I decided to mosey around for a bit and see if what I was after was close. The town seemed tailor-made for moseying.

Another block of easy striding, and there it was. A diner called, simply, Bud's. Brick-solid, there was nothing overly remarkable about it. But from the cleanliness of the windows and the swept sidewalk, it looked to be a step or two up from the usual beanery.

When I opened the door, this time I was rewarded with the dinging bell I'd been denied at the employment office. Glancing around, I grinned in astonishment. You just don't come across places like this one much anymore.

The diner held maybe six gray Formica-covered square tables scattered around, each table complemented by four tubular metal chairs topped with red vinyl seats. You've seen them, I know.

At the back of the room, separating it from the kitchen, was a long lunch counter containing eight round swivel seats, also covered in red vinyl. The floor was a black-and-white checkered-tile pattern, and on the walls all around was memorabilia from the golden age of television. Coonskin caps and Mickey Mouse ears and *I Love Lucy* posters and such. Topping off the fifties motif was a genuine Wurlitzer jukebox on the far side of the diner, banging out loud music.

The only thing keeping me from believing I'd been transported back to the time of Ike and hula hoops was the tune coming out of it, some rap or hip-hop trash or other. Its main claim to fame was a tinny synthesizer top-note setting off a bass line that almost, but not quite, drowned out the male singer (and I use the word advisedly), an angry dude who sounded like he was spitting every other word into the mike.

The place was nearly full, so I took one of the counter seats. My stomach was growling in anticipation. It was only after I'd settled my weight that I remembered that with those mouth things, I couldn't eat my meal here. Nuts. Maybe they did takeout.

It looked like I was about to find out. A moment later a chunky teenage girl with thin black hair and very pale skin loped down my way. She stopped, wiping the counter with a damp rag and stern determination before looking up at me. "Hi, mister. You hungry?"

I'd had my suspicions with her gait and almond eyes and stubby fingers. But when she'd spoken, she confirmed it. Unless I missed my guess, the girl had Down syndrome.

I've always had a special place in my heart for those folks and their courage, so I looked her right in the eye as I answered. "You bet I am. What's good here today?"

"Well ..." The girl stuck the end of her thick tongue in the corner of her mouth and stared at the floor, as if concentrating on my words. I hoped I hadn't embarrassed her. But sometimes I do that with special needs people, even though I don't mean to.

While she thought, I looked around to see if there was a menu close by.

I caught a guy standing by the kitchen door staring at me intently. He was maybe early to midfifties, and a bit shorter than me, with a shiny bullet head, hard eyes, and a tough build. Unconsciously I looked down at his hands hanging by his side. His right one held a spatula, glistening with grease.

His left one was gone. In its place hung a two-pronged hooked prosthetic.

Right then, I was awfully glad I hadn't gone with Toni's Captain Hook prop as part of my disguise, even as a joke. Talk about bad taste.

Before I could think more on it, the girl spoke up, and I gave her my full attention. "We have eggs," she said, as if from memory. "And bacon in the morning. Toast ..." She brightened. "Oh yeah, and hamburgers. I like hamburgers the best. With cheese on top."

I smiled. "That sounds real fine. What's your name anyway?"

"Wendy." She pointed at the man with the hook-hand. "That's my dad."

Again I looked his way, and this time he pushed away from the wall and came over, ending up next to his daughter. Without taking his eyes from me he said to her, "Did you get this man's order, Wendy?"

She nodded forcefully. "Yeah, I did, Dad. He wants a hamburger. With cheese on it." Well, I hadn't exactly told her that's what I wanted, but it sounded all right. At any rate, I wasn't about to correct her in front of everybody.

With a will he pulled his eyes from me and put them on her. "Did you ask the man if he wanted anything else? Think hard, now."

I jumped to the girl's defense, keeping my fake accent and persona in place. "I'm sure she was just fixin' to." Turning my attention her way, I said, "Wendy, I'd also like some fries and a Coke with that. All of it to go please."

"Fries and a Coke," she nodded again, just as hard.

"That's the way," I smiled again.

Her father waited until she'd waddled into the kitchen to put in the order before he addressed me. "New in town?" He said it as an accusation rather than a question.

"Sure am. Name's Sid Bean, fresh up from Kentucky."

"Why?"

That stopped me for a second. What was he asking? Why I was from Kentucky, or why was I here? It took me a moment to formulate an answer. I had the feeling this guy would let me know if it was wrong.

"I was kinda lookin' for work up this way," I said.

His reply was flat. "There's no work here."

"You know, that's what everybody keeps tellin' me."

"They're telling you true."

I needed an ally here, and his attitude to the contrary, I wondered if this man might be it. Taking a pure stab in the dark, I glanced at his hook. "Lose it in-country?"

He blinked, and then nodded. "AirCav, 1973." He frowned. "How did you know?"

"Me too." Before I could confuse him further I went on. "I mean, my hitch wasn't in AirCav, ridin' the friendly skies, but I did a tour there. I was an infantry grunt."

"I was a door-gunner on a slick, until the day we went down, thanks to an RPG." The guy seemed to be more talkative now. Good. I needed to keep that coming.

"I turned out lucky," he went on. "I only lost my hand. The pilot burned to death. Where were you stationed?"

"The Ia Drang Valley. Ninth Corps, Charlie Company."

For the first time since I'd sat down, the man's features eased, and he gave a disbelieving smile. "Ia Drang Valley? You're kidding. That's where I was stationed too."

Now, wasn't that interesting? Through fate or prayer I'd been led to the right guy. "Son of a gun. Y'all might have evacked us out of a hot LZ once or twice."

"We may have at that." He stuck out his good hand. "The name's Bud Spencer."

"Bud, huh?" We shook. Now that I knew he was a bro, I hated maintaining my ruse, but there was nothing for it. If I let my true business and name slip now, I might pay for it in spades later. Releasing hands I said, "This is your place then, I reckon."

"Yeah," he nodded. "Mine and the bank's." Seeming to relax some more, he glanced down at his hook. "Sometimes people look at the hand and just don't get it."

"Nobody gets it who wasn't there."

"You got that right." I could have been mistaken, but I thought I heard his voice catch as he went on, "Pity for me I can take. It's pity for Wendy that tears me up."

"She seems like a sweet gal."

"She's my life," he said simply. I was right. Bud was thawing.

He went on, as if anxious now for a friendly ear. "Wendy came to my wife and me late, and the fact she came to us different just made her more special. Since cancer took my wife two years ago, now I'm more protective of my daughter than ever."

"I kinda picked that up from the way you were givin' me the hairy eyeball when I was talkin' to her."

Bud shrugged. "Things around here weren't too bad before Cyrus Tate moved in and started that project of his out at the edge of town. The locals all knew Wendy and treated her right. But now ..." His voice trailed.

I felt like I might be onto something here, and pressed the man firmly, but gently. "What do you mean?"

He glanced from side to side, as if some of Tate's men might be in the room with us. "I mean we have pervert problems."

"Perverts?"

I guess figuring the lousy music coming from the jukebox wasn't quite enough to mask our conversation, Bud's answer was oblique.

"You really ought to rethink your idea of having anything to do with this town, Sid. I mean that. We've got a bad element running things here, and something tells me that before it gets better, it's gonna get a whole lot worse."

"Surely they wouldn't try nothin' with your daughter."

Bud's laugh was harsh and world-weary. "Don't you bet on it. I've seen men, and even worse, women, around Sunnyvale these days that'd make your skin crawl. They come in here for a snack or a cold drink and look at Wendy the way a dog looks at fresh meat."

I shook my head, still amazed at how far people could fall. "How can that be?"

The other man shrugged, as wrung-out as I've ever seen a guy. "Who knows? Let me ask *you* a question. Did you ever get leave to Saigon during your tour over there?"

"Yeah, a couple of times, when the brass was in a good enough mood."

"Ever make it over to Bring Cash Alley?"

My laugh was as rough as Bud's had been. "Did I ever. What a place. I saw things there my nineteen-year-old hillbilly eyes had *never* seen before."

"Well, this new crew hanging around Sunnyvale these days puts the creeps we saw at Bring Cash Alley to shame."

It was my turn to look in disbelief, because Bud became adamant. "I'm telling you, man, they're horndogs, every one of them. You were there. You know what I'm talking about. And I think whatever Tate's planning out at PornUtopia is gonna make the stuff we saw at that Saigon red-light district look like a meeting of the Kiwanis."

I squinted. "And you know this how?"

His reply was flat. "My brother-in-law. He worked there on the finish paint crew, and those guys are usually one of the last ones on a job. He'd come in here every night after work looking to cadge a free beer, sniggering like a kid at what he'd seen out there."

"Like what?"

Bud shook his head. "He wouldn't say. Or couldn't."

That didn't sound right. "You mean like a gag order or somethin'?"

"Yeah, kind of like that. I heard Tate has every worker there sign a confidentiality agreement, promising they won't spill the beans about what's inside the place until the grand opening. If they agree, they're each supposed to get a cash bonus the day the doors open. If just one lets the cat out of the bag, the deal's off for everybody."

"Dude's keepin' his cards held close," I said.

"With all these weirdos running around town, something tells me it's more than tickle parlors and peep shows for the tourist trade Tate's planning," Bud said. "A lot more. And when whatever it is happens, it's going to take the world by surprise."

16

*T*he Styrofoam box holding my lunch felt pleasantly warm as I headed back to where my car was parked. I remembered Wendy's words as she'd given it to me.

"I stuck an extra pickle in it," she said, her voice taking on a rough stage whisper. "'Cause you were nice to me and didn't laugh." When the girl handed over the white carton, she beamed like it held the crown jewels of Europe.

For a moment my throat closed. I managed to croak out my reply as I said simply, "Thanks, Wendy."

The grateful smile and nod I'd gotten from her father Bud as I left told me I'd secured the ally I'd sought here.

Back once more in the Regal, I drove back out of town a ways before I found a secluded enough spot where I could remove my mouth appliances and set about the serious business of ramming some groceries down my throat. And I enjoyed every bite. Not only was the price of the meal at Bud's fair, but the burger was dead perfect, charred just right outside and juicy pink inside, the fries were crispy, and the pickles pleasantly sour.

As I ate, I reflected on the man and his daughter. Bud had his work cut out where Wendy was concerned. No doubt about it. I'd never been faced with such a challenge, but I imagined it was incredibly hard, even in the best of circumstances. Having to do it in a town now overrun with "perverts," warped and twisted people who "eyed his little girl with bad intent" (to quote a line from an old Jethro Tull tune), would make it even tougher.

Maybe all wasn't lost though. Before it was all said and done, maybe somehow I could put enough wheels in motion with the authorities to make Bud's task a little bit easier.

The meal finished, I reinserted the mouth dealies—it was getting easier now—and threw the trash in the back seat, keeping up my who-cares ruse. Then I started up the Regal and put the old beater in gear, once more heading back toward town.

OK, the first leg of the mission, reconnaissance, was accomplished. Now I needed a place to bivouac (having met a kindred Vietnam vet in Bud was causing me to think again in military terms). For you civilians, I'd scouted the village; now it was time to find a place I could sleep for the night.

I discounted the two bright and snazzy new chain motels built quickly and ready for occupancy I'd passed earlier, over on the other side of the road from PornUtopia. I needed something closer in. Either a small hotel or inn right in town, near to the action you might say. Or more accurately, closer to ground zero. But where? The Chamber of Commerce might help, provided Sunnyvale was big enough to have one.

But a second later that question was answered. And in a way I hadn't thought of.

Pulling the Regal into the small empty parking lot in front of a white clapboard building, I turned it off. Then slumping my hands over the wheel I read the name written in neat letters above the structure's wide, plain, wooden double doors: Sunnyvale Community Church. And below it, in smaller letters, Rev. Mason Kilbride, Pastor.

I shrugged. Why not? I've found a small-town pastor usually knows a whole lot about a lot of things. Why not ask this Rev. Kilbride if there was a clean place nearby for a weary traveler to rest his head after time on the road? (It being only a little after one in the afternoon, I wasn't weary *yet*, understand, but you get the idea.)

I got out and crossed the lot, mounting the half-dozen concrete steps up to those doors. Knowing churches are usually kept open during the day—for whatever reason—I pulled the big, black wrought-iron handle on the right side door. It swung open with nary a creak. Cautiously and quietly I crept inside.

I found myself in a vestibule, with the twin oak doors to the sanctuary proper a few feet farther in. They were propped open. Entering the sanctuary, I found it cool and dim, but there was enough light for me to see the small altar area and podium up near the front. Past that, up on the back wall, was a large, old stained-glass window, showing Jesus holding a lamb. It let in enough illumination to let me know I was alone. Or so I thought.

"Hello, may I help you?"

I turned, not too fast, to see who'd spoken. The voice was genial and inviting, and belonged to a shadowy figure I could barely make out past the altar area.

"I hope so," I said, squinting as I began approaching whoever it was.

A few moments later we met in front of the podium. The voice belonged to a man wearing old ripped jeans and a torn T-shirt. I took him to be the janitor.

"I'm Reverend Kilbride," he said. "And you are ...?"

Reverend, huh? I guess he wasn't the janitor after all. Taking his outstretched hand, it felt warm and wet and slightly oily, as if I'd just caught the good reverend in the middle of draining the crankcase on his Chevy out back. As I've said before, I've always hated moist handshakes, and so only gave it a quick up and down before releasing it.

"My name's Sid Bean, Reverend," I said. "And like I told you, I hope you can help me."

"I'll certainly try." Kilbride pointed to a pew in front of us. "Please, have a seat. I trust you don't mind a little drywall powder on it. I'm replastering the ceiling."

"Not at all." I sat, the pastor joining me, and I got my first good look at the man.

Kilbride was slightly older than I am, and about as tall, with a narrow patrician face setting off deep green eyes, eyes which to me seemed spread a bit too far apart on either side of his aquiline nose. For some reason he seemed eerily familiar, and then I got it. He looked quite a bit like the guy who'd played Ashley Wilkes in *Gone with the Wind.*

But unlike that actor, Kilbride's wide shoulders and thin waist gave him a swimmer's build, as if from the head down his frame belonged to a younger man. Idly I wondered where a preacher would find the time in his busy day to make it to the gym.

I dove right in. "Reverend, I'm fresh up from Kentucky, lookin' for work. I ain't got a lot of money"—I snorted in self-deprecation—"heck, almost none, and I need a place in town to sleep nights that won't cost me what little I got."

"And you're hoping to find work here? In beautiful Sunnyvale?"

"Yeah, I always heard Sunnyvale was nice." What a lie. "I figure once I get me a good job, I'll bring the missus on up to find us a place to stay. You know, permanent like."

"The missus, you say ..." As if secretly amused, Kilbride lightly tugged on his lower lip. "The two of you *are* aware of our town's new claim to fame, true?"

"Yeah. Why?"

"And you'd have no problem settling here?" he pressed. "Especially your wife?"

"No." Why was I getting the feeling there was more to this supposed reverend than met the eye?

And right then my spine began tingling like a live wire. *Wait just a minute,* I almost blurted. *Why here? In a church?* That made no sense. But I'd puzzle that out later, when I had the time. Kilbride was expecting an answer.

I gave a weak shrug. "Well, y'know, live and let live, right?"

Kilbride's stare was intense. "That's an awfully enlightened attitude, Mr. Bean."

"I'm not sure what that word means," I said, still playing dumb. Something in the man's tone was causing me to stare back at him, just as hard, and I thought I'd gig him a bit. "What do *you* think about Mr.

Tate's creation, Reverend? You bein' a preacher and all. That place he's puttin' up out there has gotta gall you some, right?"

The pastor's demeanor of casual amusement was back. "At the end of the day, who cares what I think about it?"

Me for one, but I kept silent.

"I suppose you might also call me enlightened," Kilbride went on. I must have looked really at sea then, because he said, "I know it goes against the grain of most men of the cloth, but frankly I think what Tate is planning with PornUtopia is healthy. Extremely so."

My mouth appliances almost fell out at that, but I managed to keep my composure. Just barely.

"Healthy?" I said in disbelief

Now it was Kilbride's turn to shrug. "It was God's choice to make human beings sexual creatures, with strong carnal drives, true? So why would he then deny that pleasure to his own children?"

That threw me. I was trying not to sound confrontational as I said the next. But this dude's thinking was stupefying. "But … what about marriage? Like me and the missus?"

The other man's answer was smooth. "What about it?"

Good grief, what kind of a reverend *was* this anyway? There was no evidence inside the sanctuary to clue me in either. Come to think of it, maybe this wasn't even a real church.

Not anymore.

The look I gave must have been pure bafflement. "You've really lost me now."

Kilbride remained controlled and even in his reply. "Recreational sex has very little to do with the marriage covenant. They are two separate things, Mr. Bean, I assure you."

While I fumbled helplessly for a comeback, Kilbride reached into his front jeans pocket and pulled out a small notebook and pen and began writing.

"I have a friend who runs a bed-and-breakfast back in town, just off Main Street," he said. "She only takes guests on personal recommendation, so feel free to mention my name. Her name is Sarah Poole. These are the directions." Tearing off the paper, he handed it to me.

"I'm sure you'll find Sarah an ... accommodating sort." Kilbride smirked at his own wit, such as it was, and I wondered if there was a deeper meaning to what he'd just said.

"Thanks." Mouth dry, I folded the paper and slipped it inside my pocket. Before I left though, I had to know. "Sir, exactly what kind of a reverend are you anyway?"

Kilbride's smile was otherworldly. "An accommodating sort."

♦ ◊ ♦

Inside of five minutes I was back on Main Street and looking for Carlton Avenue. My brain was still reeling from Kilbride's bizarre observations. He may have considered himself an "enlightened" individual, but to me he was a grade-A, farm-fresh nutjob.

Double-checking the paper lying on the seat next to me, I saw the directions said that Carlton crossed Main at the bakery. The address for Sarah Poole's bed-and-breakfast was number twelve. A moment later the bakery came up on the right, and I made my turn.

Three houses down, and there it was, a fine-looking older redbrick Cape Cod topped with a gray slate roof. It looked a little like Angela's house back home. The hand-painted sign hanging on the small metal stanchion out front was classic in its simplicity, reading in neat, easy to read black script: Sunnyvale View, Sarah Poole, Proprietor.

I pulled the car into an empty space on the street right in front and got out. Coming up the sidewalk, I saw the front door was already opening. Had I triggered a sensor on the sidewalk, like at the grocery store? In this town, anything could happen.

Climbing the three steps up onto the gray-painted wooden porch, I saw the door now was standing wide. Framed in its opening stood a tall older woman, midseventies maybe, gray-haired but ramrod straight. A slight smile graced her full mouth.

"And you must be Mr. Bean," were her first words as I reached her.

"Yes, ma'am." I took the woman's proffered, liver-spotted hand. Like my late mother's, it was cool and dry to the touch, but with a core of strength. "And you must be Sarah Poole." It could have been she wasn't, but the possibility was strong. "How'd you know who I am?"

"Rev. Kilbride called just now and told me to be on the lookout for a tall stranger with a woebegone way about him." The woman's speech was precise, as if in her youth she'd had lessons. She stepped aside so I could pass. "Please, won't you come in?"

"Thanks." I did, walking past her. And doing so, found I'd taken a trip through Mr. Peabody's Wayback Machine.

The space stretching out was an airy, open parlor, just like the one in the movie *Arsenic and Old Lace* ... although hopefully Sarah Poole wouldn't turn out to be a Abby Brewster–type, and a poisoner of gentleman callers. The curtains slowly wafting in the gentle autumn breeze appeared to be genuine Irish linen. The furniture sitting around was heavy Victorian, covered here and there with yellowed doilies and large antimacassars.

Somewhere a radio was playing Benny Goodman, and the air smelled of pine and fresh gingerbread. On the small wooden table over by the fireplace rested what looked like a hammered brass tray holding a flowered china teapot and little cups. All the room lacked to complete the twenties feel was a wind-up Victrola with some wax seventy-eights stacked on top.

I stopped in amazement, taking it all in. Behind me I heard the woman softly shut the door.

"How do you like my establishment so far?" she said, her clear blue eyes probing. Turning, I regarded Sarah Poole more closely. Remove her gray hair, take forty years and its attendant wrinkles away from her face, and the innkeeper must have once been a handsome woman, as my Granny used to say.

"Your place reminds me of somethin' out of a magazine," I replied truthfully.

"Good. That's the look I was going for." The woman moved past me to the tea set and picked up the pot. "Would you care for some tea, Mr. Bean? It's fresh."

"Yeah, I would, please." Toni had said nothing about me not being able to drink while wearing the appliances. "But no sugar or lemon. I don't much hold with it."

Expertly Mrs. Poole poured me a cup without spilling a drop. "That's interesting. That's how I like mine, too." Done, she handed it to me.

I took a sip. Normally I'm strictly a coffee man, but the stuff wasn't bad.

The woman tilted her head a bit. "Do you like it? It's a special blend of my own."

"Not bad, Mrs. Poole." I took another pull. It really was pretty good. If there was poison in it, I couldn't tell.

"Thank you." My hostess was obviously pleased I liked her brew. "And please, call me Sarah."

"Sid," I replied.

The old innkeeper went on. "Although technically I suppose the term 'missus' is no longer true. I've been a widow now for quite a while."

Gently I set the cup down on a nearby table. "You surely knew I was comin' here this afternoon to get me a room, ma'am. Which is fine, 'cause here I am. But here's the thing. Your Rev. Kilbride told me I was s'posed to mention his name to you when I arrived. So how come he took it on himself to call you anyway, and let you know I was on my way over?"

Her answer seemed forced. "Perhaps he thought you'd forget."

You mean he was warning you, I thought.

"Yeah, maybe," was what I said.

The old woman primly folded her hands. "How long are you planning on staying with us?"

I shrugged. "Depends on the tariff, I guess."

"The 'tariff,' as you put it, is fair. Twenty dollars a night. That includes a hot breakfast in the morning, with all the trimmings, and dinner with me, if you wish. For lunch you're on your own."

I nearly whistled. "Twenty bucks a night for all that is more than fair. So—"

"I was hoping you'd think so," she broke in.

Never a master of tact, I finished. "So how in the world do you make a livin' here, chargin' so little?" Almost as an afterthought I added, "Forgive me my rudeness, ma'am."

Sarah's countenance held a bit of mystery. "Oh, a woman has her ways." She seemed to grow a bit somber then, and her next words were spoken to herself as much as me. "Even this late in the game, a woman has her ways ..." Returning from her reverie, her tone turned brisk. "Would you care to see the room before you agree to take it?"

I waved that off. "Naw, I'm sure it's fine. Just let me get my stuff out of my car."

"Yes, your car." Sarah Poole's gaze had turned strange, her eyes unreadable. Kind of a weird bird all around, truth be told. "A 1990 Buick Regal. I had one like it, when I still drove. And forgive *me*, Sid, but you've neglected it badly. It's a shame, really."

Dang, that stupid car. A second ago I'd nailed Sarah with a rude question. I guess I had it coming. Whatever damage done had happened though, and I tried to recover as best I could.

"Yeah, well ... things went south for me and the missus kinda sudden like."

That sounded stupid even as I said it, and I knew it wouldn't stand up to heavy scrutiny. How come I didn't just say the Regal was a loaner from a friend and leave it at that? Deception isn't my strong suit. Normally I play it straight up, or not at all.

Thankfully Sarah seemed to accept it. "Life tends to do us that way sometimes." From her tone, she sounded like she was speaking from hard experience. But what kind? Who cared? Another Sunnyvale secret. Big whoop.

I reached for my wallet. "Do I pay you in advance or what?"

She waved that away, apparently back in full control now. "You'll find I'm fairly unpretentious. We'll settle up the bill when you leave."

I was about to answer her when something else beat me to it. Out of nowhere a venomous voice suddenly rose up and hissed its own reply deep in my brain.

Yeah. If you leave.

Sarah stared at me as I struggled manfully to keep my face blank. Sarge and Angela both had tried to warn me about the probability of this. But in my experience, theory and reality are most often two very different things.

"Are you all right?" the older woman asked, concern filling her voice.

"Panic attack," I gulped. "I get 'em sometimes."

I suppose "panic" was as true a thing to call this attack as anything, Pan being the name of an old god of Greek mythology. An enchanter and a thoroughly nasty sort, if memory serves. With a will I tried to calm my rapid breathing and slow down my racing heart. So far it wasn't working. So I did what I should have done at first and sent up a silent prayer.

"Just give me a minute," I said, hoping it wouldn't take near that long.

Sarah nervously glanced at the phone sitting on a small table in the corner. "Maybe I should call Rev. Kilbride. He might be able to help."

My chuckle was ghastly as I said nothing. Yeah, right. The day I'd listen to that twisted yahoo's advice for anything is the day pigs fly.

"Please don't bother," I finally managed to croak.

"Are you sure? He can be here in a jiffy."

"No …" I sat there breathing hard, waiting it out. Surely it couldn't go on much longer.

It didn't. A moment later the sense of doom began lifting like mist off a lake. A few seconds more, and it was gone completely. To where, I couldn't say. But somehow I knew the dark voice's departure was only temporary. Like my nightmares, there was more than a strong chance that later it would be back, possibly worse, possibly with a vengeance.

I gave Sarah a wan smile. "I'm OK now. Really." Thankfully I was.

She cocked her head, clearly not buying it. I couldn't blame her. I didn't really buy it myself.

17

Sitting down on the edge of the old Murphy bed, I looked around the room.

Like the parlor downstairs, Sarah Poole's love for old styles carried through to here. Lace curtains graced the natural-wood windows, and the cherry waterfall dresser opposite me was obviously an antique. So was the white marble-topped nightstand to my left, which held a vase of fresh-cut yellow mums. The lamps were *faux* Tiffany, and the brown and gold woven rugs on the floor appeared to be freshly beaten. I've stayed in newer places in my time, and some that were older and definitely worse, but to me this eclectic room was just plain nice. And Sarah was only getting twenty bucks a night for this, and that included two meals a day? That bore looking into.

Later, maybe. As pleasant as the thought was, I couldn't sit here all day.

Getting back up off the bed, I hung my few meager clothes in the mahogany wardrobe next to the room's door, sticking my now-empty suitcase inside. The shaving kit containing my razor, toothbrush, shaving mug, and brush I placed on the dresser. The spirit gum and acetone for the fake mustache I'd left in the Regal. Then I left the room, gently pulling the door shut behind me.

Coming back down the stairs, I sniffed the air. Something good was baking. Brownies, if I knew my treats. As I stopped at the foot of the stairs, inhaling the intoxicating smell, I heard Sarah call to me from the kitchen.

"Sid? I'm in here. Come in, and I'll show you what I'm making for supper." If the brownies were any indication, supper would prove to be noteworthy.

Cutting through the living room, I passed the white stone fireplace. On the cherrywood mantel above it I spied some pictures I'd missed the first time around. Figuring the brownies could bake on their own for the next minute, I stopped to take a look at the faces in the brass frames.

Part of my action involved nosiness, I admit, but part of it was gathering intel. I needed to keep in mind the fact that, regardless of the gone-back-in-time feel to this house, I wasn't here on vacation. I was on a mission to find Billy's killer. And keep my own hide out of the jug.

I began scanning the frames. When a woman like Sarah Poole becomes of an age, as my Granny used to put it, she's expected to have made a lot of memories, those memories reflected in family pictures. But not here. Not in this house. There should have been at least a dozen photos up on the mantel. There weren't. And that was strange. I only counted four.

By its yellowed, faded tone, I could tell the first one was a blown-up color Polaroid from the fifties. The subject was a young blonde woman, midtwenties maybe. She was kneeling by a lake, a small bouquet of wildflowers held loosely in her hand. Looking off to her left, a slight smile adorned her face, as if someone had just told her she was pretty. The feel of it was a candid shot, done while she wasn't paying attention.

I leaned in for a closer look. Wait a minute. I'll be a son of a gun. The woman was a young Sarah Poole. I straightened. Well, so what? Some folks like to keep pictures of themselves sitting around. I don't, but some do. Weird, but there you go.

The next photograph over was much newer, showing a bored-looking young couple holding a baby. The people staring out appeared to be in their late twenties. The guy was a sandy-haired greaser, the girl a mousy blonde, both as bland as grits. Of the three of them, only the baby looked like he had a personality.

The next photo was Sarah holding that same small infant bundled in her arms. It appeared the kid hadn't aged much. The chair seemed familiar, and I glanced from the photo to the wingback over in the far corner. Yep, same chair, same floor lamp. Obviously the picture was taken here, in this room. Sarah's hair didn't appear nearly as gray in this shot. I pegged her for maybe ten years younger. But her face carried an unmistakable sadness.

The last one was of a young boy. Again I leaned close. And as I did, my heart nearly stopped.

The kid was me.

My ticker now was tripping double time. Not again. On my last case I'd found some pictures of me with my mother, a woman I'd been told had been dead for years. Those photos had nearly destroyed me. I couldn't go through it again.

Commanding my body to calm itself, once more I took in details, lots of details. Who the devil *was* this youngster?

From far back in the kitchen I heard Sarah call out, "Sid? Are you coming?"

I ignored her as I nearly willed the boy in the picture to speak.

Then peering closer, I gulped in relief. It wasn't me after all, thank God. Still staring at the kid, my pulse slowing now, I shook my head. Legend says that every person in the world has a twin somewhere. It could be this young boy was mine.

I'm rotten at judging children's ages, so if hard pressed I'd peg the kid in the picture at anywhere between six and nine. He possessed a wide, open, friendly face, with an unruly cowlick of black hair hanging lank across his freckled forehead, exactly as mine had done. Maybe that's what threw me. The kid's gap-toothed mischievous smile completed his Huck Finn look. I could picture this boy and runaway Jim poling their raft down the Mississippi.

So in the end we had four photos, and only four, to commemorate Sarah Poole's life so far. The first one showed her as a young woman kneeling by a lake. The second one featured a mystery family. The third had Sarah as much older and holding the same infant. And then the last one revealed this kid, my *doppelganger*.

"Sid?" the old innkeeper lady querulously called again.

Still staring at the picture I answered loudly, "Comin', Sarah."

Leaving the photos behind at last, I walked on into the kitchen. Before she could ask me what had held me up, I beat her to it. "Just admirin' your house some more."

"I trust you'll admire my supper just as much." She was vigorously stirring a gray steel pot that had a decidedly strange smell coming out of it.

"I'm sure whatever you fix will be fine. But when it's ready I'll take my plate up to my room, if that's all right with you. I need to look at some want ads for jobs." No, the truth was I needed to take out my mouth appliances so I could eat Sarah's grub.

"If you wish." Clearly she wasn't happy with the idea.

Then remembering some of the truly lousy meals I've had to endure in my time, including C-rats out of a can in Vietnam, I went on, "So what are we havin' anyway?"

"I've been in a German phase these days, so we're having sausage cooked in beer, along with sauerkraut, mashed potatoes, and hot slaw. How does that sound?"

"Sounds great." I knew I'd failed badly in my enthusiasm. I've lived in Cincinnati over half my life now, and in that time have never even been tempted by German food. Only the slaw and potatoes sounded faintly enticing, and then not very much.

Sarah must have picked up on it. "You're not a fan of food from the Deutschland, eh?"

"Not a whole lot," I admitted.

She gave the pot another brisk turn with the spoon. "Oh, it's wonderful in the fall. You've just never had it cooked right. I—" Her actions stopped as we both heard the phone ringing back in the parlor.

"Oh for the love of Timothy," Sarah said, blowing a stray strand of hair away from her face. "I've been meaning to have a second phone installed in here, for just these times." Turning away from the stove, she held the spoon out to me. "Sid, could I ask you to keep stirring the kraut while I get that? It's probably my friend Oneida. She always does this."

"Sure," I said, taking it.

As my host left the room I stuck the spoon back down into the pot, giving the mess inside a few desultory turns. It was brown and stringy and stunk to high heaven. So this was sauerkraut, huh? From the stench I hadn't been missing anything.

After a few moments of stirring I heard Sarah come back into the kitchen, and I turned to find her looking puzzled.

"I was wrong, it wasn't Oneida. The call is for you. It's Bud Spencer."

"Bud Spencer? How did he know I'm here?"

"Who knows? But it sounds like he may have a line on a job for you."

"A job?" Then I tried to remember, that was a good thing. "That'll work. Thanks." Handing off the spoon to the older woman, I went back into the parlor and picked up the receiver from the table. "Bud? How'd you know to find me here?"

"That's easy," he said. "When you were in my place earlier today and said you were looking for work, I kind of wondered if you were hard up for cash and needed a cheap place to stay. I put two and two together and figured you'd wind up at Sarah's sooner or later."

"Looks like you figured right."

"Yeah, good on me. Listen, Sid, Sarah might have told you the reason I'm calling. I think I may have a job for you. A strong possibility of one anyway."

"Any port in a storm. What is it?"

"Before I tell you, I need to tell you how I came across it. It's kind of funny. Remember I told you that my brother-in-law works as a painter out at PornUtopia? And that sometimes he comes in here after work to get a drink or three, on the cuff?"

"Yeah. Are you sayin' he can get me a slot on his crew? I thought you told me they were about done with that kind of work over there."

"No, it's not painting, and that's kind of why I'm a little hesitant to tell you. It's janitorial." He waited, as if he was thinking I'd balk. But I fooled him.

"I've done janitorial work before. It's not bad."

And I really had. One summer in college I'd worked as a maintenance man/janitor at a Best Western motel. It wasn't the easiest job I've ever done, or the cleanest, but it kept me off the streets. Which in a college town is a feat in itself.

"So you're cool with the job?" Bud asked.

"Beats a poke in the eye with a fork."

"Good. My brother-in-law's name is Jimmy Holmes. He said when you get to the gate tomorrow morning at six to mention his name. That should get you in." Bud's voice became worried. "Six isn't too early for you, is it?"

"Six is fine. I get up with the birds." Then I said, "If Jimmy's job is comin' to an end, how come he didn't snatch this janitor gig for himself?"

Bud's chuckle was nasty. "For being a painter, old Jimbo's kind of a clean freak. Sounds crazy, but it's true. He thinks janitorial jobs are dirty."

"He's right," I laughed, and then I turned serious. "Listen, man, I appreciate this."

"Hey, I figured I owed you."

"Owed me? For what?"

"For you treating Wendy like she was a human being."

"Any decent man would have done the same."

"We're pretty short of those around here," Bud said. "And besides, as one bro who served a nightmare hitch in the Land of the Bad Things to another, we gotta watch each other's backs, right?"

"Right."

He went on. "I mean, we may have served in different units, you on the ground and me in the air, but we sure chewed some of the same real estate, didn't we?"

That we did. And now it looked like I'd be visiting an entirely different kind of real estate, come the dawn.

◆ ◇ ◆

I drove around the town the rest of the afternoon, seeing what was what. Until my new job started tomorrow morning, time hung heavy on my hands. But in the end all I accomplished was racking up more miles on the Regal's already overtaxed odometer. I even located Sunnyvale's small police department, over on Tulip Street.

But I didn't stop. Something inside had checked me. And wasn't that strange?

The last thing Sarah had asked me was to be back by six for supper. I agreed, but I can't honestly say I was looking forward to it. As I said, something about her seemed off.

But as promised, six o'clock found me pulling the car into an empty spot on the street in front of Sarah's.

Getting out, I could smell the pungent aroma of the German food from clear out by the curb. The fragrance of the brownies, sadly, appeared to have died under the onslaught. Surely the stuff tasted better than it let on. I mean, millions of Germans couldn't be wrong, could they?

Then I remembered Adolf Hitler and answered my own question.

Sighing like a man facing a firing squad, I trudged up the steps, opened the door, and went on into the house. As I feared, the reek in here was palpably worse. And I was going to willingly eat this junk? You're a brave soul, Joe Box.

A second later that thought was driven from my mind as I was nearly knocked off my feet by a small flying form. It was almost out of reach when I grasped the back of its jacket, stopping it in midflight. The form revealed itself to be that of a young boy.

"Hey! Leggo of me!" The kid was twisting around, trying without success to free himself.

"Whoa, wait a minute, pard, not so fast. Don't you know there are speed limits in this town?"

The kid ignored me as he continued to struggle. "Let me go!" he said again, louder.

I was about to answer when Sarah beat me to it. She'd come out of the kitchen and was now standing in the classic "mom is mad" pose we all remember from our childhood—the one where she has her feet set apart, arms folded across her chest, and blood in her eye.

"Ryan Kipling Poole!" Sarah snapped. "Stop that this instant! And you apologize to Mr. Bean for acting like a hairy heathen."

"Awwww ..." Sighing in defeat, the kid turned and faced me. That's when I got my first good look at him. I wasn't surprised at all to find he was the same boy as the one in the picture on the mantel. This close, he looked even more like me. "I'm sorry," he mumbled.

"No harm done," I said gravely. "You only smashed my right leg. Good thing for you they gave me a spare one. I keep it over here." So saying, I tapped my left thigh.

From beneath lowered brows, the boy looked up and favored me with a slight grin. "You're silly."

"And you smell," I shot back. "Have you been rollin' with the dogs? Or is it hogs?" I gave him a theatrical sniff on the top of his head. "Yeah, it's hogs all right."

Turning, he addressed the old woman. "I like him, Grandma. He's funny."

"That may be, but Mr. Bean is right." Her tone had turned mock stern. "You do smell awful. Run upstairs and take a quick bath before we eat. Go on, off with you now."

The boy did as she asked, making a flat run for the stairs. But he got in one last dig before he disappeared around the corner. "I don't smell as bad that sourkrauuuutt."

Sarah sighed in annoyance, but I could tell she didn't mean it. "That boy, I swear."

"He seems like a pistol, all right," I agreed. "What did you say his name is?"

"Ryan Kipling. Named after his father, and the famous author. I call him Kip."

"He called you Grandma."

"That's because I am. Kip's father, my son, and his wife are both dead now, over five years gone. Kip's six. I doubt he even remembers them. I'm all the family he has."

Remembering being raised by my own Granny, I said, "Sometimes that's all a boy needs."

"And sometimes it's not," Sarah retorted. I could have been wrong, but it seemed again I was picking up an undercurrent of something else. Repressed bitterness, maybe? Joe Box, psychoanalyst.

"How I wish …" she started again, and then stopped, as if it wasn't worth pursuing. "Never mind. You have your own problems, Sid. You don't need mine added to them."

"If there's somethin' I can do to help …" I knew even as I spoke how shallow it sounded.

"Oh, we get along like aces, Kip and me." Sarah's tone was chipper, and her eyes shone unnaturally bright. Then the light faded as she spoke to herself, as much as to me, "We have to."

18

*P*ulling the battered Regal up to the guard shack at the gate, I rolled down my window and addressed the guy manning it.

"My name's Sid Bean," I said. "Guy named Jimmy Holmes told me to report for a janitor job this mornin'."

The guard checked his clipboard. "Yeah. Bean. Here it is." He pointed to a lot on the far left side of the PornUtopia building. "Employee parking is there. You'll need a temporary pass for today. If you get hired, your supervisor will give you a permanent one to stick up on the inside of your windshield." Reaching back inside the shack, the guard's hand came out holding a rectangular piece of yellow paper. "Put this on your dash for now. It'll hold you for the rest of the day so you don't get towed."

Taking it from him, I did as he said. "Thanks."

Pulling his head back in the shack, the guard reached down and pressed something. A second later there was a buzz, and the steel gate before me lifted up and out of the way.

Mashing the old car's throttle, I pulled through. On my way back to the employee lot the guard had mentioned, I watched the gate come back down in my rearview mirror. As it did I got the oddest sensation—the feeling was as if I'd stuck my fist in a monkey trap, the way I'd seen it done in-country. If so, I was going to have a devil of a time getting free.

Making my way down the driveway, once again I noted the flag-poles flanking it on either side. Did Tate really expect jaded pornaphiles—to coin a word—to flock here from around the globe just to sample his wares? Or did the flags mean something else entirely?

I'd check into it when and if I got the chance. Right now the employee lot was coming up, and I wheeled the Regal into the first empty slot I found.

Getting out, I cranked my head up, gazing at the edifice before me. Not surprisingly, PornUtopia was even more massive up close. It wasn't its height, of course; five stories is nothing nowadays. But it did have a presence. And not a good one.

To my right I saw a door reading Employees Entrance. That was me now. I walked over to it, finding a keypad located next to the knob. Another layer of security. Hoping there was someone on the other side of the mesh-reinforced window in the door's center, I gave the glass a couple of smart taps. The guard at the gate must have alerted whoever was inside that I was here, because the door swung open almost instantly.

I almost laughed. Well, what do you know. The greeter was none other than the Nine Millimeter Man, the second guard riding in the cart yesterday, and the one who'd unsnapped his holster on me. His lips retreated from his teeth as he gave me what passed for a grin.

"Back for more, huh? Looks like you've got friends in low places."

I repressed a half-dozen snappy comebacks, instead staying in char-acter. "Jimmy Holmes sent me here. He said I could get a job as a janitor."

Smirking, the guard stepped aside to let me pass. As I did I saw his badge listed his last name as Head. Maybe his first name was Shrunken.

The room I was now standing in looked like the employee lounge you might find in any midsize corporation, with the usual uncomfort-able leatherette chairs scattered around, along with three low knotty-pine tables littered with haphazardly folded newspapers. The far wall contained the obligatory candy and soda pop machines, along with a sink, a couple of microwave ovens sitting on a counter, and a large coffeepot.

The guard motioned me to follow him, using his first and second fingers in tandem. Don't ask me why, but I've always hated that. Maybe it's because my third-grade teacher, Mrs. Kazanjian, used the exact same gesture when I was being summoned to the principal's office for my daily beating.

As we walked, I suppressed a belch. I'd given Sarah's German cooking an all-American try, but in the end it had bested me. I don't know if it was the wienerlike things, the kraut, that hot nasty slaw, or what, but the resulting mess had festered in my gut all night long like a witch's brew. Even the two brownies I'd copped for dessert hadn't helped much. But I'd done as Granny taught, and manfully downed what was set before me. Now, twelve hours later, I was still burping the stuff up.

Please Lord, never again. Give me ham, yams, cathead biscuits, and green beans with fatback any day.

The guard and I walked for quite a long way around the inside circular hall before finally coming to an inset door marked Maintenance.

"This is you," he said. "Just knock. The head maintenance guy here, a dude named Marko, is waiting for you." With that my guide turned on his heel, leaving me there alone.

Marko, huh? A guy with a handle like that was worth meeting. Reaching out, I gave the door a couple of medium taps and waited.

A few seconds later a barrel-chested bull of a man wearing a stained blue jumpsuit opened it wide. "You Bean?" he snapped. Snapped. Bean. Snap beans. Har.

"I am if you're Marko," I said. The dude was a head shorter than me, but like I said, blessed with a solid build. The red crew cut above his pale blue eyes made his bulldog face appear even tougher.

"Funny," he scowled, pulling the door wider. "Well? Don't just stand there."

I could tell this guy was going to be a charmer, and again I swallowed a comeback. It was rapidly becoming plain that the hardest part of this case was going to be my staying in character as a dull-witted, subservient drudge.

"Yes, sir," I replied, ducking my head as I came in as if the top of the frame was going to scratch my scalp.

"Don't call me 'sir,'" the man barked. "I work for a living."

I'll be jigged. I'd have bet Noodles' last cat treat this guy had been some kind of a non-com in the service. Only topkick sergeants and the like get so incensed when someone inadvertently calls them "sir." And they almost always use a variation on Marko's line, usually with some salty words thrown in for flavor.

"You can call me by my last name, Mr. Pankowsky," the maintenance chief went on. "Later on, if we get along, you can just call me Marko." He held up a warning finger. "But not yet. Understand?"

Again I bobbed my head. "Yes, sir. I mean, yes, Mr. Pankowsky."

Still scowling, he folded his arms across his chest and looked up at me, obviously not intimidated in the least by my height. "So what makes the idea of slaving away in a glorified cathouse so attractive to you, Bean?"

"I don't care nothin' about it bein' a cathouse. I just need work."

Closing one eye, Marko gave a curt nod. "Work, huh? Well, work you'll get, pal, and plenty of it. Provided we get along. Like I said."

"No problem on my end with that, Mr. Pankowsky." I was rushing my words, as if I felt the job slipping away. "I'm a hard worker. Ask anybody."

"I did. I asked that deadweight Jimmy Holmes about you. All he said was this deal was a favor to his brother-in-law, Bud Spencer." Marko blew out a disgusted breath. "Jimmy I got no use for. Freaking layabout. But Bud served a hitch in AirCav, like me."

I nearly smiled. I knew it.

"So it's only as a courtesy to him, not Jimmy, that we're talking at all today," the chief went on. "Are we clear on that?"

"Crystal," I nodded.

"The pay is twelve bucks an hour, and the hours are six in the morning to three in the afternoon. Lunch is a flat sixty minutes at ten a.m. No more. You'll sweep, polish, clean toilets, take out the trash, and whatever else strikes my fancy. You'll answer to me for everything. Because in this place there's only one god, and Marko Pankowsky is his name."

Man, this guy was as rough as a cob.

He pointed to a row of lockers on the other side of the plain room. "The middle one is for your street clothes. You'll find some blue jumpsuits like this one in that closet over there." He made a face at my fake beer belly. "And find one that fits. You get all that?"

Yep, this guy had been a non-com all right. A DI—drill instructor— at least. "Yes, Mr. Pankowsky."

He nodded again. "Good." Handing me a clipboard with some papers on it, he said, "Fill this out at your break. Which doesn't come until eight thirty."

Taking it, I gave it a quick scan. "What is this stuff?"

"The usual. Application, insurance forms, W-2, confidentiality agreement."

"What's that last one you said?"

"Confidentiality agreement. It's a bonus deal Mr. Tate set up for us."

My expression cleared, and I gave a goofy Sid Bean grin. "I like bonuses."

"Then you'll love this. If you can keep your trap shut about what you see around here for the next few weeks, until the grand opening, you'll get a bonus. Ten percent of what your yearly salary is."

From a quick ciphering in my head I knew roughly what that amounted to. But I felt the man was wanting me to ask him anyway. "How much is that?"

"In your case, over two thousand dollars."

I whistled, still playing the bumpkin. "Holy cats. For two grand, you can bet I'll keep quiet. You can tell Mr. Tate I said so too."

Marko was still smiling sarcastically. "You bet I will. And know this, too. The agreement applies to everyone here. If one guy blabs," he held up an index finger, "just *one*, the deal's off for everybody." His eyes went Arctic. "And you simply can't imagine how little I'd like that."

Yeah I could too. "So what kind of stuff will I be seein'?"

"Never mind. Most of the hottest stuff you won't have access to anyway. Not until Mr. Tate clears you. And I wouldn't hold my breath for that."

"Has he cleared you, Mr. Pankowsky?"

The other man's expression toughened as he eyed me. "You know, Bean, for a guy as hard up for three hots and a cot as you seem to be, you sure ask a lot of questions."

I realized I'd come perilously close to blowing it, and immediately became contrite. "Gosh, I'm sorry."

Marko's voice was still as hard as baked iron. "Forget it. Go get changed like I told you. You've been on the clock now for almost fifteen minutes, and Mr. Tate has yet to get any work out of you."

My eyebrows climbed. "You mean it? The job's mine?"

"It's yours to lose, pal, if you don't get your rear in gear."

I resisted the urge to pump Marko's hand. No sense overplaying it. "Thanks Mr. Pankowsky! I won't let you down."

"See that you don't. I want you changed and ready for work in two minutes." The chief raised his sleeve, checking his watch. "The clock's running, Bean."

"Yes, sir. I mean, yes, Mr. Pankowsky." I gave a pretty credible imitation of stumbling over my own feet as I began heading toward the locker.

I hadn't gotten far when Marko's voice stopped me. "Hold it, hotshot. You're in luck. Here's a couple of fellows walking through the place you need to meet."

"Yeah? Who?" Then I saw who.

Standing there, examining me like you would a particularly unusual cut of meat, were Cyrus Alan Tate and Morris Chalafant.

For a second I was struck dumb. Talk about the moment of truth for my disguise.

And then I thought, why not? This meeting had to occur sooner or later. PornUtopia just wasn't that big. Neither was the town that hosted it. But to say I was nervous as I walked over to the two would be badly understating the case.

I tried masking my tension as awe. Maybe Tate and Chalafant would be too dense to notice how rattled I was. No, forget that. It would be a bad mistake to underestimate either of these two.

"Bean, I want you to meet the boss, Mr. Tate," Marko said as I reached them. He indicated the other guy. "And Mr. Tate's right-hand man, Mr. Chalafant."

Both men nodded at me, Tate trying to hide a superior smirk, Chalafant's eyes as dead as a bull shark's.

Tate spoke first. "Sid, Marko here tells me you're our newest hire. Welcome."

"Thank you, sir." I was trying to sound subservient. "I really appreciate this job. It means a lot to me and the missus." If I'd had a forelock, I guess I could have tugged it. *As you wish, m'lord.*

"Yes. Your wife." Tate was gently massaging his chin, his little boy simper badly needing to be smacked off. Maybe by me.

He went on, "I'm looking forward to meeting her as well. I try to get to know all my employees. It helps to foster a ... family atmosphere. Wouldn't you agree, Marko?"

"Sure," Marko nodded. Family atmosphere. The Manson family maybe.

As Tate spoke, I noticed Chalafant's gaze was still as cold as a frozen cod. When he finally did decide to address me, it almost caused my heart to stop. "Have we met?"

"Uh." *Caramba.* I swallowed a lump in my throat as big as a cabbage. *Listen, Toni, about your disguise ...* "No, sir, I'm sure I'd remember that," I managed to get out.

"Funny." Chalafant was still sizing me up. "I never forget a face."

Pursing his lips, Tate looked from him, then to me. "I can vouch for that. Morris is very good at remembering people, places, things.... That trait, among others, is what makes him so valuable."

Marko turned to me. "I guess I'd better explain, Bean. Mr. Chalafant here will be running the day-to-day operations of PornUtopia."

"Yes, he will," Tate broke in. "I'd wager you'll be seeing quite a bit more of him than you will of me, Sid. Are you sure you and Morris have never met?"

"Positive." I wished I sounded more sure than I felt. "I'm just a janitor. If I'd ever met rich guys like you, I'd sure enough recollect it, you bet."

Tate laughed at that, genuinely it seemed. Chalafant joined in a second later, but not with near the gusto. I could tell right now he was going to be a problem.

"Sid, I like you," the porn king said. "And in this town, that means a lot. Call on me if I can ever be of assistance."

"I'll do that, Mr. Tate. Thanks."

"Not at all." He turned to his toady. "Morris? Are you coming? We need to check the invoices on that latest shipment from overseas." Tate's grin aimed my way was conspiratorial. "I've learned from hard experience you can't trust foreigners." Nice to know xenophobia was alive and well in Sunnyvale, Ohio. He went on, "Truthfully, I don't trust anyone. Save for Morris, of course." He glanced at the other man. "Those invoices won't check themselves. Let's go."

The two of them began walking toward the elevator bank, heads together as they talked. It seemed they'd dismissed my existence as if I was no more than a potted plant.

But Marko didn't seem to take it that way. He turned toward me, a disbelieving look filling his face. "Man. How about that, Bean? Mr. Tate personally telling you to call him if you ever needed anything. Around here, that's better than gold."

"I guess." Fool's gold maybe. "Which locker did you say is mine again?"

And so that's how I became a janitor at PornUtopia, drawing a legitimate paycheck from the world's most famous purveyor of perverted sex. Life is weird sometimes.

◆ ◊ ◆

The day passed fairly quickly, and like I'd told Bud, the work was familiar.

The tasks Marko had given me were menial: cleaning, scrubbing, polishing, moving boxes around. Because of my mouth things, I skipped lunch. While I worked, I didn't see anything that I could hang Tate with for Billy Barnicke's death. I'd figured from the outset that just one session here wasn't going to be enough, but still I found my nerves growing taut as the day progressed.

The inside of PornUtopia, surprisingly, was pretty much as I'd pictured it would be. The first floor consisted mostly of that sex-through-the-ages exhibit Morris Chalafant had bragged about on his visit to my office. To my jaundiced eye, the waxwork figures didn't look particularly enticing. Even if they did have silent motors inside them that caused them to go through their paces—so to speak—somewhat convincingly. At any rate, the people running the Pirates of the Caribbean ride at Disney World had no reason to lose any sleep.

The second floor was a different tale. The porn superstore Chalafant had mentioned took up the entire floor. As I cleaned, I tried to avert my eyes from the salacious books and lurid videos that seemed to be everywhere. But as bad as they were, the "games and toys from around the world" were worse. Most of the rubbery things looked decidedly uncomfortable, and some even downright painful. I found it hard to fathom how one human being could use them on another. The Marquis de Sade would have felt right at home.

I'm ashamed to admit the next part, but the third and fourth floors were more familiar territory. They simply consisted of Security, plus numerous massage parlors on the third floor and whoopee rooms on the fourth, exactly like the ones I'd been introduced to in Saigon's Bring Cash Alley, as a dumbstruck Kentucky teenage boy on leave for the first time from the army. The only difference here was the sheer number of them.

The fifth floor was the puzzler. I couldn't get up there. Unlike the rest, there was no wide-stepped escalator leading up to it. Even stranger, the elevator I was in also didn't seem to want to go there. I mean, obviously it was supposed to, because there was a number-five button for the floor on the panel, with a small slot underneath to hold who knew what. But when I pressed the button, the car stubbornly refused to rise.

"Hey, Mr. Pankowsky," I called, sticking my head out of it. The maintenance chief was down at the end of the hall, running a big floor polisher over the parquet wood. Maybe he couldn't hear me. I sang out louder. "I think this thing is stuck."

"It's not stuck," he called back over the motor's noise. "You don't have clearance."

I knotted my brows. "What clearance?"

With a disgusted move Marko snapped off his machine and began stalking down my way. "Remember this morning, when I mentioned to you about having access to certain areas? Where the hottest stuff was?"

"Yeah, so?"

"So, the fifth floor is where that is. Only thing is, it's off-limits for now. Mr. Tate only lets certain employees have access, and that ain't you. Yet. You may never be."

Wasn't that interesting. "So who the heck cleans it?"

"I do," Marko said. "Until we hire a full maintenance crew when the place opens in two weeks. Using this gets me up there."

He reached down at his side and pulled a white, credit card–sized piece of plastic off his belt, holding it up. From where I stood I could see the PornUtopia logo filling the side facing me. By the clicking sound it had made when it released, the card seemed to have been stuck there with some sort of magnet.

Trying not to appear obvious, I looked again. Yep. Right there where Marko's hand had been I spied a round piece of steel on his belt. It appeared to have been either sewn or riveted in. That stud is what the card had been stuck to. So that meant it was the card itself that was magnetized.

Marko was wagging it. "This card unlocks the floor button when I insert it in the slot under five. But for now, that's all you gotta know. The subject is closed. Got it?"

"I got it."

Turning away, the maintenance chief secured the card back on his belt. I'll be switched. This case had just come alive.

The rest of the day I spent in robot mode, counting the hours until I could clock out of here and go think about this in peace somewhere. Marko's surly demeanor didn't help the day pass any faster either.

Obviously his best years had been spent in the service. And just as obviously he'd carried all his bad habits learned there over to civilian life. It seems to me some people enjoy living their lives permanently ticked off. I think he was one.

A couple of times I was tempted to ask him a question, that question being, if he was so miserable working for Cyrus Tate, why didn't he just up and quit? If it were me, I would have.

But I didn't ask it. I had the feeling I'd find out for myself why, in due time.

19

*T*hree o'clock that afternoon found me at my locker, exchanging my soiled jumpsuit for my street clothes. I looked over at Marko, who was doing the same as me three lockers down.

I felt self-conscious as I hung my work outfit on a metal hook inside. "Sorry about the stink, Mr. Pankowsky. After a day like today, this thing smells kind of ripe."

"Maybe it does. I don't smell it." He pointed at his lumpy nose. "I haven't smelled anything since 1969, the day I was trying to fix a bullet hole in the fuel line on my slick, and an NVA regular jumped up and smashed me in the face with the butt end of his AK-47."

I gave him a commiserating wince. "Yowch."

"Yeah. Like you would know anything." Marko was sitting on the common bench, pulling on his shoes. He squinted up at me. "Tell me, hotshot, were you ever in?"

"What, the service?"

"No, the circus," he mocked. "Of course the service."

Slipping back on my big, new, red flannel shirt, all the while I kept my back turned enough so that he couldn't see the straps holding my fake beer gut to me under my T-shirt. "Didn't you check what I'd put on my application?"

"Don't get smart with me. Although for you I'd say that's impossible." Marko bent low to tie his laces. "No, I didn't look at it. That's Mr. Tate's job. Answer the question."

"Yeah, I was in." My service time in Vietnam was the one true thing I'd listed on the forms the other man had given me. Why, I have no idea, unless it was perhaps a silent nod to those of my bros who hadn't made it home.

Speaking of lies, one of the things weighing heavily on my mind during work that day was exactly how long it would take somebody in Tate's organization to realize from the fake name and personal information I'd provided them that they had a ringer in their midst. There was no way of knowing for sure, of course, but I'd have bet my socks I had no more than another seventy-two hours of grace before the game whistle blew.

By then I reckoned I'd either be merrily on my way home with the Barnicke murder evidence safely tucked away in the Regal, or nailed to the wall. Figuratively, I hoped.

My answer had made Marko look up. "You were in? When? What branch?"

I undid my pants, tucking my shirttail inside before I zipped back up. "The army. Nineteen seventy-two to seventy-four. The year of seventy-three I spent in-country."

Now the maintenance chief had turned still, watching me closely, as if he knew there was more to it. He was right.

"I know what you're thinkin'." I nodded. "Yeah, I was there. The Ia Drang Valley. I was an infantry grunt."

"Ia Drang Valley? Huh." Was it my imagination, or was Marko now looking at me with a bit more respect? He went on meditatively, "That's where Bud Spencer was too. Said his was a pretty rough tour. Worse than mine even."

"If a guy spent any time at all in the bush, it was a bad tour."

The chief snorted. "I guess so. That valley took his hand."

"If I spent a rougher year anywhere, I don't recall it," I said, pulling on my jacket.

"So you saw a lot of combat?"

Smoothing down what little hair Toni had left me, I shrugged. "I saw my share."

"Ever kill anybody?"

I turned. Marko's gaze was as intense as I've ever seen on a man.

"Yeah. Quite a few, if you want to know the truth." And I really had. Now it was my turn to stare back. "How come you're askin' me all this, Mr. Pankowsky?"

As he turned away from me, his reply was evasive. "My own reasons."

Caramba. Another layer of intrigue, in a case already top-heavy with them. But I wisely kept my own counsel as I closed my locker and left.

♦ ◊ ♦

Speaking of death, I had some time to kill before supper, so I decided to take a drive out past Tate's estate. I wanted to see for myself how a porn king lived.

During our work time together that day Marko had let it slip where Tate's mansion was located, on the other side of Sunnyvale from PornUtopia. Since "mansion" was the operative word the chief had used, I didn't figure it would be too hard to spot. It wasn't.

I slowed the Regal as the Tudor-style monstrosity flanking the river drew up on my right. Like Tate's porn establishment, the smut peddler's home, which he'd cutely named "Desire Under the Elms"—I swear, that really was the title engraved over the filigreed iron gate—was an exercise in bad taste. Everything about the place seemed overblown, from the circular drive, to the guesthouse, to the putting green verge—lush even at this late season, good lawn care, I guess—right up to the brightly painted red double doors leading inside.

In front of that garish gate stood the obligatory guard shack, manned by the obligatory guard. I could see he was wearing what appeared to be an Apex shirt. Tate was sure getting his money's worth with these guys. The guard was giving me a hard glare, so I fed the car some gas as I sped by and passed him. A quarter-mile down the road I found an empty drive, where I turned around. Then I made another pass by the house.

As before, it looked inordinately large for one man, even if, as Detective Pilley had intimated, Tate had packed the place floor to ceiling with nubile young women. Oh well. Probably not important. I saw the guesthouse again, from this angle getting a better view. I couldn't be sure, but I thought I saw the shadowy forms of small deer running around outside it. Again I sped up, this time heading back toward town.

♦ ◊ ♦

Back at Sarah Poole's house, the afternoon found me taking a long, hot shower in the common bathroom upstairs. Figuring my twenty bucks a night didn't buy me washing machine privileges here, I wondered as I soaped up if it would make more sense to take my now-stinky street clothes and try to find a Laundromat, or to just let them pile up and take the whole mess home with me. Rinsing, I decided to let it accumulate. Surely in the next day or so I'd find the proof against Tate I needed.

Getting out of the shower, I reached for a fresh towel stored in the rack above the toilet. But as my hand closed on it, I realized it was a regular-size one, not a full-size bath towel.

I shook my head. If there's one creature comfort I have to have, it's a big, fluffy towel to dry off with after I bathe. Maybe it goes back to my poverty-stricken childhood, when a bath was a Saturday night occurrence in a galvanized metal tub sitting on the kitchen floor. The richness of that luxury was always followed by Granny giving me a brisk rubdown with a feed sack.

At any rate this dinky thing wouldn't do. I needed to make a mad dash across the hall to the linen closet, and hope I'd be well rewarded. I also hoped the towel would be big enough to cover me while I did it.

Holding it tightly around my midsection as I stepped lively across the floor, I found that it was. Barely. All that remained uncovered was my right leg. Well, ooh la la and hubba hubba. I hoped Sarah wouldn't surprise me as I riffled the shelves.

I'd just opened the closet door, initiating Operation Bath Towel, when Sarah's voice drifting up from the living room stopped me. From the stilted tone of the conversation, it was obvious she was speaking to somebody on the phone. Just as obvious, she was upset.

"No!" I heard her say, with a catch in her voice. Then, "I've given you all I'm going to. You'll just have to muddle along without me."

I took a couple of steps closer to the banister, so I could hear her better.

"Yes, I'm quite sure." Sarah sounded a bit calmer now. Then, "I don't care what Mason says, or does. That's his affair."

Mason ... Kilbride?

"He and Evan can take up my part," she said. "They can afford it."

She had to have meant Evan Talbott, the mayor. Straining now, I wished my ear were bigger. What was Sarah talking about, that he and Kilbride could afford?

Suddenly the conversation took a worse turn. Sarah's voice grew shrill. "That had better be a joke! And if it is, it isn't funny! I mean it, Cy!"

Cy? She had to be talking to Cyrus Tate. I should have known.

When Sarah spoke again, an edge of steel was in her voice I hadn't heard before. "You try that, and I'll kill you," she said. "So help me God, Cy, I'll kill you with my own hands. You—" But he must have hung up on her, because a second later Sarah crashed the receiver down. The name she called him would have made my Granny faint.

As quietly as I could, I snagged a bath towel off the shelf, quick-stepping back to my room.

Shutting the door before I started drying off, I thought about what I'd just heard. Evidently Sarah Poole, Mason Kilbride, and Evan Talbott had gone into some kind of a business deal with Cyrus Tate. Now it seemed he was pressuring all three for more money. The other two had anteed up, but Sarah had balked. So what deal could it have been? Maybe ... PornUtopia itself? This thing went deeper than I'd ever imagined.

I'd try to look into it later, when I was a little more rested. Now, it was time to relax, if I could. After changing into fresh duds, I figured it would be a nice finish to my workday to lie down on the old bed in my room for a nice pre-supper catnap. So I did.

The window was open about halfway, and through it on the breeze drifted in the late fall sounds of tardy cicadas strumming their abdomens, as kids played ball in the empty lot down the street. Off in the distance floated the somnolent soft buzzing of someone cutting their grass. Stretching out, I smiled lazily. This was nice. Sarah and her problems were already fading into the haze.

I'd only planned to close my eyes for a quick fifteen-minute power snooze, and so was surprised to find the innkeeper's knocking on the door rousing me.

Fuzzy, I propped myself up on my elbows. "Huh? Whazzat?"

"Sid?" Sarah said from the hall. "It's nearly six. Will you be joining Kip and me for dinner?"

"Yeah. Dinner." My head was still filled with cotton. Then my thinking cleared in a flash when I realized I was speaking to her without my mouth thingies in. Maybe she hadn't noticed. Or maybe through the door she couldn't tell.

Not wanting to compromise it further, I put my hand over my mouth and faked a yawn. "Just let me get some clothes on. I'll be right down."

Three minutes later I walked into the kitchen to find the table laden with tonight's fare. Surreptitiously sniffing the air, I was glad to discover it wasn't German food again. Life simply couldn't be that cruel, not two nights in a row. As before, I found Kip had moved his chair close to mine and away from his grandma. If that upset her, she wasn't letting on.

Standing there, I gave the antique pedestal table an appreciative scan, this time making sure Sarah saw me sniffing. It all looked tasty, the main course consisting of what was either fried chicken or rabbit—and I was betting chicken—piled on a big white round platter, with side dishes of mashed potatoes, bright green peas, and puffy rolls.

The only dark cloud over the meal was a large bowl by Sarah containing a reddish something. Beets, by the look of it. Yuck.

But I commented anyway. "Everything smells great. What's on for tonight?"

Kip beat her to it. "We're having chicken. It's fried, and I get the leg."

"Kip," Sarah scolded. "In this house, we let the guests choose first. You know that."

"But Mr. Bean's not a guest, Grandma," the boy said. "He's a customer. Right?"

Before she could be embarrassed further I jumped in. "Let Kip take what he wants, Sarah. Don't matter a scratch to me."

"A scratch," the youngster giggled behind his hand. "You talk funny."

"That's because I'm from the South."

"The south what?" he asked.

I made a general motion toward the kitchen window. "South Kentucky."

"I've never been to Kentucky. I've only been to Cincinnati."

"You'd like it a lot," I said, and I winked. "We eat our weight in fried chicken there."

Kip's eyes opened wide. "Really?" He turned to Sarah. "Could we go to there? I want to eat my weight in fried chicken."

The old woman and I both laughed heartily, while Kip frowned, not getting it.

"Well, I would," he said. Kids.

"First you have to get big and strong to travel that far," Sarah said. "Including eating not only chicken, but other things. Like these beets." She picked up the big milk-glass bowl in front of her, ladling a huge smelly mound of them on his plate.

Kip looked stricken. "Eww, beets. Not so many, Grandma!" But too late. She'd piled them high.

I couldn't blame him. To me, beets have always tasted like the dirt that grew them. But tonight I'd scarf them down, and gladly. Anything beat sauerkraut.

Suddenly the boy switched gears. "Hey, Mr. Bean. Look what I drew for you." Reaching in his pocket, Kip pulled out a folded piece of paper. Undoing it and smoothing it out with his hand, he held it up, beaming. "Do you like it?"

Taking it from him, I stared, trying to fathom what in the world it was. It appeared to be two stick figures, a big one and a small one, with something vaguely round floating in the air between them. In the upper corner was a bigger round thing, with squiggly lines coming out of it, and several curvy Vs above it all. The scrawled title read *My Best and Greatest Adventure.*

"Uh, it's great," I said. And then I asked, with my famous lack of tact, "What is it?"

"Don't you know?" Kip sighed. He began pointing out what was what. "That's you and me. We're in Mexico. And we're throwing a ball to each other on the beach. See?"

"OK, I see it now," I nodded. "What's the round thing up there with the lines?"

"The sun, silly." He pointed again. "And those are birds, flying. See their wings?"

Now that he mentioned it, I did. Pretty good picture. "Can I keep this?"

"Sure." As little boys are known to do, Kip abruptly changed the subject yet again, looking at me hard. "Do you like helicopters?"

"Who doesn't?"

He crinkled up his nose. "Grandma doesn't like them."

"Yes I do, Kip," Sarah said patiently. "I've told you, I just don't like them flying so close to us. To me, that's dangerous."

"Is there a base nearby?" I asked her. "Or a National Guard armory?"

"I don't know where they come from." She looked in alarm at her grandson. "Kip. Use both hands to pick up your glass."

"I'm old enough to use just one hand, Grandma. See?" He held his glass of milk out to her, as if to prove his point.

"Well, just be careful. Milk costs money." She addressed me again. "Wherever they're coming from, I'd wish they'd go back. But they don't. The fifth of every month, just like clockwork, one flies over our house, low enough to rattle the crockery."

"Yeah, at *night.*" Kip was grinning through his milk mustache. "Sometimes it sounds like they're gonna land in our own *backyard.*"

That didn't sound right. I'm not a pilot, but I'm pretty sure the FAA has rules about flying low like that.

Sarah must have thought the same thing. "I feel like reporting it. But seeing as how they're probably friends of Mr. Tate, I don't. What would be the point?"

"Tate?" Him again. But I had to ask. "What makes you think he knows them?"

Kip answered for her, grinning. "Because they land at his house." His voice again was filled with little kid excitement. "Isn't that *cool?*"

Yeah, cool. Why would Tate have choppers landing at his house at night? Those noisy eggbeaters aren't the easiest things to fly, even in daylight. I remember that from overhearing their warrant officers describe them, back in 'Nam. Like a puppy worrying a sock, my thoughts started rolling around the idea of what that might mean. If anything.

"That'll be enough, young man," Sarah said to Kip. "It's time to eat."

I agreed. Picking up my plate and bending over the table, I decided I'd ponder this some more later. Tonight was for more pleasant things.

As we each took our portions, I silently reflected on how *right* this felt, how natural. Sarah, of course, was an old woman, and Kip obviously wasn't mine. But if I squinted just right, I could almost picture my late wife Linda sitting there, along with my never-born son, Joe Junior, enjoying meals just like this one. Meals that I knew would never be.

Whoa, doctor. If I didn't watch it, I was going to work myself into a funk, and I didn't feel like making up a story for that. So I just smiled as I filled my plate. Courageously, I even added a few beets. What a man.

Sarah noticed me still standing as I got my food. Her smile and tone grew strained. "Another night of not eating with us, Sid? A lesser woman might be insulted."

Kip pointed at the chair next to him. "Yeah, come on, Mr. Bean, eat with us."

"There's nothin' I'd like better, son," I said. And that was the truth. "But I gotta make a call on my cell to the little woman, tell her how I'm gettin' on here. Before she leaves for her sewin' circle." And that was a lie.

Kip frowned. "Who's the little woman?" Then his expression brightened. "You mean like a hobbit, in *The Lord of the Rings?* Could I see her?"

"Mr. Bean means his wife, Kip." Sarah cocked her head, addressing me full on. "What did you say her name was again?"

My mind instantly went as blank as a sidewalk. *Had* I mentioned my shadow wife's name before? I hoped not. "Uh, Marjorie." Where the devil had I come up with Marjorie?

"Marjorie," Sarah nodded. "Pretty name."

"And she's a dang pretty gal," I babbled. Why didn't I just shut up while I could?

Before I could get in deeper, Kip piped up, "What's a sewing circle? Is it magic?"

Yeah, and I wished it could make me disappear, right now.

"Never you mind," Sarah said firmly. "Just eat your food, and let Mr. Bean eat his. In his room." The look she gave me was cool. "I'm sure he has his reasons."

Yeah, I did, because I really did need to make a call. But the "little woman"—and how she would hate me using that term for her—I was going to call was Angela.

♦ ◊ ♦

Back up in my room, sitting on my bed, Sarah's cooking caused me to dawdle in pleasure before I rang up my sweetie. I'd been wrong to judge the old woman's culinary skills based on one lousy German meal. The fried chicken was tender, and the rest just as good.

Giving my fingers a final lick, I picked up my cell phone and punched out Angela's number. I hoped the walls of this house were as solid and soundproof as they appeared. Also I hoped Sarah wasn't the type to stand outside the door to eavesdrop. What I was about to say to my fiancée was for her ears only.

Two rings and she picked up. "Hi, Joe."

"Hey, baby."

"I've been hoping you'd call," Angela said. "I miss you so much. So does Noodles. He says hi, by the way. I think he misses you too. He's been chewing on my shoes. Nerves, I guess." Her laugh was forced. "The same goes for me. Nervous, that is."

"There's nothing to be nervous about. I'm as fine as frog's hair, split four ways."

I knew she'd like that. That silly phrase is one of her favorites.

I went on. "But tell Noodles that Joe says he'd better start minding his manners around you, or I'll take the price of a new pair of pumps for you out of his Kitten Kuddle allowance."

We both chuckled, Angela sounding better now.

"I suppose I've waited this long to call you," I said, "because up until now there hasn't been a whole lot to report." In concise terms I began relating the events of the last day and a half, including the conversation I'd overheard before supper. While it was good to hear her voice, it also made me long to be there with her.

But not looking like I was now, of course.

When I was done, Angela laughed again, this time genuinely. "So Toni Maroni's turned you into a couch potato, has she? Complete with a cheesy black mustache and fake beer belly. What I wouldn't give to see that."

"I wouldn't say that the mustache is necessarily cheesy. Toni's made a pretty good effort with the disguise, considering the material she had to work with."

"You mean yourself, of course. Joe, the very idea of you wearing makeup is … priceless." It sounded as if she was about to start getting the giggles again. I figured to stop it.

"Like I said, there's no makeup involved. It's just some stuff I have to wear. The mouth inserts, the fake lip hair, the ersatz beer belly. It's all part of the act."

"Including the black hair dye?" Angela's voice took on a fake, fruity tone, like a besotted Brit. "The theatah, the theatah, my kingdom for the theatah." She began laughing once more.

As the Borg Collective says, resistance is futile, and I found myself joining in. My fiancée's sense of humor is as contagious as poison ivy, but a lot more fun. And she was right. This whole crazy thing did have an air of the melodramatic about it.

And then I remembered Billy Barnicke, dead in my arms, and was instantly sober. Billy wasn't laughing, for sure.

Angela must have picked up on my sudden change of mood. "Sarah Poole's apparent battiness aside, do you have to go back and work another day for that horrid man? That Marko whoever he is?"

"Yeah, good old Marko. He's another lost soul. This town seems to be the last stop for a lot of them. Or maybe they were all OK before Tate arrived."

"Including 'Mr. Pankowsky'?"

"I don't think Marko's all that bad." My tone was pensive. "There's something else there, a kind of, well, almost like a sadness, down deep beneath his crusty exterior. But yeah, I'm going back. I have to."

"You don't sound happy about it."

"I'm not. But something big is up on that fifth floor, Ange. Something that Tate only allows a select handful of people to see. I have the feeling it's the key to everything."

"But you'll have to get past Marko to get up to it, right? What if it turns out he's one of the 'select'? Wouldn't that cause a problem?"

"A big one. But whether he is or not, tomorrow I aim to make it up there and find out for myself."

20

*D*uring the night I'd wrestled with the idea of how to get access to the fifth floor.

I'd run various scenarios through my noggin, ranging from pulling the fire alarm and sneaking in during the chaos (stupid), to hacking the system and giving myself clearance (highly unlikely, given my nearly nonexistent computer skills).

No, as Occam's Razor—or the Joe Box variation thereof—states, the simplest solution, the one requiring the least effort, is usually the best one. Marko Pankowsky's key card was the way in. All I'd have to do was hook it.

Somehow.

Arriving at the front gate at five minutes to six, the answer to how I'd do that still hadn't presented itself. Nor had it done so by midmorning break. Or by lunch (which again I skipped). By one o'clock I was fairly chomping at the bit. Two hours until quitting time, and I was still stumped.

But at a quarter after one, the answer to the problem fell into my lap. Literally.

The solution started simply enough at one straight up, when

Marko came up behind me as I was washing out my mop in the utility room tub.

"Did you do the floor out by the visitor's entrance?" he asked.

That's why I'm rinsing this out, Einstein, I almost said. What I in fact said was, "Yep."

"Good. Hurry up and get finished, because I need your help in the basement."

Don't rush me, Slats, I almost said. What I actually said was, "Be right with you." What a fine employee I was.

A minute later I'd hung up the mop to dry and was following Marko into the service elevator. Unlike the bank of four public ones on the other side of the building, this one had been designed purely for scut work, an unadorned box with enough dings in its stainless steel walls to let me know it had been used, and used hard, in outfitting this porn palace.

But, maddeningly, just like its more uptown brethren, the elevator also had a thin slot cut right out under the number-five button. I guess that ruled out any attempt to sneak up to the fifth floor.

"You just gonna stand there?"

"Huh?" Looking around, I realized the car door had opened into the basement, and Marko was already out, impatiently waiting for me.

"Uh, sorry, Mr. Pankowsky," I muttered, sheepishly exiting the car.

"Come on." Smartly turning on his heel, the maintenance chief began walking away. I was expected to follow. So I did.

As we walked, I looked around. Down here, all pretense of fulfilling the desires of the flesh had ceased. The basement we strode through was just that, a carbon copy of one you'd find underneath any business establishment of a decent size.

To my left I spied cases of office supplies, copier toner, and blank manila folders and reams of unopened white bond paper and such like. To the right were cartons of what seemed to be medical supplies.

That was strange. There appeared to be enough of that gear for a prolonged siege by Attila the Hun.

Then looking again, I felt red embarrassment settling itself around my neck and ears. Those weren't medical supplies. By their labels, the scarlet and white boxes held tubes and jars of perfumed creams and lubricating jellies, along with their prophylactic counterparts.

On second thought, this wasn't like any basement I'd ever been in.

"Here's what I need help with," Marko explained.

We were now at the far wall, and his words pulled me back to reality. "What is it?"

He was pointing with his work-roughened finger at a steel fifty-five gallon drum blocking smaller boxes holding cleaning supplies. "That big old mother in the front is what we have to move. Believe it or not, it's loaded to the brim with disinfectant hand soap."

My tone was disbelieving. "Fifty-five gallons? Of hand soap?"

Marko nodded. "Yep. You know that big, empty, horizontal metal rack outside the utility room? That's where it's going."

"So how come the delivery guys didn't just put it there when they brought it out?"

"Because they forgot to bring the rack with them on the same truck. They had to send for it, and it arrived two days later. In the meantime, they put the drum down here." Shaking his head in disgust, he went on, "Mental midgets, both of 'em."

Mental midgets. I kinda liked that.

"So what are we supposed to do with the drum then?" I asked.

"When this place opens for business and is fully staffed, every morning we're supposed to fill smaller plastic bottles with it, and put one in each of the massage cubicles and pleasure rooms. Right by the sinks." I frowned, and Marko went on, as if the subject was as distasteful to him as it was to me. "For the customers. You know. For after."

I shook my head. "Mr. Tate must be expectin' some really dirty men to come here."

"I think he's counting on it. Well, come on. Help me bull this thing up onto that hand truck there."

Marko was indicating a large industrial dolly a few feet away. It was full of straps and buckles, like the kind used to move refrigerators. And like those, its back was flat, not curved. Back in the service I'd seen the correct kind of dolly utilized, one like we should have had, with a curved back to hold a fifty-five gallon gasoline drum in place. This gadget simply wouldn't work, and I told Marko so.

"I know. But it's all we got. Are you gonna give me a problem, Bean?"

"Nope. But if it falls off and cracks open, don't blame me."

"Of course I'll blame you." His smile was evil, or close enough. "Until we get fully operational here with more maintenance people, it's just you and me. That means I got seniority."

That he did, and I gave an exaggerated shrug. "Let's do it then."

Gripping the drum, and with mighty grunts and groans, the two of us began tilting the thing back. A minute more and we managed to get the lip of the dolly wedged underneath. But the straps didn't seem to want to cinch down.

All that was the easy part. The hard part came when we went to tip back the hand truck itself, so the drum could be moved.

"Only one of us can wheel it," Marko said, breathing hard. "I pick you."

This time I did let a remark slip out. "Why me?"

"Because you're younger than I am, Bean."

"Yeah, by maybe five years."

"And like I said before, that five years gives me seniority." He squinted at me. "Unless you'd like to draw your pay right now."

No, I wouldn't like that at all. No way was I going home skunked. Not after having sweated so much to get this far.

I just nodded in acquiescence as I stepped behind the dolly and grabbed the handles. "Ready when you are, Mr. Pankowsky."

"OK. On the count of three. One … two … *three.*"

On three I drew the machine's handles toward my fake gut as Marko simultaneously pushed the drum farther back against the frame. A second later I had it, but barely. My hands were wobbling like I was an old man of a 106, suffering the palsy to boot. Lord love a duck, this thing was stout.

"OK," Marko said with a wheeze. "You need to step back slowly maybe five paces, pivot, and then aim the dolly toward the elevator. I'll hold the drum steady while you do."

"All right." I did as I was told, letting inertia do most of the work. But I also knew inertia can be a fickle thing. If I got going too fast, the hand truck would be a beast to stop.

Marko must have known that too, as he said, "OK, you've got it turned right. Now start heading down that way." He pointed toward the car we'd come down in. "Slowly."

Concentrating hard in the less than stellar light down here, and transporting the thing at what seemed a snail's pace, we cautiously began moving the dolly and its cargo. Things went fairly well for the first twenty feet or so. Until we hit a rough spot on the floor.

That's all it took.

As I said before, the flat-backed hand truck had never been designed to hold a curved object. Especially one with this drum's weighty mass. One good jarring bump, and with a screech the big metal cylinder started sliding horrifyingly off to the side.

Marko saw it first. "Grab it!"

Right. When I'd first spied the drum against the wall, my mind—as it tends to do—had instantly calculated how much weight was there. A gallon of anything weighs around eight pounds or so. Multiplying that by a factor of fifty-five gives you a net weight of 440 pounds for the hand soap, not to mention the weight of the drum itself. Call it five hundred pounds even. And Marko wanted me to grab it. *Sure thing, chief. One hand or two?*

But he was already putting his mitts on it, and in my too-vivid imagination I saw the heavy drum falling off and landing on Marko, squashing him like an éclair. If it didn't kill him outright, it would sure put a hurtin' on him, as my Granny would say.

Against my rational thinking, my flesh took over. Jerking the dolly upright, I dropped it with a loud clang, flat on the floor. That saved both Marko and the drum.

But the cylinder was still rocking back and forth alarmingly. I rushed around to help the older man. It was a near thing, but between the two of us we managed to slowly steady the drum, and then, inch by inch, began finagling it back onto the hand truck's lip.

By that time we were gulping with effort. At last the drum settled back into place with a solid thud, and we looked over the top of it at each other, chests heaving.

"Freaking piece of junk," the maintenance chief gasped. Well, "freaking" wasn't the adjective he used. And "junk" wasn't what the dolly was a piece of, but you get the idea.

Anyway, I agreed with the sentiment, if not the words. "Who's the lamebrain that requisitioned a refrigerator dolly to move a steel drum?"

"That would be Mr. Tate," Marko said, still panting. "Mechanics ain't his strong suit."

"I'd say you're right."

After a few more minutes of standing there, our labored breathing improved. I can't speak for the other man, but my heart had slowed its racehorse pace.

"Well?" Marko was staring at me. "You ready to try it again?"

"Just a minute. Let's not have a repeat performance." I started walking the last forty feet out, closely examining the expanse as I went. Reaching the elevator, I nodded. OK. No more rough spots.

Now as I headed back toward him, Marko called out, "Everything all right?"

"Yeah, looks like smooth sailin' from here to the door. I—"

I ceased my chattering. What had stopped me was something new in the equation. A small flat object was stuck to the drum's side. What the heck was it? Some kind of shipping label? No, better. Drawing close, I saw what it was.

Marko's key card.

All right. Somehow during our frantic acrobatic dance of keeping the container upright, the card, being magnetic, had come off of the chief's belt and stuck itself securely to the nearest larger metal object.

That object being the side of the drum.

I sneaked a peek at Marko. He'd drawn a dingy red rag from his back pocket and was wiping his face with it. From his relaxed posture, it was obvious he hadn't missed the card.

Yet.

I sure wasn't about to tell him. As nonchalantly as I dared, I turned my back to him, positioning my body between him and the drum. I reached out. If I could only—

"*Now* what are you doing?" He'd stopped wiping his face, staring at me hard.

"Uh, just checkin' the lid on this thing, Mr. Pankowsky." I squinted at the drum and gave it a couple of fraternal taps. "Good enough. Looks tight."

"Maybe you're worth your kingly paycheck after all, Bean," Marko grunted, in what seemed to be a grudging respect. He indicated the dolly's handles. "OK, come on. I'm about tired of screwing around with this. Once more for the Gipper."

Thankfully, it didn't seem like he was aware I'd pocketed the card from the drum's side as I talked. I'd masked the click it had made as it let go when I'd tapped the lid.

Stepping around to the back of the hand truck, I began pulling it toward me, Marko pushing from his side. A strong shove from my legs got the dolly moving again, and with his help we got the thing to the elevator at last, and then inside, with no more incidents.

Up on the main floor, outside the utility room, Marko and I used a hanging block and tackle to move the drum into its final position on the rack. Even with the aid of that device, we both were winded once more when it was done.

"Man," Marko said, reaching again for his red rag, "let's not do *that* again for a while."

"I hope fifty-five gallons of hand soap lasts for years," I agreed.

"We've put in almost a day's work, and it's not even one thirty." He was wiping his face once more, hard enough to peel the skin. "Because I'm a generous sort, Bean, I'm gonna extend your afternoon break. Take twenty instead of ten. But no more. Got it?"

"Sure do. Thanks." Well, how about that? Things were definitely on the upswing. Now I had the card and some time to use it.

I went on. "I believe I'll head up to four and stretch out on one of the beds for a while."

Which wasn't true, but seeing that I'd been given the gift of twenty minutes to check out the fifth floor, without Marko wondering where

I was, I'd use them well. Surely he wouldn't do a bed check on me, like I was a kid in summer camp. I hoped not anyway.

The chief nodded. "The linens haven't arrived yet, so I guess that'll be all right. Be sure to hang your feet off the end of the mattress though."

"Will do." With a wave I started toward the elevator bank as Marko turned away.

Once there, I pressed the button. Noiselessly the doors to the nearest one opened. Stepping inside, I glanced back out in the hall to see if the other man had changed his mind, and I'd been followed. Nope, still nothing.

The doors slid closed. Then reaching in my jumpsuit's hip pocket, I pulled out the maintenance chief's card. Not for the first time, I was glad the modern design of the building didn't allow for showing what floor a particular car was on, or heading for.

Flipping the card over, its obverse was blank, except for a black strip along the edge. OK, time to see if this thing worked. With a silent prayer I slid it in the slot, strip side down, to where it stopped and pressed the button. There was a heart-stopping pause. My spirits plummeted ...

And then the car began to rise.

21

*T*hat ride had to have been the longest five-floor elevator trip I'd ever taken in my life.

Part of the stress was knowing that somewhere a twenty-minute game clock had started, and I knew I had to be done and back with Marko well before then. Another part was wondering what I was going to find up there. Given Cyrus Alan Tate's fancy for bizarre sexual proclivities, it could be anything. It could even—

Before I could ponder it further, there was a muted ding, and the doors opened. It appeared I was about to see for myself.

Stepping softly out of the car, I slipped the card back out of the slot and pocketed it. Stopping, I glanced quickly and discreetly from side to side. I seemed to be alone. Hoped so, anyway. If I wasn't, things would turn interesting in a hurry. But for now it looked like it was just me and my hammering heart.

I craned my head up and around, taking everything in. Surprisingly, there didn't seem to be a whole lot to see ... then I froze.

High up on the wall, pointed right at me, was one of those thumb-sized security cameras like I'd seen at Tate's employment agency. For an eternity I didn't move. But after another moment

I noticed something else. The tiny light on it, which should have been glowing red, was dark. So was the thing active or not? I had no idea, and I could grow old just standing and waiting for it to do something.

Throwing caution to the wind, I took a step to the side. The camera didn't follow me, and the light didn't come on. For whatever reason, it was as dead as Julius Caesar.

Breathing once more, I began walking again, looking around. The area appeared plain and unfinished. That was strange, considering there were less than six weeks until the grand opening. But touching the wall next to me, I saw I was wrong. It had been painted a light gray sometime in the past. Or was that the lighting playing tricks on my eyes?

I looked up at the recessed fixtures overhead. They seemed to be just like those on the other floors, but up here were quite a bit dimmer. To my eye they appeared to be dialed in at maybe 50 percent strength. Was that a money-saving gesture on Tate's part, or something else? Cautiously I took a few more steps away from the elevator and then turned and halted again.

Now here was an anomaly. Stranger still was the fact that I hadn't really noticed it before. Owing to the architect's whim—or was it?—the bank of cars was located directly in the center of the building, causing the shaft to cut through all five levels, like a toothpick spearing an olive. But why?

Angela, being an architect herself, would have had a few wry comments to make about such a floor plan. Combine the weird elevator placement with the curvature of the building's exterior walls, and it seemed that every level of PornUtopia in fact carried a 1950s, gee-whiz-Eddie-it's-a-flying-saucer, *The Day the Earth Stood Still* feel.

But nowhere more so than here on the fifth floor.

I began moving again, glancing down at the carpet. It too was gray. I guess to match the walls. What was up with Tate's love affair with that bland color up here at the top of his pride and joy? Especially given how lurid and garish the other floors were?

But that was all the thinking I did on it, because right then, a scant twenty feet out from the elevator, I encountered my next weird sight. And it was a dilly. At first my eyes hadn't understood what it was exactly I was seeing, blending in as it did with the gray.

It was a curving gray wall, completely unadorned.

What the devil …?

Stopping, I reached out my hand, tentatively touching it. For some reason I half expected the thing to be metallic and ice cold. But it wasn't. It proved to be nothing more than painted drywall.

Strangely, I was kind of let down with that. Given the freaky ambience around here, I'd hoped for something a bit more exotic.

OK, enough. I needed to get a handle on the layout here. We had an inner wall running the circumference of the building. So what lay in between them? More walls? My imaginary bird's-eye view of the fifth floor gave it a surreal bull's-eye look, with the elevator bank located dead center. Why did I think that? Who knows? Realizing time was marching on, I flipped a mental coin and turned left. And almost walked right into the field of view of another security camera. And unlike its brother, the light on this one glowed a cherry red.

Then with a soft whir the camera started turning itself my way.

No point in freezing now. In seconds it would have me. Frantically I looked from side to side for a doorway to duck into. Nothing. I was nailed. All I could do now was wait.

But right before I came into the camera's view, it seemed to hesitate. For a moment it went left to right and back again, its motor chattering. Then the light on it died, and the camera stopped completely.

For endless seconds I didn't dare move. Or breathe. But after another century of my staring at it, the camera remained as still as stone.

If this was a joke, it was a sick one. I'd either been caught or I hadn't. Either way, I didn't plan on standing there meekly. Taking a deep breath, I began walking once more.

Twenty feet down, I came to a door.

The dimensions looked right, but there was no knob, only a slot plainly designed for a key card in the wall next to it. I wondered whether, if I turned right, I'd find this door's twin twenty feet or so around the curve that way.

But why would a design plan call for two identical doors to the inner area to be placed nearly twenty-five feet apart from each other, with none located in the most logical place, directly across from the elevator bank? What would be the point of it?

I checked my watch. Nuts. Nearly ten minutes of my break gone. Knowing Marko, if I wasn't back on the job in another ten, I'd catch it. Or worse, he'd come up to the fourth floor and not find me where I'd told him I would be. Time was a-wasting, and obviously Security wasn't coming. Once more it seemed I'd dodged a bullet. Pulling out Marko's key card, I slipped it into the slot. There was a soft click, and I gave the door a cautious push.

Silently, the portal opened wide. Cautiously I stepped in, holding my breath. As I placed my foot down, high overhead some more recessed lights flickered briefly a moment before coming fully on. Even then, the huge room wasn't well lit.

I stopped dead. It took a second or two for my disbelieving brain to fully understand what I was seeing.

On the floor rested six bedlike things, fitted down inside what looked for all the world like some kind of weird, fiberglass cocoons. The beds, or pods, or whatever, were well padded. Above them, swung up and out of the way on hinges, loomed clear hard lids, made of what looked like either glass or acrylic. The pods had been arranged in a star shape, with the heads in the center and the feet pointed outward, like spokes in a wheel. *Hi, I'd like to show you the sleeping quarters of the Glaxar family, from the planet Zoob.*

The setup looked maddeningly familiar. Where had I seen this before?

Then I got it, and realized I hadn't been that far off with my planet Zoob wisecrack after all. Whether it had been the designer's intention or not, the arrangement of the whatever-they-weres mirrored almost exactly how the suspended animation chambers had been laid out in the movie *Alien*. I'll say it again: what the devil …?

I noticed something else then, just as perplexing. Positioned around the beds were huge computer workstations, their LED light banks softly blinking in the dimness. In front of them were large black chairs, ready and waiting for their operators. But to operate what?

My eyes were drawn to a new object. A book. Feeling hope for the first time, I drew closer to it. In the seat of the chair closest to me, where it appeared to have been casually tossed, lay a thin, comb-bound tome of some kind.

Totally aware of what little time I had left, I picked it up, peering at it in the murky light. But as I read the title, my good vibes fell away. The mystery had grown.

In plain black font on white stock, the cover page stated that what I was holding was a manual for something called the VE 1000 XE. I nodded. Of course, I should have known. The good old VE 1000 XE. I had one like it at home. Noodles slept on it for naps. Yep.

Beneath that, rubber-stamped, were the words VP Version, Property of PornUtopia, LLC. At the bottom of the document there was no copyright date listed, and flipping it over, I saw none on the back. Whatever this volume was, it had never been submitted for filing by the U. S. government. Obviously the thing was bootleg. But what *was* it?

Checking my watch again, I blew out a breath. Two minutes left. Rats on a cracker. Clearly I wasn't going to solve the puzzle of this book in the next 120 seconds, so I did the next best thing.

I stole it.

Stuffing the thing inside my jumpsuit, I was fully aware of the illegality of what I was doing. I was also aware that I didn't care. Figuring that more than one copy of the manual had to exist somewhere, and that Tate would just suppose the book had gone missing, helped ease my conscience as I zipped up.

OK, you battle-scarred hilljack, I told myself. *Time to boogie.*

22

*B*ut that almost didn't happen. Reaching the main floor, the elevator doors opened, and I found myself face to face with a scowling and ill-tempered Marko Pankowsky.

"I was just on my way up to get you," he growled.

"I told you I'd be down in twenty." I was trying to calm my tripping heartbeat.

"Yeah," he sneered, "and you wouldn't be the first guy in history to try dogging it on your break, hotshot."

"Not me. I'm a hard worker. Just—"

He waved that away. "I know, I know, just ask anybody. It's all you keep saying."

"That's because it's the truth."

"Whatever. I hope your rest was nice, and you have some strength left. Because you still have a little over an hour on the clock left to go, and we ain't done yet."

"Not a problem. Just let me hit my locker first. I need to get somethin'." Actually, I needed to stash something—the book I'd lifted.

Obviously less than pleased at the wasteful way I had with Tate's money, Marko sighed. "OK. Fine. But head to the utility room as soon as you get done. I want you to pick up some polish I left there, 'cause before you leave for the day I'm gonna have you do the woodwork out at the visitor's desk."

That idea didn't bother me in the least. And why shouldn't I be cheery? For the first time in this misbegotten case, I had my hands on a genuine clue. Well, not really my hands, seeing as how the book was stuffed down in my pants, but you know what I mean.

I'd just started to turn away from Marko when the older man laid his hand my arm. And what he said next chilled me right down to my socks. "Just a minute, Bean. You haven't by any chance seen my key card laying around, have you?"

Whoa, sweet mother in the morning. What a question. How was I going to answer him? *Sure, Marko, I have it right here. I stole it from you earlier, but you can have it back. No hard feelings, huh?*

Yeah, right. I don't think so. So I reluctantly did the thing I hated to do the most in this world. Especially when backed into a corner. I lied.

"No, Mr. Pankowsky, I sure haven't. Do you remember where you saw it last?" *Just don't say it was while it was stuck to that drum of hand soap.*

Staring at the floor, he shook his head again. "No, darn it, I don't. Hang the luck."

Of course, "darn it" and "hang" weren't the words the maintenance chief used, they were—well, you know the drill by now.

He went on. "The last time I had it on my belt for sure was right before we went down into the basement. And if I lost it in the middle of all that junk, it'll take forever to find."

I tried to keep my words as casual as I could. "That's a shame. What happens now?"

"Again with the questions, Bean. What do you care?"

I thought fast … as fast as I could, under the circumstances. "Well, I'd like to think that Mr. Tate thinks I'm a good worker. Maybe one of these days he'll give me one too."

While the other man paused, I fervently hoped he'd bought my bogus line. He must have, because then he replied, "Normally I'd log the stupid thing in as lost, Security would cancel it, and then immediately issue me another. But that ain't gonna work this time."

"How come?"

Marko snorted at my apparent ignorance of how things ran here. "Because we're still not fully online with all the systems, including the computers, that's why. The last time a card went missing, it turned out some low-rent private eye had taken it for himself."

My mouth went dry. He must have been talking about Billy. But I had to be sure.

"A private eye? What the heck was one of them doin' around here?"

Marko sounded disgusted. "You tell me."

No, I don't think I will.

The chief went on. "All I know is, the guy was hired to do a free-lance double-check of Apex's work, and he totally blew it."

Yep. That was Billy all right.

"And it got worse," the other man continued. "After three days of not too great work, the fourth morning he shows up here as drunk as a monkey, screaming at everybody."

Hold on a minute. That part didn't sound like Billy at all. I knew he liked to tie one on, but only after a job was done. He never even took a sip of beer during a job. What could he have seen here on that third day to drive him over the edge like that?

"As a precaution, Mr. Tate had him frisked by the guards," Marko said. "When they found the missing key card on him, that was all she wrote. Mr. Tate fired him on the spot. The guy just stood there with his pockets turned inside out, giving everybody in earshot one more good cussing out, and then he split. That's the last I saw of him. And good riddance."

That wasn't the last I saw of him. I still remembered the feel of Billy's warm, sticky, dying blood running down my hands.

"Anyway," Marko was saying, "the point of that story is, things still aren't fixed around here. If a guy loses a card, it stays lost. Until a new one can be issued."

Shaking myself out of my funk, I tried looking chipper. It wasn't easy. But what Marko had just said, about the system here not being at full strength? That was the one bit of good news I'd heard. "So we're not online yet?"

"Didn't I just say that?"

He had, but I just lifted my shoulders.

Marko went on. "I'll tell you how bad it is. Half of Security is still dark. The only TV cameras and motion detectors working with any regularity so far are the ones up on floors two and three. That is, until next week, when the rest of the equipment arrives and everything gets booted up. Maybe then we'll finally get squared away around here."

Motion detectors. Caramba. Why hadn't I thought of those? The cameras had been bad enough, even if they weren't working right. Once again I sensed the color draining from my face. If the detectors had been operational, the alarms they would have sent up would have stopped my jaunt on five cold dead before I'd walked three feet off the elevator. I tried to make my smile one of wry commiseration, but I'm sure it just came off as sickly. As unobtrusively as I could, I wiped the flop sweat coating my palms onto my pant legs.

"Oh well," the chief shrugged. "It was only just yesterday I cleaned up there, so that'll hold it until Security issues me another card. Although I'll hate explaining what happened to it." Marko cocked his head, moving closer. "You all right? You don't look so hot. Moving that drum put a strain on you?"

"I'm fine. Just a little tired."

"Well … all right then. Get to it."

I did, stashing the book in my locker first, and then finishing up my last sixty minutes of the day by putting a nice shine on the oak furniture and trim out at Reception. At three o'clock I quietly retrieved the manual from its hidey-hole. It almost burned a hole in my pants before I left the facility's grounds and placed it on the Regal's seat next to me.

Now all that was left was to find a safe spot and read it.

◆ ◊ ◆

Ten minutes later I pulled my car into a tree-lined picnic area in the municipal park along the river I'd passed yesterday.

Feeling foolish for doing it, I glanced around for snoopers before I picked the book up off the seat. At almost a quarter after three on a late October weekday afternoon, the park was deserted. Big shock.

If there had been a flyleaf in the original, telling who the author and publishers were, then whoever had bootlegged this copy had for their own reasons left it off. Flipping the manual open to the first page, I began to read.

Now with the one exception of understanding car manuals from the fifties and sixties, before they went high-tech on me, I'm not the most mechanically or technically astute person ever born. For that reason alone the more esoteric parts of the book left me as baffled as a termite in a yo-yo.

But it was the parts I understood that really caused my blood to chill.

Plainly put, the VE 1000 XE had been developed as a teaching device for the military. OK, big deal. Military teaching devices have been around since Pershing. But if what I was reading was for real, mother have mercy, what an apparatus it was. The machine would make the training I'd gone through at boot camp look like a caveman throwing bones.

First off, the "VE" part stood for virtual experience. What my brother Vincent had picked up through the grapevine, that the project Tate was involved in concerned a form of "artificial intelligence," was true. But only in a peripheral way.

According to the manual, the way the device worked was fairly simple. First the recruit would be made to lie down in the pod, which was in fact a personal-sized sensory deprivation chamber, Lord help us. The closed-cell, foamlike padding lining the thing—which was kept at the exact temperature of the human body—would cancel out the weight of the individual.

That's when the real fun would begin.

A complicated type of headgear would be placed on the soldier, covering his eyes and ears, and then the lid would be swung closed and locked. The lights in the room, which had been purposely kept dim, would be brought even lower, almost to blackout. Combine that lack of illumination with the already gray and featureless walls, and the mind's first line of defense was easily breached. A soft white noise, a type of static, would then be pumped into the earphones for four or five minutes, further relaxing the ... I almost said "victim."

And it was right about that time that inside that pod, the devil would be loosed.

Pouring into the soldier's consciousness would be a type of "streaming video." But it was generations beyond what you'd find on your home computer. As mind-blowing as it sounds, the experience entailed not only sight and sound, but also feeling.

This is where the techie aspects of the manual started to lose me, to be replaced by what appeared to be witchcraft. Cascading into the brain of the man lying in the pod would be nothing less than full-intensity, real-life combat experiences of other fighting men.

Again, according to the manual, it seemed that in some kind of eldritch, black ops scenario, volunteer (I hope they were volunteer) soldiers, sailors, and airmen fighting in Iraq and Afghanistan months earlier had been fitted with a wholly different type of headgear. A gear that didn't obscure their sight and hearing. Far from it.

That equipment recorded, in faithful, excruciating detail, every aspect of war.

My mouth was dry, but my palms wet as I kept turning the pages of this incredible book. No more stateside basic training to endure to see if he had what it took, before a soldier was thrust into the crucible of fighting. If this thing really did what it said, those days were long gone. All questions about his abilities would be removed at the very beginning.

Because the VE 1000 XE was more than just a training device. With the experience of the total sensation of every aspect of raw combat, it was the ultimate war movie. But instead of sitting in a darkened IMAX theater munching popcorn and stale Milk Duds as you watched Bruce Willis or Nicholas Cage trashing the enemy, you would be right there alongside them, lobbing grenades and pulling triggers. Only these weren't Hollywood stars you were running with, but actual fellow combatants, just as scared as you, and the bullets and pain and death flying all around you would be all too real.

The idea was incredible. And to someone like me who'd already experienced the terror of combat, the thinking behind this was completely and utterly horrifying. The poor trainee in the pod would have zero control over what was happening to him.

But it got worse. I'd only read a little bit more before I was stopped short by the next part.

The manual promised that if trained technicians manned it, if it was set up properly and calibrated right, the VE 1000 XE would cut the learning curve of military preparation drastically. How drastically? This much. Six three-hour sessions in the pod would give a spanking new recruit the same killing-edge experience as if he'd served a year in a hot zone.

I dropped the book in my lap, staring. If this thing really worked as advertised, it would revolutionize every aspect of the military. I shook my head in awe. The military, nothing. What about its use in business training, education, space exploration?

It would revolutionize the world.

With a will I tried to rein in my thoughts. The question to be addressed right now was, what the heck was porn king Cyrus Alan Tate doing with his admittedly grubby hands on a piece of secret high-tech military hardware?

Obviously the "VE" portion of the title meant "virtual experience." That part was plain enough. The "1000" though? Who knew? Maybe it was the thousandth incarnation of the system, before some skinny Silicon Valley computer geek with white medical tape wrapped around the nosepiece of his glasses had managed to get it to work. Or maybe the designers just thought "1000" rolled off the tongue easier.

The "XE" part was where I finally started to get it. The manual was irritatingly silent, so the only thing I could fathom was that it stood for "experimental edition." Not a happy thought for the poor sod locked in the pod.

But wait a minute. It could be I was jumping the gun here, so to speak. Let's chill out. Maybe this thing wasn't as sinister as it appeared. What if it hadn't worked after all? That happened sometimes. With new technology, it happens a lot.

What about this? Could it be that the alien-looking machines Tate had installed up on the fifth floor of PornUtopia were nothing more than some type of Rube Goldberg, military-thrill gizmos that had never proved operational and were later abandoned?

But that made no sense. Why install the system at all then? Whatever the answer, it wouldn't be the first time the military had screwed up with a supposedly can't-miss device.

I recalled a story about the army trying to develop yet another secret weapon, way back in World War II. To me, the plan seemed desperate enough for wartime.

The thought had been to affix small incendiary bombs to the legs of bats, of all things, and release them over Tokyo. The idea was that at a certain predetermined altitude the devices would explode, not to mention blowing the poor ignorant bats to flinders, thus setting ablaze the city's paper houses and spreading panic throughout the populace.

Not a bad plan, really, but the execution was lacking. During the first and only test, upon their release the bats, instead of flying directly to their targets, had behaved instead like third-graders getting sprung from school for the summer. They went east, they went west; a few may even have gone up a general's dress. But for sure at least one rocketed right into a nearby aircraft hangar before detonating in a merry fireball. The resultant blaze burned down both the hangar and three combat-ready B-17 bombers stored inside.

So much for that idea.

But that begged the question. As I said before, if the VE 1000 didn't work, why did Tate have it? It couldn't have been cheap, even purchased on the black market. Then a darker thought hit me. What if the porn king and his engineers had done what the military had failed to do, and gotten the blasted thing to work?

But to what end? Teaching young men how to kill? That was insane. For any guy, young *or* old, out to spend his hard-earned Saturday night whoopee cash at PornUtopia, killing people would be the very *last* thing he'd have in mind.

I shook my head. None of this made a lick of sense, no matter how I sliced it. In disgust, at myself for being dumb as much as anything else, I tossed the manual back down on the seat and angrily wrenched the Regal's ignition key.

That's when my eye, almost of its own volition, was drawn to what had been rubber-stamped on the cover, below the title. The penny dropped. Part of it anyway.

Turning the car off, I grabbed the book back up.

VP Version, Property of PornUtopia, LLC, it said. VP version … VP version …

Once more my mouth fell open. So *that's* what this was. I harked back to what my brother Vincent had said, that Tate was working on a thing that was "a new development in sexual pleasure." Something not entirely "human."

And this was it. How could I have missed it when it was so obvious? I knew Tate's secret at last. I knew what he was hiding up on the fifth floor of PornUtopia.

23

*I*f I was right, this was too big. I was out of my depth here. Time to bring in an expert.

My hands trembling with barely contained repulsion, I pulled my cell phone out of the glove box and punched out the number of the one man in the world I knew who could possibly help me fill in the gaps in the case. My old buddy, Rankin Quintus Blaine.

Three rings, and he picked up. I knew he'd be at home. He always was. "The Blaine residence."

"Quint? Joe here." I'd slipped my mouth appliances out so I could talk better.

"I know." The other man's tone was low and cultured. "Although you're aware that I have caller ID, Joseph, I know your number by heart. After all this time, I should."

"Yeah? Then how come you never say to me, 'Hey, Joe, good to hear from you, pal. How's tricks?'"

I could picture my large, rotund friend coughing discreetly into his fist at my crass boorishness. "Surely you're joking, dear boy."

I laughed. "Yeah, I guess I am. A little."

A word of explanation is called for. For the past fifteen years, "Quint" Blaine has been as close a friend as a man could want, although we remain as different as hot dogs and steak. He's obscenely wealthy, the fruits of some sort of family trust, or so I gather, but he hasn't let his vast riches spoil him—not too much, at any rate.

Although he has no need to work, Quint does lend his extensive computer expertise, for free, to those he deems worthy. I must fall into that category, because I've received his help more times in the past than I can count. And he's never asked for a thing in return. The mark of a true friend.

"I was just enjoying a repast of chateaubriand when you called," Quint went on. "Tasty, but a bit on the dry side. I must speak to Michael about it."

Michael was the latest in Quint's never-ending quest to find the perfect chef. They usually lasted about a month or so, before throwing up their hands in despair and storming out of the house. When it comes to food, and the proper preparation thereof, Quint can be a terror. And if my count on him was right, Michael was just about at the four-week point.

I figured to needle my friend a bit. "It's only three thirty in the afternoon, Quint. A bit early in the day to be eating supper, especially chateaubriand." I remembered the last time I'd had it, with Angela at the start of this case. "And it's usually for two, as I recall."

"The operative word being 'usually.' As small as the portion before me is, it might as well be for one." That was an exaggeration. I'd enjoyed Michael's cooking the last time I'd dined at the mansion. If anything, the steak Quint was disparaging was probably hanging off both sides of his plate.

"Well, let me fill you in on why I'm calling," I said, "and then you can get back at it."

"I'm finished," my friend said. "I was only eating a snack this early as I'm having Professor Ted Bronstein from the university over for cocktails and dinner at seven, and the professor usually runs late." Quint obviously turned away from the phone as his voice became muffled. "Michael, I'm terribly sorry to upset you, but this is quite unacceptable. Yes, I'm sure. Please give it to Brutus, if you would be so kind. Yes, thank you."

Brutus is Quint's purebred rottweiler, as lean and deadly as Quint isn't. The dog's a merciless killer, but for some reason he likes me. I guess he knows how I feel about animals.

Quint's voice grew louder once more. "All right, that's that. Now. As to the purpose of your call."

"Fair enough. Have you ever heard the term 'virtual experience'?"

"Of course. That's the more common term for what's known in the high-tech industry as immersive VR, or virtual reality. By any name it's savage, nasty stuff. Highly experimental."

Given his interests, I wasn't surprised he was aware of the thing. "Tell me about it."

Quint turned sly. "So you're on a case, are you?"

"Yep." That's all he needed to know. For right now at least.

"Good. I'd hate to think of your *nouveau riche* status changing you."

"Not much chance of that," I laughed. "As Popeye put it, I yam what I yam."

"Truer words were never spoken. Let's see now ..." I could almost picture Quint settling back deeper in his luxurious dining room chair. "Whichever term, virtual reality or virtual experience, the idea was first attempted by the United States military back in the mid-1960s. The thought behind it was innocuous enough, that of using a computer program to cut down the time involved in developing a recruit's weaponry expertise."

"From your tone, I take it the venture didn't work out too well."

"The will to try it was there, but not the technology," Quint agreed. "That didn't begin to change until 1989, when VPL Research came up with the first HMD, the famous 'EyePhone.'"

"Wait a minute, wait a minute. HMD?"

"Sorry, Joseph. That's the acronym for head-mounted display, a large and rather cumbersome eye and ear interfaced headset."

"It sounds uncomfortable."

"I tried it myself once, and believe me it is. For a time it was strictly backwater. But some new breakthroughs in haptics in the late nineties prompted another look at it."

"You've lost me again. Haptics?"

"From the Greek, *haptesthai*, meaning 'to touch.'" I heard Quint take a sip of something, most likely coffee or wine. "Haptics is the new science of applying tactile sensation to human interaction with computers. Once again, VE has gotten hot."

"Hang me for a pig stealer." It seemed to me we were skirting dangerously close to science fiction territory. "So using this haptics software, a person could actually feel things, not just see or hear them?"

"That's the idea."

"It's incredible. But that begs the question. Does it work?"

"That's what the military intended to find out. Once more it was ramped up. The administration at the time even awarded it fast-track status, but the project was finally abandoned as being too dangerous for continued experimentation."

Abandoned? Dangerous? Then how did Tate manage to secure one of the units? "What was dangerous about it?"

"It quickly became evident that human beings had no ready defenses for it."

I didn't answer, waiting for more. Quint continued darkly. "For the most part, Joseph, the human mind is still uncharted territory. We all might as well have 'here there be dragons' signs on our foreheads."

"I don't understand."

"It's quite simple." Quint took another sip of whatever. "In half the cases where the supposedly 'new and improved' version of virtual experience was tried on human military volunteers, it drove them mad."

Mad? I'd had the feeling that's where Quint was going. But still the word struck with an almost physical force. "Do you have any idea of how many young soldiers were affected?" I managed to get out.

"Dozens, I suppose. With as much time and money spent by the government on trying to get the blasted thing to work, you can imagine how reluctant they were to finally write it off as a lost cause."

Yeah, even with deep pockets, that must have hurt. "When did all this happen?"

"The technology was finally declassified early last year. The thinking at the time was, let the private sector take a shot at it." I heard Quint chuckle morbidly. "Pardon the terrible pun. But if some Bill Gates-type did manage to somehow get virtual experience to function properly, then it would be a fairly easy proposition to adapt it back to military use."

Good night, nurse. So that explained it. Cyrus Tate hadn't stolen the VE equipment from the government. He'd *bought* it. And why? So that after he got the bugs worked out of the system, then in turn he could sell it back to Uncle Sam, all cleaned up and shiny and running like a Swiss watch. In the meantime, he'd also make a tidy profit with it as VP. Virtual porn.

"So has anybody done it, that you've heard of?" I asked. "Gotten VE to work, that is?"

"A couple of privately funded endowments have dipped their respective toes in the water. Foundations for the blind and quadriplegics, mostly. Money tubs. If one could somehow negate dangerous elements of VE, the idea itself is quite exciting."

"How do you mean?"

"Consider this, Joseph," Quint said. "A blind person, or a handicapped person, using VE, simply flips a switch, and experiences the same thrill someone else does of looking at a sunset, or climbing a mountain. What kind of price tag would that be worth? There isn't any. Because during the time that equipment is worn, that person is *normal,* don't you see?"

I did see, and my friend was right. It was pretty wonderful. But then a cloud settled in. "That still doesn't solve the problem of the equipment driving some people crazy."

"No, it doesn't. And therein lies the conundrum. Much more time, and unfortunately, some lives, will probably be sacrificed before VE is anything more than a toy for the wounded rich, who feel they have nothing to lose."

"But you're telling me you've not heard of anyone yet who's had any luck with it."

"Well … that's not entirely true."

I stiffened. "Meaning?"

"I could be wrong, but I seem to recall hearing Cyrus Tate having some success."

I found myself gripping the small phone tighter. "Cyrus Tate?"

"You've heard the name around town, certainly, Joseph. Cyrus Alan Tate. The notorious 'Cat.' *You* know. The pornographer who's building that enormous brothel out in Claxton County."

"Yeah, I've heard of him." I lightly scratched my lip. "What would be Tate's interest in VE, do you think?" Although I was fairly certain what his interest was.

Quint laughed, "What a question, dear boy. What do you think would be his interest? Opening new frontiers in lust, of course."

Of course. Although it made me a little nauseated, I tried picturing that, without a whole lot of success. Tate would have porn actors wearing VE recording equipment while they did their thing. That account would then be played back in faithful, full-blown, sick reality on the apparatus of the customer lying in the pod. Danny the Dud would suddenly become Lance the Lover ... for as long as his credit card held out.

"Would what Tate did even be legal?"

"I don't see why not. It mostly depends on the voters in the area. For example, look at the bawdy houses operating outside the city limits of Las Vegas. They're functioning perfectly within the law, because every year they pay big money to the commissioners of Clark County for that right."

I wondered just how much it had cost Tate to smooth the skids at Claxton.

My thoughts were interrupted by my friend's laughter again. "Why all the sudden interest in VE, Joseph? Are you planning on recording the adventures of yourself and your intrepid cat for posterity?"

I tried laughing back, but it was forced. Hollow. "Why? Do you think I should?"

"No offense, but no." He still sounded wry. "I don't suppose there would be much of a market for it."

"Just as well," I said. "No one would ever believe me anyway."

24

O
ne mystery was solved, but that led into an even deeper one.

To wit: as galling as it was to consider it, what Cyrus Tate was planning on doing with those rotten pods up on the fifth floor of PornUtopia—turning them into the ultimate dirty movie—was legal. Not smart, mind you, but completely legit. I'd imagine the release forms that a patron would have to sign before climbing in one for the ride of his life would be as thick as a New York City phone book. That mystery was solved.

The deeper one was this. If what Tate was doing was on the up-and-up, why did Billy Barnicke have to die for discovering it? What did his last words, "the first two," have to do with it? In short, I was wrong; virtual porn was only part of it. What was Tate's real game here?

There had to be more to it. And that led to even more questions. Could it be stopped, whatever it was? And most important, could it be done with no more deaths?

Pulling the Regal up to the curb in front of Sarah's, my head was spinning. No matter which way I turned the problem, I'd missed something. It was something important. The final linchpin to the case. Going inside the house, that certainty grew. There was no way around it. I had to get back inside PornUtopia. Tonight.

The oppression hanging on me must have been palpable, because Sarah noticed it as I began to mount the stairs up to my room.

"Sid? Is anything wrong?"

My voice troubled, I gave her the same answer I'd given Marko. "Naw, it's nothin'. I'm just a bit tired."

"Can I bring anything up to you? I made some vegetable soup today. It's still hot."

I stopped and fixed my attention on her. Beneath Sarah's eyes rested dark circles like ink smudges, and her face was drawn and gray. For the first time since we'd met, the old woman looked every one of her seventy-plus years. In fact, she didn't look any better than I did about then. Was it something in the water around here?

No, I knew what my problems were. Bad water wasn't the culprit. Whatever had been causing Sarah Poole to lose sleep since the first day I arrived had been growing steadily worse.

"Are you tired too?" I asked her.

Her answer surprised me. "Tired? Tired doesn't even cover it. You can't imagine how weary I am, Sid. Weary right to the bone."

"Somethin' I can help you with?"

The innkeeper's smile was tinged with melancholy. "I wish somebody could. But no, this I have to handle for myself." Her voice took on a musing quality, like it had when she'd talked about herself and Kip, that first day I was here. "If I'd had only the courage then, I could have handled it years ago."

"Sounds bad. You sure you don't want to share what's buggin' you?" All by itself, my private-eye, help-all-the-people-you-can persona had stepped up to the plate. "I can be a pretty good listener."

"Listening I don't need. It's come time to take action." Sarah seemed to rouse herself. "That's enough about me and my troubles. Are you sure I can't interest you in some soup?"

"Thanks, but no," I said to her over my shoulder as I started back up the stairs. "I'm just gonna lie down for a while. I might have to do somethin' later tonight."

That wasn't entirely the truth. I'd definitely be heading back out, because I needed to be on-site at the PornUtopia facility right at six o'clock, when the guard shift changed. I figured that would be the best time to bluff my way in, when neither group would know I wasn't allowed to be there.

Climbing up on my bed, I checked my watch. Four o'clock. As much as my body didn't want to, I closed my eyes to grab a little rest. Who knows? Later I might need it.

♦ ◊ ♦

Rest I got, but the sleep was bad. The faces-in-the-wall dream made an unholy appearance.

I willed myself to wake up, because each time after awakening from that nightmare, getting back to the land of the living was getting harder.

As my body lay there, in that half-dream time, my brain was flying, running through the scenarios of how I could accomplish the task of getting back inside the building. In the end only one scheme presented itself, and it was so modest I figured it didn't have a ghost of a chance of succeeding. But it was all I had.

At five thirty I rolled off the mattress and onto my feet. Time to get after it.

For a moment I considered changing my smelly clothes before I headed over, before discarding that as foolish. Going back there still clad in my dirty street duds wouldn't affect my admittedly lame plan at all. I shut the door behind me as I went into the hall.

Taking the stairs by twos back down, I nearly ran over Kip, who was coming up.

"Mr. Bean, can you play ball with me?" His little-boy voice was high and entreating and stopped me cold in my tracks.

Kip's jet-black hair was sticking up at all angles in the back like Dennis the Menace's, his well-worn Louisville Slugger Junior bat, the shellac long gone, propped on his shoulder. Dangling precariously from the end of that raggedy bat was Kip's cracked and seamed first baseman's glove, badly in need of some neat's-foot oil.

Right then, I almost lost it. Don't ask me why.

Maybe it's because the boy looked so much like I had at his age, and triggered thoughts of how my own son might have turned out. Maybe it was the time of year, with the holidays—and the anniversary of his and his mother's deaths—just a couple of months around the corner. Or maybe I'd been so immersed in sleaze and debauchery these past few days I just needed to hear the clean crack of a bat and feel the gentle autumn breeze on my face as I instructed a gap-toothed little boy in the finer points of fielding a fly ball.

Heart right up in my throat, I turned and sat on the step, taking Kip's left hand, the one not holding the end of the bat, in both of mine.

"I'd like that, son, and that's a fact. Just let me get this one little thing done. Later on we'll play all you want."

Kip frowned, his freckled snub nose wrinkling up. "Hey, how come you're not talking like you were before? And how come your eyes are all wet?"

I realized that unconsciously I'd let my fake accent slip just then. But the wet eyes? Those I couldn't control.

The grin I gave him was embarrassed. "I've been tryin' to learn how to talk better. Do you think it's workin'?"

He shook his head. "Not much. Now it's bad again. Better keep at it."

Chuckling genuinely this time, I mussed his hair. "I'll do that."

Kip turned and thundered back down the stairs, me a couple of steps behind. When he reached the bottom, he made a beeline toward the kitchen. But I headed toward the door.

As I walked, I heard Sarah scolding him from in there. "Kip! Put down that bag of cookies. You'll spoil your supper."

"Is Mr. Bean eating with us tonight?" he said, obviously with one in his mouth.

"I don't know. I think I heard him in the parlor." The old woman came in, wiping her hands on a dish towel. When she saw me with my hand on the doorknob, she frowned. "Kip was just asking if you're eating with us tonight, Sid."

"No, I can't. Like I said, I have to go out for a while."

"Are you sure? We're having pot roast."

That was one of my favorites too, but I shook my head. "Sorry. I really gotta get a handle on this."

"I can keep it warm ..." With all her problems, Sarah really was a nice woman. If I had the sense God gave a jackrabbit I'd forget this silly jaunt and join her and Kip. But the die was cast, and I had to go with it.

"Y'all go on," I said. "I'll grab a sandwich or somethin' later while I'm out."

"Well. Please be quiet when you come in. I have a headache that's about to tear the top of my skull off."

"Graa-a-a-andma!" Kip called from the kitchen. "I'm hungry!"

I gave Sarah a small smile of commiseration. "The call of the wild."

"It never ends," she said. "Anyway. This thing you're doing tonight. Enjoy."

Enjoy? Right. To paraphrase the rat guy in the movie *The Abyss,* I'd be doing it. But I wouldn't be digging it.

◆ ◊ ◆

As I pulled the Regal up to the gate, the guard manning the booth leaned out.

Taking a look at the parking pass I'd affixed to the inside of the windshield of my sad ride, he wrinkled his brow doubtfully. "Help you?"

I nodded. "Yeah, I'm in maintenance, day shift, workin' with Marko Pankowsky."

"I know Marko. You, I don't know."

"Check your employee list. I'm there. Name's Sid Bean."

He did, and then frowned again. "OK, here you are. But according to this thing you clocked out today at three-ten."

"Yeah, I know. I forgot somethin' in my locker."

He shook his head. "Well, that's your problem. I can't let you back in. Rules."

"It's a present. For somebody special."

"Still can't do it."

I almost said, *It's for my wife,* before checking myself at the last second. Something about this man, this place, told me that would carry little weight with him.

I gave a lascivious grin and coaxed. "Come on, dude. Have a heart.

I met a sweetie in town last night that made my tongue hang out. I bought her some perfume, but stupid me, left it in my locker. Me and her have a hot one booked for tonight. That stuff would sure make things go easy."

Reluctantly the guard gave in. "Trying to get to first base, huh?"

My grin expanded. "First base, nothin'. I'm goin' for a homer." I jiggled my eyebrows. "And this girl ain't never even been inside the ballpark, if you know what I mean."

I chuckled nastily, the guard a second later joining in, just two rough-cut horndogs getting a kick out of the ladies. When this case was finally over, a hot shower wouldn't do it. I'd need to be steamed off at the car wash.

Still chortling, the guard pushed the button, and the gate swung up. "Never been inside the ballpark. I'll have to remember that." So saying, he waved me on through.

For hopefully the last time I made my way down the flagpole-lined drive, parking in an empty slot near the employees' entrance and getting out. Remembering my five-digit access code, I punched it into the keypad on the doorframe. It buzzed loudly, and I turned the knob, walking in.

At this time of night the lounge just inside was deserted. It took me a second to locate the light switch. Once I did and flipped on the overheads, I crossed the room, opening the final door that led me to the visitor's lobby.

The lights in here had been dimmed, but not so much I couldn't easily locate the elevator bank. Standing in front of the nearest one, I pressed the button, at the same time pulling the key card from the front pocket of my jeans. A second later a muted bell dinged, and the doors slid open. My pulse racing now, I walked in, turned, and slipped the card into the slot. The number-five button lit. I thumbed it.

Here we go.

25

*T*hankfully the lights up here had been left burning, albeit still at their otherworldly dimness. If they hadn't, locating the door to the pod room would have been a problem.

On a hunch, I turned opposite the way I'd gone earlier today, and started walking. Thankfully the TV cameras remained dark and still. Just as I thought, the door's twin to the one I'd entered earlier was located almost twenty-five feet farther down the hall.

Still operating on intuition, I slipped in the key card. There was a soft click, and I pushed the door open. As in the other barnlike room, six empty pods, arranged in a star shape, rested on the floor, their attendant computer consoles silent.

Standing there, I began running some admittedly crapshoot numbers through my mind. OK, six pods to a room, making twelve in all. Let's just say, to keep things symmetrical, that there were two other pod rooms on the other side of the building; I'd check that in a minute. Twenty-four pods. Let's further allow an hour session in each pod, at a hundred dollars a shot (again, both ideas completely arbitrary).

Roughly totaling it up, my mouth fell open. *Ka-ching and caramba.*

If, as the company literature had promised, PornUtopia was running twenty-fours hours a day, seven days a week, the income from those pods alone would net Tate somewhere in the neighborhood of well over a million and a half bucks a month, or a cool eighteen million a year.

Eighteen million.

Say what you will, that was one *nice* neighborhood.

Still …

I looked around, gauging what I was seeing. No doubt about it, this building was big. Eighteen million a year was a good amount of cabbage, but to fund a place with this much square footage, would it be enough?

Let's keep the numbers game going. Add in the estimated input from the massage cubicles, the whoopee rooms, the infamous "toys and games," and lastly the tickets to the museum. Then deduct the cost of running PornUtopia itself, with its salaries, upkeep, taxes, and inventory.

I stopped my figuring. This was intriguing. If I'd done the blue-sky ciphering right (no guarantees there), I'd missed something. No matter which way I noodled the numbers, Tate's monumental salute to bad taste would be profitable, but not spectacularly so.

There had to be more. And it had to be up here.

I began circling the pod room, looking around for … whatever it was. But there was nothing. And nothing to be found in the remaining three rooms either (as I'd thought, the other ones were found around on the backside of the building).

To my frustration, that appeared to be that. Those four large surrealistic rooms and their attendant equipment were all that comprised the fifth floor of PornUtopia. Except, of course, for the utility room. But that was pointless. Every floor had one of those.

With that I stopped and suppressed a grin. No. No, it couldn't be. Could it?

Hurriedly retracing my steps around the back of PornUtopia, I halted in front of the room. With such an ordinary-looking door sealing it, I wasn't surprised to see it didn't need a key card for access.

There was only a garden-variety knob. I wrenched it, jerking the door wide. I'm not sure what I expected. The entrance to Shangri-La, maybe.

But I drew up short in disappointment once again. There was no inner sanctum here. Just a rudimentary closet.

I was amazed by how small it was. The room basically was a four-by-five rectangle, wider than it was deep. It contained only a utility sink at the back, with some metal shelving to the left, holding various bottles of cleaning supplies.

And that was it. No Shangri-La. No inner sanctum. Nothing nefarious at all. And I would have bet my last dollar I'd been right too.

But it was just a plain old storeroom, like you'll find by the millions in office buildings around the world. I almost laughed at my naive foolishness. Well, idiot, had you really expected anything different? No, I suppose not.

That's when my eye was drawn down to the floor, and the laugh died on my lips.

Under the sink, running left to right and ending at the metal rack, I spied a thin worn area on the floor, like an arc. I frowned. Marko had told me all the carpet that had been laid in PornUtopia was new, less than a few months old. What could have caused that worn spot?

Squatting down, I tried peering underneath the basin. In the dim light, that wasn't easy. But what I saw deepened the enigma. The arc ran from the front right leg around the left rear leg's position, splitting the arc exactly.

The only thing that made sense about this setup was if the entire sink swung left. For maintenance maybe? But that was crazy. How would the plumbing work?

Getting all the way down on the floor and lying on my back, I wriggled my way underneath the sink, resisting the itching urge to check my watch. By now the next shift had begun. Who knew, maybe the new guard at the gate hadn't been told I was even in here. Maybe.

Once there, I ran my fingers from the drain, down the curve of the S-pipe, and then up to where it should have gone into the wall. But it didn't. It stopped right up against it.

What the—?

Still on my back, I reached into my rear jeans pocket and pulled out my wallet. From it I extracted a dollar bill. Stretching up and holding it taut, I slipped it between the end of the pipe and the wall. It met no resistance, coming out the other side.

I'll be a monkey's second cousin. The pipe was a fake, a phony, a PVC dodge.

Making my way out from underneath and standing again, I leaned over the sink and opened the taps all the way. Nothing. Dust city. No water had ever flowed through them.

I fought the urge to shake my head in consternation. What in the Sam Scratch was going on here? The entire setup in this closet was as fake as a kid's dollhouse. But why?

I've been known, even among my closest friends, to be a bit slow on the uptake, so excuse me if it took a moment longer before I got it. But taking a look at the sink again, and the useless water hookups, and the arc gouged in the carpet, I finally understood. So *that's* what this was about.

But there was one more piece of proof needed before I was sure.

Again leaning over the basin, I examined the wall behind it. Where the abutting walls joined, there was a definite crack running down each side, ceiling to floor. *Yowza.*

What we had here, ladies and gentlemen, boys and girls of all ages, was every spy novel's chestnut, and every little kid's dream.

A secret door.

26

OK. That had to mean there was a secret way to get in the room behind it.

But during these past few days at PornUtopia I'd grown mighty weary of secrets, and the people keeping them. I reckoned to give myself exactly thirty seconds to figure out how the doorway operated. If that didn't work, I'd go down in the basement, grab myself a ten-pound sledge, come back up here, and have at it.

Even as my fingers probed the cracks, I realized what a dumb statement of bravado that was. The name of the game was to get the proof I was after by stealth, not to alert every guard on the grounds. And with this fake room setup, how could Marko not be in on it?

The thirty seconds grew to sixty. All I'd gotten for my trouble so far was ripped nails and torn cuticles. *Come on, Box,* I thought. *Sean Connery as secret agent 007 would have had this thing open and enjoying a shaken, not stirred, martini by now.* Well, that was him not me. I straightened up, almost wanting to run my fist through the wall in frustration.

Twisting from side to side, I tried to get the kinks in my back to loosen. It seemed brute force was out. What was next?

In the movies, there'd usually be a book or something the hero would tilt out, releasing the latch. But there were no books in here. Only cleaning supplies on the shelves.

Feeling like a prize chump, one by one I started lifting the bottles. Nothing.

Nothing.

Nothing.

Click.

With that sound the wall behind the sink opened my way an inch. I couldn't believe my luck, almost bursting out laughing. It *worked.* Thank you, Hollywood. I looked at the jug that had turned the trick. A gallon of bleach, sitting on a pressure switch.

Still grinning, I unscrewed the cap to see what was really in it. As I took a deep sniff, the fumes almost knocked me back. Whoa. Bleach, all right. I remembered Granny using the stuff on washday, trying to get the red Kentucky clay out of my dad's work clothes.

Well, Cyrus, old sock, I thought, *you're going to need plenty of bleach to clean up the mess in your life I'm about to cause.*

Pulling the sink fully toward me, it smoothly followed the groove in the carpet, easily swinging open to reveal a three-foot-wide entrance. That's why the room was of such an odd dimension. It had to be this wide, so that it could allow the basin to be moved aside far enough that a person could get past it.

As the sink reached its stopping point, automatically some dim lights in the room beyond came on, beckoning me. Nervously I licked my lips. *Well, boy howdy.*

Heart going like a freight train, I stepped through.

Three paces past the threshold, I stopped and stared. The reality of this room dwarfed whatever fantasies I'd had about it. The area before me had to have finished out at least twenty feet by twenty. But it wasn't its relatively large size that threw me. It was its design.

Unlike the grayish carpet covering the rest of the fifth floor, the one I was standing on was a rich blood red. It complemented the walls perfectly, which were as black as sin. At first glance it reminded me of Prince Prospero's seventh room in Edgar Allan Poe's *The Masque of the*

Red Death. But there was no iron sconce here holding a brazier of strange fire.

There was only a solitary pod in the center of the floor, its computer console next to it. But no, there was a difference. This console had no chair for an operator, and the pod had no lid. What there was, in fact, was a thin cable coming from underneath the console, ending in a hand controller resting on the pod's cushioned interior.

Meaning that whoever lay in the pod controlled the game.

Cotton-mouthed, I tore my gaze from the apparatus and took in more of the room. I'd missed something at first glance. Lining all four walls, including the one I'd just come through, were high wooden bookshelves. So Tate was a man of letters, was he? Let's just see.

I turned to the shelf on my right. Though obviously well made, the dark wood was unfamiliar. Finished in rich satin varnish, the bookcase was only a couple of shades lighter than the wall behind it. From the cracked look of their spines, the volumes filling the case appeared to be old. Trying to be mindful of the brittleness of the pages, I pulled out the first one my hand touched and opened it. Holding it up so the light hit it better, I tilted it to get a closer look at the frontispiece. Doing so, I almost dropped it.

The photograph was that of a child, a girl of nine or so.

Being ravaged by a man.

Involuntarily I sucked in a breath. It was like I'd been hit squarely in the gut by a battering ram. What in God's name was *this?* For a second the air froze in my lungs, and the room swam.

With an effort I forced myself to look again. Opposite the photo was the book's flyleaf, proclaiming the title to be that of *Juliette's Ecstasy*. The author—most likely the gleeful bearded beast in the picture—was listed as Unknown, and the publisher was an entity called New Era books, based in London. The copyright date was 1883.

What I was holding was child porn, pure and simple. Old child porn at that.

Every fiber of my being resisting it, I pressured myself to once more look at the girl in the picture. She seemed terrified, agonized, humiliated, and if I could have found the man doing those unspeakable acts to her, I would have shot him in the face.

Stomach rolling, I leafed through the book at random, savagely turning the pages, not caring much now if it fell apart or not. I'd like to have taken a flamethrower to it. The contents were precisely as advertised, and exactly as I feared. It was a journal, a diary really, of the yearlong sexual domination of a little girl.

Even though I didn't want to, I flipped to the last page. I had to see for myself how it had ended for her. Had she been released?

No.

As I gripped the book tight enough to tear it, the final words exultantly told how that after the final act, mister "unknown" had strangled the child with her own underwear.

Thankfully there was only that one nightmare picture, but that was enough. I knew I'd never forget that little girl's face as long as I lived. If God was just—and he is—she'd found a place beside him in paradise. And the man who'd treated her so viciously would have spent the last century and a half of his eternal sentence barbequing himself in hell.

With trembling hands I slipped the book back where I'd found it and took a couple of steps back. Surely that book was a fluke. Surely.

Walking to the opposite side of the room, I came to another case and yanked from it the first book my hand touched. From the lurid bright-yellow cover, this one was clearly a lot newer than 1883. But I didn't need to open it. The title said it all.

Lollytots.

Rubbing a roughened hand over my mouth, I tried to comprehend this madness. But there are some things the sane mind will never understand. No matter which way I sliced it, Cyrus Tate was a pedophile.

Stumbling like a blind man, I circled the room, taking in bits and pieces of Tate's obsession. Most of the items on the shelves were books, but not all. Interspersed with them were old VHS videotapes and newer DVDs, all with the common theme of child abuse. Some of it featured little girls, some showcasing little boys, some with both groups suffering together, every perverted bit of it as illegal as it gets.

There was enough intense black-hearted evil stored in this room to put Tate behind bars for the rest of his natural life. Which, if the stories I'd heard of the harsh treatment regular prisoners inflicted on child molesters, wouldn't be long at all.

And what a shame that would be.

OK, get a grip. The main question here was straightforward enough. Was the stuff found in this room damning enough to have caused Billy Barnicke's death? The answer was, I didn't know. Because that still left that different-looking pod on the floor.

Fully mindful of how much time I'd spent up here, I squatted down beside it.

At first rush, it didn't look too awfully different from the ones in the other rooms. But as I said, the differences were there nevertheless. The padding, for one, looked richer in this one. And why not? It was the boss's. He could afford the best. The walls in this pod, too, looked a bit higher. Not much, maybe a couple of inches. The fact that it didn't have—or maybe need—a lid, I didn't think too much about. Maybe it was a later version.

But the thing that really set this one apart was the controller resting innocently in it, like the devil's TV remote. Picking it up, I examined it critically. This was like no remote I'd ever seen. In place of numbers were arrows, right and left, up and down. Centered in the middle was a small, thumb-operated joystick. Beneath that setup were two more right and left buttons, where the volume control would normally be. I switched the thing from hand to hand. A rightie or leftie either one would be comfortable using it.

That Cyrus Tate. What a scamp. Who'd have thought he was ambidextrous?

I realized something else was different about this pod. It was a moment more before I got it. Where the heck was the headset?

Still squatting, I pivoted around, glancing up at the console. Nope. Turning again and looking deeper into the chamber, I even lifted up the small pillow. It wasn't under there either. I tossed the remote back inside and stood, scratching my head.

Maybe it didn't need one. Maybe the whole inside of the pod itself was wired. Maybe Tate had taken it with him. And maybe I just didn't give a flying … fig.

And with that, clear out of the blue, the craziest thing happened. Suddenly I was gripped with the crazy desire to climb inside the thing and find out for myself what all the fuss was about.

That was the very definition of insanity. What purpose would a stunt like that serve? It could be it wasn't just naked women videos I'd see. What if the very act of lying down in the pod would trigger something worse, and the kiddie porn I was certain it contained would start pumping into my brainpan?

But lynch me for an outlaw if I didn't stand there a moment longer and consider it.

I can't explain it. It was as if the floodgates of perversion had sprung wide, and every dirty thing I'd seen in this place for the past few days had come roaring up. The magazines. The videos. The toys. All of it.

Even as I struggled with the deluge, a part of me was arguing back. Wait a minute, what century was this anyway? Unless I was mistaken, we'd crossed the new millennium mark a while back. Look at it logically. It was only sex, right? And like Rev. Kilbride had said, sex was the most natural thing in the world. How else was the planet populated? Through phone orders to the Monkey Ward catalog?

And speaking of which, how long had it been for me, since I'd been with a woman? A while, for sure. And never with Angela. She and I had never done anything wrong. But again, wait. Whoever said crawling into the sack with Angela would be wrong?

I could feel my defenses crumbling like a graham cracker in milk. Deep inside, part of me was fighting back like a Turkish prisoner of war. Was this how it had been for Tate when he'd been snared, like with Sarge's plastic-wrap allusion, as a kid living with his aunt and uncle?

Wordlessly I breathed a prayer as the back and forth struggle raged. I knew I wasn't strong enough for this.

Why had I blown off the warnings from both Sarge and Angela? They'd tried to tell me about what was in store for me at Porn Central, but I knew better. Oh, yowza, I sure did. Joe Box, moral centurion. Look how well I was doing.

Still the battle flared, and I could feel myself slipping. And then it got worse.

Come on, something new whispered. *One excursion inside the pod, just one trip down the rabbit hole. Who's going to know? Besides, kiddie porn might be a kick.*

That made sense. How would I ever be able to help others, unless I was willing to experience what they did? Right?

It sounded reasonable, even as part of me gibbered in horror at the thought of losing my mind in there.

How many men did you say went crazy trying to make VE work, Quint?

Half of them, Joseph. Oh sweet mother ...

I wasn't going to make it through this. I was going to give in, crawl inside that pod, flip the switch, and come out a crazy man.

But wait. Suddenly I heard someone say, "No." It was me. And with it, did there now seem to be a lessening of the pressure?

There was. Like the dark attack I'd undergone my first day at Sarah's, it appeared the onslaught was reluctantly lifting by degrees. It was another minute or so before it was gone completely, and I found myself gripping the bookcase, dripping with sweat.

It looked like the battle was over. For now. Like a kid trapped in a haunted house, I had to get out. Now. Before the whatever-it-was came back.

Because next time, I might just surrender.

My feet had almost turned back toward the door when I stopped. Wait. Not so fast. I'd seen a lot up here, but nothing concrete yet to link Tate with Billy's death. And also nothing to explain just how Tate was funding PornUtopia. I'd come in here looking for proof on both, and so far all I'd gotten was a case of the whim-whams.

I looked around one more time. Where was it? *What* was it?

That's when my eye caught the last big item in here. Tucked catty-ways in the far corner sat a combination desk and workstation. I walked over to it. Compared to the soul-killing porn stuffed chockablock all around me, along with that weird pod on the floor, the workstation I was approaching looked fairly prosaic.

To my untrained eye the IBM computer clone appeared new, or newer anyway, and from the soft hum I could tell it was in standby mode. At least, I think that's what it's called. Quint and my library friend, old Mrs. Brake, have been trying to drag me kicking and screaming into modern times for a while now.

But what really got my attention was the ledger book lying next to it. I picked it up. A ledger book. Huh. I used these in my own business. Now this was more my speed.

But as I began flipping the pages, once again I felt gloom settling down. They were covered in gibberish. The double-entry columns were the only things familiar. Everything else looked like just random numbers and letters, a dog's breakfast of clutter. Tate had encoded it.

I almost threw the thing. Give me a freaking break already. A cryptologist I ain't. It was with a growing sense of helpless frustration that I started to put the book back where I'd found it. Wasn't anything about this case going to go easily? Slapping the book down, my aim was off, and it bumped the mouse next to the keyboard.

With that, the computer came alive.

Drymouthed, I leaned in. On the screen was a spreadsheet. With a start of recognition I saw that what was shown there was a copy of what was on the first page of the ledger. Kind of.

I ran my finger under the first entry found. *B-STO 1g 12yoG D u.p. 1K US*. Like I said, gibberish. But as I compared it to the first line shown on-screen, my face paled, and I nodded in grim triumph.

Tate, you useless, worthless sack of flesh. I've got you.

The *B* stood for Bangkok, the destination of the shipment. *STO* was the name of the buyer there, a guy named Soon-Tai Oh. The *1g 12yoG D* notation really made my fists knot up: *1g* equaled one gross, while *12yoG* was a twelve-year-old girl. The *D* was shorthand for DVD. And the last part, the *u.p. 1K US*, meant the unit price for each was one thousand U.S. dollars.

So what that tallied up to was clear: Cyrus Tate had sold 144 copies of a bootleg DVD, showing a captive twelve-year-old girl engaging in illegal sex acts, to a Mr. Soon-Tai Oh, located in Bangkok, Thailand. Presumably for resale there.

For that, he'd been paid one thousand dollars for each disc, or a grand total of 144,000 bucks for the transaction.

As they used to say on the old radio shows, even if you said it fast, it was a lot of money. And that was for just one sale. The page held the records of dozens of sales, the book itself composing a hundred such pages. And who knew how long Tate had been at it?

He wasn't just a pedophile. He was a broker.

And that explained PornUtopia, and the flagpoles. It was Tate's sly dig at normal humanity, as well as a tacit advertisement of his wares. The building and its debauched offerings were just window dressing, to hide Tate's real agenda. That of spreading child pornography to others of his kind around the world. And turning a buck or three in the process.

At the far right corner of the screen was a heading called Notes. Figuring to get all the intel I could on this place, against the time I turned the case over to the cops, I moved the mouse over and clicked on the link.

Instantly another screen popped up, giving details about that shipment to Bangkok. This one listed the date of the order, the date of transfer by truck to a Los Angeles shipping port, even the name of the container vessel. A lot of people had their fingers in this particular pie. It was the line at the end of the listing that confirmed what I'd already thought: "terms payable in advance, FOB Bangkok, approved by Morris." Morris Lester Chalafant, the Sydney Greenstreet of porn; I knew he must have had a piece of this.

Quickly I cross-checked the next entry in the ledger with the listing on the screen. It showed a shipment to New Orleans of fifty DVDs featuring a little boy of five. So Tate and Chalafant sent the stuff to cities here in the states as well, huh? FBI, here we come.

But it was the next entry that literally caused me to freeze in place.

I blinked, my disbelieving mind twisting like a reed in a hurricane. In the ledger, the listing was almost sterile: *C-EV 2 9yoG 1 10 yoB L u.p. 50K US.* It was the fact that there was an *L*, not a *D* before the *u.p.* that brought everything into screaming reality.

Final delivery point of shipment, Curacao, Venezuela.

Buyer, one Enrique Velasquez.

Items shipped ...

Eyes stinging, I tried it again. Items shipped: two nine-year-old girls, one ten-year-old boy.

Three living, breathing children.

Unit price for same: fifty thousand dollars. U.S. currency.

I went to the notes link. "Terms payable in advance, FOB Curacao, approved by Morris." FOB meaning freight on board. Well, of course. They weren't kids. They were freight. Unconsciously my fist had cocked back, all the way back, ready to smash that smug screen. I only stopped myself at the last possible second. *The proof is there; don't destroy the proof,* I had to keep telling myself.

Billy had obviously found what I had. And though he may have been an obnoxious, womanizing drunk, I also knew that, before his priest had molested him as a child, he'd been an altar boy. There must have still been a core of something moral and decent there, and Tate's obsession with kiddie porn must have struck it. That's why Billy had come in wasted and raving the next day after he'd been up here. He'd found his worst nightmare locked away in this room. And that's why Tate had ordered that Billy be beaten to death, and to make it look like a house robbery gone wrong.

But something else had gone wrong that night. Billy hadn't died, at least not right away. He'd lived long enough to tell me who'd done it.

Only one thing was left to decipher. Who or what were "the first two"?

27

My guts were churning over the horror as I pulled the Regal up to the gate on my way out. Sex slavery. Involving children. Where was Tate getting them? They were too young to be runaways, at least the way I understood it. Had they been snatched at malls or ball games, maybe when the parents were distracted? I'd heard of such things, but I'd always thought they were urban myths, like snuff films or alligators growing in the sewers.

But what I'd found secreted away on the fifth floor of PornUtopia was all too real.

With that cheerful thought foremost in my mind, I pulled the car up to the guard shack. Even the air seemed heavier now, as if a portent of change. This deal had better go smoothly. My .38 was in the glove compartment, and I was in just the right mood to use it.

The guy manning the booth, an older and fatter version of the one who'd let me in an hour earlier, leaned out, a scowl clouding his harsh features. "Who the devil are you? And how'd you get in?"

I pointed to the parking pass on the dash. "Name's Sid Bean. Maintenance. The other guy let me in earlier."

"Bean, huh?" The guard reached back into the shack, his hand coming out bearing the employee list. "OK, here you are." He seemed disappointed at that. "Says here Randy clocked you in. But his note also says you were only going to be checking your locker for something." The guard lowered the clipboard, suspicion filling his face. "Now are you gonna tell me it took over an hour for you to do that?"

"No, I'm gonna tell you I fell asleep."

"What?"

"It's the truth." No it wasn't. "Marko worked me like a dog today, and when I bent down to close my locker, my back seized up." I was getting pretty good at making up lies on the fly. Not that that was something to be proud of, understand. "I sat down for a minute in a chair in the lounge, and the next thing you know, I was sawin' logs."

"Anybody see you?"

"If they did, would I know it?" My reply seemed reasonable, but it only made the guard's face scrunch up even more.

Raising the clipboard to his eyes once more, he savagely checked my name off, at the same time muttering, "The guys Mr. Tate's been hiring to work here, I swear." When he lowered it, he seemed surprised I was still there. "Go home, Bean. Do your sleeping there."

"Sounds like a plan," I said, nodding and putting the Regal in gear. With a yip of tires I fed it some gas. As PornUtopia receded in my rearview mirror, I hoped the next time I saw the place would be on the evening news, with Tate being led away in handcuffs.

♦ ◊ ♦

Pulling the Regal up to the curb in front of Sarah's, I was still consumed with what I'd seen. I needed to get proof of the crime, but couldn't seem to get a handle on just how to do that. A couple of ideas came to mind.

First off, I should have taken the ledger. There's nothing like the printed page to get the authorities' attention. But I discarded that one almost as quickly as it had come. The ledger was gibberish. Encrypted gibberish at that.

Then how about getting some disks and tomorrow make copies of what I'd found on the computer? Computer proof is also pretty solid these days.

That thought also went by the wayside. Quint had told me once about the electronic locks he'd put on his own system to prevent unauthorized copying. Considering the subject matter involved, I imagined what Tate used was even stronger.

Owing to my brooding confusion, I didn't notice the strange old biddy just shutting Sarah's front door until I'd almost run into her.

"Goodness, you startled me!" she said, putting her hand over her heart.

She was short, round, and plump, a human basketball of a woman. As I met her weak and troubled brown eyes, I apologized. "Sorry, ma'am, I didn't see you."

She looked past me, wringing her hands in distress. "It's all right. No harm done."

I looked where she was looking and didn't see anything, so I turned my gaze back at her. "Are you sure?"

"Yes. It's just that I'm about to go out of my mind with worry." As if to prove that point, she despondently shook her head. "Poor Sarah."

That drew me up short. "Sarah? What about her? Who are you anyway?"

She returned the look, her answer sharp. "I'd ask the same question of you. But since *I'm* polite, I'll go first. I'm Oneida. Oneida Firch. I live next door."

I remembered Sarah mentioning her name. "I've heard of you, ma'am, and I'm sorry if I made you mad with my remark. That wasn't my intent. But again, please, what about Sarah?"

"Wait. I know you. You must be Mr. Bean." The old woman went back to gazing past me. "Sarah mentioned she had a new boarder. I was just inside, watering her plants. I know she'd want me to." Her hands were still twisting around like snakes.

"Yes, ma'am. Can you tell me what's goin' on?"

Her head snapped around. "Why, it's like I said. Sarah's in the hospital."

The *hospital?* She hadn't said that at all. I reached out and touched the woman's hands, stopping their aimless motion. "Ma'am? Oneida? Could you please start from the top?"

I guess it was my using her name that caused the old woman to finally draw a breath.

"It happened an hour or so ago. Sarah called me right after dinner and asked if I wanted to join her and Kip for an ice cream over at the Dairy Flip. She said if I'd drive, she'd buy. Sarah doesn't drive anymore, you know."

"Yes, ma'am." I wished she'd get on with it.

"I told her that sounded fine. I asked her to give me a few minutes to clean up my own dinner dishes, and then I'd be right over. But when I did, and knocked on the door, there was no answer."

That didn't sound right. "What happened then?"

"I let myself in. Sarah and I have keys to each other's doors, and have for years. I called her name, but she didn't answer. I started going through her house, room by room, and that's when I found her."

"Found her? What do you mean?"

"Just what I said. I mean I found her, lying at the bottom of her basement stairs. She must have stepped funny and fallen all the way down. She's been under such a *strain* lately—"

I almost grabbed Oneida by her shoulders. "Fallen all the way down? Is she all right? Where is she now?"

"My nephew Freddie works on the life squad, and his unit was dispatched," the old woman said. "They were the ones that took Sarah to the regional hospital, over on Garrard Street." She sniffed back tears. "I've called them and called them, but they won't tell me a thing, not a thing. I've been waiting for Freddie to show up. He'll tell me."

Man, this on top of everything else. And then— "Where's Kip?"

"Why ... I suppose at the police station. Where else would he be?"

This time I did grab her. As gently as I could. "He's not here? With you?"

"No. In the confusion with the stretcher and all, I saw one of the responding officers place him in the back of his car."

I had to know. "Local or state?"

"What?" She looked at my hands. "Please, Mr. Bean. You're hurting me."

227

I blew out a breath, released her, and tried it again. "I'm sorry. The police that responded. Were they state police, or Sunnyvale?"

"Sunnyvale, of course. The name was right on the car door." She frowned at me. "You're not from around here, are you?"

"No ma'am," I gritted. *That's why I'm staying in a boarding house.*

"Well, there you are then," the batty old woman said. "Everyone knows the state police haven't come to our town for years. Not since they caught those awful Mexican boys trying to bring drugs across the ferry at Ripley. Land sakes. The ferry! Can you imagine?"

I didn't bother to answer, because I was already pounding back down the steps to the street, and my car. Ten seconds later the Regal and I were a half a block down from Sarah's house and accelerating. If the Sunnyvale cops pulled me over for speeding, fine. They were the ones I was on my way to see anyway.

But no cops appeared in my cracked and dusty rearview, and a couple of minutes later found me pulling up in front of the police station on Tulip Street.

As I stormed in, the young sergeant manning the visitor's desk looked up in surprise.

"Can I help you?"

"Two things," I said, panting, the humidity making my shirt itch. "One, I want to see Kip Poole, and make sure he's all right."

"Who?" the cop frowned.

"Kip Poole. The little kid who was with Sarah Poole when she was taken to the regional hospital, after her fall."

"Sir, I—"

"That brings me to point two. I'd like to speak with the officer who got the call about that. Now."

The sergeant lifted his hands in puzzlement. "Sir, I have no idea what you're talking about."

My tirade died in my throat. "What did you say?"

About that time the door behind him opened, and another cop stepped through it, older and tougher-looking.

He addressed the younger officer, but was looking at me. "Farley, what's all the commotion out here?"

The younger man, Farley, pointed at me offhand with his pen. "Drew, this guy here—what did you say your name was?"

"I didn't. It's Sid Bean. I'm stayin' over at Sarah's place."

"Anyway, this Bean here is asking if we're holding some kid."

"I didn't say you're holdin' him. I said he was probably brought here when his grandmother was taken to the hospital. He's only six."

Drew was still looking hard at me. "Mr. Bean, I think you were given some wrong information. We have no child here, six or otherwise."

"What?"

"Maybe you'd better start from the beginning," he said.

I did, rushing my words. At the end, the older cop was nodding his head.

"I get it now. At least, I think I know what's going on. Chief Stryker must have been the responding officer. That's why it was never logged in here."

"I don't understand."

"Sunnyvale is a small town, Mr. Bean, and we only have three squad cars. One of them is Chief Stryker's. Whenever an officer-assist call comes in, it's routed to whichever car is on duty at the time. When Miss Poole's fall occurred, it was right at shift change. The chief must have been on his way home, took it, and just hasn't called back to log it in yet."

As an ex-cop myself, that sounded like an incredibly sloppy way to run things. But maybe in Sunnyvale it worked.

"That still doesn't answer the question of where Kip Poole is," I argued.

Officer Drew Whatever-his-last-name-was sounded patient. "No sir, it doesn't. But knowing Chief Stryker, he probably has the boy with him. The chief loves kids."

I picked up the desk phone receiver and handed it to Farley. "Good. Let's be sure. Call him."

The younger cop took it from me, but looked questioningly up at his boss. The older man seemed to be trying to hold in a laugh. I guess they thought I was a head case.

"Do as the man asked, Farley," Drew said. "Call the chief."

"OK." Farley shrugged, punching in the number, obviously humoring me. He listened for a second, then said, "Chief Stryker? Farley. Listen, I got a guy here says he has some questions about a kid."

Farley listened again, then placed his hand over the mouthpiece and looked at me. "He says, 'What kid?'"

My fists knotted. It was only by concentrating that I made them unclench. "Tell him the boy's name is Kip Poole. He was there with her when his grandmother Sarah fell."

The young cop spoke once more into the phone. "The dude says the kid's name is Kip Poole. He seems kind of wound up about it. The guy's staying at the Poole bed-and-breakfast." He listened again, nodded, and then said, "I'll tell him, Chief. Thanks, you too."

Farley hung up and began writing something on the pad in front of him, talking as he scribbled. "These are the directions to the Alice Bain Memorial Hospital, over on Garrard Street," he said, tearing off the paper and holding it out. "Turns out you were right about there being a kid. The chief's there with him, and when you have a minute, he'd like to talk to you. Something about your stay at the Poole house."

Playing dumb, I said, "Kip would?"

"The chief."

"There, you see, Mr. Bean?" Drew boomed. "One missing child located, and we didn't even break a sweat. Mystery solved."

It was far from solved, but I showed both of the cops my teeth. "Thanks guys." Taking the paper, I turned and headed for the door.

As I pushed it open I heard Farley say to my back, "The weatherman's saying a cold front's coming through, and it's liable to ice up tonight, Mr. Bean. Drive safely."

"Tell him not to forget his skates," I heard Drew say to the younger man, then he muttered, "And his tinfoil hat." He and Farley both laughed like it was slapstick.

I merely waved as I crossed the sidewalk and went around to the Regal's driver-side door. Getting in, I savagely wrenched the key before I put the car in gear and hit the gas. Idiots. God save me from buffoons and jackanapes.

Pulling away into the night, I thought about Officer Farley's last mocking words. *Drive safely.* Right. Sarah's fall was no accident. I knew that as sure as I knew my name was really Joe Box. She and Kip were in the kind of danger that if you're lucky, you see only in nightmares.

And if the tingling on my spine was any indication, nobody would be safe in this town ever again.

28

The directions weren't hard to follow. Five minutes later I wheeled the Regal into the hospital's visitor's lot. The Alice Bain Memorial Hospital was more grandiose in name than in reality. The building was only two stories high, and the sooty red brick and black casement windows pegged it as a midforties vintage.

Because the lot by the emergency room doors only had spaces for four cars, and they were all filled, I had to put the Buick into the main lot and use the front entrance.

Inside the automatic glass doors, off to my immediate right I spotted the gift shop. It was staffed by what we used to call a gray lady, an older female volunteer. She was just locking up and gave me a cordial smile as I approached. "Yes, may I help you?"

I figured her for around Sarah's age, mid-to-late seventies maybe. Both her manner and voice put me in mind of the sweet little old gal who owned Tweety Bird. The plastic name badge listed her as Mrs. Phillips.

"Yes, ma'am. I'm looking for the emergency room entrance?"

"Oh dear. Those words always send a chill down my spine."

Mine too.

She pointed past me. "Down that hall, and to the right. You

can't miss it. But perhaps I can help you with whoever it is you're looking for. I know almost everyone in Sunnyvale."

"Maybe you can at that. I'm tryin' to find Sarah Poole."

Mrs. Phillips looked stricken, and she tsk-tsked. "Sarah, yes, I heard about her fall, poor woman. At her age, a slip like that can be terrible."

It wouldn't do you much good either, I thought.

"I was on duty when they brought her in," she said. "Poor dear. When you see her, please tell her Flo wishes her well."

"I will." Heading down the hall, I found the emergency room information desk just where she'd said it would be.

Seated there was a middle-aged nurse with sparkling blue eyes and copper-bright hair, a fair daughter of Eire. She smiled professionally as I approached. "May I help you?"

"Yeah, I'm lookin' for information on Sarah Poole's condition."

"Are you a relative?"

"Just a friend."

Leaning in, the nurse checked her computer screen. A moment later she shook her head. "I'm sorry, the system says she's still in surgery."

"Surgery? Does it say for what?"

"We're not allowed to give out that information. Her doctor should be able to tell you though. Dr. Brandywine."

"Good. I'll wait."

"That won't be for a while. After surgery she'll be in recovery. They won't put her in her room for hours yet. Perhaps you should come back tomorrow."

"Does it say what happened to her?"

"I'm sorry. That's privileged information."

I must have looked frustrated, because the nurse smiled sympathetically. "As I said, Dr. Brandywine is the surgeon on duty tonight. That's a piece of luck. He's really very good."

I was about to say something to that when the woman looked past my shoulder. "Chief Stryker!" she called out. "You asked me to let you know if anyone requested information on Sarah Poole's condition. This gentleman just did."

I turned to see she was talking to a large guy in a blue Sunnyvale police uniform—like Farley and Drew had worn, but with a lot more hash marks running down its sleeve—and he was coming our way. The cop appeared beefy, but it was a hard body past its prime, now going to fat. Hatless above his ruddy boxer's face, Stryker's brown cop eyes were regarding me like a worm on a hook.

Oh boy. This was going to be a treat.

"You were asking about Sarah Poole?" Stryker's voice was a shock. At odds with his menacing build, it was a high, clear tenor. His tone, too, seemed friendly.

But it didn't go with those flat, cold eyes.

I figured to run with it. "Yeah, Chief, my name's Sid Bean. I'm a boarder at Sarah's. How is she?"

"Bean," he mused. "I was hoping you'd stop by." Then he snapped his fingers. "Say, I know where else I've heard your name before. You're Marko Pankowsky's new helper over at PornUtopia, right?"

Come on, he knew I was. I'd bet a kid couldn't light a firecracker in this town without Stryker being there to pinch off the fuse.

"Anyway, Sarah is still in surgery," he added. "Like the lady said."

"Can you tell me what happened?"

"At this point, you know as much as we do. All we can say for sure is, earlier this evening she took a tumble down her basement stairs. She's being treated now."

"So where's her grandson, Kip? We kinda hit it off. I'd like to see him."

"*You'd* like." Stryker's helpful manner faded. "No offense, but you're just her boarder. A paying customer. You really have no standing in this at all."

I'd come dangerously close to overplaying it, and I gave the cop what I hoped was a reasonable nod. "Yeah. You're right. It's just that I've grown kinda fond of the kid. This has to be pretty tough on him."

"That's true," Stryker said. "That's why he's over at county children's services."

Don't ask me why, but that statement, said just that way, sent an iciness coursing through me. "But Officer Farley said he was with you."

"He was. Up until about five minutes ago. That's when the caseworker came and took him with her."

Caseworker. I tried to keep my tone steady. "Is that normal procedure?"

"Sure it is. He's got no other living family. Sarah's all the kid has." Stryker's fake amiableness was back. "Don't look so shook-up, Bean. The county folks are all right. They'll feed the kid, calm him down, give him a nice bed for the night."

That's not why I was looking at him that way. Stryker was lying. It was hard to spot, deep in those cold eyes, but it was there. It appeared we had another player in the game.

I was out of my depth. Though part of me wanted to knock this guy to the floor and beat the truth of Kip's whereabouts out of him, I let the notion go by. Patience. For now.

"I guess he's safe enough there," I allowed. "But gettin' back to me. Officer Farley said you wanted to talk to me?"

"Yeah, I do. And it's not a pleasant duty. As much as I don't want to, I'm going to have to ask you to vacate the Poole house."

I'd kind of figured that was coming. It's called tying up loose ends. And Stryker had looked almost genuinely pained as he said it. He'd missed his calling—acting on the stage.

"How come?"

"Since Sarah's laid up in here for the duration, and since she's the owner, technically that makes you a trespasser."

"But like you said, I'm her boarder."

"Uh-uh." Stryker held up a finger. "Guest. Sarah doesn't settle up with boarders until the day they leave. Everybody in town knows that. So according to the law, until then you're her houseguest. And seeing as how she's unconscious now, and can't vouch for you any longer, and also since she probably won't be going home for a while ..." He spread his hands. "Do you see the dilemma?"

"Yeah, I guess so. Can I at least get back in to get my stuff?"

"Sure. I'll let you in there myself. I've got keys."

I didn't doubt that for a second. He probably had keys to every house and store in the village, against just such a contingency. What a swell fella. What a helpful guy. *Right.* Stryker was about as chummy as a scorpion. One with lingering constipation. And hives.

I knew the real reason he wanted to be there with me when I got my gear. Although I'm sure he'd pegged me as a drifter, he also struck me as a man who left nothing to chance. If so, it'd be a useless trip for him. Granny didn't raise a fool, my present persona to the contrary.

I merely nodded. "Let's go."

We left the hospital, Stryker staying exactly one car length behind me as we made our way over to Sarah's. Arriving there and getting out, the cop still kept his distance, staying three steps to my rear as we mounted the porch steps. Stretching past me, he already had the door key in his hand.

"I'll get that," he said, slipping the thing in the lock. Of course he'd get it. Had he expected me to kick it in?

Coming inside, we crossed the living room. "My room is upstairs," I said.

"I figured that."

Casually Stryker began mounting the stairs, following me up. Once in my bedroom, I made a big show of pulling my suitcase out of the wardrobe before I started opening the dresser drawers. As I tossed my stuff in the grip, the man watched my every move with a beneficent beam. He didn't miss a trick.

If I'd had anything in here pertaining to the true business of that porn palace at the edge of town, I knew the cop would have been on it instantly. Not for the first time, I thanked God I'd stuck both the key card and the VE 1000 manual in the Regal's trunk.

A second later I had the valise closed and the locks snapped shut.

"Is that it?" Stryker asked.

"I travel light."

"Smart man. Listen, Bean, I feel terrible about this." *Sure you do, buddy.* "Have you checked out either of those new motels at the edge of town? I hear they're nice."

"Not yet," I replied, picking my suitcase up off the bed and heading out into the hall. Stryker was right on my heels as we went back down the stairs.

He was still yammering. "And since PornUtopia hasn't opened for business yet, I'm sure getting a vacancy at either place won't be a problem." Then he chuckled. "I don't think they'll give you as good a deal as Sarah was giving you though."

"No, probably not."

He followed me out onto the porch, pulling the front door solidly closed behind him.

"I guess I'll do a little look-see around. Earn my city paycheck," Stryker laughed, but his mirth was as fake as a game show host's.

"You do that." I left him standing there with his arms casually folded across his chest as I walked down the steps to the curb and to my car.

Getting in, I heard him call out, "Listen, you take care of yourself, Bean. I'll be seeing you around."

"Count on it," I muttered, starting the Regal and wheeling away.

It wasn't until I was on Main and heading out of town that something Stryker had said registered. *Earn my city paycheck,* he'd said. As if he was drawing another paycheck. One with Cyrus Tate's name scrawled at the bottom.

I shook my head, holding back a weary chuckle. On further consideration, I doubted Tate paid his flunkies with anything so mundane as checks. Cash, liquor, drugs, sex? Yeah, any or all of those. But not checks. They call it leaving a "paper trail" for a reason.

As I drove, I pondered Sarah's condition. And Kip's. Where *was* he? Not at children's services. I'd have bet Noodles on that. When I called them, come the morning, they'd have no record of him staying there or with a foster family. And that wasn't a slam on them; surely the conspiracy didn't go that far. They'd simply plead ignorance, and rightly so. It'd be interesting to watch the dance Stryker would perform to account for that.

The answer to all this lay with Sarah Poole. I wasn't exactly sure how I knew it, but she was the key.

◆ ◊ ◆

I ended up taking a room at the Golden Oaks Lodge. The next morning I awoke to find the sheets soaked in sweat. Mine.

I'd dreamed about Kip, and it wasn't good. We were on an ocean liner, the *Lusitania* of all things, right after the patrolling German U-boat had sent a torpedo into her amidships. Panic was rampant, and I kept losing the boy among the throng of frightened passengers.

Then the dream shifted, as they tend to do, and I found myself thrashing in the water. The liner had sunk before the lifeboats had been unhooked from their davits, leaving us all to drown like rats. Uppermost in my mind was, *Where was Kip?* I felt him slipping away.

Then, off to my left, I saw him. Sarah Poole had him, cradled in her arms through her bulky kapok life jacket. They were both screaming. Looking closer, I saw why. The group they were part of was being circled and attacked by sharks. Man-eaters.

Heedless of the danger, I started swimming as hard as I could over to them. For some reason, the sharks were leaving me alone. Too greasy, I guess. But just as I reached the two, suddenly the dream shifted again. Now it wasn't Sarah holding a sobbing Kip.

It was my dead wife, Linda, holding our son.

I stretched out for them as they floated and bobbed just out of reach. My screams of frustration matched theirs. Then a second later, their cries turned to shrieks of fear. Another shark, bigger than any of the others, if the size of the fin sticking up out of the water meant anything, was closing in like a rocket.

I made one more supreme effort to grab them, but too late. With a flip of its tail and a roiling of water, the beast pulled them down. All that was left was a bloody disturbance as the waves sloshed, leaving me alone and shrieking in the vast ocean.

Calling Doctor Freud, we have a live one for you.

The dream wasn't hard to figure. Things were spinning out of control. The passengers being eaten alive were the men and women and children who'd be devoured by the shame and degradation patiently waiting for them, like the sharks in the water, at PornUtopia. The ocean was the uncaring world they lived in. And the giant shark, of course, was Cyrus Alan Tate. *Go back to your journaling, Doctor. I can take it from here.*

At 7:00 a.m. I was up. The promised ice had held off, but the sky was still sullen, and as gray as lead. After an unremarkable breakfast at the motel coffee shop, eight o'clock found me cooling my heels in the visitor's room at the Sunnyvale cop house. I didn't much care that I wasn't at work yet. I was most likely done there anyway.

A middle-aged officer afflicted with dishwater-blond hair and a pinched face had told me to take a seat in one of the chairs while he called the county welfare people. I examined my nails while the conversation went back and forth. Not surprisingly, when the cop hung up he told me they'd never heard of Kip Poole.

"Big shock," I muttered. Flicking away a piece of dried skin, I raised my voice from where I sat. "Could you call Chief Stryker? He's the one that saw the boy last."

The cop, whose name was Keller, chortled, revealing grayish, inward-tilting teeth. "At this hour? Not me."

I got up and walked over to him, hand extended. "OK. Let me do it then."

"I don't think so. The chief's number is unlisted."

Trying to keep the aggravation from filling my voice, I said, "Then you dial it, and hand me the phone." Still the cop balked, but I just shot him an impatient look.

Obviously anxious to have me gone, Keller shrugged. "Your funeral." Picking up the receiver, he began punching numbers. "Where would you like the body sent?"

"Lord save me from funny policemen."

We waited for the call to go through. I heard Stryker say hello, and Keller handed over the phone. "Here you go."

I took it. "Chief Stryker? Sid Bean."

"Bean. Why am I not surprised?"

"Listen, we got a problem. County services said they've never heard of Kip Poole."

Stryker's tone wasn't nearly as friendly as it'd been last night. "*We* got a problem? You're like a scroungy dog with a bone, aren't you? It's only a paperwork snafu. I'm on it."

"You mean he's there after all?" I didn't believe that for a second. "Could I pay the kid a visit? See how he's gettin' along?"

The chief's sigh sounded huge and exasperated over the phone. "No, you can't. They don't have him anymore."

"Really." I looked at Keller, who wasn't hearing Stryker's side. "That's no good."

"It's as good as it's going to get. He's at a foster home now. And before you ask which one, that's privileged information. The boy's safety is paramount."

Stryker sounded like he'd really meant that. *Not.*

"Are you sayin' I'd put him in danger, Chief?"

"I'm saying it's none of your concern, Bean. Now go to work. I believe you're a couple of hours late by now. Or go have breakfast. Or go get drunk. Whatever you do, do it before I run you in on general principle. This conversation is over." The sound of Stryker's receiver crashing down was like a cannon going off in my ear.

Keller was grinning as I handed the phone back. "Shot you down, huh?"

"You know, I heard the bakery over on Carlton Street's runnin' a special on day-old donuts. Better get some before they're gone."

Before the cop had a chance to fire back a reply, I turned and stalked out the door.

29

Once outside, I immediately opened my cell phone and called the hospital, asking if Sarah Poole was up for visitors yet. The admitting nurse said that she was now in ICU, and that unless I was a relative or clergy, I couldn't see her. Frustrated, I bit back an acidic reply. It wasn't the nurse's fault I was stymied. I did manage to get her to tell me that Sarah was probably going to be moved to a private room in a few days, and that I was welcome to come see her then. I curtly thanked her and hung up abruptly.

I called Angela next, telling her I'd hit a snag in the case, and that I was going to be in Sunnyvale for a little longer than I'd planned. To her everlasting credit, she didn't tell me, "I told you so," though she probably thought it.

The next couple of days I puttered around town, not even bothering to ring Marko to tell him I'd quit. Maybe that makes me a jerk. You call it. What I know for sure is I don't do the hanging-around-with-my-thumb-up-my-nose bit very well. As a kid, I drove Granny to distraction with my edginess. But, as she used to say with a shrug, it's just the way I am.

The third day found me back at the hospital, standing before the main information desk. I'd dinged the little metal bell sitting there (thankfully not one of Toni Maroni's joke items), and was waiting for somebody to come by and answer it. From the deserted waiting room, the residents of Sunnyvale either must have been disgustingly healthy, or very lucky.

I glanced over at the gift shop. Not open yet. I couldn't even commiserate my woes with old Mrs. Phillips, the gray lady who'd helped me. I was just about to give the bell another smack when a female in casual business attire came bustling around the corner.

She was a younger, attractive blonde woman, extremely pregnant, and her wan smile was apologetic. "I'm sorry. I heard someone out here, but I was in the ladies' room. Can I help you?"

"Yes, ma'am, I'm lookin' for Sarah Poole's room. Can she have visitors yet?""

"Poole …" The woman was typing Sarah's name into the system as she said it. Looking at the screen, she nodded. "Yes, she's allowed. Room two-twelve."

Two-twelve? That shouldn't be hard to find.

"The elevators are that way," the receptionist went on, pointing. "Second floor, first right." The smile she awarded me was the sunniest I'd seen since I'd arrived in town. It sounds dumb, but from that alone I'd bet she was going to be a great mother. As a good place to raise a child, though, this burg sure wasn't it. If the EPA rated toxic porn dumps, Sunnyvale would top the list.

"Thanks." Following the woman's directions, I took the elevator and turned right. A couple of minutes later I was standing before the nurse's station.

The sixtyish woman there wasn't nearly as pleasant as the young lady downstairs. She frowned like I wasn't quite right in the head when I mentioned I was there to see Sarah.

"She's only been in the room a few hours," the battle-ax said.

So what? I almost retorted. But I held my peace.

"Does she even know you?" the nurse grilled.

This time I let a bit of my famous Joe Box temper out for a romp, like a little red dog on a frosty day. I'd had just about a gutful of this town. And its residents. Fully using my six-foot-three frame to my advantage, I leaned in.

"Yes. She knows me. Not well. But she knows me. And unless there are doctor's orders to the contrary, I want to see her. Now."

The nurse's hazel eyes widened just a bit, and she fumbled with Sarah's chart for a second before she found her composure. "Uh. This says Mrs. Poole is in room two-twelve. My instructions say any visitors must sign in." Sign in? I'd bet anything that was Stryker's doing. The battle-ax said it as if she'd used it to score a point for bureaucrats everywhere.

"Thanks," I replied, as civilly as I could, signing the form before I turned and began walking away. Two doors down was room two-twelve, and I pushed the entry open.

Before I go any further, let me say this. I hate hospitals. That's not meaning any disrespect to those who work in them. The hours they put in are generally long, the pay generally short, and the appreciation next to nonexistent. So it's not the people. I just can't stand the thought of all that pain and suffering and dying held tightly in one place.

Maybe as a kid I had a bad time in a hospital and just don't recall it. Unlikely, but possible. For sure I hated the field hospitals I visited in Vietnam, paying calls on buddies who'd been shot, stabbed, burned, blown up, or otherwise mutilated and insulted by the enemy.

So it was with less than joy that I approached Sarah's bed. She was covered with bruises and seemed to be asleep. I swallowed a bit of bile as I took in all the hoses and wires attached to her, running in and out. *Maybe I'd better come back later—*

But she must have only been dozing, because just as I began to step away from her bed, Sarah turned and favored me with a pale, pain-racked gaze.

"Sid ..." she croaked, lifting up a frail, bony hand that waved helplessly around in the air before I gently stopped it with my own.

"How are you, Sarah?" I asked gently, softly patting her hand. I said before that I hate hospitals. And the two groups of patients I hate to see there most of all are the elderly and little kids. Both are so utterly defenseless. But I tried to make my smile warm.

"I've been better." She ran her pale pink tongue around her dry lips. Unbidden tears filled her eyes as she went on, "They tell me my pelvis is broken."

"Here, let me get you a drink." I poured some ice water from a small carafe that was sitting on the bedside table, into a squat plastic cup. As I placed the end of the straw into her mouth, the old woman placed her chilly hand over mine and took two long, deep gulps.

She released my hand as I pulled the cup away, and nodded. "That's better. Thank you, Sid."

Glancing over my shoulder to make sure the door was still shut, I looked back at her. "Sarah, I need to ask you a question." How she got hurt wasn't it. I'd come back to that.

"A question?"

"Several questions, actually. First, though, do you have any idea how much pain medication they have you on?"

She swallowed. "I'm not sure. Something fairly strong. And that's what's making this so difficult. I know it'll be wearing off soon. And I can't have more until sometime this afternoon. My heart, you see."

I felt bad for her pain, but the fact that she appeared to be clear-headed, at least for now, prompted me to take advantage of it, for as long as she could hold out. Pulling up a nearby chair, I sat down. I wanted to look her in the eye. She deserved that, at least.

"I need to ask you some things, Sarah. I also need to say some things to you. Hard things. And it may be difficult, but there's no time to waste."

Dread filled her face. "Dear God. Is it about Kip?"

"Indirectly."

"But ..." The poor gal looked completely lost. I couldn't blame her.

She went on, still in anguish, "What does 'indirectly' mean?" Unconsciously she began knotting up the sheet in her fists. "Where is he? Is he all right?"

I blew out a breath. "I wish I could say yes. The truth is, your Chief Stryker has been giving me the runaround. All I know for sure is, Kip was seen being placed in the back of Stryker's car as you were put in the ambulance. After that, he vanished. I'm sorry."

Huge tears welled up in the old woman's eyes. "Oh, Kip, my baby. My poor little child."

"Don't worry. I'm going to get him back for you." Those words fell so easily out of my mouth. I hoped I'd find it just as easy to make them come true.

She blinked. "Why are you sounding so ... I don't know, so different, Sid?"

"That's the first thing I need to come clean with you about." My palms grew moist. I was about to give her my complete trust. And that's never an easy thing. Still gazing into her eyes, I confessed, "My name isn't Sid Bean."

Staring back at me, Sarah's filmy eyes were enormous, and she sounded like a lost little girl. "It's not?"

"No. It's not. It's Joe Box. I'm a private investigator."

Now she looked totally bewildered. "Investigator? I don't—"

"Shh." I gave her what I hoped was a reassuring look. "Wait. Just let me tell it. Tell you why I'm here. Then you can talk, and maybe fill in the gaps about this town."

She nodded, plainly still unnerved. "All right. But then please, you must get Kip."

"I will." With that I dove in, hoping she wouldn't be calling my buddy Cyrus Tate as soon as I left. If so, I'd be signing my own death warrant with my words.

♦ ◊ ♦

Starting with Morris Chalafant's visit to my office two weeks before, right up until my run-in with Chief Stryker last night, the telling of it took a lot less time than I thought it would. Fifteen minutes later, and I was done. Strangely, during my speech nobody from the nurse's station came in to chase me out. Maybe Hilda the Battle-ax had forgotten me. Or maybe she was on break. Stranger yet, the more I talked, the better Sarah looked.

But when she spoke at last, her words surprised me. "You poor man."

"Poor man? Now I'm the one that doesn't get it."

She ignored that. "Morris Lester Chalafant. I wondered how deep he was in all this. Cy, of course, we already knew about."

I raised my eyebrows. "We?"

"We. The three of us. Bud Spencer. Marko Pankowski. And me."

Huh? Bud Spencer? And *Pankowski?* "But what—"

Maddeningly, before I had the chance to get any more out, the door swung wide, admitting a swaggering Doogie Howser Junior. I'm not kidding. The guy looked like he wasn't even within spitting distance of puberty yet. I took him to be a doctor, until I noticed he was wearing hospital greens, and noticed the initials RN on his ID badge. I stood. Doogie tried to make up for his wet-behind-the-ears appearance with a harsh look. "Sir? Are you a relative?"

It was tough not to laugh at his Beaver Cleaver voice. "I didn't know I had to be," I answered, as straight-faced as a deacon.

Before the guy could reply, Sarah jumped in. "Nurse Boudine, this is my cousin Albert. He just got here, and we're discussing some family business. Could we have some privacy, please?"

"You can have all the privacy you want after I take your vitals."

"Vitals," Sarah said. "At my age, it always comes down to that, doesn't it?" She tried sounding reasonable. "Listen, my cousin can't stay long. Come back later. Then you can take vitals to your heart's content."

Boudine was holding the metal clipboard out like a beggar with a tin cup. "But, my chart—"

"Can be completed later," Sarah finished up, and she softened her words even more. "Please, nurse. This really is quite important. Humor an old woman."

Dropping his hand, Boudine set his jaw. "I'm sorry, I can't. Rules."

At that, Sarah caved. "Oh, all right," she sighed, giving me a look. "But please hurry."

I guess Boudine hurried. I don't know how long taking vitals is supposed to take. But five minutes later he was done and had hung his stethoscope rakishly back around his neck.

As he scribbled his notes on her chart, Sarah's words to him were arch. "Neatly done. But the next time, please warm up that instrument before you use it on me. Warm your hands as well. You're a cold young man."

Stung by her rebuke, Boudine pulled himself up to his full height of five foot three. "I'll return in one hour." Turning on his heel, he yanked the door open and left.

I waited until I was sure he was gone, and then I looked down on the old banged-up lady in the bed. "Albert?"

"It just came to me. And I got rid of that undertaker in short order, didn't I?"

"As my Granny would say, Sarah Poole, you got grit."

She smiled weakly. "I've been told that before. A long time ago."

My lighthearted banter faded. "A couple of minutes ago, you'd started to tell me about you and Bud and Marko. You also called me a 'poor man.' Words like that tend to get a guy's attention. What exactly did you mean?"

"I mean this whole thing goes deeper than you could imagine," Sarah said. "And now I've gone and involved Kip in it." Her voice grew rough. "He's my life, Joe. You have to get him back. You *have* to. He's all I have left. You've come clean with me." Sarah's voice was cracking with strain. "And if you're to have any chance at all of getting my grandson back, I need to do the same."

I waited. She'd made the odds of my success sound pretty bleak. But what Sarah said next blew my conceptions of her, the case, and the entire town, clear out of the water.

"My name hasn't always been Sarah Poole." It seemed she was drawing deep on a well of strength I didn't know she had. "You see, back in the fifties I was an actress. In the movies."

An actress? Along with being a fan of classic jazz, I've been a movie buff for as long as I can remember. I've seen a ton of them, from blockbusters to grade-Z turkeys that should have been left on the cutting room floor. I'd never seen her in anything.

She must have seen my puzzled look, because she continued. "My screen name was Selena Shock."

Selena Shock? For sure I would have remembered an off-the-wall handle like that. Nope. I was drawing a blank.

Noting my confusion, Sarah's countenance carried eight kinds of embarrassment. "I don't blame you for not recognizing me. The years haven't been kind. As Selena Shock I made ... stag films."

Country boy to the core, I felt my face redden, like I was still twelve. Stag films. That explained why I'd never heard of her. That's what movie porn was called back then.

But surely I'd misunderstood her. Still stunned, I sat back down. "Stag films?"

She choked. "Do I have to spell it out?"

No. She didn't. "We all have pasts, Sarah. Things we'd rather forget. You. Me. Everybody. And it's called 'past' for a reason. It's gone." I paused. "If you want it to be." That was the truth. I was Exhibit A.

"You're wrong, Joe." She sounded bleak. "It's not gone."

In her condition, I wasn't about to argue with her, so I let her go on.

"A long time ago, I was christened Sarah Ann Poole, in Madisonville, Wisconsin." Sarah was speaking in a monotone, staring straight ahead, like she was making a demo tape for the History Channel.

Totally at a loss, I said, "I hear Madisonville's a nice town."

"It is. Like a lot of kids, I wanted to be an actress as far back as I could remember. Unlike them, I took the plunge. As soon as I graduated high school, I took what savings I had and hopped a bus to Los Angeles."

I pretty much knew where the rest of this was headed. Sarah didn't disappoint.

She related the poverty she endured, the bit parts and walk-ons that barely kept her alive. It was at her lowest point, when she was seriously considering bagging her dream and going home, that fate stepped in. That was the day she answered an open casting-call ad she saw in the back of a discarded *L.A. Times*. The next morning, bright and early, she showed up at the door of a rickety movie studio on lower Sepulveda Boulevard, along with a couple of dozen other hopeful small-town kids.

Sarah wasn't stupid. Right out of the gate she realized this wasn't going to be legit work. The studio chief, an oily, cigar-chomping guy by the name of Fernandez, made it plain he was looking for pliable men and women who needed some quick cash. A few of the hopefuls read between the lines. Realizing they weren't up for that, they left. But a disappointing number of them, including Sarah, stayed behind for a "screen test."

"It was about like you'd imagine, Joe." Sarah was failing to keep the shame out of her voice. "Even as I rutted on the floor with one of Fernandez's cameramen, I kept telling myself, 'I'll only have to do this for a while, until I get my break.'"

"Which never came," I said gently.

"Never," she replied shakily. With a will her voice grew strong again. "After a few weeks of working for him, Fernandez was the one who came up with my screen name."

Give the guy credit. I had to admit Selena Shock was forceful and to the point.

"We all had them in those days," Sarah was saying. "The films we did were silent. Shot in crude color in eight millimeter, sometimes in sixteen. Finished in a day, and then distributed to grind houses across the country. Who knows, maybe even other countries."

My mind flashed back to Tate's VE pods I'd seen on the fifth floor of PornUtopia. The technology now was newer, but the audience was largely unchanged.

"I sold my soul, if I ever had one, for porn." Sarah's voice was full of shameful regret. "After a while, I just grew numb with it. I was a cog in the machine, cranking out product. And my dreams died. But unlike most of the others I knew, I didn't sink my pay into drugs or liquor. I knew my looks wouldn't last forever, so I became Fernandez's partner."

That drew me up short. "His partner?"

Her laugh was bleak. "Funny, isn't it? The same industry that had killed my dreams, I now was helping to kill the dreams of others."

"Funny" wasn't the word I would have used. But I didn't say anything. Sarah went on to tell of how the money started rolling in. So much cash in fact that, ten years later, she bought out Fernandez's interest. That's when she really started to make it hand-over-fist. By the midsixties her porn company profits had made her a millionaire. And that's about the time she launched the career of one Mason Kilbride.

"Wait a minute." I wasn't sure I'd heard her right. "*The* Mason Kilbride? Are you saying the good pastor of Sunnyvale Community Church was once a *porn star?*"

"The screen name I gave him was Randy Riggs. Cute, huh?"

Cute, no. Kilbride had struck me as a weirdo that first day I'd met him, but I'd just written him off as some kind of a kook. A crackpot, a fallen, would-be man of God. Now she was telling me I'd pegged him completely wrong. He was a magnitude beyond that.

Sarah's demeanor carried more guilt than a human should have to bear. "I'd met Mason as a twenty-something, good-looking hunk, bussing tables at the Brown Derby. The original one, on Wilshire Drive in Hollywood. One thing led to another, and soon he was making movies for me."

I wouldn't have paid ten dollars to think there was such a dark area to her life.

And that's when her story got even worse.

30

*F*or the next few minutes Sarah told all the dirty details of her business, and lurid they were. I won't bore you with them. She went on to say how she'd met Cyrus Tate, a competitor, at a gala event for porn awards. I didn't even know there was such a thing, but she assured me there was. Tate told her of his grandiose plans to build the world's first porn superstore. At Mason Kilbride's suggestion, he'd decided to build it just outside of Sunnyvale.

"Why Sunnyvale?" I asked.

"Mason was born not too far from here, over in Peebles. When he retired from acting, he came back, figuring no one around here would remember him. He was right. He got himself a mail-order degree and became a pastor. Just for laughs and easy money."

"Yeah. Real funny."

"He encouraged me to move here too. I'd already sold my movie and magazine businesses and wanted someplace calm and quiet to spend my final years. So I did."

Calm and quiet? Sunnyvale? Not if Tate had his way.

Sarah went on. "Mason had heard about Cy's plans and suggested this place to him as a possible site because it was close to both a major city, Cincinnati, and an international airport. Cy's people did a demographic study and found that to be true. But in the end he put it here for his own reasons."

I had a pretty good idea of what those reasons were. Tate putting up his porn palace in the heart of the Midwest was the ultimate slap in the face to his probably long-dead father. And to the traditional pastoral values his dad had betrayed.

The porn king proved to be a good salesman, and Sarah ended up sinking a sizable chunk of her money into his vision. Plans for the facility were drawn up, and slowly and surely the blight that would come to be known as PornUtopia began taking shape.

During this time Sarah injected more cash into Tate's enterprise when he needed it. She even told me how her own illegitimate son Ryan—she'd lied, she'd never been married—got a job as a cameraman in LA for Tate's films. His wife, Crystal, did the makeup. Kip, their only child, remained blissfully unaware of how they kept him in formula. Those three faces, she told me, were the ones in the second picture up on her mantel.

And then, five years ago, to his horror but not great surprise, Ryan discovered he'd contracted AIDS. Not willing to face a slow death, he opted for a quicker one, taking a vial of sleeping pills. The LA cops found him, dead in his Corvette, high up along the Pacific Coast Highway. The same day Crystal, knowing she was also infected, blew her brains out in their garage. Baby Kip, miraculously clean, was left an orphan.

And people say porn is victimless.

"With the deaths of my son and his wife, I'd had it," Sarah sighed wearily. "To my thinking, Sunnyvale was just the place for me to try to give Kip some kind of a life."

"But that doesn't make any sense. You knew Tate was putting up his smut temple right outside of town. With a whole country full of nice places for you to raise the boy, you picked here. Why?"

"I was torn." Again tears were welling in Sarah's eyes. "For nearly fifty years porn had been my life. I'd put a ton of money into Cy's venture. I thought that by being close to it, I could gauge if he was making a go of it. And I thought that since I'd gone back to my original name when I moved here, I could regain a part of the girlhood innocence I'd left in Wisconsin. Mistakenly I believed raising Kip here would help."

"And you found out the tentacles didn't come loose as easily as you'd hoped."

She stared at a spot on the wall past my shoulder. "Not even a little."

Lord above. She sounded so *hollow.*

"I tried to reinvent myself as a genteel innkeeper." Sarah sadly gazed out the window. "Even to the point of outfitting my home in an older style." Looking back at me, her voice grew impassioned. "I wanted a normal life for Kip. Something pure and clean. Something his father, my son Ryan, hadn't known. Can't you see that?"

"Sure I can. I'm not the enemy here. You know that." She buried her face in her hands, totally lost in her grief. I went on, "So when did the wheels finally fall off?"

Her words were haunted. "A few months ago. June fifteenth. I'll never forget the night. Cyrus had called an emergency meeting of his investors."

"Investors," I interrupted. "Who are they?"

"Myself. Mason, of course. Evan Talbott, the mayor. Chief Paul Stryker. That's it."

That struck me as a pretty small circle, and I told her so.

"I know," Sarah said. "Cyrus wanted it that way. Mason and I were the majority investors. Paul and Evan came in on pocket change and became his willing puppets. Cyrus told me months earlier he'd mainly brought them in to buy their silence."

Now we were getting to it. "Silence about what?"

Again, the old woman's voice grew guarded. "About what was really going on at PornUtopia."

"You mean the pods."

Her eyes widened in surprise. "You know about those?"

"I saw them. I can be a pretty good sneak when I need to be."

"That's what the meeting was about. Cyrus told the four of us the pods were malfunctioning, and he needed us all to kick in more cash to work out the problem."

"How did the others take that?"

"Not well. Mason was agreeable, but Paul and Evan balked, even though their contribution wouldn't have been a tenth what mine and Mason's was." Sarah's laugh was grim. "But Cyrus Tate is nothing if not persuasive. He kept pressuring them, saying how much money could be made from the pods. At last, they gave in."

"But not you."

"No. I told Cyrus I'd think about it. Something about the way he was acting … it scared me. I realized I was having second thoughts about the whole thing."

"And that's when he started amping up the pressure on you to toe the line."

"It was like he was possessed. His coercion turned into threats. Vague. But they were threats all the same."

"I think I can figure the rest. Tate became more and more demanding. Finally he started threatening the boy if you didn't ante up."

"The day before you arrived, we had a terrible argument about it. I turned Cy's threats back at him. I said if he harmed one hair on Kip's head, I'd see him in hell."

I grinned at her. "Good for you."

"Not so good. Because I'm in here, and Kip's gone. I'd say Cy made good on his threat."

"How *did* that happen to you anyway?"

"I was in the basement, putting in some laundry, when I heard Kip yelling in the backyard."

"What was he yelling?"

"I couldn't make it out. I went over to the basement window, thinking he was most likely fighting with this neighbor boy again. They were always getting into it."

I tried not to smile. Kip sounded just like me at his age.

Sarah's tone darkened. "I wish a fight was all it had been. But it wasn't. It was Cy's bodyguard Candi. She had Kip by the shoulder, pulling him along. He was twisting and crying. Calling for me to help." She gulped. "And for you."

My fists knotted up of their own accord. Cindi and Candi, the

Bobbsey Twins from Gehenna. I'd known they were bad news from the start.

Sarah was still speaking. "I ran up the steps to stop it. And that's when someone slammed the basement door in my face. I lost my balance and fell all the way down."

What brave thugs Tate employed, abusing old women and children.

"And of course Kip couldn't get away from Candi," Sarah went on. "She being a man."

That one stopped me completely. "Who's a man?"

"Candi." Sarah spoke as if it was common knowledge. "She and Cindi both are men. Or they were, before their surgeries."

"Uh, they are? I mean, they were?" My ears were burning. I felt like the biggest rube in six states.

"Of course. Couldn't you tell?" Before I could answer, Sarah said, "No, of course you couldn't tell. The clinic they used was good, to make that dramatic of a change."

Change? What, like butterflies after their metamorphosis? I doubted that.

She went on. "I'm telling you this, because it may be important in helping get Kip back. Cindi and Candi are what are known as TGs, or transgenders. They're women who started out life as men, before they were chemically and surgically altered."

I'd heard of such people, but had never met any. "And you know this how?"

"I'd met them in LA, when I still had my business. They made special movies for Cyrus. You'd be shocked at the strength of the market for TG sex romps."

After my experiences in this town, I doubted I'd ever be shocked by anything, ever again. No wonder I'd felt there was something off about those two. And how.

"Later Cyrus decided to have them take martial arts and firearms training," Sarah was saying. "He felt they'd be more exotic as bodyguards than as actresses."

Exotic. I could see Tate putting a premium on that.

"It's easy to spot a TG if you know what to look for," Sarah said, holding up her hands. As she did, I frowned. They appeared to be shaking. "Th-these, for instance."

"Their hands?"

"A man almost always has bigger and bonier hands than a woman does. Surgery can't fix that. Neither can it fix this." Sarah was pointing at her wrinkled throat, the shaking growing worse. The pink color now was leaching from her face. Obviously the painkiller's effects were lessening. We were running out of time.

Still I pressed her. "The Adam's apple." I was starting to see it now.

She gulped. "A surgeon, a *good* surgeon, may be able to carve it back. Just a little. But a man's voice box will always be bigger than a woman's."

"Giving us deeper voices," I finished. So that's why Cindi had sounded so weird to me that day at the employment office.

"That's right. It—" Suddenly Sarah's eyes grew wide, and she pointed her chin at the ceiling, hissing in pain. "Oh, no. The stuff they ... gave me is wearing off quicker ... than I hoped." The shaking grew worse. "I'm sorry ..."

"Let me call Boudine." I reached for the buzzer.

Sarah placed a clawlike hand over mine, her grip surprisingly strong as she gasped her words in fragmented sentences. "That ... won't do any good. I can't get another one ... until later." She'd told me the same thing just a few minutes ago. But still it was hard, watching her writhe in agony. A few seconds more passed. Finally I couldn't take it anymore.

"I'm getting the nurse," I insisted, picking up the buzzer and giving it a squeeze.

"No." Her gasp was feeble. "I'm ... not finished. Marko ... and Bud ... they—"

"Yes you are."

Right then the door opened, and Boudine bustled in. "Mrs. Poole? You rang?"

"I did," I said. "She's torn up here. She needs another shot."

"But—"

I held up a hand. "I know. She's not supposed to have another one yet." I looked down at the tormented old woman and then back up at the nurse. "She's really hurting here. Just do what you can for her. OK?"

His expression softened. "Let me get Dr. Callahan. We'll see what he says."

"Thanks." Again I turned to her, not sure if she could understand what I was saying. I bent low and said it anyway. "I'm going to get Kip back for you, Sarah. I promise." Pushing past Boudine, I left him to it.

As I took the elevator down, my brain was doing loops. Virtual reality pods. Child porn. Transgender bodyguards. Murder. Why hadn't I just been an auto mechanic?

31

A few minutes later found me pushing the door to Bud's diner wide. Since it was now midmorning, the crowd in here was sparse. That was good. The fewer ears, the better.

Bud was wiping down the counter and smiled when he saw me. "Sid. Top of the morning. Can I get you some coffee?"

"Could we talk somewhere?"

His smile faded as he saw my expression. "Sure."

Bud turned to the window behind him, which opened into the kitchen. Wendy was there, filling the saltshakers.

"Honey?" he said to her. "Could you bring Mr. Bean and me a couple of coffees? We'll be back in the office."

She looked up from her task, a huge grin splitting her thick features as she saw me. "Hi, Mr. Bean."

I returned it. "Hi yourself, Wendy. How are you?"

"I'm filling up the saltshakers." She held up the one in her hand. "I won't spill any of it either. See?"

"That's real good," Bud said. "Don't forget the coffee, OK?"

Tongue tucked into the corner of her mouth, Wendy resumed pouring the salt. "I won't, Dad."

I followed Bud through a door at the end of the counter, into a small, nondescript room. From the boxes stacked neatly inside, I saw it served both as an office and inventory space. It was a far cry from my brother Vincent's digs.

Bud took a seat behind a battered metal desk and pointed to a folding chair in front of it. "Have a seat."

I did, and the other man folded his good hand over his hook. "What's up?"

I was about to reply when the door opened, and Wendy shuffled in. She was carefully holding two steaming white mugs. "Here's your coffee, Dad."

"Thanks, hon." Bud took one, me the other.

I waited until the girl left, pulling the door shut behind her, before I spoke. "I just got back from seeing Sarah Poole over at the hospital."

"Yeah, I heard about her fall. How's she doing?"

"Hurting." I took a pull of coffee. Strong. "She had a lot to say though." Setting the mug down on the desk, I leaned back, gazing at the other man. "Before her meds wore off, she was just starting to tell me about the three of you."

He blinked. "The three of who?"

"Her and Marko. And you."

Bud's laugh was unconvincing. "Tell you about what?"

I glanced over my shoulder at the door and then back at him.

Ignoring his coffee, Bud wasn't laughing now. "You'd better tell me what's going on, Sid."

"Joe," I said.

"What?"

"It's not Sid Bean. It's Joe Box. And I'll be happy to tell you. Because you need to hear this. All of it."

◆ ◊ ◆

I must have been getting better at relating the story, because it only took me half the time that I'd spent on it with Sarah. As I finished, Bud was shaking his head.

"I ought to break your neck for pulling the wool over my eyes. And Wendy's. How come you didn't say who you were right from the start?"

"I didn't know a soul in town. What would you have done, if you were me?"

"I wouldn't have set foot in Sunnyvale in the first place." He dry-washed his face. "Man. You've really stepped into a nest of hornets here, haven't you?"

"Hornets don't bother me. Guys like Tate do."

The other man's chuckle was grim. "Brother, you don't know the half of it."

"Probably not," I allowed, pulling out the wet mouth appliances and sticking them in my jeans. "Man, that's better." I rolled my tongue around, enjoying the space.

Bud looked more disgusted than surprised. "What was that?"

Wiping my hand on my pants leg I said, "Part of what's kept me alive in this town of yours. Up till now anyway. But getting back to Tate and his shenanigans. Let's just say I know enough. What I don't know is where you and Marko figure in."

Setting down his coffee mug, Bud leaned back in his chair, putting the point of his hook into a well-worn spot on the desk. He rocked his prosthesis back and forth a few times before he said, "I've told you already what my main problem with Tate and PornUtopia is. She's out in the kitchen now. Filling saltshakers."

"You've done a good job of keeping her safe from him and his kind."

"I hope that's good enough." Bud had stopped rocking his hook. "I keep dreaming that one day I'll slip up and find Wendy gone. Lost somewhere in Tate's operation." Lifting his prosthesis, he critically examined its business end. "I'll plant the pointy part of this in the dude's skull before that happens."

"OK. That's your beef with him. But what about Marko Pankowsky?"

"How much of this do you need to hear?"

I slipped off my glasses and laid them on the desk. "As much as you've got."

Bud picked them up, examining them for a moment before putting them back. "Fake too?" I nodded, and he went on. "Did you get them from the same outfit you got those nasty things you just jammed in your pocket?"

"Yep. This too." I indicated my mustache. "I'd rip it off and show you, but I'm not much into pain."

"Leave it," Bud said. "I started to say, I'll do anything, if it'll help stop Tate."

"Speaking of that, let's get back to Marko."

"We should. Because his deal with Tate is a lot worse than mine."

"What do you mean?"

"Marko's a widower, like me. And like me, he has a daughter." Bud held up his index finger. "Correction. *Had* a daughter. Ania."

Oh good. Just what I wanted to deal with. Another dead person. I harked back to my recurring dream, the one with the faces floating in the walls.

The other man looked at the floor and sighed. "Man, Ania was sure a pretty girl. The kid turned the head of every boy in town. A willowy blonde. A few years older than Wendy. Headstrong though. Always looking to stretch her wings."

"And always held back by Marko," I ventured.

Bud nodded. "The day Cyrus Tate pulled into Sunnyvale, that pretty much spelled the end for her. Tate had barely gotten settled in when he started building that mansion of his out on the highway. He said he was going to make it party central."

"I'm not surprised."

"He threw a wild one almost every night," Bud said. "Money was no object. Drugs, liquor, music by bands you've actually heard of. Tate's parties had it all. Somehow Ania caught his eye, and she wrangled herself an invitation. Marko told me she emptied her bank account to buy a fancy outfit in Cincinnati, and she arrived at the party dressed to the nines. When she got home later, a *lot* later, she told Marko she'd made a hit."

"I think with Cyrus Tate, anything in a dress would make a hit."

Bud scowled. "Or out of one. Anyway, the next morning over breakfast Ania and Marko got into it. Bad. She told him it was high time for her to make her own way. Without daddy's rules. Marko threatened to disown her, but it didn't make a dent. That same day Ania packed up what few things she had and moved in with Tate."

There was a sick familiarity to the story. It bore the same marks as the one told by Doris, Detective Pilley's secretary. And I had the feeling that, like her daughter Brandy, things had gone south for Ania too.

"Ania's leaving, especially like that, broke Marko's heart," Bud said. "He and I've been friends for years, right after we found out we'd both served in AirCav in Vietnam. Anyway, the day the girl left, Marko went bughouse. Crazy. He said he was going over to Tate's house that night and personally blow him away."

"You obviously talked him out of it."

"Yeah." Bud looked disgusted. "With the way Tate's people have been sizing up Wendy lately, I'm thinking I should have let him go ahead and do it."

"Stopping him was probably smart. Apex trains their guards to be pretty good shots. Marko would have gotten himself drilled coming across Tate's lawn. The guards would have just gone on record as saying it was a righteous shoot. Taking out a dangerous nut. In the eyes of the law, they'd be right."

Bud gave me a puzzled look, and I sipped some coffee. "I used to be a cop."

"A cop, huh? Too bad you couldn't take Stryker's place, so we could get a handle on things around here."

Take Stryker's place? Right.

Bud continued, "Killing Cyrus Tate was never far from Marko's mind, whether it was against the law or not. Especially with what ended up happening to Ania."

As I said before, I had the feeling I knew where this was going. But I asked anyway. "What happened?"

The other man paused a moment before answering. When he did, his tone was somber. "It was a couple of months ago. This past May tenth to be precise, around three thirty in the morning. Marko got an anonymous phone call. The caller said there'd been an accident, involving Ania, and that Marko should get out to Riverside Park right away."

Riverside Park. I knew that place. That's where I'd parked the Regal that day, to read the manual I'd hooked.

"Before Marko could ask them anything more, they hung up," Bud went on.

"Did he get a phone number on his caller ID?"

"Nothing showed up. It just read 'caller unknown,' and listed an eight-hundred number."

No doubt about it. Tate's people were good.

"Marko called me, frantic, and I met him out there." Bud seemed to be having trouble getting the rest of it out. "That's where we found Ania. She was dead. Nude. Lying face down, sprawled on top of one of the picnic tables."

"That had to have been rough."

"Rough isn't the word. Poor old Marko went completely ape." Bud's eyes were haunted. "I'd seen a lot of dead men in Vietnam, but never a woman. I believe I took it almost as hard as him. All I could see was Wendy lying there."

"What did she die of?" A hundred things came to mind.

"About what you'd think. The coroner said she'd OD'd on a mix of crystal meth and cocaine. The kids call them fireflies."

Drugs had topped my list. "Brother Cyrus had thrown another party, huh?"

"Like I said, he threw one almost every night. Marko and I were both convinced Ania had died at Tate's place and then been dumped in the park. Chief Stryker, of course, was no help. He gave the picnic area a quick once-over and said the evidence was 'inconclusive.'"

"Spoken like a true marionette. What did Tate have to say for himself?"

"Nothing. All he did was tone down his shindigs some. But I think he was going to do that anyway. PornUtopia was really starting to take shape by then, taking up more and more of his time, and he was giving fewer parties out at his mansion for that reason."

"So whose idea was it to have Marko get inside Tate's operation?"

"Both of us." Bud was finally getting to it. "Marko had been retired from General Electric out in Evendale for five years. He'd worked in maintenance there, ever since he got out of the service. A week before Ania's death, he'd seen a job listing in our paper for a supervisor at PornUtopia."

"If he was looking for part-time work, that should have suited him to a T."

"He wasn't looking for anything. As I said, he was retired, and happy. He'd seen the ad and shrugged it off. But later, after we'd buried Ania, he started looking at Tate's job listing as fate. As a way to avenge her death."

Fate. As good a name as any for it. "Revenge can have a nasty way of coming back to bite you."

"That's what I told him. Marko finally realized that killing the guy wouldn't bring his daughter back. But we both had the feeling there was more to that porn place than met the eye. We figured that with him on the inside, we could dig it out."

"Wait a minute. That doesn't make sense. Pankowsky isn't exactly a name you hear every day. Wouldn't Tate have connected Marko to Ania?"

"I doubt it. A few months before she left home, she'd started using the name Richter for everything. Spite, I guess. You know, as a way to get back at her dad. For him being so overprotective. It was her mom's maiden name, and the one Tate knew her by."

"So him getting a job there wasn't hard at all."

"Not even a little. We worked it out pretty good. One night, after the funeral, the two of us bought a case of cheapjack Mexican beer and drove up to the top of a high bluff not too far from here. We drank and planned the thing until dawn. With his experience, he was the obvious choice to go."

I took another sip of my coffee, which had cooled to room temperature. Setting down my mug, I said, "If you ask me, he's a pretty good actor. I had him pegged as one of Tate's hardcore faithful."

"Marko's hardcore all right. Hardcore in his hate for Tate and everything he stands for."

"Did he tell you about the pods up on the fifth floor?"

"Yeah." Bud curled his lip. "That has to be the sickest thing I've ever heard of."

"Not half as sick as what Tate's got stored away in that secret room."

"What secret room?"

Without really meaning to, I let a smirk cross my face. "Son of a gun. I can't believe it. For the first time in this case, I know something nobody else knows."

Bud motioned impatiently. "So out with it, Sid, or whatever your name is."

"Joe. I think I told you that." In as few words as I could, I told him about Tate's dealings in child porn. Bud blanched as I talked.

"God Almighty. I *knew* there was more to this. Somebody has to stop him."

"My thoughts exactly. The longer Kip stays missing, the less I like it."

"We gotta call the state police. Maybe even the FBI."

"You're right. We should. The problem with that is getting a warrant."

"A warrant?" Bud's eyebrows climbed his shiny head. "That won't work. Tate owns the county judge. He'd never issue one. Tate has to be stopped *now*."

"I can't argue with that. But as far as anyone on the outside knows, what Tate's doing at PornUtopia with those pods is legal. Twisted and perverse. But legal. Also you've heard the phrase, money talks and the other stuff walks?"

"Usually the other stuff is called something else."

"There's the hang-up," I said. "Cyrus Tate is a rich man involved in what looks like a perfectly legal venture. The cops and the Feds don't like cutting warrants on men like that. Not unless the proof is overpowering."

Bud stood. "So what are we waiting for? Let's go get it."

"Fine. I'm with you. But let's do this smart and not stupid." I checked my watch. "It's almost ten. Marko should just about be leaving for lunch. Call him. Tell him you need to meet him somewhere to talk."

"Should I tell him about you?"

"Let me do that."

Bud unconsciously glanced toward the door and the kitchen.

"Take it easy," I soothed. "She's going to be all right. Trust me."

I sure was making a lot of promises to varied and sundry people. I just hoped I'd live long enough to keep them.

32

*U*sing Bud's Ford Taurus—figuring the Regal would cause suspicion—we met Marko outside PornUtopia's front gate. That is, Bud did. I stayed slumped down in the passenger seat, trying to keep away from the prying eyes of the guards. Mr. Nine Millimeter and his partner were on duty this time of day, and I didn't feel like bracing them. Yet.

I cranked my head around. It felt like I had a croquet ball buried deep between my shoulder blades. For the last few nights my sleep had been bad. The nightmare about the faces in the wall competed with the one about the sinking ocean liner and my inability to reach my dead wife and son. On top of that, the tingling along my spine was now almost constant. One way or another, the end of this case was coming. And fast.

From my position I could make out the two of them talking: Bud waving his arms around, Marko slowly shaking his head. A couple of minutes later they came over and got in the car. Bud retook his place behind the wheel while Marko climbed in the back.

Slamming the door shut harder than necessary, Marko leaned over the front seat, his tone sarcastic. "Bud tells me it turns out you're some kinda mystery man, Bean."

"Box," I corrected as Bud put the car in gear. "And we can talk about this at the park."

"Oh good," the ex-DI said. "I can't wait."

Three minutes later we pulled into the gravel lot there and parked and got out. I looked up at the sky. It was still cloudy, as if it couldn't make up its mind to rain or not. Although the air was cold, it could have been worse. It could have been snowing.

Marko jammed his hands into his pockets, all our breaths blowing small plumes of fog in the air. I knew time had gotten away from me, that Halloween had come and gone while I'd been on this case. But I wasn't sure if today was November fourth or fifth.

At this hour of the morning, there was almost no traffic on the highway to yell over. Marko's words were clear. "All right, Box. I'm listening."

Like a salesman with a pitch, I started. I was finding the telling of it growing easier and faster each time. As I spoke, Marko's scowl deepened. I don't know if that was more at my story, or the fact that I'd removed the mustache and slipped off the fat suit belly as I'd talked.

"I *knew* Tate was hiding something worse than those pods up there," Bud exclaimed when I'd finished, pacing back and forth on the small rocks. "I *knew* it."

"Yeah, you knew it," Marko shot back. "So what do we do about it?"

That brought up a question of my own. "Are you saying you never realized the sink in the utility room on the fifth floor was fake? You, the maintenance chief?"

"That's exactly what I'm saying. Tate told me to only clean up there with that real mild stuff I keep on the main floor. I never had a reason to try the taps."

I guessed I believed him. I tossed the last of my disguise onto the Taurus's backseat. "I say we head back over to PornUtopia, go up on the fifth floor, and get the proof. If need be, I can show you how the catch works on that hidden door to get in the secret room."

Marko rocked his head. "That won't fly. That day you didn't show up for work, I fired your worthless butt. I can't very well get you back in now."

"Fine, then you do it."

"Can't." His tone was still flat. "Tate and Chalafant are both squirreled away up there doing who knows what, and probably will be the rest of the day."

"What about tonight then?"

"Maybe. But with that stunt you pulled the other night, showing up way after your shift was over, getting in there now is going to be ten times harder to do. Tate reamed me good for that."

I looked at Bud, and he lifted his shoulders. "So now what?" he asked.

"Let me think ..." I started walking away a few steps. And then something awful occurred to me, and I spun back around. "Wait a minute. What's the date?"

"The fifth," Marko replied. "Why?"

"Oh no ..." My spine was tingling so hard I thought my shirt was going to burst into flame. What was it Kip had said? *Do you like helicopters?* And Sarah had piped up, *The fifth of every month, just like clockwork, one flies over our house, low enough to rattle the crockery.*

"What's the matter, Joe?" Bud asked. "You look like you've seen a ghost."

I stared at them. "I know how he's doing it. I know how Tate's moving the children."

♦ ◊ ♦

We were back in the car, driving fast (as fast as we could, without Bud getting a ticket from one of Sunnyvale's finest) down Main Street toward the opposite side of town.

"Tell me again how you figured this out," Marko said from the backseat.

"I didn't figure anything. I feel it."

"Great. You feel it. You want to get out your crystal ball next? Or would reading tea leaves work better?"

"A crystal ball, no." Spying Evan Talbott's hardware store coming up on the right, I pointed. "But your buddy Talbott might have something just as good. Pull up there." Wheeling the Taurus into an empty slot a few spaces down, Bud parked the car and shut it off.

"*Now* what are you up to?" Marko asked pointedly.

Ignoring him, I reached in my back pocket for my wallet and pulled out a couple of hundreds. While Bud just stared, I handed them over.

Bewildered, he gingerly took the bills with his hook. "What're these for?"

"I can't take the chance of going inside there. Even with most of my disguise off, he still might recognize me. But you can."

"What have you got in mind?"

"Simple. When I first arrived in town, I drove out past Tate's mansion, just to see what's what. Right next to it, mostly shielded from the road by shrubs and trees, I saw a small guesthouse. Patrolled by dogs. Dobermans. I wasn't sure of that at first. But these past few days I've had some time on my hands. So after driving past it a few more times, I am now."

Bud made an I-don't-get-it face. "Yeah, so?"

"So it hit me. Why would a mansion as big as Tate's even *need* a guesthouse? Especially one patrolled by dogs? Unless its occupants weren't guests. But something just the opposite." I looked at the other two men. "Prisoners."

Marko paled, and Bud's voice thickened. "You're saying that's where he's keeping Kip."

I nodded. "It's the only thing that makes sense. Besides squeezing his investors to cover his cost overruns on PornUtopia, he needs to move some merchandise."

Marko looked bloodless. "You mean the boy. *He's* the merchandise."

I nodded, feeling like I was a million years old. "Sarah's the only one that didn't ante up, so Tate plans to get it from her another way. From the records I saw on the fifth floor, the going market rate for a sex slave these days is fifty large. Each."

"Man, this is *insane*," Bud muttered. I'd have bet anything he was seeing Wendy's face.

"Tate'll take every nickel he can get for Kip," I said. "And love every minute of it. And that's why I think he's going to be moving the boy from the guesthouse tonight."

"Why tonight?" Marko asked.

I quickly told them about Sarah's tale of a helicopter flying low over their house, late at night, on the fifth of every month. They'd heard them too. I guess the whole town had.

"Kip seemed excited about the prospect of seeing one," I finished. "Any little boy would." I went on, my voice darkened, "Tonight he'll find himself *on* one. Sold into the worst slavery imaginable, bound for God knows where. Along with who knows how many others Tate's got stashed away in that house."

Marko cocked his thumb at the hardware store. "OK. So what are we doing here, wasting time?"

"I'm hoping Talbott has a strong pair of field glasses for sale," I said.

Bud said, "Because without them there's no way we can get close enough to that guesthouse without tipping off the guards." Marko nodded in agreement, finally seeing it. As a former DI, he should.

"Sounds good," he said. "With a decent set of binocs, we can spot the bad guys before they spot us."

"Buy the best pair the guy has," I instructed Bud. "If two hundred bucks doesn't do it, I've got more."

Now Marko stared. "Just who the devil *are* you?"

"I'll be right back," Bud said, opening the door and getting out. We waited.

Ten minutes later he returned, holding a nondescript box, which he handed to me. "The cash you gave me was plenty. Evan said these are the best he had on hand. But he sure was nosy about it."

"How do you mean?" I asked.

"He knows darn well I'm not rich. The idea of me buying a brand-new two-hundred-dollar pair of binoculars just for grins got his radar up. Even if it did mean a nice sale for him. I told him they were for Wendy, for bird-watching. That calmed him down. I think. He knows I don't deny that girl anything if I can help it."

"What kind did you buy?"

"Steiner, eight by thirty, military-marine."

"Those'll work." I took the glasses out of the box. They were rubber-coated desert camo, with a good heft.

Putting them up to my eyes, I aimed them down the street and turned the focusing knob. Tate's employment agency sprung into clear, disgusting view.

What a sight.

Laying the binocs back in their box, I said, "Let's do it." Bud twisted the ignition key. The Ford's old engine turned over with a mean, butt-sprung growl, as if it was just as anxious to get this dirty business done as the rest of us. Bud fed it some gas, and we pulled away.

◆ ◊ ◆

Five minutes later Sunnyvale was behind us, and Tate's mansion was coming up.

"Go past it easy," Marko said. A true backseat driver.

"I've done this before," Bud retorted.

We cruised past the place. The guard manning the booth didn't even look up. After drifting down another hundred yards or so, Marko reached over the seat and tapped Bud on the shoulder. "Slow down. I think I see a spot."

Coming up on the right was a long, rutted gravel driveway. At the top, its peak toppled over at an impossible angle, was what was left of an old farmhouse. Bud pulled the Taurus into the drive and put it in park, and then we fixed our attention on the structure.

"That's the Rafferty place," Bud said. "It's been abandoned for years." It looked it. "Who owns it now?"

"The city took it for taxes after old Mrs. Rafferty died. With it being this close to Tate's place, I'd bet anything he bought it."

"Let's check it out."

Putting the car back in gear we slowly made our way up the drive. It circled on back around the farmhouse, which made it handy for us. Shutting off the engine, the three of us got out. I was pleased to find the car was completely blocked from the view of the highway.

"So far so good." Marko leaned in and took the binocs from their box on the seat. Hanging them around his neck, he said, "OK. I'm ready."

We turned right and began our reconnaissance, tramping through the high weeds toward Tate's place. At this time of the year the undergrowth was dry and crunchy, and Marko and Bud sounded like a herd of wildebeests coming through. AirCav pukes. What're you gonna do.

"Let's keep it as quiet as we can, guys," I said, and I used a phrase from Vietnam I knew they were intimately familiar with. "We're in Indian country now."

The other two men began mimicking the way I placed my feet, the way I'd been taught when I'd first arrived in-country. We kept moving, repeatedly checking the terrain every few seconds. Within another thirty yards the weeds had given way to a thick grove of winter-bare maples. The going was slower as we navigated our way around the trunks.

Another few minutes and I held up my hand, stopping. "We have to be getting close. Tate probably has fencing set up around his property line. Along with who knows what else. Let's not stumble into it and set off any alarms."

"Or get fried if he's running juice through it," Bud said.

"Yeah, that would be a bad thing too," I agreed.

Going much slower now, we started moving again. We didn't get far.

Another twenty feet, and there was the fence. It was wire mesh, six feet tall. With all my know-it-all yakkity-yak I'd almost run into it myself. It was dark brown, almost indistinguishable from the late-fall landscape. I held up a hand. The area might have been wired with motion detectors.

Through the fence were more trees. Beyond them, flat grassy terrain. Centered in that clearing I could make out a huge structure, looming. Tate's mansion. "There it is."

"Where's the guesthouse?" Like me, Marko had lowered his voice, as if he were afraid there might have been microphones stashed up in the branches. Who knew, there just might have been.

I paused to get my bearings. "Let's go left."

We did. Another fifteen feet down, the trees began thinning. A hundred feet away from the mansion, but still in the clearing, from this angle the guesthouse stood out plainly.

"I don't see any guards," Bud whispered. "Where're those dogs you mentioned?"

I didn't know. And that worried me.

Marko put the binoculars up to his eyes. Turning the focusing wheel, he muttered, "I don't see any dogs *or* guards. And if these things can't spot them, they ain't there."

"Give 'em here." Taking the glasses, I looked too.

The binocs were a honey, presenting a sharp, clear image with no prismatic distortion. Marko was right. If any guards or dogs were on station around the guesthouse, they couldn't have hidden from these. But there was nothing. I hoped we wouldn't turn around to find them right up on us, jaws slavering and hair bristling.

A second later that was answered when four black, unleashed Dobermans came trotting around from the back of the guesthouse. Part of the patrol, I guess.

Handing the glasses back to Marko, I squatted down, examining the fence critically without actually touching it. Apart from its camo color, it appeared to be plain chain-link, just the kind that Robert Frost had said made for good neighbors.

Spying something else, I looked closer. When the poet had made his famous comment, I don't think this was the kind of fence he had in mind. Across the top ran a thinner wire, with ceramic knobs bulging along it every foot. Bud had been right. This fence was hot. And if the size of those insulators was any indication, most likely real hot.

"What're those things?" Marko asked, reaching toward the barrier.

I slapped his hand away. "Don't. They're insulators. I grew up in a rural area. I know an electric fence when I see one." Pointing at the knobs, I said, "By the size of those, this thing must be carrying one whale of a load. If you don't believe me, touch it and see for yourself."

"No. I don't think I will."

"So how do we get past it?" Bud asked. "I'm not much into turning into a Toaster Treat."

Neither was I. "We don't get past it," I said. "We get under it."

◆ ◊ ◆

Forty-five minutes later the three of us were back in Bud's office, deep in strategy.

"I think we're agreed the dogs have to be taken care of first," I said.

"And I don't know about you two, but I'm not into killing innocent animals if we can avoid it."

I harked back to Noodles, and to the poisoner who'd almost planted him. With PornUtopia, we were dealing with another kind of poison. Slower. But just as deadly.

"How about this," Bud suggested. "When my wife was in the last stages of cancer, the doctors at the hospice in Ripley gave her some heavy-duty pain medication. Really strong stuff. After her death the law prevented them from taking any of it back, so I've got a lot that's never even been opened. I bet it's enough to put the dogs to sleep."

"How do we get it in them?" Marko asked.

Bud cocked his thumb over his shoulder. "Hamburger from the fridge."

"Sounds good to me," I said. "We'll mix up a batch of meatballs before we leave." I leaned over the table, folding my hands on it. "There's something we need to address here. And it's important."

Marko frowned. "What?"

"This. Tate's not about to let us just waltz in and take his meal ticket away from him. He's going to fight. And fight hard. I think Sarah was wrong when she said Tate's circle was small. With this child porn ring, he has to have some of the guards in on it."

"So we fight back." Bud's eyes were hot as he slammed his hook down on the table. "Nobody's taking Wendy from me. Nobody."

"And if he thinks I'm going to let him get away with what he did to my Ania, he'd better think again," Marko added darkly. "It's payback time. Way past."

"Tough talk," I said. "But when it hits the fan, and it surely will, let's make sure it's more than that."

"Not a problem on my end," Marko spat.

"Or mine," Bud added.

"We're gonna get bloody on this one." I was remembering Billy Barnicke, lying broken and dead in my arms. "And that's too freaking bad. But it's time to stop Tate. Stop him flat in his tracks. Remember the old phrase from 'Nam?" The others nodded and my voice grew rough. "Tonight, boys, we get some."

33

I checked the luminous dial on my watch. Nine p.m. It had been dark now for nearly three hours. Still no sign of the chopper. I'd called Sarge earlier, asking him to be ready to call Detective Pilley when I told him to. Pilley could take it from there with the state police.

Looking over at Bud and Marko lying prone on the dead leaves, it was hard not to smile. Like me, under their ebony parkas the two men were clad in sooty jeans, black work boots, and blacker sweatshirts. Under our coal-colored watch caps, our faces were smeared with dark blotchy camo paint. Second-rate ninjas are what we looked like. After the meeting had broken up at Bud's we'd stopped at the mercantile to buy these duds we were wearing.

We'd caught a break when it turned out Marko was a deer and turkey hunter, with all the trappings. He'd readily supplied the face paint, entrenching tool, electric socks, and Jon-E hand warmers when we'd stopped at his house after our shopping.

Under the cover of darkness, using the E-tool, Marko and I burrowed a wide opening under the fence. Considering the high voltage we were dealing with, we made double sure we dug the thing deep enough to clear it. With plenty of room to spare.

Because of his prosthesis Bud couldn't help us, so he'd kept an eye out for guards while Marko and I made like moles. The digging had gone fast, thanks in part to the edge Marko had put on the small folding shovel. I'd seen that done before; it was an old Special Forces trick from 'Nam. That sharpness turned the thing into a deadly slicing weapon.

Now we were done. And waiting. The air temperature on this still night was right at the freezing mark. But with our layers of clothing and the warmers jammed down our pants, we were relatively comfortable.

I'd taken the first three-hour watch, which was drawing to a close. I'd used some of that time to probe the other two about their spiritual health. Since there was a better than even chance none of us would make it past this night alive, I was curious.

Not surprisingly, neither man had considered his final destination for years. Marko said he'd frankly never thought much about it one way or the other. Bud blamed God for Wendy's condition and his wife's death. They seemed open though (as anybody is before an action), and we talked without rancor. I flatly told them Jesus was their only hope. At the end, they said they'd think about it. That's all I could ask for.

Using the binocs from my position with my back against the tree, legs stretched out in front of me, for what seemed the hundredth time I scanned the guesthouse and grounds. Owing to two big blue-white halogen spots mounted on each corner of the roof, the area was lit up like Broadway. Every few minutes the dogs would cross the light, sniffing the ground, ears pricked, before heading back into the dark. Other than that, zip.

"You're sure that chopper's coming tonight?" Bud whispered from where he lay, looking up into the icy blackness. The cloud cover over us was dense as a blanket.

"I'm sure." I stood, my knees creaking in protest. "I'm also done. Your turn."

With a sigh Bud exchanged places with me, Marko remaining as still as a stump. "You alive there?" I asked, giving him a light prod as I sat down next to him.

His reply was a soft grunt. "I'm alive. Just thinking about Ania."

I didn't answer. He appeared solid, but it would bother me greatly if Marko froze up when things turned interesting. As I settled myself, my hip struck the heavy duffel bag between him and me. Trying to lighten the mood I said, "Some pillow you brought."

"I hope Tate and his boys think so," the other man muttered. "I truly do."

He'd get no argument from me. That bag held our armory.

The last thing we'd done before we left Marko's house was to go on a tour of his gun collection. I know it would give any antigunners a case of the vapors, but the man owned quite a little arsenal: rifles and pistols and shotguns aplenty, all well maintained.

"You were the infantry grunt," he'd stated. "Tell us what we need to pack."

I tried answering him with a quip. "You're the hunter. Don't you know?"

His eyes went hooded and unreadable. "Outside of 'Nam, I've never hunted men."

I had. And wished I hadn't. "I brought along my Smith and Wesson .38. It's in the Regal's glove box. But that's only for close-in work. Let's see what we've got here."

For the next few minutes the three of us sorted through the collection. At the end Bud had foregone a long gun, saying that with his hook he couldn't guarantee his accuracy. Instead he'd chosen a Sig Sauer P226 pistol, sporting a .40-caliber S&W barrel.

Marko had chosen three weapons. The first two were long barrels: a twelve-gauge Remington Express slug gun, a real man-stopper, and an AR-15, which was essentially an M-16 that could only fire semi-auto. His third piece was an old standby, made famous for nearly a hundred years: a Colt Model 1911 .45-caliber handgun.

I'd opted for something nearly as prosaic. A Henry Big Boy .44 Magnum lever-action rifle. Plus my Smith, of course.

At the last second the turkey hunter remembered his old dog whistle. We needed something to call the Dobermans without alerting the guards. And as a final thought, we'd each taken a large hunting knife from his locker. Just in case.

Staring through the glasses at the guesthouse, Bud asked, "What time do you think we ought to throw the burger balls to the mutts?"

"Your guess is as good as mine. I've never drugged a dog. I have no idea how much time it takes to put one down." I turned to Marko. "You must have used dogs to hunt. What do you think?"

"Who knows? My dogs aren't as big as those beasts. From the amount of crushed-up pills Bud packed in each one, it shouldn't take long."

Pensively I said, "If Sarah was right, we should hear the chopper coming quite a ways off. As soon as we do, I say we toss the balls over the fence. That should give us two or three minutes anyway. If the dogs aren't completely knocked out by the time it arrives, they should at least be good and wobbly." The other two agreed. We went silent again, each alone with our thoughts in the darkness. Passing the time. Listening for the chopper.

At exactly 11:47 p.m., it came.

Hearing it first, I nudged Marko and Bud with my boot. "Show time."

They were instantly alert, peering up into the blackness. "Where?" Bud asked.

"Low. Out of the east."

"Yeah. I hear it now," the other man said. Marko nodded once.

Turning away from the noise, Bud took another look through the field glasses. "Uh-oh. We got some Apex guys coming out of the main house."

Just as expected. "How many?" I opened the duffel, pulling out a small plastic trash bag.

"I count six."

"How about the dogs?" Marko asked.

"They're just kind of running around aimlessly. Like they're excited." Bud pulled the binocs away and looked over at me. "I don't think the guards are paying much attention to them. Looks like they've been distracted by the slick."

Lifting out some meatballs, each the size of a small potato, I said, "Call 'em."

278

Marko put the ultrasonic whistle up to his mouth and blew. Instantly the dogs stopped their capering and as one looked toward the tree line. At us.

I held my breath. If just one guard got suspicious and followed the dogs' lead, this mission was over. We'd be lucky to escape with our skins.

But that wasn't the case. As the Apex boys began moving toward the guesthouse, the dogs started trotting our way.

"Let them get closer. Out of that ring of light and into the shadows," I said.

Bud was peering through the glasses once more. "Well. Looky who we've got. Tate and Chalafant just came out of the mansion." His smile was savage. "Along with those freaks, Cindi and Candi. And bringing up the rear is our good friend Chief Paul Stryker."

"Evan Talbott's not with him?" Marko asked. Like me, he had a meatball in each hand. The dogs were almost in range.

"Nope."

That made sense. Talbott was good for cash when he thought it was just going into making the VE pods work. Tate, though, needed Stryker to keep the authorities away from his child porn operation.

Marko looked at me. "Now?" he asked, and I nodded.

Tossing the meatballs in a high arc over the fence, they landed just where we hoped. In a flash the Dobermans were on them, gulping them down nearly whole. Just as fast Marko and I lobbed four more their way. These too were snapped up. The last four joined them, wolfed down by the dogs, and we looked at each other.

"Mutts were starved," Marko murmured.

"I guess they keep them lean and hungry, like yon Cassius," I said.

"Huh?" He obviously missed my reference to Shakespeare's play, *Julius Caesar.*

"Forget it." With the soul-shattering sound of the approaching helicopter nearly drowning out everything else, it was next to impossible to hear one another any longer. *Rattle the crockery,* indeed.

Reopening the duffel, I pulled out the guns. "Time to saddle up."

From the mansion's roof a couple of huge spots suddenly snapped on, illuminating the riverside helipad and grabbing our attention. The trees overhead were whipping back and forth in the monstrous downdraft, leaves and debris whirling everywhere, nearly blinding us. Just like when I'd been in-country. Some things never change. We raised our arms over our faces, protecting our eyes from the onslaught.

Into the circle of light the helicopter slowly descended, a *deus ex machina* from hell.

To our right, well within the shadows, two of the dogs were already prone on the grass, the other two shaking their heads in dizziness. Bud was right. The stuff was strong.

Wordlessly the three of us had taken off our parkas. By then the chopper had landed and was throttling down. The name of the game now was mobility. Not warmth. If we pulled this off, there'd be time enough later to get warm. If we didn't, it wouldn't matter. We'd never be warm again.

Not on this earth.

I tugged on my shoulder holster, settling the .38 deeper in the pocket. Holding the Henry Big Boy, I rocked the lever once, placing a .44 round in the receiver. That left nine more in the magazine. If that didn't do it, too bad. I hadn't brought any more.

Pulling out my cell, I flipped it open and punched in Sarge's number. He said hello, and I only grunted one word. "Now." Tucking it away, I looked up, breathing a heartfelt prayer. "Help us, Jesus." Then dropping down, I positioned myself to go under the fence.

The other two men had readied their weapons: Bud flipping off the safety on his Sig, Marko inserting his twenty-round clip into the AR-15. The Colt hung snug on his hip, the slug gun resting in its sling across his chest.

Pulling back on the AR's charging handle, he said, "This should go quick."

Something in the offhand way Marko said that drew my attention. "What do you mean?"

He returned my gaze. "I mean quite a while ago I filed the sear down on this thing. The day I buried my Ania." He was looking back toward the clearing. "Now it's full auto."

The baldness of that statement stopped me momentarily. "You know that's illegal. Right?"

"I'd sooner be judged by twelve than carried by six," he said simply.

"The chopper's on the pad," Bud broke in. "And Lord help us, it's a Bell JetRanger. Those things are *fast.*"

"Then we can't let him get away, can we?" I said over the machine's thrumming. Holding the Henry on my chest, I flipped over on my back. "Time to get after it, boys."

Adrenaline pumping, I scooted under the electrified fence, and then was up and back on my feet. Seconds later Bud and Marko were standing by my side, all of us still hidden in the trees.

I squinted. "The guesthouse door just opened. Here come the kids. Looks to be two guards herding them."

There were seven children. Kip was third in line, staggering along as if he'd been drugged. Or worse. Seeing him that way made my blood boil.

I was surprised to find that not all were little like him. At least two looked to be young teenagers. I didn't know if that was going to make what we were about to do easier or not. I guessed we'd find out soon enough. Silently we started toward the clearing.

We'd gone over the game plan regarding this moment for when it came. Obviously keeping the kids safe and out of any line of fire was paramount. The idea was simple. We'd come up behind everyone, guns bristling, and catch them all by surprise. Marko and I would disarm whoever needed it while Bud kept them covered. After that it would just be a matter of keeping the kids warm and dry while we waited for the state police.

Anyway, that was the idea. But Napoleon had said it nearly two centuries ago: "A battle plan never survives first contact with the enemy." I believe that's true.

Because less than a second later, our battle plan died.

"What the—!" Bud's eyes were staring, his voice filled with horror. "They've got *Wendy!*"

"*What?*" Marko and I looked where he was pointing. My blood temperature plummeted to zero. Things had just gotten personal. Last in line, and being shoved along by none other than our pal the Nine-Millimeter Man—AKA Shrunken Head—was a crying, disoriented Wendy Spencer.

How in heaven's name had they gotten her? They had to have snatched her on her way home from the diner, while her dad and Marko and I were shopping at the mercantile. The "why" of it though, I didn't know. Right then, it didn't matter.

"Son a of a—!" Bud was already starting to move when Marko and I grabbed him.

"Hold fast, you idiot!" Marko said frantically. "You want them to see us?"

Too late. The guards had turned, and one of them was pointing our way. We were close enough we didn't need the field glasses anymore; everyone's expression was well defined. Cyrus Alan Tate in particular did not look pleased. He was stabbing his finger our way, his screams garbled over the insane beating of the helicopter's rotor.

Mr. Nine Millimeter Man, grinning like a kid at the zoo, set his feet wide apart in the classic, bent-knee pose he'd seen on every TV cop show. Holding his gun two-handed, he cranked off a round.

And that's when everything went straight to hell.

34

The guy was a cruddy shot—all hat and no cattle, as the cowboys say—and the bullet went wide, ricocheting off a tree trunk. Hard on its heels a couple of more rounds came at us. One of them zinged over my head so close it sounded like an angry hornet buzzing past.

Brother, that noise took me back. A split second later a full fusillade from the rest of the guards flew our way.

Almost too late I yelled, "Take cover!"

Bud and Marko may not have been infantry like me, but they'd been under fire once or twice. They didn't need my instruction and wasted no time diving behind the trees.

"Don't hit the kids!" Bud hollered, just as an incoming round tore a huge hunk of bark off the tree he crouched behind.

Thankfully the kids looked to be out of the line of fire. At any rate, I couldn't see them anywhere. As soon as the shooting had started, the children, screaming in terror, had broken ranks and run off in all directions into the night. We'd round them up later, when this was over. I hoped.

Marko must have seen that same thing. He roared his words. "Clear field of fire!" Stepping out from behind the tree, he locked his AR-15 down on full-tilt boogie, spraying hot lead far and wide, his rounds cutting fiery trails of death through the dark.

One of the guards flew backward, his perforated chest gushing blood. Another one clutched his guts, cursing. Oh God. We'd started something now.

Well, in for a penny, in for a pound, as my Granny used to say. Time to rock 'n' roll.

I rose up, put the Henry to my shoulder, sighted my target, and pulled the trigger. The recoil from the big .44 kicked like a mule as the round rocketed from the muzzle. As a boy back in the Kentucky hills I'd been a pretty good shot. In the lean times that skill had put meat on our table. When I was sent to Vietnam, my marksmanship had saved my life more times than I could count. Later as a street cop too.

Even so, I never got used to killing people. My stomach rolled as I saw my bullet catch Mr. Nine-Millimeter Man right in the bridge of his nose, the top of his head vanishing in a spray of gray and crimson. I gagged. I should have figured Marko had put hollow-point shells in the rifle.

Puke later. Right now we had to save those kids.

The remaining guards had taken cover behind some boulders that had never been cleared when the mansion was built. They blazed away, and we blazed back. Something tugged hard at my side, the impact sending me sprawling. I felt warmth, then a burning. Struggling to my feet, I risked a glance. Just a graze. But jeez Louise, it hurt. Obviously the guards were hoping their superior numbers would drive us out of our cover. I wasn't surprised to see Cindi and Candi had joined them in throwing lead.

The only point in our favor was that all they were packing were handguns. With Marko's two long guns and my Henry, we had the range. If we could keep them pinned down in those rocks until the state police showed up, we might make it out of this yet.

Suddenly that equation changed. Now we were taking fire from a new direction. The chopper. With its engines throttled back to a slow mutter, the pilot was leaning out of his window with a pistol, viciously firing away at us. And why not? He was in this as deeply as the others. He had nothing to lose.

From that distance it was doubtful he'd be able to hit anything of consequence. Especially with a handgun. But I've learned never to take anything for granted. That proved itself as there was a wet smack, and I heard Bud scream in pain.

"You all right?" Marko hollered. What a stupid question.

There was a pause. Bud's reply was shaky. "I'm hit … my leg."

"Stay down," I called over the din. "We'll get you out."

"No." Even from where I was, I could hear him pull in a shuddering breath. "It's a through and through … I just … plugged it with my finger."

Tough as nails, that boy. That left Marko and me.

I saw the old DI eject a spent clip and slap in another one. Again he fired downrange at the remaining guards while I spun to my left and opened up with the Henry on the chopper. The gunfire from the cockpit instantly ceased. I didn't know if I'd gotten the pilot or if he was just reloading.

Now with the blades from the slick throttled down, I could make out the confused voices of the enemy. They were chattering, excited, yelling over one another. It was plain they'd never been in anything like this before. There didn't seem to be a leader.

And that's when I realized that Tate, Chalafant, and Stryker were gone.

Marko apparently was on the same wavelength. "Where are they?"

I just shrugged. How should I know? With the Apex guys leaderless, we wouldn't be presented with a better chance to get the kids. Using hand signals, I placed my finger on my chest, and then indicated the rocks. Pointing at Marko, I made a little let-your-fingers-do-the-walking-through-the-yellow-pages deal with my hand.

He understood, nodding once.

Leaning around the tree, I opened up with the Henry again, firing and cocking the lever and firing and cocking the lever and firing and cocking the lever, as fast as my hand could move.

I may have mentioned that those heavy .44 rounds packed some authority. With bullets ricocheting like hail off the rocks, the guards didn't dare lift their heads. Marko used that lull to break cover and quickly start moving to his left.

The roar from the last round I'd fired was still echoing down-river when the Henry's firing pin clicked on nothing. I'd run dry. I could have kicked myself for not having brought along any spare cartridges.

That just left my Smith. And as reliable as the .38 revolver was, it put me on the same footing as the Apex men. Thing was, there were more of them than there was of me. I hoped Marko was quick in find-ing the kids. Then we could all scoot out of here and let the staties clean up the mess.

The guards must have figured nothing more from the Henry was coming their way. They were right. Dropping the rifle on the ground, I pulled the Smith from its shoulder holster. I sure wished I'd hear something from Marko. Soon. I figured to give him another ten sec-onds. Then I'd make a break to the right and hope the other side would be too surprised to do anything about it.

It didn't take ten seconds. It only took four. Suddenly the AR-15 made its characteristic barking, along with an altogether different gun blasting back its reply. The sound was heavy and harsh, and although it made no sense, I knew it was a BAR. A Browning Automatic Rifle. Those things had torn up jack on the Pacific atolls back in World War II. Marko was now clearly outgunned. Caramba. Where had Tate's people gotten that weapon? More to the point, what kind of mess had Marko gotten himself into?

Whatever it was, it was over quick. Once more Marko's machine gun rattled, and I heard strangled cries. I knew I was asking for it myself, but I had to find out.

Taking a quick peek around the tree trunk I saw three bullet-riddled figures sprawled lifeless on the grass. The BAR was lying beside one of them. Lazy smoke curled up from its barrel, but that's not what caused me to gaze longer than I should have.

Two more guards were forever gone. And one, the person spread-eagled dead next to the BAR, finger still on the trigger, was none other than Cindi-the-freaking-bodyguard.

That was all the thinking I could do on it. Off in the distance came the sound of approaching sirens. A lot of them.

The next few things all seemed to happen at once.

From the chopper arose a clattering windup of the rotors, the engine rapidly building power. I saw Chalafant and Tate and Stryker and two other people make a break for it from behind the guesthouse. The fourth person looked to be dragging the fifth. It took a moment for me to understand. The one heading for the helicopter was Candi, and she had Wendy by the hair.

Instinctively I found myself running toward them like a moon-shiner with a revenuer on his tail, the wound in my side filed away under "later." The three remaining guards had the same goal, but I'm sure theirs was to grab some seats on the whirlybird.

From behind me I heard a curse and a gunshot. With that, one of the guards stumbled and rolled, dead as a hammer. Taking a quick glance, I saw who the shooter was.

Bud Spencer.

He was leaning against the guesthouse wall, his Sig held in a shaky hand. Bud's eyes were wild, and his leg was drenched in blood. With the shock from his wound, and the fact he'd used a handgun, there was no way he should have pulled off that shot. But he did. Sometimes it's better to be lucky than good.

Slumping to the ground, the gun slipped from his fingers. He was done fighting. I'd come back for him later. If there would be a later. Closing in on the chopper, I wasn't sure of anything. It still seemed a long way off. I was close enough now to hear Wendy's faint screams. Except for her, I had no idea where the other kids were.

I heard footsteps running beside me, and risked a look. It was Marko, knees pumping, carrying his big-butt Remington high.

"You see Bud get off that shot?" he panted as we pounded sod. I just nodded as I feinted right, Marko following.

By that time we were close enough to see that the situation had deteriorated. Chalafant, Tate, and Stryker were already inside the red and white JetRanger, frantically motioning to Candi. Over the big engine's roar I could make out Tate's words as he mouthed them. "Leave her."

Because Candi was nearer to us, it was easier to hear her terse reply. "No way! She's mine!"

We'd see about that. Marko and I poured on even more speed. We'd tightened the gap to less than thirty feet when some sixth sense must have warned Candi.

She whipped around, and I was surprised to see a big automatic filling her left hand, her right fist still tangled in Wendy's thin dark hair. Before either of us could dodge, she smoothly ripped off a shot, and Marko clutched his chest. Sheer momentum carried him another few feet before he dropped with finality facedown, like a sack of meal.

No time to grieve. I grabbed the Remington from his limp hand. The old turkey hunter had surely known my Smith was no match for Candi. The slug gun was. But a second later the game shifted again as Wendy's foot got entangled in a tree root. She went down hard, screaming in agony as her hair tore loose, leaving Candi with a handful of it.

The bodyguard threw the mess down, shrieking something unintelligible as she kicked Wendy hard in the ribs. Then she made her own dead run for the chopper.

I really couldn't afford to, but I holstered the Smith as I stopped to attend the child. Wendy was writhing on the ground, wailing like a banshee. Her hands were mashed tight against her right side, her scalp torn and bleeding.

The girl's terrified, pain-filled eyes looked up and found mine, not comprehending this deal at all. And who could blame her? Right here we had Cyrus Alan Tate's perverted world in microcosm. If the pain and degradation of pornography ever had a voice, hers was it.

That just left me now. Of the three of us who'd started this, Marko was most likely dead. Maybe Bud as well.

Standing there alone, sixty feet from the chopper, I saw it begin lifting off. I was losing them. Tate, Chalafant, Stryker, and now Candi were safe inside. A wide-eyed and jabbering guard hung from its skid, as the last one still on the ground frantically tried to yank him off. All the while the pilot wrestled with the controls, vainly trying to balance the ever-shifting weights, his huge machine screaming and bucking like the baddest, meanest bull in the rodeo.

And I was going to stop it? Right. Me against that thing. David against Goliath.

And then, incredibly, the peace that Angela had said would surely come, surely did. As I stood stock-still on that killing field, sweetness began settling on me like a mantle, like soothing oil running down. I wasn't alone, that Presence said. I never had been.

"No way you're leaving, Tate. No way." Methodically I put the slug gun up to my shoulder. Earlier I'd counted the shells Marko had used. Four. I knew he'd taken out the sportsman's plug, and the gun had held five. Computer brain that I am, that left just one.

And that was all right. One was all David had needed to bring down the giant on that ancient Middle Eastern battleground, all those years ago. One would do it again.

With steel in my eye and a prayer on my lips, I lined up the tip of the Remington's barrel with the JetRanger's engine housing. Exhaled my breath. And squeezed the trigger.

The blast and recoil were brutal, but not as brutal as what happened to that housing. With a blast of fire it blew apart, throwing pieces of itself as big as my hand fifteen feet out.

That should have been the end of it. It wasn't. The chopper should have dropped back to the helipad and died. It didn't.

From my time riding slicks in the jungles of Vietnam, I'd known that the Bell Company made tough machines. But that JetRanger gave a new meaning to the term.

Still less than a dozen feet off the ground, it made a hard, tilting cut to the left, the engine revving up with an almost cicadalike screech. Past the canopy, framed in the bright glare of the halogen spots, the pilot's face was pulled into a rictus, his eyes bulging. As he fought the useless controls, through the open door I could see the four passengers, Tate, Chalafant, Candi, and Stryker, thrown violently back.

The guard dangling from the slick had hung on just a second too long. Brutally the torque slung him off and straight onto the frozen spike of a long-dead, lightning-blasted oak, impaling him like a bug in a sixth-grade science-fair exhibit. Zowie. Give that man a Tums.

The last of the Apex men had wisely let go of his partner's legs when I'd fired and was still on his hands and knees on the ground.

For a moment it looked like the chopper was going to beat the odds and fly, as straining skyward, its nose lifted. That's when, still at altitude, and still slipping left, the spinning rotor blades encountered the unyielding trees.

It was like I'd been dropped into a blender. With a horrific shearing sound the chopper's blades broke into a dozen, a hundred, a thousand razor-sharp pieces, flying out in all directions in a deadly arc. Somehow, miraculously, not one touched me.

The last guard alive on the ground, the one who'd dropped safely off, wasn't so lucky as he clambered to his feet and tried to run. He hadn't even made it two steps when a piece of jagged steel as big as a pirate's cutlass windmilled into him at waist level. The wicked blade cut him in half as neatly as a cucumber, his blood spraying wide.

At that, his fate was better than the others still trapped inside the JetRanger when it plowed nose first into the ground and exploded.

Two days before my tour ended in Vietnam I'd seen a medevac slick, full of our wounded, take an RPG round through its tail rotor and spiral into the earth. If anything good had come of that crash, it was that all the men inside that slick had died on impact.

They were spared what I was seeing now. And hearing, as a blazing figure stumbled out of the broken doorway, its body sheathed in bright orange hellfire.

It couldn't have been the pilot; there was no way he could have made it out of the squashed cockpit. It had to have been one of the others. But I couldn't have told you which one if you'd threatened to toss me in there with them. The raw animal screams tearing from the person's throat as the figure staggered and capered and flailed were so high-pitched it could have been either sex. But whoever it was couldn't match the shrieks coming from inside the chopper.

Watching that, hearing that, I stood trembling, utterly unable to help. Not again. How many times in my life was I going to have to endure this? As a boy of nine I'd been on the scene when a house fire took the life of a childhood friend and her whole family. In Vietnam my platoon had called down an air strike on some murderous NVA regulars from a couple of patrolling F-4 Phantoms packed with nape. Nearly a year ago the serial killer I'd been after died a fiery death right in front of me. And now this.

Welcome to hell, folks.

The flames were so hot it didn't last long, for any of them. Aviation fuel is like that. And that's when I heard the sirens from the cop cars pulling into Tate's drive.

I couldn't be found here, not yet. Wendy had been located, and I'd pulled her out of harm's way, but Kip and the others were still who knew where. I'd promised Sarah I'd bring him back. And I'd do that very thing, the police and their probing notwithstanding.

I softly called his name. Nothing. I called louder. Zip.

From somewhere far back I heard a rough man's voice call out, "You there, stop! Police!"

Forget it, pal. I ran a few more feet without calling Kip. Neither he nor any of the others had answered yet. Maybe they couldn't. Maybe they weren't still around here at all. If so, I had a pretty good idea of where they were.

Ducking low and staying in the shadows, I managed to circle the approaching cops. But to their credit, the helicopter's blazing hulk would have grabbed anybody's attention. As I moved farther away into the dark I heard another man's voice say, "Let him go, Ed. He can't get far." The man's tone got worse. "Mother have mercy. Look at this. Bodies everywhere. And a crashed chopper to boot. Better call for some ladder units and EMTs. Plenty of each."

Mother have mercy indeed.

Another little bit of skulking found me coming up behind the guesthouse. Once in the Stygian gloom I slipped and almost went down on something nauseatingly squishy. Regaining my footing at the last second, I didn't bother trying to see what it was. No doubt some guard's blood. I'm sure he was long past minding me stepping in it.

The children coming back to this place made a sad sort of logic. They'd been held prisoner here, true, but they'd also been safe. Why not? As Tate's ledger had said, they were merchandise. And every storekeeper worth his salt knows the importance of keeping his shelf stock safe and ready for purchase.

Coming around to the front, I was glad to see the door was still hanging open. I went in low, the Smith back in my hand, hoping there wasn't a leftover guard hiding inside who'd be all too happy to blow my head off. But it was clean. I didn't dare flip on a light, not yet. Just in case some trigger-happy cop should see it and make me just as dead.

"Kip?" I whispered. Nothing. Moving from room to room, first the ground floor, then the second, I called his name. Silence. I was starting to get a sick feeling that I'd been wrong about this place. Although the guesthouse was blandly nice, in a woman's magazine sort of way, it looked more and more like it was all for show. With the pristine cream walls and un-sat-on ultramodern furniture, it seemed the place had never housed a living soul. Unless …

The basement. That had to be it.

Clenching my hand tighter around the Smith's grip, I made my way into the unused kitchen. I'm no architect, but from my experience, that's where most basement doors are found. I was right. Approaching the massive oak door in front of me, I felt my guts twist up in anger. There were no less than three solid locks on it. Unless Tate had been keeping Bigfoot stored down there, to me that seemed like overkill. He'd sure been scared spitless his little prisoners might have made a break for it. Given half a chance.

All three locks were opened, obviously done when the Apex guys had brought the kids up earlier. Putting the Smith in first, cautiously I pulled the door wider a few inches. I hadn't turned on a light since I'd come in. I didn't want to give a clear shot to any missed guard that might be lurking down there. I waited. Still nothing.

No, that wasn't quite right. Something. The muffled sobs of children crying.

Mouth dry, I softly called to him. "Kip? Are you down there?"

There was a pause, and then a tiny, hopeful voice spoke up. "M-mister Bean?"

Thank God. I flipped on the light, not caring much now if the cops came running or not. In the circle of light at the foot of the stairs, I could see Kip standing in a knot of kids.

Realizing they'd all seen enough guns for one night, I slipped the Smith into my shoulder holster before making my way down. As I reached them, only Kip was brave enough to come close. His eyes were lit up in joy. "I *knew* you'd come, Mr. Bean, I *knew* it—"

But then the joyous light left as he stopped and got a better look at me. He backed up then, his face pale as he began screaming. "Y-you're not Mr. Bean! Stay away from me! Stay away!"

What had Tate and his people *done* to these kids, to put so much fear into them? The others around him had picked up on Kip's fear. Their cries of terror joined with his turned the air heavy and sour.

"Yes I am, Kip," I said reassuringly, speaking up over the appalling din. "It's kind of a game. I look a mite different now, don't I?"

He didn't answer, his eyes wide as he pressed himself against the wall.

"Speaking of games, we still need to play some baseball, don't we?" I nattered on. "Before it gets much colder. You remember us talking about that at your Grandma's house? Right?" I was babbling, but the crazy night seemed right for it. Whatever, it seemed to be working.

"I remember ..." Kip had stepped away from the wall, but still kept some distance. The noise from the others grew less as the gutsy little boy's face hardened. "If you're really him, what is it I don't like to eat?"

Don't like to *eat?* Brother. Don't like to— And then I remembered. "Beets. I hate 'em too. And your Grandma Sarah sure fixed a mess of them for us that night, didn't she?"

That did it. As Groucho put it, I'd "said the secret woid." With a sob Kip hurled himself onto my leg, grabbing it desperately. The tears were coming hard and fast from him, and as I looked up, I found myself surrounded by children. All weeping in relief.

The six of them, three racially mixed boys and three girls, ranged from Kip's age who appeared to be the youngest—to a girl of thirteen or so. Wendy, of course, was still on the grounds somewhere. I prayed she was being looked after by the EMTs.

The kids clustered close. But not too close. Like skittish horses, it was as if they craved a friendly caress, but had had too many of the other kind. So although I wanted to, I didn't touch any of them except Kip. I was surprised to find them not too much worse for wear. They all appeared thin, but not overly so, and seemed relatively healthy.

Oddly, they all were wearing identical outfits, white cotton trousers with matching long-sleeved shirts. On their sockless feet were sandals. In the excitement I hadn't noticed any of that when we'd spotted them being herded out to the chopper. From their dress, it was clear that once Tate had gotten them aboard, their final destination was to have been somewhere tropical.

But Marko and Bud and I had stopped it.

Marko and Bud.... My chest felt hollow. I'd told them we would get bloody tonight. We had. Some bloodier than others.

I went to make a motion to the kids that we should all start heading upstairs, when something about the room caused me to stop. And stare.

Kip looked up from where he still clenched my leg. His face was wet and streaked with little boy grime. "What's the matter, Mr. Bean? How come you're looking funny?"

It was the room. This basement. But that was—again my mouth went dry.

It was the place from my nightmare.

The dank stone walls were identical. I had to look twice to make sure there were no shifting faces in them. Feeling the pressure on my leg, I glanced down, hoping it was still Kip, and not a morphing, scorpion-filled python. Nope, thank God. Just Kip.

He was still clinging to me as again I took in the room. In some ways, it was worse than the one in my dream. The dirt in here was worse, and screwed into the walls were big iron rings, obviously for restraint. Along with some other items I didn't have a clue about. In the far corner sagged a filthy, stained mattress. One guess as to what it was for.

One item in particular stood out. A thin, whiplike object tipped with a small bulbous protrusion, hanging on a tether from a hook. Without even knowing exactly how I knew, I was certain this thing, or one like it, was what had been used on Billy.

There would be plenty of time later to figure out what this room's main purpose was. Right now the number-one task was to get these kids out of it.

"Nothing's the matter, Kip," I said, wishing I meant it. I looked around at the others. "Y'all ready?" Silently they nodded. I nodded back. "Good. Let's go home."

With the kids lined up behind me like ducks, I'd just placed my foot on the first step when the basement door flung wide with a crash. Filling it was an older state trooper the approximate size of Montana. In his mitt was clutched a department-issued handgun. And it was pointed straight at my chest.

"Freeze!" the cop roared, just like in the movies.

He didn't have to ask me twice. I turned to stone.

35

Outside Angela's warm house, the November weather had turned blustery. The wail of the wind-hurled sleet against her windows sounded like the business end of a sandblaster, and in the corner Noodles looked up from his nap in alarm.

"Settle down, boy," I called from where I sat, at the head of the dining room table.

"Offer him some turkey," Sarge suggested from the opposite seat. "That always works with me." Next to him, his wife, Helen, snorted back a laugh.

"He won't eat it," Angela replied from my left. "Not to say Joe and I haven't tried."

"That's true." Picking up the bowl of mashed potatoes, I spooned a glop of them onto my plate. It was my third helping. But who was counting? This was Thanksgiving. Setting the bowl back down I went on, "Unless it's sweet breakfast cereal, or that nasty Kitten Kuddle junk, or the occasional odd squirrel, he won't touch it."

"Crazy feline," Sarge muttered, taking another huge bite of his drumstick.

He'd get no argument from me. These past couple of weeks I'd been in a pretty expansive mood altogether. Especially considering how things could have gone.

The big, unsmiling state trooper had hustled me into the back of his squad car, after first handing off Kip and the other kids to a bunch of EMTs. Tate's once palatial grounds now looked like the day after the circus had left. The area all around was trampled and torn by what looked to me like a hundred or more cops' feet. There were staties in the mix, county mounties, even a couple of Sunnyvale's finest, Drew and Farley, all vying for their moment in the sun. Because, let there be no mistake: The collapse of Tate's empire was Big News.

The troopers won the prize and took me to the closest barracks over in Ripley so they could get the full story. I didn't disappoint them. Once there, I told it all, starting with Chalafant's visit, right up until the time I was discovered in Tate's basement. Even as I spoke I knew it wouldn't be enough. Sure enough, before it was over I had to tell it twice more to some higher-ups.

The biggest surprise as I sat in that bright, stark room at 3:00 a.m. was the arrival of Detective Max Pilley. I didn't even bother asking him how he knew I was in on this. As a former cop, I can attest to the reality of the secret information network they share. But since I was still a suspect in Billy Barnicke's death, they'd brought him in as a courtesy. So I had to tell it yet again. Surprisingly, as I did I found him taking my side. Mostly.

Pilley told me of arriving at the Tate estate sometime after I'd already been led away. He'd seen the BAR lying on the ground next to Cindi. Being somewhat of a World War II buff, he'd realized how out of place it was. Inside the mansion, he'd found more combat memorabilia. It turned out Tate had a veritable arsenal in his basement, including other automatic weapons. Pilley said that while the staties continued to secure the place, he'd gone down in Tate's guesthouse basement, looking for more guns. Once there, he told me he found it as dungeonlike as I did.

But it was to be three days after I'd been released from custody and back home when I'd finally get the full story from him, the day he arrived in person at my office.

After I'd seated him and gotten us coffees, Pilley told the tale dispassionately, which made the horror of Tate's operation just that more real. He started with a report about the firefight's final body count. Thirteen. An unlucky number for all concerned.

The bad guy dead included the six rogue Apex guards, the chopper pilot, Cindi and Candi, Paul Stryker, Morris Chalafant, and lastly Cyrus Alan Tate. It turned out the person who'd come to that grisly, fiery end in front of me was Tate himself. I tried to decide how I felt about that. Nothing. Only dryness.

The good guy dead was just one. Marko Pankowsky. Poor Marko. I knew when he took that round to his chest from Candi's handgun he was a goner. But happily, Bud Spencer had survived, and Pilley said he and Wendy were being treated for their wounds in the same hospital where Sarah Poole had been treated.

When his questioning me that night at the barracks was done, Pilley had gone back to his home in Cincinnati. The next afternoon a couple of computer whizzes from the FBI geek squad were turned loose up on PornUtopia's fifth floor, given *carte blanche* to dig up whatever they could. They didn't disappoint.

First off, it turned out I'd been right about the sex-slave angle. It seemed Tate and Chalafant had been working hand in glove with an interstate ring of kidnappers, who kept them supplied with street kids or poor kids or any kids who otherwise wouldn't likely be missed. Or so the thinking went. After a child was snatched, his or her introduction to what would be an admittedly short life as a sex slave began right down in that guesthouse basement.

Tate had kept a meticulous diary of it all, no doubt influenced by the "Unknown" who'd penned *Juliette's Ecstasy*. Overconfident, he'd kept it right next to that fifth floor computer that housed his damning data. If I'd only turned my head a bit that night I was up there, I would have seen it too. In it he told of those who'd bagged "first rights" to the captives. Usually it was Tate himself, but sometimes Chalafant, and on occasion Chief Stryker. Only after the children's wills had been broken by leaving them chained up to the basement walls were they considered prime cut and ready for sale. Sometimes that breaking took hours. More often, it was days. After Tate and his pals had finished with them.

There was more to it, of course. A lot more. But I won't tell it. Your imagination has probably already filled in most of the gaps. Suffice it to say, between trafficking in child porn and handling sex slaves for the world market, old Cyrus had been doing all right for himself. His only headache had been those stupid virtual porn pods.

"The Feds say it's unlikely he would ever have gotten them to work correctly," Pilley told me. "Evidently there's a basic flaw in the programming codes. They pretty much lost me there. Whatever it is, it's sufficiently bad that the pods will probably never be anything other than experimental."

"Looks like Uncle Sammy got a good deal in unloading them on him," I said.

Pilley snorted. "Yeah. For once." Then he said something that drew me up short. "By the way, they found the murder weapon that killed your friend Barnicke."

I stared at him. I had the feeling I knew what it was. But I asked anyway. "What was it?"

"It's kind of a weird thing, found in the basement, where Tate and his pals had kept the kids. A skinny gizmo." Pilley stretched his hands eighteen inches apart. "Maybe yea long. Bendable, made out of hippo hide."

I'd been right. But the material threw me. "Did you say hippo hide?"

He nodded. "After the Feds were done, our forensics guys worked on it. They tell me dried hippo skin is an unusual substance. It's as flexible as leather, but almost as tough as Kevlar. The lead weight woven into the thing's tip is what clenched it. That, and the fact that it had traces of your friend's blood on it."

"I remember seeing it hanging on the wall. I had no idea what it was."

"A martial arts guy on the force recognized it right away when we took it in for analysis," Pilley explained. "It's called a *dugong*. From Indonesia. The cops over there use them for crowd control."

"I'll bet it works too."

"Oh yeah. It's a pretty versatile weapon. Flick it softly, and it just leaves a welt. But use it with force, especially with that lead weight sewn in the end, and you can beat a man to death without even raising a sweat."

"Exactly what was done to Billy."

"The prints we lifted off of it matched those of a couple of transgender actresses—and sometime prostitutes—from Los Angeles. Candi Birdwell and Cindi MacIntyre were what they called themselves out there. Their pre-op names were Carl and Chad. Both were found dead in that bloodbath at Tate's place. I may have mentioned that."

"It was a crazy night," was all I said.

"What we can't figure is why Barnicke let them in his house in the first place."

"Who knows? Maybe the two freaks showed up, said they remembered him from his work out at PornUtopia, and told him they liked him and wanted to party. As sex-crazy as Billy was, it wouldn't have taken much. However it played out, he paid for his stupidity with his life."

"There's just one last unsolved bit before we can wrap this up," Pilley said. "Back at the state police barracks, you mentioned your friend's dying words: 'the first two.'"

"I can help you out with that." Then I paused. "But you're going to find it hard to believe."

"After what I saw at PornUtopia, I can believe a lot."

"Let me start with this, Detective." I leaned forward. "Did you know that not only was Billy Barnicke an altar boy, he'd once seriously studied for the priesthood?"

Pilley's expression clouded. "As a practicing Catholic, I find that joke distasteful."

"It's not a joke. He really did. As a young guy, he even spent a year in seminary."

"What does that have to do with his last words?"

"Plenty. Before he gave up his religion and turned to hedonism, Billy studied the Bible. He told me one of his favorite things was biblical history. Especially studying the tribes that gave the Israelites such fits. The Canaanites, the Moabites, and the Ammonites."

"I still don't—"

"A lot of scholars think the Ammonites were the worst. They were into some seriously bent stuff, including placating their god by sacrificing their own children to him. The god's name was Molech."

"So what?"

"'The first two,'" I said. "Billy had given us the key, and we all missed it." The cop still appeared lost, so I said, "Consider the letters comprising Molech's name, taken in groups of two. MO–LE–CH." I gazed at him as I said the next with a rhythmic beat. "Morris. Lester. Chalafant."

Pilley's mouth fell open. "*What* did you say?"

"Of course, that's not the name he was born with. Chalafant's birth moniker was Eli Herman Stein."

"How do you know this?"

I picked up my mug of now cold coffee and took a sip. "After I'd been released from custody and was back home, I couldn't get Billy's last words out of my head. So I had a buddy of mine who owns an almost mini-Cray home computer run full backgrounds on all the principals. Buried in some old records he found Stein's beginnings. That's when I knew."

"His beginnings?"

I nodded. "It seemed Stein at one time had also been religious. Like Billy. But Stein was Jewish and was studying to be a rabbi. Somewhere along the line Stein—like Billy—lost his faith. But instead of turning to the bottle, he found satisfaction with a different kind of false god. Molech. That's when he changed his name. Obviously to honor him."

The cop was shaking his head. "Incredible."

"Not as incredible as this last part. It turns out the real brains behind Tate Enterprises was Chalafant himself."

"What? Seriously?"

"He did it as a way of securing children for his fantasies. Cyrus Tate was just as sick. But his face was only for show. Your hotshots must have missed it. It seems the two had met in college and realized they made the perfect team: Chalafant's brains and Tate's magic way of making money. Early on they decided that Chalafant would be much more effective as the power behind the throne, rather than the king himself. So Tate became the figurehead. But it was Morris Chalafant who was the one pulling the strings of that particular puppet."

I stopped talking then. Detective Pilley stared at the floor in silence as he digested all this. I didn't interrupt his meal.

At last he put his hands on his knees and stood. "You've given me a lot to think about, Mr. Box. When I return to the office, I plan to reopen Tate's file. In the light of what you've told me, there's probably a *lot* we've missed." He held out his hand, and we shook. "I owe you."

"And I'll collect," I grinned devilishly. "Someday."

That was ten days ago. Now I was enjoying Thanksgiving dinner with my three favorite people in the world. I told them Max Pilley had said the state police and the Feds were working closely with both Interpol and the Missing Children's Network. Happily most—but not all—of the kidnapped kids had been traced. In a matter of days their buyers would be facing some hard time, and the kids would be reunited with their loved ones ... those, that is, who had them. But getting safely back to their homes would be just the start. After that would come months, maybe years, of counseling and therapy to rid themselves of the lingering effects of their ordeal.

Speaking of ordeals, my nightmares had stopped at last, beginning with the first night I'd gotten home from Sunnyvale. Cyrus Alan Tate—the Cat—was well and truly skinned.

Pilley did say that Wendy Spencer was bouncing back better than most. Why, is anybody's guess. In his interview with her, he'd mentioned me, and told me she wanted to tell me thanks. And that she'd fix me a cheeseburger whenever I wanted it.

So it seemed the case was over. Kind of.

The past few days I'd been in a sort of funk. Some of the vets coming home from their tours in-country had suffered it. The shrinks had even given it a name. Post-traumatic stress syndrome. Maybe that was it. Or maybe it was just that the psychic stink from my time in Sunnyvale was going to take a while to dissipate.

Even Noodles had picked up on it. When I'd pulled up in the drive I saw him sitting in the front window, as if he'd been watching for me. But when I'd come in, he'd sniffed my clothes, and then looked toward the door. It was as if, along with me, he was expecting someone else. The rest of that day he'd hung close. Closer than even he usually did.

And then just yesterday he'd done the strangest thing. I'd come into my bedroom to find him on my bed, curled up on top of the picture Kip had drawn of the two of us. Stranger still, he was purring. Cats. Who can figure them?

I'd smiled. "You like that, huh? Me too. Good picture. Good kid." Noodles just closed his eyes and purred louder.

Anyway, that was then. And today was Thanksgiving. The day before, I'd taken a trip back out to Sunnyvale, to pay a call on Sarah and Kip, along with Bud and Wendy. Sarah was asleep, but I found Bud sitting in a wheelchair next to Wendy's bed. Both of them looked way better than they'd had any right to. Bud said it was due to God's mercy. It turned out that after he'd fired that last shot and had slumped to the ground, he'd realized he might not live to see his daughter again. And that was unacceptable. Right there on that frozen dirt, he'd taken the step and given his heart to Jesus. I just wished Marko had done the same. Who knows? Maybe he had.

Anyway, as the song says, today the weather outside was frightful, but in here, it was so delightful. In the soft glow of the candlelight, Angela looked like a vision. I know Sarge and Helen caught me staring at her. But I just couldn't help it.

A beautiful woman, good friends, excellent food, gracious surroundings ... I'd come a long way from the hills of eastern Kentucky. I was made for this.

And then my cell phone going off broke the spell.

"Oh, Joe," Angela scolded. "I thought you'd have that turned off. Especially today."

"I thought I had too," I replied, reaching for it. I'd make short work of this. Then I saw the number on the screen, and I frowned.

"Who is it?" Sarge asked.

I looked at him. "The Sunnyvale Convalescent Home."

"Well, answer it already," he said. "Maybe it's Sarah Poole, and she's calling to wish you a happy Thanksgiving."

"Right," I laughed. But I said hello anyway and began listening. By the looks the other three were giving me, my expression must have reflected my confusion. Because my end of the conversation consisted solely of two "uh-huhs" and one "I see." Two minutes later I ended it with, "See you then," and flipped the phone closed.

"Well? Was it Sarah? What did she want?" Angela asked.

"It was her. Poor gal sounded strange. Her voice was weak, but her words were plain enough. She asked me to drive back out there tomorrow. To visit a spell with her." I chuckled, even though it wasn't really funny. "She said she wants to ask me a favor."

"A *favor?*" Sarge's eyebrows went up. "You already broke up a sex-slave ring and got her grandson back. What more could the woman want?"

"You're not going, are you?" Helen asked.

I looked at Angela. She was smiling, but it was wry. She knows me so well.

"I'm going," I said, and I pointed at her. "And you're going with me."

"I wouldn't miss it," she grinned. "From all you've said, Sunnyvale sounds like a treat."

"Forget it being a treat. The woman just has me curious, that's all."

"You know curiosity killed the cat, don't you?" Sarge grunted.

Noodles looked up, eyes wide.

"Relax," I said. "We're not talking about you."

Cautiously he put his head back down on his paws. But his single ear twitched.

36

*P*ulling the Cougar into an empty slot in front of the Sunnyvale Convalescent Home, I parked, and Angela and I got out. The weather was still crummy, windy and cold. And unless I missed my guess, those fat-bellied clouds hanging just above our heads were jam-packed with the first snow of the season.

As we'd driven through the streets, to me the town had a battened-down, Leningrad appearance. And why not? For a while there it had occupied the attention of news agencies around the world. It looked a lot different in this gray light than it had the first day I came here. Hard to believe that had been less than a month ago.

We walked up the steps to the entrance, pushing the door open. But the person who greeted me wasn't Sarah Poole. It was Kip.

His face lit up, dispelling the gloom. "Mr. Bean! I mean, Mr. Box! Hi!"

"Hi yourself," I said, genuinely happy to see him. Maybe this trip wouldn't be a bust after all. I motioned to Angela. "Kip, say hello to Miss Swain."

"Hi, Miss Swain." The boy's nose crinkled up. "Miss Swain. That's hard to say."

"Not for much longer," Angela smiled. "One day soon it'll be Mrs. Box. And it's good to finally meet you."

Kip grinned again. "Mrs. *Box?* Does that mean you two are gonna get *married?*"

"It sure does," I said.

His smile grew. *"Gross!"*

About then I heard a querulous voice. "Kip? Who is it?"

"It's Mr. Box, Grandma," he yelled. "And some really pretty lady with a funny name. They're gonna get *married.*"

"Bring them back here, for heaven's sakes."

Kip grabbed each of our hands and began tugging us along around the corner. When we got there, I wasn't too surprised to find Sarah sitting in a wheelchair in a nearly deserted brightly painted sunroom, a red plaid blanket lying over her legs.

She held out a withered hand. Taking it, I tried to hide the expression on my face. Plainly put, she looked awful. It seemed breaking her pelvis had sent Sarah on a long downhill slide. Or maybe it was almost losing Kip that had done it. Either way she was drawn, gray, and worn-out. It was only then that I noticed a taller, well-dressed older man seated on the far side of the room, next to a young woman clad in hospital greens. They stood and walked over.

Sarah released my hand and took his. "Joe, I'd like you to meet an old friend. Brian Sutter. Brian is my attorney. And this is Cara Worthington, my nurse."

Attorney? Now what? Exchanging pleasantries, we all shook anyway. Realizing the ball was in my court, I introduced Angela to them, and then Sarah asked us all to have a seat.

"Me too, Grandma?" Kip asked.

"No, I want you to go with Miss Worthington," the old lady said.

"But I wanna stay in here."

"We'll send for you in a few minutes. Please, Kip." Sighing hard, he left with Cara.

Once he was out of earshot, Sarah dove right in. "Let me be blunt with you, Joe. About several things. First, don't let Kip's cheeriness fool you. He's been having terrible dreams about what was done to him. Every single night." I knew how that was. "Second, my bones aren't knitting the way they're supposed to. The doctors have said they might never be right again. Until they do, I'll be in this wheelchair. And that's not fair to Kip."

Angela glanced at me.

"I'm sorry to hear that," I said. And I was. I'd kind of expected the bad doctors' report, but had no idea what it had to do with me.

Sarah turned to Sutter. "Brian, show him."

The attorney reached into his briefcase, pulling out a manila folder. From it he withdrew a sheaf of legal papers, which he silently handed over to me.

I'd only gotten to the second paragraph when my mouth dropped open.

Angela frowned. "Joe? What is it? What's wrong?"

Looking up, I stared hard at Sarah. "Does this mean what I think? Do *you* mean it?"

"Every word," she nodded.

A frown creased Angela's brow. "Will somebody tell me what's going on?"

I turned to her, my words disbelieving. "Sarah wants me to adopt Kip."

"What?"

"Not adopt," Sarah said. "Only take temporary custody of him. Until I get better." A pained expression crossed her face. "If ever."

I stared at her. "What are you saying, Sarah?"

"I'm saying I may not come back from this. As a matter of fact, I have a strong feeling I won't. With my injuries, and my age, I'm a prime candidate for a stroke."

"Please, Mrs. Poole, don't say that," Angela said, touching her hand.

Sarah smiled, gripping Angela's hand in return. "It's all right, dear. You know, they have the most wonderful chaplain here. A minister from the Baptist church over in Byer. We've prayed."

"And?" I asked.

"And I'm ready," Sarah said. "For however things work out for me."

She turned brisk. "And that brings me back to Kip. And his welfare. The thing is, he's very fond of you, Joe."

"It's mutual. I'm fond of him, too."

"That makes you his only hope."

Only hope? Surely not. I began handing the documents back. "I'm touched you'd consider me for this, Sarah, but I can't do it."

At that the old woman's eyes teared, and Sutter spoke up. "I'm afraid you don't understand, Mr. Box. It's you or the county foster home for the boy. Sarah has no living relatives. According to the law, she must make arrangements. Those are her choices."

I jumped to my feet. "Those are no choices at all. And no offense, but it's not my problem." Running my fingers through my still-stubby hair, the custody papers crumpled in my other hand, I blew out a harsh breath. "You can't ask me to do this, Sarah. What in the world do I know about raising kids? Nothing, that's what."

Angela reached up and touched my hand. "Joe. Please sit down."

I did, but only because I didn't know what else to do.

Sutter and Sarah wisely kept quiet as Angela's soft words penetrated my whirling thoughts. "Think of the little boy. Is what she's asking really so awful?"

"It's not awful at all. It's just that I'm exactly the wrong guy for this."

"No you're not," Sarah said, drying her eyes with a tissue. "After what you risked to bring Cyrus Tate down and Kip back to me, I'd say you're perfect."

I could feel the tide in the room running against me. "But—"

Sarah looked at my fiancée. "Miss Swain, you'd help out, wouldn't you?"

Again Angela grasped the old woman's hands. "I'd be honored."

I frowned. "Wait a minute—"

Releasing her, Sarah turned to Sutter. "Brian, would you have Miss Worthington bring Kip back in here, please?"

"Now hold the phone here—" But it was too late. Sutter had already left the room. I sat there and steamed. Intelligent woman that she is, Angela kept her yap zipped.

Less than thirty seconds later the attorney returned with the nurse and the young boy. Laying her wrinkled, skinny arm around her grandson's shoulder, Sarah said, "Kip, I want to ask you something. And it's important. Would you like to stay with Mr. Box until I get better?"

His eyes were dancing. "Could I, Grandma? *Really?*"

Sarah looked at me. "That's up to Mr. Box."

Trapped like a rat. Kip walked over and took my hand, looking up. The expression he was giving me I surely didn't deserve. "Is it OK if I come and stay with you, Mr. Box? I don't eat much. And could I call Grandma sometimes? Hey! We could finally play ball like you promised!"

I threw Angela a helpless glance. "Don't just sit there. What should I do?"

"You know full well what to do," she smiled.

Looking down at the boy, I gave him as stern a face as I could. "One question. Do you like cats?"

"You've got a cat? What's his name?"

"Noodles. I've had him forever. Thing is, he's an independent booger. We'd have to make sure the two of you could get along."

Kip grinned at Sarah. "He said booger."

"Another thing," I said. "What I say in my house goes. You go to bed when I say, eat what I eat, and watch John Wayne westerns when I feel like it."

"Who's John Wayne?"

"Who's John—? Oh, brother."

Angela was hiding a smile behind her hand, while Sarah and Cara Worthington and Brian Sutter were grinning at me openly.

"Well, who is he?" Kip demanded.

Strike the colors. I was licked.

♦ ◊ ♦

After saying our good-byes to Sarah and the nurse, Angela and I waited until Kip said his.

I think he must have picked up on something, because after he'd kissed her and we were leaving the room, Kip turned to her and spoke, as seriously as I've ever heard a person, child or adult. "I'll always love you, Grandma." Sarah only cried a little at that, while I felt a lump swelling up in my throat the size of a navel orange. We left then and followed Sutter and Kip over to the Poole house to get the boy's clothes and whatever else.

As we drove, I could feel Angela's gaze on me. "Are you all right with this?" she said at last.

"I guess I have to be. I was kind of roped into it."

"It's a good thing you're living in a house now. It's not like you don't have the room." She smiled. "I'm thinking it might be kind of fun for you. Guy stuff and all that."

"Yeah, room's one thing I have plenty of." I glanced at her. "But we're talking about *me*, here. What kind of father figure does everyone think I am, anyway?"

"A good one," Angela answered at once. "I've always thought you would have been a great dad, Joe …" Thankfully she let that thought trail off.

"I don't even have any toys for him to play with. What about that?"

"There's a new thing around. It's called a toy store. You may have heard of it."

"Sarcasm ill becomes you, woman." I paused for a moment, then said, "I guess I could always let him play with Mister Monk Junior."

Angela said nothing. She knew my wife, Linda, and unborn son had died on her way back from buying the stuffed sock monkey toy for me. Since their deaths, Mister Monk Junior had only been touched by me, when it came time to dust the place where he sat.

Before I could say more, we'd arrived at the house. Parking and getting out, we waited until Sutter had opened the door before following him and Kip on in.

Sarah's house had that dusty, unlived-in smell any place does when it's been unoccupied for a while. With Kip leading the way, chattering nonstop like a magpie, we went up the stairs to his room.

I found myself battling my own dark thoughts. Part of me was as grudgingly excited as Kip at the idea of the two of us palling around together. But another, bigger part was more cautious, reminding me that I'd never had the chance to be a dad. The odds of me being a decent one were long.

As I trudged, I found myself praying something short and heartfelt under my breath. "Look, Lord, I know it's unbelief, but I really need you to show me a sign that I'm doing the right thing here. The right thing by the boy." I paused. "And by me."

Angela glanced at me. She'd heard it. But had God?

Reaching the top of the stairs, we went past my old room, Kip still nattering on. Pushing the door to the next one wide, he shouted, "And this is my room! Look at it! Isn't it *cool?*"

Cool it was. The room was a bit smaller than mine had been. Eight feet by eight or so, decorated in Early Kid. There was a child-size chair, and a desk in the corner, covered in crayon-scrawled paper. On the floor his large area rug doubled as a track for his little race cars. Above Kip's action-figure-littered dresser top was a big *Lord of the Rings* poster, featuring Aragorn and Legolas and the rest of the boys ripping the holy liver-lights out of some snarling orcs. My kind of poster.

But it was when I saw his inexpertly made-up bed that I stopped and stared. The breath froze in my lungs.

Picking up on it, Angela turned abruptly. "What?" Then she saw what I did, and clapped a hand over her mouth, her eyes wide. "Oh, Joe ..."

Kip and Brian Sutter exchanged glances, and the boy walked over, following my gaze. "Yep, I make my bed up all by myself," he said.

That's not what I was gazing at. On the bed, propped up on Kip's pillow, was a smiling, red-muzzled, long-tailed sock monkey. And I'll be jigged if it wasn't a dead ringer for Mister Monk Junior.

Angela grasped my hand, squeezing it hard as she gazed up at me. Her beautiful eyes welled with tears. "Looks like you got your sign," she said huskily. Had I ever. In spades.

I turned to Kip. "Your stuff won't pack itself," I said, my voice as rough as Angela's. "Let's get started."

Between us all it only took ten minutes before we had Kip's suitcases packed and a couple of boxes we'd retrieved from the basement stuffed with his "most favorite toys that I can't leave here." Included in the box, along with his slot-car set, baseball bat and glove, Nerf football, Hungry Hungry Hippos game, and Silly Putty egg, was Kip's sock monkey, whom he called Marvin. I didn't care. A man has the right to name his sock monkey whatever he wants.

It was as Brian Sutter and I were placing Kip's gear in the Cougar's trunk that the long-promised snow finally arrived. The flakes now pouring down were the size of postage stamps, and it seemed there were jillions of them being blown along by the capricious wind.

"Look at this," Sutter said to me in disgust. "This junk is going to make travel a mess. Man, I hate winter."

"Oh, I don't know." I was looking at Angela buttoning Kip's coat tightly around him, up on the porch. He was still talking a mile a minute, his Best and Greatest Adventure begun, while she beamed at him like a Madonna.

Tilting my face skyward, I grinned like a child, letting the drifting flakes land where they willed. "It feels like spring to me."

READERS' GUIDE

*For Personal Reflection
or Group Discussion*

Readers' Guide

Warning: This Readers' Guide reveals key plot points.

Private investigator and new Christian Joe Box is pretty confident about his skills in bringing criminals to justice. But his ability to withstand temptation is put to the test when he takes on porn king Cyrus Alan Tate. As Joe unearths one layer after another of secrecy and evil, he learns the tentacles of sin go very, very deep.

In chapter 1, Morris Chalafant tells Joe everyone has a price. What would make it difficult for you to say no to something you knew was wrong? What would help you to stand fast and resist the temptation to be bought? How can you fortify yourself against being bought?

In chapter 2, Joe recommends his friend Billy Barnicke for the job he turned down. Why might Joe consider it acceptable to recommend a friend for a job he felt was wrong for him to take? What parallels can you draw between Joe's rationalization and the way many Christians perceive non-Christians? What does Ezekiel 33:1–9 say about our responsibility to others?

In chapter 3, when Joe's cat, Noodles, is poisoned, Joe does everything in his power to save him. In the following chapter, Joe calls Billy and tries to talk him out of taking the "poison" job at PornUtopia. What kind of parallel is the author trying to make between Joe's attempts to save Noodles and his attempt to save Billy? See 1 Corinthians 6:18–20. If Joe had felt as much for Billy as he did for his cat, what more might he have done to save him?

Cyrus Tate shows up in the least likely place—a church parking lot—to try to talk Joe into taking the job he'd turned down earlier. What about that is surprising? How far into Christian territory is the enemy willing to encroach? Where can we find sanctuary and a fortress from evil?

Just before he dies, Billy tells Joe that Tate is responsible for his beating. Why doesn't Joe pass that knowledge on to Detective Pilley? How would you handle the murder of a friend? Would you trust it to a higher authority to deal justice, or would you feel the need to take action? Explain.

Detective Pilley tells Joe his secretary's daughter is dying of AIDS. Describe the downward spiral that led to her death. What does it say about the power of the sex industry to enslave its victims? See Proverbs 5 for a description of a similar descent into sin.

In chapter 8, Joe realizes avenging Billy's death and finding his killer are "two sides of the same dingy coin." What does he mean by that? When is it right to pursue justice? When is it wrong? See Romans 12:17–21. Why is it so difficult to leave vengeance to God?

Joe's half-brother, Vincent Scarpetti, is a mafioso boss who barely tolerates Joe, yet Vincent is persuaded to give Joe information on Tate. Why? What weakness does Joe exploit to get information? Why is Vincent concerned about his reputation? Before Joe sees Vincent, he has to get past Carmine, a giant with a less-than-welcoming face and manner. Yet Carmine treats Joe warmly. What does this say about the nature of relationships?

Describe Carmine's physical appearance. What would be your first impression upon seeing him? In chapter 9, the author humanizes Carmine, making him more likable. How does he do it? Why does he bother to make him likable? What does it say about how we are to view people, especially those who seem intimidating or on the wrong side of the law?

Vincent says in chapter 10 that porn has always been the "third rail" among his Mafia elders. It's OK to commit adultery, he says, but it's unmanly to engage in pornography. It seems absurd to engage in crimes such as murder, yet consider porn inexcusable, but many people believe the one unforgivable sin is the one they personally won't commit. Why do we think another's sin is worse than our own? In light of Romans 1:18–32, Romans 2:1–4, and 1 Corinthians 6:9–10, how does God rate sin?

What would it take for "regular folks" to turn the tide of smut and porn around—and what hampers us from doing so?

Joe's friends warn Joe he's heading into more danger than he's prepared to handle. Joe's nightmares also seem to warn him about the environment he's entering. Why is this job so much more dangerous than anything Joe has tackled before?

The wholesome-looking town of Sunnyvale seems to make no attempt to shut PornUtopia down. Why? What does Sunnyvale have to gain from PornUtopia? What does it have to lose?

The Reverend Mason Kilbride holds some unorthodox views on sexuality and marriage vows. What are your impressions of Kilbride? God has harsh words for false shepherds like Kilbride (see Ezekiel 34:1–10). Why?

Sarah Poole's bed-and-breakfast has a charming, old-fashioned feel to it. Yet neither Sarah's inn nor the town itself is what it appears to be. What is the author telling readers about surface appearances?

In chapter 18, Joe begins work at PornUtopia as—fittingly—a janitor responsible for cleaning the building. Note the way perversion progresses from floor to floor. Why would Tate have designed his building with a museum on the ground floor and rooms for prostitution on the fourth?

In PornUtopia's basement Joe helps move a fifty-five gallon steel drum filled with disinfectant hand soap for customers to use before they leave. What irony do you find in this focus on cleanliness? What does God say about washing away sin?

Tate is planning to modify military virtual-experience pods for porn use. If no one were exploited in the process, would it be morally wrong to use such a pod for sexual fulfillment? Would it be morally wrong to run combat experiences for paying customers? Explain.

Joe later learns that virtual-reality technology has been jettisoned by the military as too dangerous—it drives half its users insane. Yet it's also seen as a potential blessing to people with severe disabilities. What technologies can you think of that have the potential for both great harm and great good? What is our responsibility when dealing with such technology?

On Joe's second trip to the fifth floor of PornUtopia, he's repulsed by the thought of child porn, yet almost gives in to the impulse to watch it. Why? What rationalizations nearly bring him down morally? When was the last time you found yourself rationalizing something you knew was wrong or reckless? What safeguards do you take against temptation?

After Sarah's "accident," Joe reveals his true identity and learns of her long involvement in the porn industry. How successful has she been in reinventing herself as a genteel innkeeper? How successful at shedding her past? How has Sarah's involvement in porn affected Sarah's family?

In chapter 31, Bud tells Joe why Marko hates Tate. Including Marko's daughter, how many direct victims of porn are there in the novel? How about indirect victims? How accurately do you feel the author has described the danger and destructive quality of the porn industry?

Recognizing the serious physical risk he, Bud, and Marko are taking in attempting to rescue children held captive at Tate's mansion, Joe tells the two men about their need for Jesus. When have you felt a need to prepare friends or family for their eternal destiny? What would help you communicate the gospel message to them? How can you develop relationships that make it easier to share the good news of Jesus Christ?

Joe is willing to undergo life-or-death risks to save children being sold as sex slaves but when it comes to giving a home to a small boy, he has serious misgivings. What makes laying his life on the line so much easier than accepting a child into his life? Why is it many people find it easier to give a check or donate time to a cause than to love people up close and familiar? How did Jesus respond to people in need? See Matthew 8:1–17.

What sign does God give Joe that taking custody of Kip is the right thing to do? Has God ever given you tangible signs of his love or leading? Give examples.

Additional copies of *To Skin a Cat*
are available wherever good books are sold.

If you have enjoyed this book,
or if it has had an impact on your life,
we would like to hear from you.

Please contact us at:

RIVEROAK BOOKS
Cook Communications Ministries, Dept. 201
4050 Lee Vance View
Colorado Springs, CO 80918

Or visit our Web site:
www.cookministries.com